DELTA: REDEMPTION

CRISTIN HARBER

www.cristinharber.com

CHAPTER ONE

"NO!" *Roar!* "NO!"

Ten little girls, ranging from junior kindergarteners to second graders, slammed their heels down. They gritted their teeth and pushed both hands in front of them.

"Good, girls. Keep your eyes open." Victoria Massey paced the front of the focused line, mimicking their efforts, her hands also outstretched. "Remember to push with the bottom of your hands. You won't get in trouble."

A few kids tried the move over and over again. A couple recalibrated their insole heel step and smashed the floor of the community center at Sweet Hills' town hall. From the side, the row of parents looked on in rapt attention, both uneasy that this was the world that caused self-defense classes for kids to be necessary and proud that their little girls were taking to it without the bashful, ridiculous thought that *girls can't do that.*

Still, it had to stay age-appropriate and fun. Victoria walked to the side and grabbed the face mask made to look like a yellow smiley emoticon. "Remember, just because I look friendly"—she knocked the cheesy face with a closed fist to show it was padded—"doesn't mean I'm a good person. Is anyone allowed to touch you without permission?"

"No!" the class yelled.

"Should a grown-up ever ask you for directions?" Victoria asked, tilting the cartoon-like face back and forth like she was bantering with the kids.

"No! Keep walking!" They didn't even giggle, and she appreciated they'd listened and let it sink in.

"What if it's a secret?" She leaned forward as if she was telling one.

"No secrets!"

"Okay, line up single file." Victoria walked over and donned the rest of her protective gear. They might be kids, but she'd taught them to fight like hell with the expectation that they could. *And they could.* She needed that layer of foam.

After slipping on the boots and padding, she stepped to the first girl who had a huge smile on her face. "Ready?"

The smile turned into focus, and Victoria couldn't have been prouder as the kindergartener nodded.

"Remember, I don't know you right now."

"I know. I remember."

Last week's class had done a great job their first time with the role-play. "Hey, sweetie. Have you seen a little puppy? I thought I saw him run down the street? But…" She looked around. "I can't find him."

The little girl walked away quickly, and Victoria followed.

"Sweetie?" She carefully placed a hand on the girl, cupping the kid against her hip.

"No!" The little girl spun in, both hands smashed together in an open-handed punch to Victoria's crotch then ran away. "No!"

The move had a surprising amount of force behind it, throwing her off balance. "Good job."

The parents and kids both clapped as the girl ran to the end of the line.

After the remaining kids did their role-play, they ran over to the table where the families had brought snacks and drinks for afterward. Victoria pulled off her gear. The mayor came over, all smiles. His boy had been in her class the day before.

"I can't wait to have the joint class." He turned around and saw the little girls, who were warriors mere moments ago, back to being little girls. "It's like they take everything you taught them and tuck it in the back of their heads."

"That's the point."

He nodded and popped a homemade snickerdoodle in his mouth. "You talk to the sheriff's office lately?"

"Yup."

"I will *not* let gunrunners take over the outskirts of my town just because they've found a nice partnership."

"What is it that you want?" she asked.

"Lee Marrow is a pain in my ass. You know what he does?"

"Mayor, with all due respect, what other bounty officers do is *their* business."

"Cutting deals—"

"We all cut deals."

"The dirty kind, Victoria. Not like the ones you work out. I get the good-old-boys club. But there's a line, and at some point, I have to call a spade a spade. He's jumping in bed with the Russians, with Mayhem, with everyone."

"The Russians are starting to be a big problem. That's what I hear." She tried to watch him out of the corner of her eye. Mayhem had always been Sweet Hills's biggest concern, but now there was a new player in town. The status quo might not be the same anymore if what Victoria heard was true.

The mayor shrugged, avoiding eye contact. "I don't see the gunrunners' future as profitable as Mayhem's."

Fair enough. The Russians were newer on the scene and rumored to stick to guns, whereas the motorcycle club dabbled in everything and were a multi-club force with a national network. Strictly from a business point of view, the mayor was probably right. "I plan to keep on keeping on."

"You know what bail-jumper Lee's hunting?"

"Don't know, don't care," she mumbled, stuffing her mouth with a snickerdoodle. If she couldn't speak, she wouldn't get herself into a pickle.

"Sheriff heard some scuttlebutt that—"

"Scuttlebutt, really?"

"Now you sound like my wife."

"Marjorie knows when you sound ridiculous, sir." Victoria took a step back, wanting another snickerdoodle more than Sheriff Turnball's *scuttlebutt.*

"In all seriousness, I'd prefer if I had both you and Lee searching for this one." He pulled a folded-up paper from his back pocket. "One of Vashchenko's right-hand men."

She unfolded it and read over Yuri Maysak's sheet and the amount attached to it. That was a decent bit of money. More than normal. "Call me interested."

"Maysak's woman is a bartender at the Ice House out on Route 209."

"I'll check it out." And she would too, because that cash would be a solid paycheck. "Thanks."

"They're due a new shipment at week's end," the mayor mumbled. "Then another later this month."

She screeched to an internal halt, surprised that half the room didn't hear the sound of the record scratching that was in her head. "I assume that's not going to happen?"

"It is."

His lips barely moved. For everything he said about wanting to keep crime away and Sweet Hills safe, he was letting them set up shop and plant their roots. "You're going to *let them* sell their guns? That's such bullshit."

"Nothing we can do about it. There are forces beyond my control on this one."

She glared at him. "I'll go after Maysak but not because I'm competing with Lee or because you told me to." She was trying to float a business, a mortgage, all kinds of things that people didn't do at her age, when they were normally thinking about graduating college.

"That's all I was suggesting, and I knew that."

"You did not." She rolled her eyes.

Why did it feel as though her sweet town always had criminal SOBs circling it in the near distance? As every real estate agent within a dozen miles always said, location, location, location. Sweet Hills was at that special juncture in the middle of the country that made it a crossroads Mecca for the criminally traversing. Then again, there was always that chance that the mayor was trying to play some political move, thinking she wouldn't see it—or couldn't—simply because she was younger than most everyone involved in the community.

Though… she didn't see it. Letting a gun sale go through? All she saw was a BS olive branch to some criminals. The 'why' evaded her.

Victoria shifted, the awareness of her past always sitting on her shoulder like a silent voice, pushing her to do whatever the mayor asked in order to always prove she was a good girl. She *was* good, and nothing anyone did could change who she was.

The door to the community center opened, and Seven, Victoria's closest friend, walked in. Half the cookies and pastries that covered the table were from her mom's coffee shop, and her friend's bright blue-and-pink hair matched some children's summer outfits.

No one thought Seven would be able to keep the Perky Cup open when her mom had a stroke, but no one knew Seven the way Victoria did. Everyone underestimated them because of their age and "life decisions," as the scuttlebutt crowd liked to call it, when Victoria decided to get a PI license instead of go to community college, and Seven continued on, brightly, with her family's long-steeped, gossip-inducing history in Sweet Hills.

"Think about what I said. Bye now." The mayor, one of the first people Seven won over, waved to her as they passed.

"Another success." Seven held up a hand. "Nicely done, my kick-ass friend. Nicely done."

"They're here for the sugar rush."

"Don't downplay." Seven clucked at her then tilted her head toward the mayor making his rounds. "What was that about? Your face was all kinds of what-the-fuckery."

Victoria choked on a laugh. "What?"

"With a side of you-have-something-to-prove—which you don't, by the way."

She always had something to prove, even if everyone said she didn't. "He's trying to help me out on a jumper."

"Oh, money, money, money, honey, I like."

"Yup. I still have that silly mortgage to pay."

"Yours hasn't gone anywhere either?" Seven winked.

"Nope. Might as well help keep our little town clean." Victoria watched the kids run around and decided that next week, she'd bring superhero capes for everyone to wear. The town's seamstress kept reminding her that she wanted to repay her for finding out who was siphoning money from Sew Me.

Victoria always waved away her offers to pay. Most times, her PI work was a steady part of her income, but for Miss Betty, she didn't charge a thing—not because she couldn't pay, but because the woman had such a kind heart had been taken advantage by a local church treasurer. *The asshole.* When all was said and done, underprivileged kids had lost out, and Betty anonymously redonated every penny lost to the treasurer's personal greed to the church. Victoria figured out what Miss Betty had done and kept it to herself.

But Betty could pull together enough capes for both the boys and girls self-defense classes. How hard would it be? Cut fabric, make ties? *Voila.*

Seven grumbled as she continued to track the mayor. "But there's always a catch."

"Yup." Victoria focused back on him. "And the one he presented is too easy."

Seven's bangles clinked as she bumped shoulders with Victoria. "I know you, and you'll figure it out. You'll always do."

"Maybe..."

The windows vibrated with a semi-familiar rumble—familiar in that she knew the sound, unfamiliar in that this was the wrong place to hear the roar as motorcycles came up Main Street and slowed. Kids ran to the windows and cheered as the club idled out front. They never had business in town.

Seven's bright eyes widened. "Well, that's something."

Certainly was. *A power play.* Victoria's gut twisted. She respected the boys on their bikes, and they respected her, but it was all business, and respect or not, she was still the enemy. Still law enforcement. A bounty hunter. A private investigator. But they weren't making a show at her self-defense class; that much she knew.

Engines idled outside, revved, and took their time as they rode off.

The mayor strolled over, eyes locked on Seven. "Good day for a ride?"

Seven smirked. "You can save your 'all is safe in the land of unlocked doors' spiel for someone else, sweet pea."

Victoria watched the dynamic between them. Seven's family, the

Blackburns, were synonymous with Mayhem Motorcycle Club, and she was the MC's princess, whether she actively took ownership of that role or not. Either way, what Mayhem had done was unexpected enough that the mayor and Seven traded passive-aggressive barbs. Victoria had never seen that before.

The MC were sending a message. Victoria had no idea to whom. A few wayward eyes were still cast toward windows, but the kids were back to their games. Some parents even seemed not to notice. But the mayor did. She felt his anxious gaze latch onto hers the second the first window rattled—and the reality of what was happening hit her.

Two rival gangs.

One prime location.

Turf war.

They were in the middle of Iowa, and Sweet Hills was going to be a battle zone.

CHAPTER TWO

"IF THE BAIL-JUMPER weren't important, the mayor wouldn't have said anything." Victoria gnawed on the stale granola bar and knew it was sacrilege to eat that while talking to Seven on the phone. Her pastries weren't more than a five-minute drive away. "There's something he doesn't like about what the sheriff's up to."

"Sheriff came in this morning," Seven said. "Ordered three dozen donuts. Cleaned me out. What does it mean? His day for donut duty? Or a nefarious sugar scheme?"

Victoria rolled her eyes at her friend mocking her and took a bite of the old granola bar, facing her cell phone as though Seven could really see her. "Why's this jumper important?"

"Why are any jumpers important?"

"Good question." Victoria chewed the inside of her cheek. "Some are worth more than others."

"So-so answer and better question: why's he playing politics and involving you, who gives no hoots about town gossip and politics?"

Seven was right. Victoria would sooner die than be a conversation piece. That anxiety was nearly debilitating. She cut favors and played the game with criminals, law enforcement, and attorneys at the bare minimum to keep the steady flow of information flowing, and that was that. No gossip. No BS. She never wanted the limelight when it came to chatter.

"Besides the fact," Seven started to answer her own question, "you're better than Douche Bag McDoucherson. Maybe he just wants a clean pickup."

"Maybe." But it felt like anything but.

"What are you going to do?"

"Snoop around. Check out his old lady."

"Want some company?" Seven asked. "I know, I know. You work better alone."

"Not always." Victoria crumpled the wrapper over the half-eaten granola bar and pitched it into her trash can. "But I'm heading to the Ice House—"

"Ew, that place smells like year-old peanuts, beer breath, and armpits. Hold your breath, and don't stay long enough to pass out."

She wrinkled her nose, remembering the last time she'd pushed past the Ice House doors. The stench of stale beer and fermenting barrels was bad. "I thought it might not be your cup of joe."

Seven giggled. "Not yours either."

"The places I've seen."

"And probably smelled. Pee-ewww."

"Agreed." Victoria reached into her office desk drawer and grabbed the subcompact 9mm that tucked nicely at the back of her jeans. "If you don't hear from me by day's end, you know where I am. Bring smelling salts."

THE HEAVY WOOD door had layers of paint that had peeled and been painted over far too many times, and yet the section near the door handle was completely worn away. If Victoria had to guess, it was from too many drunks falling against the door, going in and out. She smelled the stale beer before she toed the swinging door open.

The lights were low. The television broadcasted boxing from satellite—or so she assumed because she couldn't understand the commentator or read the words on screen. The bartender, casually refilling a draft and lifting a phone to her ear, had a harsh glint in her eye. She smiled and made small talk, replacing the receiver, slinging the beer, paying no mind to the mess she made.

Victoria pulled up a bar stool, and the bartender made her way closer, dirty rag in hand. The cloth was more for show since she seemed to ignore the old sweat marks from glasses long gone.

"What can I do you for?" Her black eyelashes had on too much mascara for what Victoria thought such light eyes needed, but she wasn't one to judge.

"Whatever you got. Just needed a break. My boss is riding my ass this morning."

Pink-lined lips pressed into a fake smile as the bartender stepped back and drew a glass and filled it without taking her eyes off Victoria. "What kind of boss is that?"

"Sales."

The woman slung the beer toward her. "Starting a tab?"

"The way my month's been going? Yes and no."

"Which is it?"

Victoria forced down a long gulp of crappy, piss-poor beer. "Yes."

"What kind of sales your boss barking at you about?"

She looked side to side then leaned forward. The bartender took the bait, inching closer and leaned too. Victoria whispered, "Couples' products."

The woman leaned back, not registering what she meant.

Well, hell. The plan to girl-talk the dirty deets over orgasm sales wasn't going to fly if she didn't clue in. "As in, pleasure."

Even if the woman was ultra-conservative and pooh-poohed the whole idea of *couples' products,* she would at least broach the topic of a boyfriend, and they could go from there.

"You sell pornos?" Her lip curled up as if she didn't believe it.

And neither did Victoria. "No." She laughed, actually embarrassed, and not needing to feign it for the purpose of forging girl talk. "Maybe this is why my boss is on my ass."

The lady laughed. "I got one of those too."

"Who doesn't?"

"What is a couples' product, if not porno?"

"Do you watch porn with your man?"

"Do I look like the type?" The bartender scowled.

Was she saying she didn't watch porn or didn't like men? "I'm the one failing at the lube and toys biz. I don't know."

"Ah, honey." She slapped the rag down, finally wiping away the old glass sweat rings. "You're barking up the wrong tree."

"Why?" Victoria made a face, leaning close again. "It's *awesome*."

"Might be, but my man is old school. *Awesome* ain't old school."

She lifted her eyebrows. "Maybe you bring him some *awesome* and change his mind."

The bartender cackled and leaned back, shaking her head. She reached over for a pack of smokes with the lighter shoved in the plastic wrap, pulled a cigarette out, and let it dangle unlit on her lip. "He likes what he likes, when he likes it, how he likes it."

That sounded like it sucked. "And you?"

The lighter flicked, and she drew deeply until the red ember crawled down the paper. After letting the smoke out her nostrils, she ashed in a bottle. "I get mine."

"The way you like it?"

"This is your job?" She gestured with the cigarette. "To talk to folks about how they diddle each other?"

"Guess when you put it like that, it is today."

"Vanna," a man at the end of the bar bellowed.

"Well, good luck with your boss." She dropped the cigarette into the bottle and headed to the yeller.

Victoria forced down as much of the crap beer as she could in order to get the woman back for a refill. *Damn.* The place was called the Ice House. *Think the draft could be a few degrees colder than room temperature?*

She took another couple huge gulps as the door opened. Two people entered. They meandered slowly, taking time to sidle up to the bar, one on each side of her. Jeez, she had no time to be hit on, and it was about noon. Why did they want to make a move on a woman slamming back beer on her lunch hour? *Because* she was slamming beer at her lunch hour. *Hello…*

But her ears pricked as they chatted to each other. Russian accents. Definitely the right bar, though neither were her bail-jumper.

The bartender hustled over when she saw them, her eyes worried, almost guilty. They quickly glanced at Victoria, but their eyes didn't stay on her long. An instinctive burst of chill bumps cascaded down her arms, and the woman behind the bar quickly went to work getting what seemed to be the men's usual drinks. There was tension in the air.

Victoria slipped her purse open, extracting a ten-dollar bill and tossing it on to the bar. "Thanks again. I better get back to work, now that I think about it."

The bartender gave a flat smile, showing no recognition that they'd ever spoken. Again, Victoria's instincts roared to life. She remembered how the woman picked up the phone when she walked in, and how her guilt seemed pronounced, even as she ignored their couples'-product-forged acquaintanceship.

"Where do you work?" the man to her right side asked.

His tone wasn't flirtatious or conversational; it was downright interrogational.

"Home product direct sales." She closed her wallet and slipped the purse over her shoulder.

"You work for yourself." The other man came up too close behind her.

They shouldn't be able to tell that she had a weapon tucked at the small of her back, but if one of them felt her and knew what they were looking for, they'd identify it as a gun. Awkwardly, she hopped off the barstool. "I've got a man, boys. He don't take kindly to me smiling where I shouldn't."

"It was a simple question." The first man's accent was heavier as the directness came on strong, and the rest of patrons quieted down.

She looked around the bar. No one turned or spoke.

"Don't worry about them."

Victoria raised her chin. "I'm not worried."

"Do you know who we are?" the first man asked.

She knew he wasn't her jumper. "It doesn't matter to me who or what you are. I didn't come here for you."

"But you did come here for Yuri Maysak."

Victoria remained still, waiting to see where this conversation would go. Who was their attorney? Most clubs and gangs had a firm on retainer. But these guys were so new to the scene that she didn't know if they had roots deep enough. "What do you want?"

They said nothing, but cold radiated from the man next to her. Bounty hunters sometimes worked in packs, other times alone. She would do takedowns with someone, depending on the mark and their threat level. But strictly on recon work? She wasn't too worried. Same with PI work. Stakeout. Asking around. Lookie-loos. Nothing more than gathering intel. These guys though... They screamed that a sinister showdown loomed.

"Nice chatting." She made it two steps before a hand clamped on her shoulder. *Asshole.*

Her elbow slammed back and elicited a solid oomph as the other man came forward. Two against one—not what she wanted. She swung the flat palm of her right hand up, hitting the man under his chin. His teeth snapped together as she popped her knee into his nuts.

As that one doubled over, the second man wrapped his arms around her chest.

"No!" she cried out. Victoria used him as leverage, kicking both her boots forward and smashing the heels into the face of the other man as he rebounded, holding his crotch, growling.

"Bitch." The man's arms tightened, and he bit her ear.

"Oh—ow!" Pulling from his vise grip made the pain worse, and she curled her legs to her chest then slammed her boots to the ground, desperately trying to hit the man's feet. Success on one foot, and he lost his bite on her ear, shouting and spitting.

He threw her onto the ground, and her ribs cried out in pain when she crashed into a table and chair. Up onto her hands and knees, Victoria broke for the door, pushing off the dirty floor. A hand caught her foot, dragging her back. She kicked, stabbing the air with her free leg.

"Let me go!" Damn it. "Let me go! Now!"

A bar of onlookers, and no one did a thing.

"What are you going to do?" she shouted, still kicking from the floor. "Scare me away? You don't want him picked up? That's what this is about?" She kicked harder, jamming the heel of her boot onto the man's fingers.

The other man came close to the one holding her on the floor by her ankle. The bartender came forward. Victoria stilled, watching her with an eerie feeling that shit was about to get a whole lot worse.

“She came here about my Yuri?” the bartender asked coolly.

Her Yuri didn’t bode well.

The one with her ankle nodded. “You did good to call. We knew they were making a move.”

The bartender handed the other man the rag in her hand, but it wasn’t the same one she’d been mopping the bar top with. She squatted next to Victoria’s face. “He may fuck me whenever, however he likes it. But I said I liked it.” She spat to the side. “No way you’re going to like whatever these psychos do. You’re about to be fucked.”

The man crouched on the other side as Victoria thrashed and pulled away. He held her forehead to the floor, and forced the rag over her mouth, its bitter taste abrading her tongue and burning her nose. She couldn’t breathe without her lungs burning. A heaviness wrapped an invisible blanket around her limbs. She couldn’t kick, couldn’t move, even though she wanted to roll over and throw up. She couldn’t. Her eyes wouldn’t focus; they spun around the room like she was spiraling. Slow, fast, she didn’t know. Gray clouds closed closer, closer, closer…

CHAPTER THREE

LIGHTS FLASHED. EVERYTHING went down. The room spun as the hot air seemed to go ice cold then scorching again. Victoria rolled on her side and got sick. Her arm dangled; her hand reached and found nothing. Blips of the attack burst into her skull alongside the pounding headache that shot daggers behind her eyes, but she struggled to sit up, desperately blinking away the blindness that held her down.

Out of breath, she collapsed again, the sweet darkness of passing out begging her to come to the other side. "No," she moaned.

Shaking, Victoria pushed up again, needing to fight, to get away. She gasped for breath even as her neck wouldn't support her head. Falling backward, Victoria hit a wall, and it held her up, its harsh texture a welcome relief.

"Oh, God…" Slowly, her head stopped spinning, and she tried opening her eyes, slits only at first. The room was light but not bright, and it smelled. *She* smelled, and the shocking revelation nearly knocked her back out as she caught her jeanless legs and dirty shirt. The room reeked of urine and vomit, and her mouth was so filthy and parched the idea of drinking water was both fantastic and foul.

"Get up." A man stepped into the room, and his heavy Russian accent sounded as ugly as he looked.

She stared, limbs shaking—not just from nerves but an uncontrolled weakness.

"Up. When you wake up, you clean." He strode over and had her on her bare feet, knees almost knocking, then half-walked, half-supported her down a dimly lit hall.

Her raw throat burned with every attempt to swallow, but she managed to whisper, “Where are we?”

“Don’t speak.”

He understood English and spoke it haltingly, and his Russian accent was thick. Very unlike the Russian gunrunners she was investigating. Where had they been hiding this guy? He certainly wasn’t skirting the town limits of Sweet Hills. Someone would have mentioned it.

They entered a bathroom, and he turned on the shower. There was no question about what she was supposed to do, about what she wanted to do, but with him standing there, watching, Victoria couldn’t. *Until he drew his weapon.* She stripped off the urine-soaked underwear, embarrassed, and trying to cover herself, her shirt, and bra, then stumbled. He didn’t help, seeming not to notice, as she crawled to the tub and pulled herself over the edge.

The lukewarm water rained down, and she opened her mouth, swishing and spitting, then rubbing her eyes. She found bar soap and a small bottle with writing she didn’t recognize and started the process of washing as best she could without standing. She didn’t have the strength to do both.

Once all the lackluster bubbles washed away, the man turned the water off, dropped a threadbare towel on her, and helped her out onto the cold floor. Shivering and shaking, she dried off, trying to stay covered. A dress, somewhat resembling a cloak, landed by her, and she glanced up.

“Dress, dress,” the man ordered.

Victoria shed the towel, tugging on the rough cloth over her still damp, chill bump-covered skin. He yanked her by the arm back onto her feet, and into the hall they went. Victoria felt exhausted beyond what her mind could comprehend. He deposited her in a room, physically lifting her and leaving her on a cot.

Eyes closed and heartbeat pounding in her ears, she tried to catch her breath—and felt eyes. Instincts desperately trying to keep up and keep her alive, Victoria jolted, pulling her legs beneath her and bracing her arms in front, ready as she could be for whatever came next.

Girls.

Women.

She let her gaze sift across the room as they all studied her. What on earth was… *Oh, shit.* This was a prostitution house? Her foggy mind tried to clear. Not a prostitution house. Prostitutes were pros. These were slaves. Sex slaves? Victoria looked down at herself then at them, at their rows of cots, and the door where the guard had disappeared.

"Where are we?" she asked, willing her voice not to crack. She wouldn't show fear, not even a sliver of the horror she knew could be found in places like a sex trafficking hellhole.

"Russia," someone whispered.

Then the whole world turned upside down.

THREE DAYS. THREE days in this God-forsaken bleary room, and Victoria was crawling the walls—on the inside. Externally, she was the face of calm resistance. Maybe it was because she was the oldest one at entrepreneurial billionaire pig Ivan Mikhailov's Russian estate, but the rest of these girls here had been handpicked. She, on the other hand, was captured and sent away, an offering to the big man like a gift.

But she'd yet to meet this Ivan jackass. Some of the guards were more talkative than others. The older ones were stoic, old guard. They'd die before breathing wrong against the former soviet intelligence official, now some higher-up in the Russian government. Talk about corruption. But the younger ones? They didn't buy into the bullshit nearly as much.

She'd learned a lot from them. Namely, Ivan was a prick of epic proportions. He wasn't home much, and he was trying to talk his daughter, Taisia, into working this part of the "family business." What kind of monster would involve his daughter in sex slavery?

The man who brought their food clambered in with two sacks' worth of meals for everyone in the room. Victoria hastened over, hoping there was something of substance to get them through the night. No. Not only no, but there wasn't enough to feed all of them now.

"Hey!" She jumped up, rushing toward the doorway to catch the man.

"Victoria. Hush," whispered worried voices behind her.

The hell with that. None of them had been touched yet, no one had been hurt, but they still needed their strength.

"Excuse me!" she called down the hall.

Nothing. *Well, damn.* "Let's divide up the—"

She saw eyes go wide before she heard the grunt of the meanest guard. He seemed not the least bit concerned.

"What?" he barked.

She straightened her spine and pushed her shoulders back. "That's not enough food. Nowhere near enough."

He looked over her shoulder and shook his head. "Eat."

"We would if there was enough. We need more food."

He walked farther into the room, his gaze crawling over the young ladies. "You have needs?"

Dread curled in her stomach. They were supposedly Mikhailov property. No guard had dared to touch them, the younger guards admitted, because Ivan Mikhailov was fanatical about his possessions. He hadn't returned yet, and Victoria gathered they were still in the start-up stage of this endeavor. What started as only a few girls days ago had almost doubled.

"You get more food." He grabbed a young girl by her hair, yanking her down onto her knees. "I get what I want."

"No," Victoria roared as the young woman sobbed.

All around them, the room balked. Gasps reverberated. The guard drew his sidearm, pointing the barrel at her face, and snarled his, snapping at her in Russian.

"We just want food," she tried again.

He caressed the gun against the girl's face then gestured to his belt. Sobbing, she cried that she didn't want to, but her hands shakily went to her chest as though she were considering undoing the bastard's pants.

Fucking hell. Furious anger coiled inside Victoria's chest. "Food. That's all we asked for. We didn't cause problems. Leave her alone."

The man laughed and pointed the gun back at her. *Good.* At least it was off the poor girl who was shaking like a leaf—Victoria was too, on the inside.

"It was my request, if that's what it takes to get fed around here." Carefully, she stepped toward the Russian pistol. What was she thinking? She didn't want to blow the guy. She wouldn't. But she wasn't going to let the girl do it either.

The man cackled. "You are Ivan Mikhailov's gift."

She'd heard that so many times at this point it was almost a shield of protection. "So what? I'm hungry. Get up," she said to the young girl who'd gone so pale Victoria thought she'd pass out. All of these girls were too young, too innocent to be here. What awaited them if she didn't figure out a way to get them out was going to ruin their lives. "Go, honey. I've got this."

A string of Russian fell from the guard's angry, bellowing mouth. Spittle flew, and the veins at his temples popped.

If she was Ivan Mikhailov's gift, the bastard wasn't going to kill her, was he? Victoria walked face first to the barrel of the gun. "Honey, get to your cot." The risk was high he would always kill another girl who wasn't a billionaire's gift. "We're all his property. Are you really supposed to use any of us before he sees us first?"

Victoria sent up a prayer that Ivan Mikhailov was a possessive, controlling bastard who didn't like to share his toys or investments. Each woman was unique in her features. They were all beautiful. They were handpicked. This was the sex trafficking stable of a billionaire, and she knew when Mikhailov got his new business venture up and running, it would be bad for them, but right now, it was almost as though they were wrapped in a protective layer.

"We need food," she demanded, "before Ivan Mikhailov arrives to find us wasting away."

The unexpected sound of footsteps broke the tension as the other man came back, two more sacks of food in hand. Victoria turned to see his face falter as he tossed them down. The two men scowled, bickering back and forth, voices dropping in angry tones, but she didn't understand a word.

The guard slammed his jaw shut and holstered his weapon. Without saying another word, he stomped out. The other man simply gestured to the new bags of food, turned, and left as well.

"*Merci.*" The girl who had been on her knees rushed over, wrapping her arms around Victoria.

The chatter in the room began, and the realization dawned on all of them that they were from all over the globe. It also seemed that Victoria was their chosen leader for as long as they were in this situation. They hadn't talked much, but maybe it was time to change that. "My name is Victoria, and I will do whatever I can to make sure we survive this."

CHAPTER FOUR

One Month Later

RYDER GLANCED OVER his shoulder at the woman tucked soundly asleep on the safe house couch. Delta team had not pulled much information out of her since they rescued her from the trafficking ring in Russia, and she was the last victim left. All Ryder knew was that her name was Victoria, and every other girl that had been subject to the Mikhailov sex trafficking ring held her in high esteem. She had protected them, reportedly stepped in their places in some cases, defended them, and made sure they had food, and she had held her own when Delta raided the billionaire sex trafficker's businesses.

Apparently, she had been holding it all together and was now taking a mental break. From the moment Ryder had pulled her out of Mikhailov's basement and torn away the gun she'd had trained on Ivan's head—thereby also saving one of his teammates—she hadn't said much.

"What are we gonna do about her?" Ryder asked his boss.

Brock shook his head. "We can't just turn her out to the world. There are people who can help her."

Ryder knew all about the organizations, rehab groups, and victim-assistance programs. She had done so much for other people, and he hated simply turning her over to strangers. It was as if he owed her something more. He didn't, but still, guilt lodged in his chest. He'd talked her out of shooting her rapist. Ryder might never forgive himself for that, but he'd also saved Locke's life. The survival of one of his teammates was more important than a victim murdering her perpetrator. Ryder had to remember that. Still, they had a connection that he couldn't explain, and he didn't want to turn her over to some faceless organization because the woman had gone into a catatonic state in which she refused to divulge who she was beyond a first name.

"What if…" Hell, he didn't even know how to suggest the idea that was never too far from the tip of his tongue. They could bring Victoria back toward HQ with them, where he knew the therapist and trusted the surroundings.

Brock gave him a side-eye. "I had a feeling you were going there. And I already talked to Winters."

"Yeah?" There was no one better than Mia Winters to help, and he liked the idea of Victoria staying where he knew every square inch of the property.

"You say the word, we'll let her rehab and pull her shit together with them."

"I'm saying the word," Ryder said, without even thinking twice.

"I CAN FEEL you staring," Victoria said with her head buried in the pillow.

Ryder had been across the room, posted in an uncomfortable chair he'd grabbed from the safe house's kitchen for the last couple hours, keeping an eye on her and thinking about their options. Not that he needed to, but Ryder had called Mia to pick her brain. It was nice to have a pseudo-shrink on Titan Group's payroll. Almost. Since she was Colby's wife, she knew a lot of what Delta team did through Titan, and since she already worked as a military therapist, he didn't have to hold back. She got it. Mia's advice had been simple: feel the girl out, and listen to his gut.

Ryder's gut said Victoria wasn't ready to share where she came from or who she was and would balk at the suggestion she stay with them in Virginia, but in the end choose to go with Delta because she wouldn't end up with some nameless, faceless rescue group.

"Wasn't staring." He stood up, dragging his chair closer to the couch. "I wanted to be around when you woke up."

She sat up on the couch and tucked the blankets and pillow around her as if she was building a fabric barrier between her and the world. After running her fingers through her hair and underneath her eyes, Victoria turned her attention to him. "I guess now's the time that I say thanks and go about my business, huh?"

"Are you headed home?" he asked for what felt like the thousandth time, and he could predict the answer.

She lifted her shoulders but stared straight through him. "Yeah, sure, maybe."

"That's awfully noncommittal, sweetheart. You know we'll take you there."

"When I'm ready, I'll go back home."

She still didn't want to go home, and he wasn't going to try again to ask what her last name was. They could easily enough figure out who she was. They could track down her home life—or criminal life, who or what she was running from or avoiding. Facial recognition was easy enough. They could lift fingerprints. There were any number of ways the Delta team, by using Titan Group's resources, could figure out who Victoria No Name was. But she didn't want to tell, and sometimes, people who were that victimized deserved to hide in their silence for as long as they wanted to. *At least for now.*

"Fair enough."

Finally, her eyes made contact with his, and Ryder knew that what he was going to offer was the right decision.

"Am I the last one?"

He nodded. "You are. And we can take you anywhere in the world."

Her eyes shifted down as she tucked the blankets around her. What he wouldn't give to get into her head and figure out her thought processes right then. What was she so worried about? Or who? So often, the people they saved wanted to get home and run into the arms of the people they loved, but not this woman.

"Look, Victoria. There are people who can help you."

Before he could continue and explain about Winters's place, her eyes widened, and she shook her head.

"No, I'm fine." Panic colored her words. "I'll just head out."

"Easy."

"I—"

"Give me a minute. Would ya, please?" He tilted his head, dropping his chin. "You don't know where you are. You have no money, no ID. What are you going to do?"

"I…" She glanced about the generic safe house's nondescript room. It held no answers.

"You're going to walk to wherever you came from?"

"Maybe."

"We're in Virginia."

"Virginia," she repeated, obviously not excited that she wasn't able to walk home.

"Let us help you out. At least, hear me out. I have another option."

Her head dropped into the pile of blankets and pillows in front of her, and she mumbled, "I want to sleep until I don't feel this anymore."

Would that ever happen? He didn't know if people recovered from what she'd gone through. Her words pierced the invisible layer of armor he kept around himself to keep people at bay and dug tiny spikes into in his chest.

The beautiful woman before him with tired bags under her eyes was unwaveringly strong in the face of what terrified so many. He'd heard about it, seen her face her monster. Victoria simply needed to recoup.

But *how* he understood that about her, barely knowing her, blew his mind. It had to be that first fierce encounter with her in that basement in Russia. Living, breathing fire—and he'd had to calculate quickly what the odds were that she'd pull the trigger and decide how to talk her down. Psychoanalyzing someone on the fly was never easy, and she was fascinating. Life wasn't fair, and she had been through the worst.

"Can you give me your eyes?"

Tired but trusting eyes met his, and he wanted to promise she'd feel life would be okay, back to whatever it had been soon enough. But… maybe those weren't the right words for someone who wouldn't share her last name or hometown.

"I want you to meet Winters."

"Is that his real name?"

"Is that snark?"

"No."

"Too bad. I was hoping you'd have a little attitude to toss my way." He grinned. "He works on a different team and has a place not too far from here. He and his wife, their kids, have a ton of room, spare rooms."

"Why would they do that?"

"That's what they do."

Victoria smirked, and it wasn't the kind of attitude he was hoping for. No, it was the kind that hated on herself, and he wanted to shut down her words before she even spoke.

"They take the leftovers from your jobs? The people you can't place in a good home, like a rescue dog? No thank you. Like I said, I'll head out—"

"Would you cut that crap!" Ryder snapped.

Surprised, she inched back and her mouth formed an O, but her pale complexion grew the slightest shade pink, as though the blood finally found the ability to flow faster than a step above living dead.

"I'll put up with a lot of stuff, and you need me to. But that bullshit?" He shook his head. "No. I don't know the right thing or the wrong thing in situations like this." Ryder stepped forward. "But I know what you just said was wrong. Don't talk about yourself that way, Victoria."

"I wasn't." She rubbed her face. "I was, I guess. I don't normally."

He stepped to the couch, leaving enough room between them. "Can I sit with you?"

Joining her on the next cushion over, he considered how to tone his lecture down, not wanting to scare the poor woman. Lord knew what kind of hell she had been through, but the idea of her saying that and not being able to comfort her was more than he could handle. He closed the distance, inching closer. "Look, they're good people. Winters doesn't mind, and Mia would love it. You're not ready for whatever your next step is. I thought it was a good idea."

"It was your idea?"

He nodded. "I mean, hell, you can walk out if you want. We're packing up, and you can't stay here. I can't stop you from splitting, but I'd like to try."

"Why?" she whispered.

Good question. "Because you've earned so much more help than you realize."

What felt like an eternity passed. What was going through her mind? It wasn't as if he could make her go to Winters's place. And if she wanted to walk out the door—no ID, no money, no plan—he couldn't really stop her, and he would keep an eye on her on his own time.

"Okay. Thanks, John."

Ryder hesitated then put his hand on the blanketed mass. "If we're going to do this, there's something that I need to tell you. My name's not John. It's Ryder… Ryder Hall."

Her lips parted as though surprised, but no words came out, and her eyes squinted like he had stolen the small amount of trust that she managed to have in the only person she had interacted with since her run in with Ivan. "What? Why?"

"Generally, we keep a level of distance between ourselves and the unknown," he tried to explain, "with the people we interact with in these situations. But not telling you who I really am feels… like a violation. And you have had enough…"

"Violations," she spat out, her voice rasping.

He nodded. "I wasn't trying to hurt you but rather protect the people I know and myself, to a certain extent. We don't know who we interact with, who is on the other side of these jobs. So that wasn't my name. But I'm Ryder."

She looked away, as if sensing the irony of her reaction and the fact that she wasn't explaining who she was. "Nice to meet you, Ryder."

"Nice to meet you too. And you're still just Victoria?" He hoped maybe she would give a last name.

"That's my name."

"It is, love." His fingers flexed into the blanket as though a strong grip could offer any reassurance after the hell that she'd been through. "Want to blow this place, yeah? We're not that far from where we need to be, and you can go back to sleep and stay there until you're ready to wake up and deal with the real world."

Victoria turned back and leaned the slightest bit closer. "What if I'm never ready? What if that bastard destroyed me?"

"No. You just need to recoup. Real food, not safe-house-pantry shit. You need to sleep in a real bed, not where people are wandering in and out."

She seemed to agree that the parade of Delta team in and out hadn't made snoozing easy.

"But more than that, you probably have to talk to somebody. I'm not that person, but I know who is."

"Someone who lives at Winters's place?"

"I promise you Mia's the best person I know. One day, it'll be okay. Real food and real sleep aren't a cure, but they help—and now I sound like her."

"Mia?"

"My go-to girl on all things I don't know how to handle. She's rock steady. Knows her shit and bonus, loves having people stay."

"Promise?" Victoria sounded as though she felt like the world's biggest burden.

He lifted his hand from the pile of blankets, tucking her to his side. He put his chin on top of her head. "Yeah, I promise, love. I promise. Mia will take good care of you."

CHAPTER FIVE

WINTERS WALKED INTO the side door of the safe house and threw his truck keys down on the kitchen counter. All night long, Ryder had checked on Victoria, and she was sleeping. Now, posted in the kitchen, he was handing her off. Damn if he didn't want to do that.

"How's it going?" Winters beelined for the fridge and grabbed a bottle of water. "How's she doing?"

"Same. Sleeping."

"Jared said we're going to wait her out."

Ryder nodded. "Yup."

"He knows something about her that we don't?"

"Guess so."

"Locke said she was in beast mode with the PSM pistol on Mikhailov."

He nodded again. "She knows her way around a weapon. That's for sure."

"Well, she's not CIA, or any of those farm boys would have grabbed their girl, or Nicola or Beth would have slipped by to take her away."

"They haven't stopped by once."

"Not government at all?"

"I don't think so."

"If Boss Man and Brock want to wait this one out, they must have their reasons to keep it in-house."

Yeah. *Him*. Special request. "You don't mind?"

Winters chuckled. "Does Mia mind having someone she can dote on? No."

"Hey, listen."

"Yeah?"

"She's a good one, that girl."

Winters nodded. "I get it. Heard about everything she did over there."

Ryder looked at the wall on the other side where she was sleeping and ran his hand over his jaw. "She..." Felt familiar in a way he couldn't place his finger on.

"I get it. Some of these jobs, man? They're gut punches."

"Yeah—" His cell phone chirped, and he slid it from his pocket.

BROCK: *Need your help on a Titan job. Haul ass to HQ.*

"Well, shit. I gotta run," Ryder grumbled, not wanting to leave without telling Victoria bye, and having no idea where or how long he'd be gone. By the time he surfaced, she could be long gone too. Though, he reminded himself that would be a good thing—back to her real life. That was the point of what Delta did. "Let me introduce you two before I jet."

Winters agreed, following him into the living room.

Victoria had cocooned herself again, walling away the world with blankets and pillows, and Ryder squatted in front of her. "Hey, sweetheart."

Her eyes fluttered before focusing. Those poor eyes. She kept sleeping, and she never looked as though she'd rested.

"Colby Winters is here, and it's time to get up," he said.

Slowly, Victoria sat up, and Ryder joined her on the couch as Winters walked over, grabbing the chair and taking a seat. Both men were on her level, and that seemed best. Winters extended his hand, and after a groggy moment, Victoria did too. They exchanged hellos, and being the great guy he was, Winters had her almost smiling a few minutes later.

Ryder should feel better than he did. But damn it, he didn't want to leave her side. He couldn't tell her he had a job. His phone buzzed, and he glanced at it.

BROCK: *ETA?*

Shit. Ryder had to run. Winters gave him a knowing glance. There weren't too many people who would be blowing up a Delta cell phone.

"Okay, sweetheart." Ryder wrapped an arm around her. "Relax at

Winters's place. Okay?"

She glanced between the two men. "Okay. We're leaving now then?"

"I'll drive you over," Winters said. "Do you have anything to bring with you?"

"Nothing." She shook her head. "The clothes were here, and… I don't have anything with me."

"We can get going then." Winters lifted his chin to Ryder. "You taking off too? Need me to close this place down?"

"Yeah, that'd help."

"Can do." He stood. "I'm going to go find that bottle of water I left in the kitchen."

As soon as Winters left, Ryder's flood of thoughts evaporated. So many things to say to her, but none came. Instead, he carefully pulled her into a hug. "Rest, okay, love?"

"I will."

He pushed off the couch then took her hand, unwinding it from the blankets, and ran his thumb over her knuckles as she stood. "Take care, Victoria No Name."

Winters came in, fist up, and Ryder gave her a last glance goodbye, ignoring the knot in his throat, knocking knuckles with Winters, and headed out the door before he could focus on how each step seemed lead-lined.

ORDERS WERE SIMPLE. Get in. Get out. But this was too simple. There were three of them, Colin, Javier, and him. But none of this felt right.

"What is that, man?" Colin, blood flowing down his face in little rivers, panted and nodded at the paper in Ryder's hand. "I always see that shit when things go wrong."

Ryder pushed his head back, gritting through the pain. He folded the note and tucked it close to his chest, as close to his heart as he could put it. "Nothing."

Sweat poured down Javier's face. "Prayers. He's got his prayers written down." He chuckled, slowly shaking his head. "When shit hits the fan, no one needs to rely on his memory. Just read that shit off a paper."

"Smart." Colin coughed.

Ryder sucked in a breath, finally able to do so without white lightning rocketing in his rib cage. "Not prayers. Jackasses."

"I wouldn't knock anyone right now for praying," Javier said. "Hail Mary…"

"Jesus Christ," Colin muttered.

Javier grabbed a rock and tossed it. "That's what I'm talking about."

"—team. Do you—" The ear piece squealed.

"Shit!" Ryder lurched to the side as Colin and Javier reacted similarly, tearing their com pieces free also.

"We almost had coms," Javier said. "That means they can pick us up on GPS."

"Maybe." Colin groaned.

"Brother, you know the last two seconds are going to be the only two seconds Parker was able to hear." Javier laughed, and Ryder had to agree. There would be shit to pay for doubting Parker's skills.

"Neither of you are bleeding. Jackasses." He patted the computer they'd taken from a drug lord's mansion. "But we have what we need."

"Can you imagine living in that place?" Javier asked.

"I didn't know places like that existed when I was a kid." It might've well been a castle. The thing had a moat, an army of guards… All had gone well until the dogs. Dogs sucked. Dogs that acted as though they were rabid, fire-breathing dragons sucked more. Ryder rolled on his side and laughed. "Should've seen your face."

Javier scowled and ran his hand over his forehead. "If you aren't praying, what was that?"

"What?" Colin grimaced.

"His paper." Javier gestured his head toward Ryder as he pushed his earpiece back in.

Ryder could feel where the folded note was safely stowed away against to his still-racing heart. Adrenaline and endorphins had bled through his system under the hail of gunfire as they escaped. "A list."

"What kind of list?" Colin asked.

Ryder looked toward the setting sun as the thick jungle trees began to darken around them. "Of reasons to live."

Colin propped himself up. "Well, fuck yeah. Don't we all need a list like that?"

"My list is one line: Sophia," Javier said.

"Not all of us got a Sophia, man," Colin added.

But Ryder'd had someone who could have been, long ago. He didn't want to think about her, and instead, focused on his earpiece until it was back in place and didn't bother him. He lost track of Colin and Javier's back and forth, waiting for Titan HQ to patch back in. They needed air support to get the hell out of Mexico.

A rock hit his chest, and Ryder startled back to the conversation at hand.

"You going to share?" Javier asked.

"Share what?"

"Your reasons to live, mate?"

He laughed at the Brazilian feigning the Aussie accent. "Nah."

But Ryder could recount the list in his head that he'd held onto since he was sixteen and had to outrun the train out a tunnel. He'd heard it coming when he started running and knew better than to go in there. But he would never let Zoe go in to save whatever animal she swore she saw. Too bad, it nearly left him dead…

Top Five Reasons To Live

One. We've yet to go skinny-dipping. Bucket list!

Two. We promised to do everything together, twice. Everything is a lot.

Three. Get out of this house. Together. No more watching other kids going. (But good for them!)

Four. One day, we won't want for anything. We'll have our own place, decide our own meals… Wait. I don't want anything other than you now. Scratch #4.

Five. You have to always be around to make your special girl happy.

Silently, he would always laugh at "special girl." They'd heard it once, when a teacher called her "special girl" as if she was anything but, and Ryder owned it, taking back the meaning because she was special. Seemed like a funny word, but they were funny kids.

On the back of that note, he'd written everything he loved about the girl he planned to make happy, and he made it in a list, just the way she loved to. He didn't have much to give her, but that, a list, he could give her—though she wouldn't take it and made him keep the paper he still brought on every job to this day.

Top Five Reasons You're That Special Girl

One. You're tough and didn't need me before I came around.

Two. But when I did, you let me help you out.

Three. You take care of people—unconventionally.

Four. No fear!

Five. Except with me—and I'll never tell your secrets.

"You know. Typical stay low, go fast," Ryder said as his com piece crackled in his ear. "One shot, one kill."

Javier smacked a branch out of his way. "Sniper CliffsNotes."

"He checks it afterward, making sure he's done it right," Colin added, busting Ryder's balls.

"—read me?" Parker Black's voice mixed with static.

"Almost," Colin muttered.

"Delta team here. Do you copy?" Ryder called in.

Nothing but silence.

"Do you read me? Delta team, got your ears on?"

Finally. Decent sound quality. "We got you, Titan. This is Delta."

"Nice to hear you, Delta."

Ryder smiled, relieved that they weren't spending the night here. He wanted back to home base. He wanted to check in with Victoria. Ryder read off their coordinates, and Parker returned with a rendezvous location and update on Colin.

Two minutes later, the three of them were on their feet and heading half a click southeast for a helo pickup.

"Your girl write you your note?" Javier asked as they pushed through the brush.

"He doesn't have a girl," Colin said, breathing heavily and sounding as though he'd sustained more injuries than they realized.

"You don't know, jackass."

"You have a girl?" Colin asked.

"Nope." Branches hit his face as they surged forward.

"You got on good with Victoria No Name." Javier's voice lifted at the end with the suggestion that Ryder thought about and hated that his mind went there.

"We just pulled her out of hell!" His molars ground as he rounded on his teammate. Now his pulse pounded like Colin's, but Ryder's was confusion mixed with lust. The jungle humidity was getting to him—Javier's suggestion too. He *couldn't* think about a woman who'd been trafficked. He shouldn't think of anyone Delta rescued. It was wrong. Wasn't it?

Javier threw his hands up. "Didn't mean any disrespect."

"She's dealing with a lot," Ryder said.

"I know, man. I only meant you two got on well."

"That could be taken a lot of different ways." Ryder inched forward, needing to defend Victoria's honor, Javier made it sound like Ryder had been doing her in the back room.

Javier gave him a chin lift. "Chill, brother."

"I'm chill."

"Then don't take that shit for anything more than the chick did some badass things over there, and she's got my respect. Special girl, is all."

Special girl. The words were a sucker punch that pushed Ryder away as he mumbled an agreement. He inched back through the underbrush and thicket.

"We good, brother?" Javier trailed him. "Nothing but mad respect for her."

"Same."

"I wonder where she came from?" Colin's voice cut with pain he wasn't complaining about.

"Better question. Where the hell is she going?"

No shit. Soon as they returned back to the States and debriefed, Ryder would forgo sleep. His first stop would be to Winters's place, and he hoped to all hell she was still there.

CHAPTER SIX

Australia
Eight years ago

ZOE WALKED INTO the bedroom of the overcrowded foster home holding a cupcake and a birthday card, a smile dangling on her face like she knew that she had snuck one over on Ryder—because she had.

"Happy birthday!" She shoved both the card and cupcake into his face and jumped beside him on the bed.

"How did you know?" Surprised, he sat up, feeling heat in his cheeks and that very present feeling that accompanied her when she walked into the room. She was the closest friend he had—the prettiest too. That didn't matter, though. He liked that she was tough, could keep up with him when they ran the train tracks, and could skip rocks behind Mister Gregor's pond. "Where'd you get a cupcake?"

Because no one in this foster home or any one of the government-run, orphan-packed operations he'd been stuffed into would spend a dollar on his birthday.

"I'll never reveal my sources," she said triumphantly.

"Spit it out!"

She shook her head, ponytails slapping her cheeks. "All you need to know is the sketchy nature of its acquisition should make it taste all the better."

He raised his brows as he drew close, and she did too. They placed it between them, and he looked up. "Then we'd better do it again, yeah?"

"Card first."

He rolled his eyes. "Only because I want a stolen cupcake."

"Didn't say stolen. I said sketchy."

He snagged the handmade card from her hand and opened it.

Happy Birthday, Ryder!

For your 14 years, I came up with 14 things that make you my best mate.

Ryder looked up. "You made me a list of reasons why I'm great?"

"A broke girl has to be creative." She nodded.

His fingers pinched the paper, and he didn't know what to say. "No one's ever got me a present before."

The corner of her lips curled like she understood because she did. "Just read."

One. That time I met you. You covered for me when I snuck in.

Two. That time I snuck in and you said I owed you for covering for me.

"Hey." He pushed her shoulder and vividly remembered the night Zoe had been locked out after their ward locked down the doors. He'd put on quite the distraction when he saw her working the door and windows. "I saw a person in need."

"Ha!" She pushed him back. "You like collecting favors."

He smirked. He could never have too many people who owed him one in a place like this. "Maybe."

Three. Sneaking beer by the Gregors' pond.

Four. When you took back my blankets from the fuckwits who kept taking them.

Ryder laughed. "Arses, all of them."

"They never took my blankets again."

"Guess they didn't." He went back to his card.

Five. Because you eat my eggs every morning when Ms. Briddle says I can't be excused until I eat them.

Six. Because you let me have your toast even though I know you want it.

"That's true."

"I know." She nodded, laughing.

Seven. Halfway through the list and I'm not sure if you're really reading this.

Eight. Never mind. I know you. You are.

Nine. Because you're the strongest guy I know—with muscles—but also on the inside. I don't know how I would've survived being thirteen without you.

He glanced up, his chest feeling tight. "Of course, I'm going to read your card." But what he wanted to say was "Of course she would survive thirteen." He'd never met anyone stronger.

"I know," she repeated.

His stomach felt tingly, his cheeks and hands warm, and Ryder went back to his card. "This thing is long." But he liked it.

Ten. Ten times I've written this list, and I wonder if this will be the one I finally give you. We will see!

"It was." He winked.

"Almost wasn't."

Eleven. We both love vanilla icing and Leaven Heaven.

He dropped the card and grabbed the cupcake. "Is that where this came from?"

"Yup."

Bugging his eyes, he knew that she'd lifted it but had no idea how. Before she could say a word, he took a bite *then* peeled down the wrapper. "Yeah. That's why they call it heaven."

"I know you're going to share."

Before he could give her a chance to read his mind, he smooshed it against her lips—not enough to ruin it. He wasn't stupid!

"Eek—Oh, yum." She licked her lips, taking his wrist and controlling the cupcake so she could take a normal bite as he laughed.

He finished the thing off in three more bites while she protested.

"You're supposed to share more!"

"Ha ha, I did!"

They licked fingers and lips clean, still laughing. "Thanks, Zoe. No one's ever stolen a cupcake for me before."

She fluttered her eyelashes and made a prissy smiley face. "Just call me the cupcake crook, at your service."

He brushed his hands off and balled the wrapper, tossing the evidence into the trash can. "Okay, what else you got for me?"

Her face flushed as she reached for the card. "Oh, that's it, I think."

"Hey, hands off my card."

"No, it's stupid." She pulled it to her chest. "I don't know why I even made it."

"Because you're you, and you're awesome." He wrapped an arm around her neck, knocking them both to their sides, and took it from her.

Twelve. Because once upon a time, you told me that we might only be in this place for a few days, a few months, or years, but that it would be okay if we were buds.

Thirteen. I like you. A lot.

Fourteen. More than friends. Happy birthday, I hope you don't hate me.

The tingly feeling in his stomach flooded his mind. He read the last line over and over before he noticed that Zoe was still as a log and quieter than she'd ever been. They were both laying on his bed, side by side with only the handmade card in between him. He slowly took it down and stared at her. She didn't make a peep. Her unsure eyes were unlike anything he'd experienced before. She was worried he'd back away—that he'd say it wasn't like that between them, and everything between them would fade away?

"I don't hate you," he promised.

But that wasn't what she'd said, just her biggest fear. Ryder swallowed, unsure what he was supposed to say. These things, they didn't come up between them. He didn't know the right words. But he knew she was the closest person to him. He felt as though he was supposed to be hanging out with her, getting in trouble with her, helping her stay out of trouble, sneaking in, out. Stealing cupcakes.

Nerves swarmed in his chest, but words didn't form on his tongue. Ryder leaned forward and wanted to explain but couldn't. His lungs pounded, and the echo of his pulse drummed in his ears as he leaned to her and pressed his lips to hers.

A surge, a thrill, unlike anything he'd ever known ran through him when the softness of her mouth met his. His nerves left as he eased closer, having never tasted anything sweeter than icing on the lips of a girl. *His girl.*

She kissed him back, and they stopped, laying side by side, eyes open.

"More than friends," he said, and his best mate became his girlfriend for his birthday.

CHAPTER SEVEN

THE MID-MORNING SUN pushed through the east-facing window, and Victoria cringed against the new day in the giant, welcoming house. She could've been there an hour, could've been there a year. At this point, it was all the same in Colby and Mia Winters's guest bedroom.

Victoria was smart enough to realize that her complete exhaustion was dangerously close to a mental breakdown. By the time Colby picked her up and Mia greeted her at the door, Victoria had been positive that her arms weren't functioning properly, her mind had moved the pace of sludge, and her legs were baby deer weak. Somehow, she'd showered and slipped into bed in clean clothes.

Yawning as she fought the decision to wake up or force herself back to sleep, Victoria pulled a pillow over her head. Had one day gone by? Or was it two? Embracing sleep was all she wanted to do—with occasional trips to the bathroom and eating because she had to. That was the only way she was surviving because the sleep wasn't working.

Damn it.

Detaching from reality was the only option for recovery because so far, closing her eyes and fading away in the lush blankets and thick pillows had meant nothing but fitful, nightmare-riddled sleep. Not even the sound of kids laughing and playing from somewhere in the house woke her up, and Victoria loved playing with kids. She didn't know whether to scream, cry, or give up.

"I'm a fake."

She rolled over in the thick comforter and pulled the soft fabric to her nose. The Downy-fresh scent should have semi-comforted her while sleeping, but awake again, she didn't want to deal with life.

It wasn't that she was raped. It wasn't that she'd been imprisoned. It was that she'd been taken against her will—that she hadn't seen it coming and couldn't figure out a way to escape it once the play was in motion.

What kind of bounty hunter had she been? How good were her self-defense skills?

A light knock on her door interrupted the career-questioning spiral she was prepared to go on. Maybe, if she didn't answer, no one would bother her. Or maybe she should because if there was one thing Victoria had learned in the short time she'd spent awake, it was that Mia Winters was a pint-sized force of nature who got what she wanted. That whole deceptively innocent act was bull. If she knocked, she was coming in.

The door cracked. Mia poked her head inside with her brown hair curling around her chin. "Are you alive?"

"Questionable."

Mia stepped inside, closing the door behind her. "At least you're awake."

"That's debatable too." Victoria burrowed under the covers and cringed. What kind of bitchy nut job did she sound like? Mia let her stay in her house, eat her food, and found her clothes that fit, sight unseen, and still Victoria was a wreck. What kind of woman would put up with her BS?

Her eyes went wide under the covers. *Maybe... someone who had been there before?* Victoria pulled the blanket down, eyeing the petite lady as she padded past the bed with a tray of food.

"Ah, um." She cleared her throat, thinking of ways to apologize for the bitchiness while still somewhat paralyzed. "That came out different than it sounded in my head."

"How'd it come out?" Mia turned from the side table where she'd placed the tray.

"It came out..." Victoria propped herself up on an elbow. "Super bitchy for a woman who's sleeping in borrowed pajamas."

Mia lifted a cardigan-covered shoulder. "I don't know much about what you went through, but bitchy is probably the least of your concerns."

Victoria breathed in as the scent of coffee slowly filtered into the room, trying its damnedest to entice her to the land of the living. The temptation was there, but her muscles and her mind were still on protest. Only her coffee-addicted taste buds were on red alert, desperately trying to remind the rest of her body how great caffeine was.

"Sleep's a good thing. No one's telling you not to sleep for a few days. Your body has to recuperate. Survival mode is depleting. Add in how you helped others, and Victoria, you need to sleep, eat, and if and when you're ready, deal with what happened."

Helping others rang out in her head. God, she had another one fooled, and this time, Victoria had done so without saying a word. Guilt bubbled under her skin. *First Ryder, now Mia.* Victoria should clear up this misconception, if only she could force herself out of bed.

"Ryder's here," Mia mentioned, turning back to the tray, moving the cup, and unwrapping the silverware from the napkin. "He wanted to stop in."

Victoria froze. *Ryder*. She'd never wanted to see him again and suddenly couldn't wait to say thank you. He'd been her savior, her believer. He'd been fooled by the belief that she was as strong as Victoria had once thought of herself. She wanted to run, fast and furiously, away from him because of everything that she was dealing with, because he said a simple goodbye and sent her off with a hug that she could still feel after she met Colby Winters. That was that. She didn't know why she'd thought Ryder would drive over with her. All she knew was that lonely sadness was almost worse than knowing how she could never go back to the career and life she'd known before.

"Can I sit?" Mia asked after assessing her for a moment too long.

"Of course." She nodded. "It's your bed."

"But you're in it."

"Everyone asks me now if they can come next to me. On the couch, on the bed." Victoria smoothed her hand over the sheets. "Is this what it's going to be like when I go home?"

She could barely remember her hometown—nothing more than a distant memory of a place that tricked her with its safety and security.

"We're just being cognizant of what you went through."

"The idea that people are treating me with kid gloves..." *Yet, I can barely get out of bed.* "Deservedly so, though. So thanks."

Mia sat and scowled. "You are really hard on yourself, aren't you?"

"Well… Yes."

"You need to eat." Apparently changing her mind, Mia jumped off the bed. "I'll tell Ryder to come back some other time."

"No. It's okay." Victoria wanted to see him more than she wanted to sleep or eat. She realized she was finger-combing her hair into something semi-presentable and quickly slapped her hands down, burying them under the covers.

"Here." Mia poured juice into a glass. "You need a little sugar in your system."

She needed something, alright, and juice was probably not the answer. *Sleep. Xanax. Something.*

One of Mia's eyebrows arched as she handed the glass to Victoria. "Might help."

"With what?"

"With whatever you need it too."

That was awfully cryptic. Maybe Mia read her mind and crushed up a sedative. She took the glass and carefully sipped it. "Oh, that's good."

"Thanks. I squeezed it with my kids." She waited until Victoria placed the glass on the nightstand.

"Grapefruit juice and something else?" Though the chances of pharmacology juice making with kids was probably not what happened.

"Lemonade too," Mia said. "There's a bacon, egg, and cheese biscuit wrapped up in that linen napkin, and if you want to take shower, I'll tell Ryder you'll be ready in an hour or so. He and Colby can go do guy things."

"Why is he here?" She quickly bit her lip, not wanting to know what Mia thought the answer was.

"Maybe he's here for the same reason that I just saw signs of life." Mia leaned against the wall.

A blush hit Victoria's cheeks. "I don't know what you think, but—"

"You've been here for almost two days and barely said two words. I've done most of the talking, and I've never seen you smile."

"I've sm—"

"You haven't," Mia corrected her. "If I didn't know where you came from and why you were here, I would have assumed you were a friend of Delta, brought home to recoup after two busted legs."

"That happens?"

"Sometimes. But look at you: ready to jump up and shower." Mia grinned.

"I barely know him."

"Either way, he's a good one to barely know."

"He is?" Victoria scooted to the edge of the bed, letting her legs dangle. "I mean, not that I'm asking *about* him. It's just nice to know he is what he seems."

"He is."

Victoria's mind raced, and she couldn't wrap her mind around why she even cared—other than the obvious. He was an attractive man, and he had an accent that could stop a woman in her tracks if the guy—the *bloke*—opened his mouth. But that was that. It wasn't as if he'd asked her on a date. No, he'd rescued her from her rapist and kept her from killing him. She should hate him...

A knock on the door pulled Victoria out of the clouds. There was Ryder, cracking the door with a winning smile and eyes that latched on to her. *Oh, whoa.* Victoria's heart stalled.

"Well, come on in, Ryder," Mia drawled. "I thought I asked you to wait."

He finally tore their gazes apart and gave Mia a saccharine grin. "Waiting wasn't working for me anymore, Mama Mia."

"Ask me how much I care what works for you, handsome."

"I will later, right after I beg for your forgiveness. Can I come in?"

"You're already in." She raised her eyebrows, looking pointedly at the carpet where he stood inside what might have well been a green zone he wasn't flagged to enter. "She'd like food, privacy, and a shower. Think you could give her a few minutes?"

"Think I could do a lot of things." He stepped further into the room as if angling to get a better look at Victoria. His silent inquisition was altogether unnerving and somehow reassuring, though his emerald green eyes darkened. Whatever he found while searching her face, she wasn't sure he was pleased.

"Is listening one of them?" Mia pushed off the wall.

"Victoria?" Ryder slowly lifted his eyebrows. "A word, love?"

The nickname ran over her like flames licking across a brush fire. A generic nickname, she was sure, but she'd heard it once before falling off his lips, and she'd just about fallen.

Weren't people like her—assault victims, due to be put in a grouped category—supposed to be unable to feel and think like the hot flash that just ran through her? She was feeling and thinking in a way that caught her off guard.

She nodded since her voice was caught in her throat.

"I'll be back." Mia smoothed a hand over the edge of the bed. "If you need anything, Ryder can find me. Or you can get out of bed. Your call."

"Thanks," he said.

Mia ignored him and waited until Victoria gave a quick nod.

"Don't forget to put some food in your stomach—something more than that juice."

"Mia can cook better than anyone I know," Ryder offered. "Bet that's hand-squeezed."

"It is, and Ryder's kissing my cute butt because I explicitly told him to wait downstairs." Mia crossed her arms and gave him one of the best mom voices Victoria had ever heard.

"Aw, c'mon now." He gave Mia an apologetic head tilt that seemed genuine. "You know I love you."

"Did you hear how thick he laid that accent on? Doesn't work for me, buddy. I'm immune to your charm."

"You're killing me." He clutched at his heart.

"Alright, don't die on my watch." Mia relented semi-jokingly and moved to the door, hanging onto the knob. "If I didn't love you, I'd kick you out myself."

"Don't I know it." He turned back toward Victoria as Mia let the door click shut.

It was just the two of them, and carefully, as though he had to plant one footstep in front of the other, he made his way closer but stopped parallel, not coming close to the edge of the mattress.

"Hi."

"Hi." She finally managed to get over her aversion to the spoken word around him. "I didn't think I'd see you again."

Odd, how there was a two-foot gap between him and her bed, but he seemed miles away. Ryder had seen her in her most needy, most vulnerable moments, but now they had this awkward threshold of appropriateness. Forget that he pulled a gun from her hand so she didn't murder a bastard. Forget how she fell apart, crying and shaking, exhausted after weeks of living in fear of Ivan Mikhailov.

Ryder had barely said a word, and that was what she needed: to be held for hours and cry. He didn't make her talk about it. Not a single word. She let it all out. But why was he here now?

God, he was such a beautiful man. *A protective one.* Her eyes dropped to his arms, and she remembered how safe they made her feel.

She sank back into the mess of covers, letting it swallow her alive. If she wasn't broken or depressed, she'd be attracted to him. But she was so damn tired. Victoria closed her eyes. *Tired, broken. Ruined, probably.* Would she feel anything again except for this all-encompassing shame from not keeping herself safe? No. The likely answer was no.

"Mia mentioned you hadn't come out much."

When she'd been held against her will in Russia, living in a room with a dozen other girls, she'd been the strong one, the one they turned to and relied on. She was strong for them, for herself. Victoria had promised there would be a way out of hell, that they would go back to wherever they came from, and she'd been right.

Except now she didn't want to face Mia and could barely look at Ryder.

"Victoria?" Ryder's low voice was like a soothing touch. "Is there anything I can do?"

She wanted another hug. Instead of asking, she squeezed her eyes shut. "I don't know."

"I'm going to sit right here." The side of the mattress dipped slightly under his weight.

She didn't say anything, but she nodded, not trusting her voice to lie to him again. What was it about him? Needing him close? Of course, she cared. He protected her, saved her when she couldn't do that for herself.

Her eyes burned, tears escaped, and she swatted those bastards away, hating how out of control her mind spun. *Raped three times by one of the most powerful men in the world.* This, she knew, would affect her. By training, by career, by natural logic, she should know this and accept it.

"You should cry. Kick. Scream. Whatever you need to," he said quietly.

"I don't want to," Victoria gasped, unable to contain her choking tears. Her shoulders shook. Memories of Ivan's face, his hands—they were too much. Once, she fought him and was hurt far more than the other times. Then she lay there and was mentally worse off. The last time, she did both and had both the bruises and the mindfuck to remember Ivan by. *God! Why? And how did this happen?*

The tears came. She couldn't stop them, and she hated the path they burned down her cheeks, hated that Ryder was witness to her unraveling, just like he'd been in Russia.

He rested his hand on her back, not speaking, and he didn't move to shush her. His palm simply rested there.

"Ryder." She fell against him, and he wrapped his arm around her.

"Easy, love," he whispered. "Take a breath."

"I can't."

His chin touched the top of her head, and the arms that she knew could hug her like all hell did the job, wrapping her away from the world until the tears stopped.

"Feel better?"

Nodding, Victoria drew in a deep breath, wiping under her eyes. "Could you hand me a tissue?"

He was already halfway off the bed as if reading her mind and handed her the box. Again, Victoria wiped her face. With another fresh tissue to cover her eyes, she could barely look at him.

"This can't be what you signed up for," Victoria mumbled. "Sorry."

"Stop apologizing."

She balled the tissue up and hazarded a glance in his direction. "Why did you come here?"

"I was worried about you." Ryder tilted his head back to the bed. "Can I sit again?"

Victoria's eyes squeezed shut, but she nodded.

"I don't have to. Never mind."

She blinked and refocused on him. "What?"

"I didn't mean to invade your space."

Her head dropped. Ruined. He saw nothing but a ruined woman who was so fragile he misread what she meant with a simple look. "I didn't—I wasn't… I made a face. Or I didn't mean to make a face." She cringed. *Such a mess!* She couldn't even get her words right. "I sound like an idiot!"

"You don't."

"I do. I'm not someone people worry about. Ever. I worry about people. That's what I do. *Did!* I took care of people, and now look at me. I'm broken." A sob caught in her throat. "I thought I was strong, and now, I'm *this*."

He came to her bedside, swooping next to her. "Victoria."

"Something happened to me. Over there." She sucked a breath as she collapsed against the pillows. "And I can't."

He put a careful hand on her forearm. "Listen to me." He ducked down close. "I don't know what's the right or wrong thing to say now, so I'm just going to say this."

He came closer so their eyes met. His head was almost level with hers on another pillow, but he held her gaze and didn't let go.

"Please don't tell me to get up," she whispered. "To get back to my life."

"I wouldn't dream of it." Ryder shifted so his weight was semi-on the bed, but he didn't break their stare. "We brought everyone home, and every girl said you were their savior, that you put yourself in front of guards for them, that you made sure they had food. If nightmares struck, you coaxed them back to sleep. You were their guardian angel in hell."

Her eyes burned again with tears, but she wouldn't look away from his emerald ones.

"Whoever you are, love, wherever you're from, you take as long as you need to get back the strength it took to become you, and I will stay by your side to help you if that's what it takes."

"Why?" Her voice broke along with a stray tear.

"Because I admire warriors." He pushed away loose hairs she hadn't noticed sticking to her tear-soaked face. "If you don't want to eat, then get some rest. Real sleep. Not this fitful, nightmarish dozing Mia's told me you're fighting through."

Her face fell, unable to lie to him when he believed in her for whatever confused reason. "I can't."

"Try again. For me," he ordered softly. "I'm not going anywhere. You trusted me once to help you. Trust me again."

Ryder shifted, placing both of his shoes on the bed and toeing them off. "I'm going to stay here, and if you need me, you'll know I'm here. Unless you want to eat something first."

"Not hungry." She shook her head and snuggled back against the pillows. He put his steady hand on her shoulder, and she shifted, grabbing onto his forearm like it was a stuffed animal, and pulled it close to her chest. It was warm and muscular. *Safe.* She could almost feel his pulse, or maybe that was hers as she curled against him and could finally breathe.

He curled around her, and she breathed in the scent of his shirt's detergent and maybe his cologne or deodorant as she finally fell asleep.

CHAPTER EIGHT

VICTORIA WOKE IN the dark with her arms wrapped tight to her chest and her mouth sandpaper dry. Relaxing, she rolled to her side and stretched as the distinct memory of Ryder rushed back the same time she registered that the change in temperature wasn't the lack of covers, but rather the lack of Ryder's arm held tight between her breasts.

"Oh." She jolted upright and felt all the blood rushing to her cheeks. "Oh! Oh, God. Ryder. I'm so sorry." Face on fire, there wasn't much to say that wasn't an apology.

"Hey," he mumbled as though maybe he'd been asleep too. The room was dark with a slice of light from the adjoining bathroom. "Easy."

She blinked in the darkness as his hands sleepily ran over her body. She tried to find her bearings. What time was it? How long had they been asleep? Did she drool on the poor guy? But as her mind rushed to make sense of clinging to Ryder as she slept, she took into account that her muscles and mind didn't hate her. Nothing moved like sludge, which had been the case before she'd gone to sleep, a tearful mess.

He pulled a hand overhead, readjusting his pillow, then ran it over his face. "Morning."

She moved from his wandering hand. He'd been asleep, maybe not knowing *who* he'd been asleep with, and he didn't need that kind of awkwardness. Out of reach, she propped herself against the backboard. "I'm so sorry."

His low, sexy laughter didn't sound annoyed, only tired. "Stop apologizing." He almost seemed to find some kind of amusement in her panicked awakening. "How are you feeling?"

Other than her racing heart, which was easily explainable as she woke up clinging to the tan, muscled Aussie with great hair and sweet things to say, she was… better. *And hungry.* That was a huge improvement from that last time she'd been awake. "How long was I asleep?"

"I conked out after a couple hours, so—"

"Oh, God. I'm so sorry." She'd held him captive?

He picked his head off the pillow, eyebrows up. "What for?"

"I'm just, um, I had you pinned. I feel bad you couldn't leave."

His hearty chuckle fell easily from his lips. *Nothing quiet about that bit of laughter.*

"What's so funny?"

He turned on to his side. "I wouldn't call it pinned." He poked her arm, and she tipped sideways an inch or two. "Point proven."

"Oh, well." She stumbled for words. "You know what I mean." Her stomach growled. "If not by holding you down, then by guilt."

"Ha. Hungry?"

"Mia left me a plate." She swung her legs away from him. "I'll—"

"So am I. You're the best excuse I have to raid her fridge. Let's go."

"I don't want to be more of a burden than I've already been." She searched for the plate, but it was gone.

"Mia took it hours ago."

"Oh." And that meant Mia also saw her clinging to Ryder like a needy lunatic. Classy. "I really should get going anyway."

He laughed. Again. "Sure thing. After you eat. Then you can walk back to wherever you came from."

She bit her lip. Maybe to the closest ATM and from there she could—no. That wouldn't work. She could call her bank, but it wasn't like they'd wire her cash. She could call Seven, and her best friend would send the closest motorcycle army to swoop for a rescue. Then she'd have to explain something to Seven about where she'd been and to Ryder and the Winters about the gang of bikers. There'd likely be police to deal with since she was a missing person. So much to talk about that she didn't want to. Her head began to spin.

"Come on," Ryder quietly said, taking her hand. "We can deal with everything in pieces. Don't let it overwhelm you. First, we eat."

The overwhelming totality hit her like a landslide. Again. This time, she didn't cry. It wasn't Ivan's face that held her in place. It was the reminder that eventually she'd have to go back to Iowa and deal with the fact she was a sham. There would be so many questions, and her face would be the centerpiece of the eleven o'clock news for the foreseeable future. None of that brought tears, but it did bring paralysis.

He wrapped an arm around her shoulders, tugging her to the side of the bed. "Mia's kitchen is like Shangri-la. You want that."

He had her unsteadily on her feet. She wasn't sure she remembered the last time she'd been there except for the rare trip to the bathroom. "I don't know."

"I do. Let's go, warrior woman."

"Don't call me a warrior. If you even knew who I was, you'd know it never should've happened." Her face twisted in disgust. "Happened? *Happened.* God, I can't even say it." Victoria groaned dropping her head back before bringing it back up, along with the truth and all the pain. "He raped me."

Ryder sobered. All laughter dissipated into the dark. "You know what I do. I know what happened out there. You don't have to say it."

"More than once, and then I couldn't pull the trigger. He took his time, and I couldn't end him."

Ryder braced a hand on her bicep as she faltered.

"They kidnapped me."

"Who?"

She couldn't explain how she went after a bounty and failed, how if she'd been smarter, more aware of what was happening, not as aggressive or something… If she had not decided on that bounty target to hunt—a high-level Russian gang member—they never would have passed her to the Russian gunrunners who were making inroads with Mayhem on the Highway 35 corridor. "No idea…"

"Sorry."

"They traded me, sent me to another country and when I had the chance to take Ivan's life, I failed." The pathetic words ran off her tongue, and she had to get back to the point of reliving all of this.

"Victoria—"

"I'm weak. I don't deserve whatever misplaced attention or respect you're giving me." She pulled back.

Ryder leaned an inch forward. "Say whatever you want to say as often as you want to say it, love."

"Why aren't you listening to me?" Frustration seared her throat. That Australian accent of his, thick and low in her ear, made her ache in irritation almost as much as she wanted to lean closer. The feel of his presence acted like a security blanket in a way she couldn't explain.

"Did you feel better after you slept?" His low voice rumbled.

"Yes." She nodded.

"You'll be even better with food in your system. Let's go." Ryder's thumb stroked her skin before he urged her forward. "Trust me."

Victoria wanted to, and there was something in his voice that reminded her of sleeping in his arms.

"Off we go, love."

Not much of a choice, and they passed an alarm clock turned away from the bed as they walked out. 1:32 AM. She'd slept for almost twelve hours. Ryder didn't leave her side for that long?

Her bare feet padded next to his socks, and they moved down a long hallway to stairs. There was a child-safety gate at the top of the staircase, and he took her hand as they went down in the dark. There were nightlights along the way, and at the bottom, they hooked a right, and he led them into the kitchen.

"The holy grail," Ryder mumbled as he hit a few light switches. The bright overhead lights blasted on, and he cursed, slapping them off. "Too much. Hang on." Finally, he found the under-cabinet lighting. "Better, yeah?"

"Yes, thanks."

"Good." He beelined for a mammoth fridge. "All right. Let's see what we have." After a quick pull, he perused the side door and began to pull out Tupperware containers, occasionally pausing to read labels.

"I'm not sure how hungry I am." She eyed all the food he was removing.

"You're starved. I heard your stomach. And so am I."

Her cheeks flashed hot. Well, all right then. "My stomach might not physically be able to hold as much as yours."

"Either way, no one will accuse me of not feeding you. Mia's cute and all, but she's also scary deadly too. Don't let the manners and smile fool you."

Victoria laughed, and Ryder stopped, stared, and went back to the fridge.

"What?" she asked, suddenly self-conscious.

"Nothing." He didn't turn around, peeking behind the milk in case a rogue vat of leftovers had escaped his inspection. "Just hadn't heard you laugh before. It's a good sound."

Warmth ran through her as she smiled. It wasn't the same as the hot flash of embarrassment earlier, even though the fact he said that made her even more self-conscious about… everything. It was just nice. Or something. She didn't know.

"Okay, I think that's everything we could possibly want." He turned with his hands full, two longnecks threaded in one hand and a gallon jug in the other. "Drinks? Beer or milk? I'm sure they've got Coke or juice somewhere too."

"A beer works for me too."

"Good choice." He put the milk back and shut the fridge, then went to a drawer for a bottle opener, flicking off the tops. "Here."

She took the bottle, and he held out his. "What are we 'cheersing' too?"

"You, love."

"Me? Why?"

"Because, Victoria No Last Name, sometimes warriors need reminders that they're badass." He clinked his bottle against hers before she could protest. "Plates, and then there is roast beef and fried chicken. Two different kinds of potatoes…"

Whatever else Ryder said didn't matter. She didn't hear anything else but "sometimes warriors need reminders that they're badass." How was he this confused? Or maybe she was? Once upon a time, not that long ago, she'd been confident enough in herself that maybe she was a little too cocky. And that's what got her in all this trouble to begin with. Correcting him didn't seem to work.

"Victoria?" Ryder stepped closer. "Fine. You get both. Roast beef and chicken. You won't regret it."

He put his bottle down and grabbed a fork from the drawer, peeling back the lids from two containers.

"I can get it." She put her bottle next to his.

"I assume you could too. But not if you keep drifting off." He paused and flicked a piece of chicken into the air and caught it with his mouth. "I'm telling you. Mia makes wonder food. Soon as you eat, you'll feel better. And whatever's bouncing around in your head? Put it on pause. You can deal with it after you get a full stomach."

She deflated. Was she that easy to read? Back in the day, she could keep her cards close to the vest if she wanted to.

With minimal effort, Ryder packed two plates with far more food than she could ever hope to eat. He microwaved both and placed them at the breakfast bar.

"I'm feeling helpless," she muttered and stood in search of silverware.

"Second drawer on the right."

"Thanks." At least she wasn't a total dunce in the lend-a-hand department.

"Now we feast."

A minute later, Ryder pulled a bar stool next to her, and they both sat in the dimly lit silence. As leftovers went, this was some of the best food Victoria had ever had. She barely tamped down a groan of satisfaction.

"Told you," he mumbled through a mouthful of potatoes. "Mia's the shit in the kitchen."

This time, Victoria mumbled an agreement even though her mouth was full. "Mm-hmm."

After a few more minutes of silent eating, she took a sip of the beer. "Maybe you were right."

"Of course I was right." His forked clinked quietly against the plate. "About what?"

She smiled against the opening of the beer bottle and let it rest against her bottom lip. "That food would help."

"That's common sense." Ryder stretched and grabbed his beer. They took long sips and placed their bottles next each other. "But Mia's kitchen is like Titan's secret weapon."

"Titan and Delta are the same thing?"

He nodded. "Titan signs the paycheck. Delta is my team."

"Ah." She wondered about her paycheck. Or lack thereof. Being self-employed had always been a bonus, and getting her little company off the ground had been hard. Hell, being a woman bounty hunter and private investigator wasn't easy to start with. But she'd never shied away from a challenge. Now who would hire her? Someone who couldn't protect herself? Someone who never saw this attack coming? No one. Sure, she could pick up bounties. But that wasn't enough to pay the bills and live the life she wanted. That was barely enough to live paycheck to paycheck. The PI work was where she flourished—that and teaching self-defense classes, acting as a pillar in the community, as what a strong, single woman business owner could be. And now look at her.

She was a sham.

Still, a well-rested sham with a full stomach.

"Where's your mind?" Ryder asked quietly.

"Home," she finally admitted.

"Why won't you tell me anything about that place?"

"Because I'm not ready to face it." She picked up her fork and drew lines in what was left of the gravy on the plate. "Because they think I'm something that this whole… situation proved I'm not."

Ryder crossed his arms and let her think in silence. She took a deep breath and made crisscross lines in the gravy remnants.

"You don't have to tell anyone what happened to you," he finally said.

"Oh," she chortled. "Where I come from, everyone's business is your business, and vice versa."

"Small town?"

"Not that small, but maybe small-minded?"

"Maybe you aren't giving them the chance. I'm sure they'd rather have you come home." He paused. "I'd rather have you come home."

Her heart skipped a beat, and she tilted her head, holding the fork still, trying to understand why he said things like that. "Sure. They'd love me to come home. I probably meant something to them."

"Did you mean something to somebody?"

It felt like a loaded question. The way his eyes held hers said it *was* a loaded question. And maybe that made sense, why he thought she didn't want to go home: that she'd been raped and couldn't face her boyfriend or husband. "No. Not like that."

Ryder nodded, not responding, and grabbed his beer, downing another long pull.

"What do you do? For Delta? Something specific when you're not sitting in kitchens at two a.m. with random women?"

"We're a ghost team. We disappear."

"What does that mean?"

"We surface to do our job and go dark again."

Her chest squeezed, and she couldn't understand the meaning behind what he explained, but the tone of his voice urged her to push. "How's this job going? Never-ending, I guess."

"Job's over." He lifted a shoulder. "Everyone's home."

"Except you."

He rolled the bottle between his hands. "Actually, I had a job and came back here. It was a quick one. In and out. Nothing too messy, except Colin. He got messy. But for now, we're all dark again."

She bit her lip.

"You could go home whenever you want. Delta, for all its bravado and badassery, has a soft center. Until you're ready, you can stay where you are."

"Right." She worked over what he said. "What does that mean? You're dark?"

He lifted a shoulder and winked. "We're a ghost team. You never saw me. I wasn't here."

"Boo," she whispered and laughed quietly.

"Boo," he chuckled and quickly drained his beer.

If he was dark, he was here on his own accord or maybe doing a favor for Mia? What did that mean? "Why are you here if you're not on the job anymore?"

"I already explained that, Victoria." He stood and picked up his plate. "You done?"

She nodded and watched as Ryder collected her plate, testing her beer and finding it not empty. He left her bottle, gathered the silverware, and dumped it in the sink then returned with fresh beer for himself.

"I'm sorry if I gave you the impression I'm something that I'm not." She toyed with her beer, hating that she could disappoint him.

"Are you tired?"

"Um, no. Not really."

He leaned against the breakfast bar. "Me either. Grab your beer. Do you want another one?"

"What for?"

"We're going outside." He pointed his new bottle toward the back door.

"Oh. Uh, no. I think I'm good."

"Come on. Let's see if Winters's alarm system is going to go off if I do this..." He pushed off the bar and went to a wall panel, pressed a few buttons, and turned back to her, looking rather impressed with himself. "Guess I remembered—hang on."

A minute later, he returned with a blanket and grabbed his beer bottle. "Now we're ready."

She didn't know what to protest, but she wasn't tired. They were just going to go for a walk with a blanket in the middle of the night? This was unconventional at best, but Victoria followed Ryder's lead. They stepped out onto a back porch, and he shut the door. Her eyes adjusted to the country night. It reminded her of her parents' house growing up in Iowa and not her house off Main Street.

He grabbed a flashlight from a table in the middle of the deck, and they made their way with the beers and a blanket. Night bugs chirped, and the sky, full of diamonds, sparkled overhead.

"Your feet okay?" He tugged off his socks and tossed them aside.

"I think so. Where are we going?" she whispered so as not to disturb the eerie quiet that always descended at night.

"We'll know it when we find it."

Grass crunched under her feet after she stepped off the deck's final stair, and she wriggled her toes into the ground. "You haven't been there?"

"Not at night."

Nerves swirled in her stomach as her eyes darted. "What about snakes or something?"

"If there's a snake, it'll hear us moving and get out of the way."

Really? But she trusted him. What was the worst thing that could happen? Since when was she scared of walking in grass without shoes on? Was this a repercussion of the rape? That she would second-guess something as simple as walking in the grass when she couldn't see what was in front of her? Her heart rate increased but not that much. Was that because she hadn't moved in days? Maybe because Ryder made her heart race for any number of reasons, none of which she wanted to think about. Or was she scared of grass now? *Damn it.*

They walked side by side for a few minutes, the flashlight illuminating their path through the grass and down a slight slope until she could see what looked like a small lake and maybe a deck ahead. He held her hand as they stepped onto the boardwalk. The smooth wood planks under foot felt well worn and cared for. Still, she was extra careful not to stub her toe. The flashlight beam caught a few kids' toys, and it made sense that Ryder didn't seem worried about walking through the grass and boardwalk.

Ryder slowed. "You okay?"

"Sure." But was she? The walk to the lake could've been relaxing, but instead, she was trying to figure out if she now had a fear of walking in the grass.

"Relax. That's the point of this."

"Couldn't be more relaxed." Even the way she forced the lie past her lips made her muscles hurt from the tension building in her limbs.

Ryder laughed out loud, and the way he did it was so honest, so brutal in calling her out, that she had to admit he knew her truth. *Some of it.* "Trying to relax."

"Better." He tossed the blanket out on the edge of the boardwalk, killed the flashlight, and dropped to dangle his legs over the side. "Want to have a seat?"

Carefully, she sat down and scooted next to him then dropped her bare feet over the edge, letting them swing back and forth. Somewhere in the water, something jumped, and a bullfrog croaked. A warm, summer night breeze picked up long enough to let the leaves rustle but not to give her a chill.

"What's home like?" His voice floated on the night's gentle breeze.

"You jump right to the deep stuff?"

He gave a quiet chuckle. "You want to talk football instead?"

Soccer or pigskin? "I guess I'm probably thinking of the wrong kind of football?"

"Actually, I don't bloody care what you talk about because it's not what I want to hear."

"Yeah." He didn't hold back much, even if he was polite and sweet or laid on his Aussie accent.

"What's home like?" Ryder tried again.

She tried to remember how it was when things were good, anything she'd be willing to admit to—though why she wanted to sugarcoat the truth for Ryder, she had no idea. "My parents' place was something like this."

That was true. It was also bullshit, true only in the fact that Iowa had lakes and bullfrogs and that she dangled her feet over the edges of lakes. But that was about where the similarities ended.

"You should call them." His inflection was earnest, and it killed her the way he simply believed that because she lived in a place like this that might mean her folks were good.

Victoria wanted to swipe away the urge to let him know more about her. *Absurd, really*. She hadn't shared her last name. But the fabric of who she was? Why not... She almost shook her head at the silliness. She spent the night in his arms, let him watch as she panicked under the covers, and yet she could barely bring down the wall on her true self. "I don't know how to get ahold of my mom, and my dad's... hard to explain. My dad is…"

"Dads are a tricky one sometimes," he finished for her.

Her dad wasn't a conversation topic she wanted to bring up. Maybe Ryder would forget he even asked if she stayed silent long enough.

"Is he dead?"

"Sometimes it seemed that way." She sighed.

"How many guesses do I get before you tell me?"

Maybe it was easier to talk about this under the protective barrier of the night. "Federal lockup."

"Ah." His body shifted as the short word drew long into the evening.

Not knowing what he thought, how that now colored his opinion of her, everything that she hated about her dad's constant run-ins with the law twisted in her gut. "I'm not a bad person."

"Didn't say you were, Victoria."

She twisted toward him in the dark. "He's probably not a bad person either, just not a great person. Just, I don't know," she rambled, hating how Ryder's opinion of her was likely lessening by the second, but she had to say something positive about her dad—or as positive as she could muster. "He's just a person who can never get it right."

Embarrassed, she wished she could lose herself in the night. Victoria put her hands behind her and dropped her head back to stare at the stars when all she wanted to do was curl into a ball and pretend she hadn't admitted that part of her family history. Why did she share that? Unsettled emotions bubbled under her surface, and she focused on the sheet of stars overhead.

"There are so many," she whispered about the brilliant, sparkling lights that beckoned for her attention like there were so many paths one could take in life. It was easy to focus on one star, but what if she chose wrong and wasted the entire time she spent there staring at some man-made satellite or hunk of human garbage reflecting the sun? Her dad went down the wrong path, and now his life was gone. But Ryder wouldn't think of it that way. He was, in a way, in law enforcement, and he wasn't saying much now that she'd clued him in on a small portion of who she was.

"More than we can comprehend."

"Does my father's history make you think less of me?" She turned her head, waiting expectantly for the usual answer. *Of course not!* But it was always a lie. She could tell in their voices no matter what their words said.

Ryder inhaled as though he considered her question. "Should it?"

"No."

He dropped back on his elbows, not looking at her, but still mimicking her position. "I wouldn't think less of you. How long's he got?"

"This time?" She fed him more information with that bit of a question. "No idea. A while. I stopped asking or counting, I suppose."

Ryder nodded.

"You have something to say about everything, advice to give, but nothing about my dad?"

"Do you need advice?"

"No." She lifted a shoulder. "You asked about home. I guess you're trying to figure me out…" A light bulb went off. "Look at what happened to me. I was a statistic waiting to happen."

Ryder jolted. "I don't believe that."

"Why not?" *Damn.* She hadn't even seen the irony until now. Not wanting to become her parents, she'd tried so hard to be the opposite of them that she became a statistic. If it weren't pathetic, she would've laughed. "God, it was only a matter of time before something like this happened to me."

He put his hand across her back, consoling her. "Stop, love. You're getting worked up. Change of subject. What do you do for a living?"

"Obviously, it doesn't matter." Victoria clamped her back molars down. Too many emotions came at her from different directions. Her job. Her past. Her parents. Her inability to avoid being a statistic.

"It matters." His hand smoothed circles between her shoulder blades.

"I could've been a superhero, and I'll still be the woman who was trafficked and raped. I was powerless to stop it when everyone thought I could."

"Are you a teacher?"

She shook her head. "Stripper."

"I'm not here to judge, love, but bullshit."

"Waitress."

He hummed and shook his head. "Maybe part-time. But no. You're hiding from a successful life at home, wherever your home is."

"Nowhere, USA."

"Nowhere, USA, for Victoria No Last Name. Sounds like a very generic place."

"Must be," she muttered. "Except for the traffickers."

"Who are you, love?"

"What do you want from me?"

"It was an easy question. I want the truth." A bullfrog croaked. "I want to know more from the girl who won't tell me anything."

She brought her knees to her chest and wrapped her arms around them as she ducked her head. "I was a sham. It doesn't matter. I didn't realize it. But now I do."

Tears she thought she left under the covers before a lack of good sleep and food crept back up and threatened to fall again.

Ryder put an arm around her shoulder. "Why is this so hard for you to admit?"

She squeezed her eyes tight and couldn't handle her own truth. "Delta can easily figure out who I am at this point, can't you?"

"Yeah, we can."

"Have you?"

"Not yet."

"Will you?"

"I don't know. Not my call."

She was so embarrassed at how much she'd failed despite all her training. It was best to leave Mia and Colby's place. Victoria would thank Mia and hit the road as soon as she was able to figure out how and where to go start over. Surely, she could do that by the morning.

"Pick." Ryder's low voice rumbled close to her ear. "Someone to trust."

Pick me… The words seemed so close to falling off his lips but didn't. Or maybe those words were only in her imagination, and she wanted someone to cling to. No one would blame her for hoping this handsome, subtly sweet man would try to make the nightmare fade away. She'd trusted Ryder enough to sleep next to him and to tell him the secrets about her family. Ryder was the person she wanted to trust.

"That person could be you, huh?" she mumbled, knowing the answer.

"Could be," he returned with a quiet, humorous lilt.

"I'm from Iowa. I was a bounty hunter and a private investigator." Inwardly, she cackled at the irony of how she could do these great things and now was nothing more than a joke. Outwardly, she waited in stoic silence for his cackles.

"Victoria," he breathed her name in reverence, holding her closer. "Love."

As much as she wanted to fight him off, the breath of her name from his lips was like a burst of shared strength. She wanted to disagree with how he inflated her downtrodden ego, but for the moment, it felt so good to have someone believe in her, even after telling secrets in the middle of the night. She hadn't seen his disgust and disappointment before, and now she had expected it—and again, was wrong.

"Ryder." She straightened. "That's the truth. Hardy-har. I'm such a fake. A sham." His embrace didn't loosen. "Feel free to stop with—"

"Relax."

"Why are you reacting this way? I teach people self-defense and was kidnapped. I hunt bounties, and they turned that around on me, didn't they?"

"My parents are dead. I killed them."

Her heart stopped.

He shifted away and leaned back onto his elbows. The night went dead around them as the stars dulled and the frogs held their tongues. Not even the fish splashed. All was silent in the country darkness. "You're not a sham, and I don't get why you think that. Who gives a hoot if your dad's a familiar face in lockup? Bounty hunters aren't invincible. What more do you want from me? Nothing is wrong with you."

In the distance, something splashed into the water, breaking her trance, but she couldn't get past what he'd said before that. "Ryder—"

"You think because you're around criminals that you're unshakeable? That people can't hurt you?" He shook his head. "Your logic is flawed.

Hell, sweetheart, humans are inherently flawed. That's a fact of science. You're gonna fuck shit up."

"Uh, um." She swallowed her thoughts about his parents. "Yes. I suppose we are."

"A person can be outnumbered, out-forced, outmaneuvered, outgunned, outwitted. It doesn't matter how talented they are, and it doesn't negate who they are."

When he said that, it made sense. But inside her heart? It didn't matter. "In theory. I still can't go home."

"Because someone took you?"

"I help protect my community. I track bounties, and families turn to me. Why should they now?" she admitted to the night, unable to face him.

"That's a bogus question, and anyone who asks that isn't looking for a real answer—just like I didn't really kill my parents."

Her forehead wrinkled as she turned toward him. "You didn't?"

"I killed them as much as you can be blamed for your situation." He draped an arm over her shoulder. "I wasn't born yet, actually. But I was breech. My mom went into labor. Everything was going wrong. Fast labor. I was upside. We didn't live close to a hospital and so on. My dad rushed her to the emergency room. There was an accident. They died. I didn't."

Victoria blinked, taking in the ramifications of what he said. "You were born..."

"An orphan," he answered. "Into the system in my part of Australia. Funny how it works. No relatives and no one wants the baby who kills their mother."

"But that was the accident?"

"My mother would've died anyway."

"Oh." She bit her lip. "You were adopted?"

"No. Never quite worked out."

"Oh."

Ryder turned and put both hands on her shoulders, squaring them in the dark. "My point is, I'm to blame for their death as much as you're to blame for being trafficked to Russia and raped."

Her chin dropped at his bluntness. "You don't know what I was doing—"

"I don't care if you were hot on a bounty—"

"I was. That's a lot different than being born."

"No. It's not. That's living your life and getting caught up in something you can't control."

"I *could*."

He put two fingers under her chin, lifting her to face him. "You were dealt a hard blow. But it doesn't change who you are."

"It might." It seemed as though it had. How many times could she question whether she was ruined and broken inside? Too many to count. But the truth was, she hadn't come up with an answer. She didn't feel the way she thought she was supposed to. Victoria kept waiting for the panic from Ryder's touch. That didn't come. No, what was inside her, curling and growing deep in the pit of her stomach like an ugly cancer, was uncertainty in her talent, her career, who she was, because her job was who she had been.

In her hometown, she'd fought to make a name, to be a single, professional woman who owned a business, who spoke at chamber events, who ran with the boys' clubs, and triumphed. Now, she was nothing more than a punch line.

"If you want." He gave her shoulders a light squeeze, rooting her in the moment. "I'll help you be whatever, whoever, you want to be."

Her throat tightened. He couldn't understand all that she had done on her own, but the generous offer—no one had ever made such a gesture before. "Why would you do that?"

Ryder let go of her and turned for the water.

"I wouldn't have an answer either," she volunteered after what seemed like an eternity.

His head hung down, slowly shaking before he picked it up and stared. "I've never wondered if I made the right decision. But you... I held you and didn't know if I'd screwed up."

The air in her lungs escaped before she realized it was gone, and her head spun at his confession. She wanted Ryder to keep going but was suddenly terrified about where the conversation might go.

"I know what I was supposed to do." His whisper scratched at her memories. "But I don't know if it was *right*."

"Ivan." A cold chill ran across her skin as his name made her sick.

"Yeah. Letting you do it. Doing it myself."

"You wanted to kill him?" She was unaware that had been an option.

"Never in my life had I ever wanted to put a bullet in a person before so badly." He pulled in a long breath. "That's saying a lot."

"Why?" Throat aching, mind spinning, she found her voice was barely audible.

Ryder let long seconds linger before he answered amid the peaceful country night buzz, "I'm a sniper, love. For the good guys, but still. Make no mistakes about who and what I am. I'm a specialist."

She leaned closer. "What do you mean by that?"

"I'm a contract killer."

She leaned back, soaking in that knowledge.

"Still want to sit next to me?" he asked.

"Yes."

"Still trust me with your secrets."

"I do."

He turned away, and she couldn't tell if he had anything in his focus. Something splashed by her feet as they dangled over the boardwalk's edge, and Victoria wanted to say something to let Ryder know that it wasn't just her secrets she trusted with him. It was her.

He drew in a long breath and let it out. "Have you ever killed someone, love?"

She shook her head.

"Didn't think so." He ran his hand into his hair and leaned back, bringing his attention back from wherever he'd been lost. "Even for the best of reasons, taking someone's life changes a person, and I don't know that's the road you needed to go down."

"I wanted to." The world didn't need Ivan Mikhailov breathing its precious air.

"Shooting him while he was unarmed..." Ryder shook his head. "There was a good chance you could've hurt one of Titan's men, and there would've been blood splatter at that close of range. The spray."

"I don't care about that. Don't try to protect my delicate feminine sensibilities."

"It's not that. It'd have been a messy kill." He shifted. "Literally or figuratively. That's the stuff that gives people nightmares, no matter how much the bastard deserved to die."

She blinked, trying to wrap her head around all the ways he was protecting her.

"You don't want that on your hands, even if you really do."

Victoria swallowed around the lump in her throat. "That's why you're helping me?"

He lifted a powerful shoulder. "I guess."

"Then you should leave."

Surprise marred his chiseled face. "What? Why?"

Or maybe she should. Victoria scrambled to her knees. "I don't want to be protected. I want to be… propelled. To be lifted, empowered."

Ryder caught her arm. "Killing someone isn't empowering."

"Neither was letting the bastard live," she challenged him, tense and feeling it in every muscle.

"Victoria." His thumb moved, smoothing back and forth, and his grip wasn't harsh. But he didn't let go. "You were in a no-win situation, and I hate that for you."

Her head dropped. Why couldn't there be a simple answer? Almost like a get-out-of-jail-free card from a game, and if she found it, the burden pressing on her chest would melt away…

"Let's drop it. For now."

She brought her head up and let him meet her eyes. "He's alive."

"A painful truth that I hate you have to live with."

Reality made her cringe, caving toward him like he might hold her up, which was absurd because she could survive herself.

"How about," Ryder said quietly, letting go of her arm and leaning close, "we go back up, raid Mia's kitchen, and find ice cream or something?"

She wasn't hungry. She wanted to… to… she didn't know what she wanted to do. But there was something about their proximity, the blanket of the night, how his hand eased her mind, and the comfort she found in his touch. Sitting next to Ryder in the dark was better than a bowl of ice cream. "Tell me something?"

"Hm?"

"How often do you hang with women you save?"

"You're my first." He leaned enough so that their shoulders kissed. "Not my standard operating procedure."

She smiled. "What is?"

"Opened my big, fat mouth, huh?" He dropped his head back. "Guess I don't have one."

"Ever been in love?"

"No."

"That was quick."

"Have you?" he returned.

She shook her head, still smiling. "But I didn't choke on my tongue to get it out."

"Any guy would be lucky, love."

"Ah, now you're just being nice because you're stuck out here with me. Used, ruined, couldn't-save-herself-when-it-counted, little old me. Such a prize."

Ryder moved close and cupped both of her cheeks. The startling move was so careful—but serious—she forgot to breathe as pale moonlight cast a dreamy haze over his face. "Victoria. I'm here because when I held onto you in that basement of goddamn horrors, I didn't want to let go. I don't want to forget why you were upset, and I don't want to play down how you felt or how many women I've pulled out of hell over the years. It's what I do. Stopping trafficking is Delta's specialty." His fingers tensed on her cheeks for a breath of a second. "But I didn't want to walk away from you because, yeah, love, you are a prize."

He stole his hands away, and she followed them like a moth to light on the country landscape. They didn't share another word as Victoria sank into his embrace. This time, she didn't sit next to him. She sat with him, thigh touching thigh. It wasn't romantic as much as it was intrinsic. They needed to touch in the dark, to feel the cadence of the other's breathing as insects skipped over the lake, and a warm breeze circled round them with the sweet smell of cut grass and summer nights. She needed him, and for whatever reason, right then, he needed her too.

CHAPTER NINE

THE SCENT OF coffee and bacon pulled Ryder down the stairs, and he rounded the corner to face a pint-size inquisition. Clara and Ace sat cross-legged on the edge of the kitchen, eyeing him expectantly as he rolled up. Behind the tiny-human gate, Victoria sat at the kitchen table with Mia and Winters.

"It's late, sleepyhead." Clara lectured him as if he were one of her dolls, and that was something Mia had once said to her.

"It's late," Ace repeated in his copycat toddler-speak. "Sweepyhead. Sweepyhead. Sweepyhead. You're a sweepyhead."

Ryder reached down and ruffled Ace's unruly blond hair. "I had a late night, old man. And while you were sawing logs, I was out doing things."

Ace scooted over and wrapped his pajama-clad legs around Ryder's bare foot, snaking himself around it like a little monkey. "I'm not a lwog."

"Eating and playing in the backyard isn't a good reason to get out of bed," little Clara lectured.

He bit his tongue not to laugh, though Winters did. Clara's serious face surrounded by the blond ringlets was almost too much to take. "Was I the conversation of breakfast?"

She nodded. "You left your socks outside."

He laughed. "Sorry, Mia."

"Wasn't me who found them." Mia crossed her legs on the chair as one of their golden retrievers trotted through the kitchen and ran out the other side.

"Not like I picked 'em up." Winters made a face.

"Good morning." Ryder trained his gaze on Victoria. "Glad to see you up."

"Are you hungry?" Mia asked him, barely pulling his attention from the quiet woman.

"Of course he's hungry." Winters gave his wife a look and stood up, causing both of their dogs run into the kitchen. "I wasn't talking to you. Who wouldn't be hungry in this house? But you two have been fed."

Mia muttered at the dogs. "Think he feeds them off the table much?"

"Never." He walked toward the counter, grabbed a plate then held it to Ryder. "Pick your poison. We have blueberry pancakes, sausage, and grits."

With Ace still attached to Ryder's leg, he made giant steps, each one lifting the little boy into the air as though he weighed a ton, complete with random noises. "I'm starved. But how… can… I… make… it… there with this monster on my leg?"

"I'm not a mwonster!" Ace roared.

Ryder took the plate from Winters and offered Ace a sausage link before making a plate. "Really? Only monsters eat links like that."

"No!"

Clara jumped on his back.

"Oh, no!" Ryder faked like he was going down, easing the plate next to the pancakes before he dropped to the floor. "I'm getting it from all sides."

One of the dogs swooped in and stole Ace's sausage, making the little boy squeak with louder laughter. Clara and Ace both moved to Ryder's back, bouncing on top of him as they tickled.

"I haven't eaten!" He laughed. "Don't… have the strength… to go on!"

"You did!" Clara cried. "You had a picnic!"

The memory of Victoria on the boardwalk in the middle of the night made him smile, even as Winters's kids climbed all over him. "Okay, you're right. You win! I picnicked!" This made him laugh more. Who ever thought he'd go on a picnic. Ryder rolled to the side, tucking both of them under his arms, and lumbered up. "What'd you eat for breakfast? Rocks?"

"No!" they both screamed.

"Rocks. Definitely rocks." He walked over to Winters. "I believe these rock-eaters belong to you."

Ace launched onto his father, and Clara climbed over to her father in a manner much befitting a serious five-year-old, making both men chuckle. He glanced at the table, and Mia and Victoria had grins reaching both their ears too. Not that he put on a show for Victoria. *But wasn't that a reaction to see?*

She picked up her mug of coffee as he stared and held it against her face as though maybe she wanted to hide behind the few inches of ceramic. Prior to last night, she hadn't seemed shy. But under the cover of the dark, they'd shared secrets, maybe the kind that a person didn't tell a stranger. Was he that to her? No. They'd had a few deep moments. This morning was the first time they weren't in some kind of crisis—no gun in hand nor lack of sleep. He wondered if she had been talking much before he walked in.

"These rock-eaters need to put their clothes on," Winters announced. "And brush their teeth."

"My tfeef are cwean." Ace peered down from his dad's shoulder and opened his mouth. "Cwean."

"You shared a sausage with the dog. Clean them again. Let's go." With both kids climbing him like a jungle gym, Winters grabbed a pancake and headed down the hall.

"Are you good, Ryder? You know where everything is? Coffee, juice, whatever?" Mia stood up.

"I could map your kitchen in my sleep."

"Think you did, darlin'."

"Right," he admitted. "But I cleaned up."

"Except the socks," Winters called from down the hall.

"Jeez." Ryder forked pancakes onto his plate and grabbed a small bowl for grits. "Who knew you were such a neat freak?"

Winters didn't answer, and the sound of galloping feet upstairs suggested he was out of hearing range.

"If you need anything, look for it or find me." Mia topped off her coffee from the pot labeled decaf and turned to Victoria. "Good chatting with you. I'll catch up with you later this morning."

With a full plate, Ryder joined Victoria at the table. "Who knew my socks would be such a scandal?"

She raised her eyebrows and sipped her coffee. "One of the dogs brought them in. The kids thought it was hysterical."

Ryder laughed and went for coffee, returning quickly. "Only because Winters probably had to force the dog to spit them out."

"How'd you know?"

"Not my first time here."

"I gathered that when the kids brought you to the ground."

"Brutal, those little buggers. Tough as they come." He winked. "Their daddy's taught them a lot of good moves. But it's their mama who's taught them the ones to look out for."

"I like Mia."

"She's impossible not to like." Ryder downed a syrupy bite of pancake. "I don't get here nearly enough. But even when we're not brought into HQ, we work with her sometimes. She has a good relationship with Boss Man—"

"Who's that?"

"Jared Westin. He owns Titan, which runs my team. They're kind of buds. Jared and Mia."

Victoria nodded. "She said she's a therapist."

Now it was his turn to nod. *Why had Mia said that?* Feelings and therapy were like a minefield, and Ryder didn't know which direction to take that conversation. He took a too-large bite of pancake instead of conversing, figuring that was the safest bet. Choke and die: better than talking.

But Victoria didn't follow up.

He swallowed a scalding sip of black coffee. "Just passing talk? Or she do what she does best?"

"I don't know." Victoria let the coffee mug rest against her lips. "Maybe what she does best. But more than that, she's a gracious hostess. Said I could stay as long as I wanted."

"She is that," Ryder agreed. "And you can."

"When do you go back to work?"

He shrugged. "Whenever there's a job."

"No set schedule?"

"No. We work like all hell when there's a contract, and then we're off, free to do whatever until the phone call or text comes. Then we go."

"Just like that?"

He snapped his fingers. "Just like that."

"Do you like it?"

Funny. He'd never thought about his job in terms of liking it. He was good at it, the best. It was immensely satisfying. There was always an adrenaline high. The team was the best. The rescues made the world better; the takedowns made it safer. He had the opportunity to meet people like her. "Yeah, I think so. Never thought about it in terms of like or dislike before."

She put the mug down. "Really?"

"Really."

"Then in terms of what?"

He drew in a breath. "It's what I'm supposed to do."

She blinked, tilting her head. "I get that."

"I know." They were cut from the same cloth. The more he watched her mind work, the more he believed that. "I know you do."

She tore her eyes away. "I wasn't talking about me."

Yes, she was. "Didn't say you were."

Victoria kept her gaze trained on her coffee. "About last night…"

"What happened on the boardwalk stays on the boardwalk. I'm not going to say anything to anyone. Like Mia said, you stay here until you're ready to go home, and when you are, we'll make sure you get there safely."

She nodded. "Thanks."

His chest tightened. The idea that she could go back to Iowa and disappear from his life didn't sit right. They'd rescued many people over the years, and never had he wanted to stay in touch. Never had he wanted to be close to them in any way… But he did with Victoria, and maybe it was because of how he'd rescued her, the circumstances with Ivan.

Last night, Ryder had said as much—almost. They'd connected. That was obvious, and they'd both needed his arms, him as much as her, until he walked her to sleep and put to her to bed like the gentleman that he was—though it nearly killed him.

Right now, though? That gentleman shit? There was none of that type of behavior revving in his blood. Ryder sucked his cheeks and inhaled deeply at the thought of her soft skin, feeling the impulse to brush the loose strands of hair dangling beside her face.

There was nothing gentlemanly about any urges coursing through his system. *But hell.* No question, it wasn't platonic, but it couldn't be sexual—or was it?

He wasn't trying to get her in his bed. He wouldn't dare, knowing where she'd been and what had happened to her in Russia. His reaction to Javier's suggestion in Mexico had stuck with him though. Man, he hadn't been able to let that thought go.

Whatever their energy, it made his muscles twitch and ran him back to Winters's. He cringed away from the echo of *special girl* in his mind and didn't likc how Victoria treaded close to those memories. Still, there wasn't a chance he'd be anywhere else right now.

He pushed away his plate. "How long might you stay?"

"I'm not—"

The barreling commotion of two dogs and two kids running down the stairs collided with the sound of the front door opening.

"We're here," Rocco's familiar baritone carried through the house.

This house served as a central meeting place for the team, and it was Saturday morning, but Mia had likely put the kibosh on random visitors since Victoria had been in bed and hiding. That meant Rocco and his wife, Caterina, were strategic. *Or not.* Ryder didn't always know how Mia worked. But she was a maverick of healing. He would have to wait and see.

Victoria's eyes bugged. Still wearing the pajamas, she faced the front of the house. "Guess I should go change."

He saw from the set look on her jaw that didn't mean she planned to come back downstairs.

"Catch up with you later then. Maybe we can go do something if you're up to it? An adventure?"

"Maybe." She shuffled out the other side of the kitchen and headed the back way upstairs to the addition that Winters had recently added.

Not that this house wasn't big enough. It was. The place had enough bedrooms to house a bunch of the team when they came in, and the basement would camp the rest. The whole damn property was huge. But for purely tactical reasons, Winters wanted multiple egress points, and Mia wanted something more than a main staircase. Thus, she had a new addition, and he was able to outfit the house with more options. Talk about relationship goals.

Where could he bring Victoria? Outside of a few Titan guys' homes, HQ, and GUNS, it wasn't as though Ryder knew the area. She didn't seem in the right headspace to go to a gun range.

Maybe just out to lunch or something. Or back down to the boardwalk.

They could go swimming. That was how he blew off steam. It would be like a vacation until she got her head in a good spot.

He pressed his lips together. He was prepping her to go back to Iowa. He rubbed his temples then pushed back from the table. "What am I doing?"

Nothing smart was the answer. He tossed a fork onto the table, and it bounced onto his plate, clattering as Rocco came in.

Again, Ryder heard the front door open and the dogs go nuts. Voices filtered down the hall—Luke and his wife, Madeleine—and Ryder knew Mia had put a play in motion. Caterina and Madeleine had both been in very different, yet very similar situations to Victoria's.

Worry clouded his thoughts, and he couldn't focus on his teammates' arrival or Rocco in the kitchen as all the small talk went in one ear and out the other. He couldn't focus on anything but the woman he'd met in Russia and how she'd devolved into this quieter, untrusting version of herself.

Delta didn't rehab people. They saved them.

End of story.

And he didn't want to *rehab* Victoria either. He wasn't a fixer. But she didn't need to be fixed, even if he believed that and she didn't. Whenever she was ready to bounce back, she would. *Wouldn't she?*

All Ryder knew was that he liked sitting next to her in the dark, liked when he had excuses for her to fall asleep against him. Even when he was so tired he couldn't stay awake, he had, and he had watched her sleep.

Jeez… What was wrong with him? Ryder rubbed a hand over his face.

"Does that look mean you don't want to?" Rocco stood practically in front of Ryder.

He blinked, trying for the life of him to recall anything that Rocco had said. *Nothing.* "Sorry, mate. What?"

"Swimming? You down to go in the lake?"

Victoria in a bathing suit flashed through Ryder's mind. "Absolutely."

Apparently, his thoughts were far less platonic than he wanted to believe.

CHAPTER TEN

THE WINDOW OVERLOOKING the backyard had a cushioned chair, and Victoria was curled up in the highback with extra pillows and a blanket, a romance novel, and a cup of coffee. But reading about a sexy alpha male who wanted to sweep a woman off her feet was surprisingly not holding much interest—or maybe, not surprisingly, considering what had happened to her in Russia. Maybe a romance novel would never hold her interest again. Or not. She had thought men might never hold her interest again. And Ryder was interesting.

Backyard was a poor choice of words to describe what Victoria was looking at. Colby and Mia had land. Some of it was mowed and manicured, and out past the lake before the tree line, high grass waved in the breeze. This was less like a house and more like an estate, except it felt like a home—something she didn't have much familiarity with. But she knew it when she saw it.

Victoria held the book in front of her face and stared at the cover model. "You don't have anything on Ryder." She tossed the book over her shoulder, dropping her head back as she thought about how they'd sat on the boardwalk, and everything in her felt aflutter.

Knock. Knock. Knock.

"Come in," Victoria said as she shifted her legs and faced the door. She had become accustomed to Mia's knock and Ryder's, but this was new.

A slender woman she hadn't met yet pushed the door open, and the first thing Victoria thought was that her eyes were exotic and had seen burdens beyond her years. There was something about people who worked with Delta and Titan. They were warriors and saviors, but they dealt with hell. That could age a person's soul even if it didn't leave so much as a wrinkle.

"Hi, *bonjour*," the accented English and French flowed off the beautiful woman's tongue in a lyrical fashion, yet there was nothing dainty or stereotypically French about her until she spoke. "I'm Madeleine, and I go by Maddy. You came upstairs before we arrived."

"I'm Victoria. Who is we?"

"Luke." The woman's features softened, and it wasn't that she had a severe hold on her face, but it was clear that even his name made her that much happier. "My husband."

Victoria didn't know how to react to hearing Luke's name. She didn't know what Luke would tell Maddy, but it seemed as though Titan and Delta were an open book with their families as to what kind of jobs they worked and where they went. But he wouldn't say what had happened to her, would he? That was personal and humiliating. Then again, anybody could assume that a woman who had been kidnapped and trafficked had also been raped. "I've met him."

Maddy didn't say anything, and Victoria wondered if maybe she didn't know or was curious. It didn't matter. "Luke was with Ryder..." Volunteering that much seemed both appropriate and too much. She had no idea how to follow that up. Luke and Ryder had been together as they wrestled the gun from her hand before she could blow Ivan's brains out? Before she chickened out after taking too long, Luke and Ryder had watched as she played judge, jury, and executioner, but hadn't reached the sentencing portion because she hadn't decided if she could pull the trigger on Ivan because she would have also killed their teammate Locke.

Ivan had hurt so many people. He'd hurt her far past the physical way he'd raped her. But in those seconds as she held the gun to his face and knew that there was a very good chance killing Ivan would also kill Locke, whose only crime was holding him in place until his teammates arrived. She didn't know if pulling the trigger on Ivan was worth his death and also Locke's, who she now knew was a very good person. That bullet would've been a through-and-through. Victoria wondered what Luke had told Maddy about his introduction to her and if he'd mentioned how Victoria almost killed Locke.

"We're going to go swimming."

Victoria's eyebrows arched. That wasn't what she expected Maddy to say. "Where? In the lake?"

"It's fun. Mostly, we kick around in the water off the side that has sand and the boardwalk."

"I didn't exactly come prepared for a vacation and don't have a swimsuit." Victoria tucked the blanket around her knees, suddenly very aware that Maddy had no clue where she had been or what had happened to her, and that was not so much embarrassing as it was a testament to who Victoria used to be—confident, powerful, and unquestioning.

"You don't need a bathing suit to get in the water," Maddy stated as though she were discussing basic facts Victoria should have known.

"Are you going to wear a bathing suit?"

The woman raised an eyebrow, relenting. "Yes."

"And Luke, Colby? They'll probably wear trunks. Mia has her swimsuits. Whoever else arrived earlier when I came upstairs—"

"Rocco and Caterina."

"If they knew we were going swimming, Caterina probably brought her swimsuit."

"She probably did," she agreed. "But are those your pajamas?"

Victoria's eyes dropped down to the clothes she'd borrowed from Mia. Maddy was right. Nothing Victoria wore was hers. "There's a difference between Mia making arrangements for me to have clean underwear and me asking someone to run to the store so that I can have a bathing suit. That seems ridiculous."

"Borrow a bathing suit top from Mia, and wear some shorts in the water. You're making a mountain out of a molehill, as you Americans say." Maddy walked further into the room and let her hands run along the edge of the bed. "May I sit down?"

"Sure." Again, everyone insisted on asking if they could be near her. She was damaged goods, and that confirmed that Maddy knew about Russia.

Victoria looked out the window at the lake surrounded by the perfect green grass, and she watched two dogs run in a field and wrestle each other as four men stood in the distance and tossed toys for the dogs to chase. A longing hit her, similar to what she'd found herself thinking the night on the boardwalk with Ryder.

It wasn't only what had happened to her was overwhelming. But now she had an added problem: enjoying this too much. Another reason why she shouldn't be awake. Iowa was great, and she had worked so hard to be a pillar in her community, respected by everybody. There were men who gathered and threw toys to dogs next to lakes, women who sat with others when something had hurt a friend, kids who ran around, food that was put on tables, but she'd never seen it with her own eyes, and it felt… intoxicating. Soon, it would be gone.

Iowa had friends. She missed Seven. The community, from the mayor to the grocery baggers, all knew her, but that was very different from this happy life that she didn't know existed outside of TV shows.

"They're not bad people," Maddy said softly.

Surprised, Victoria's head snapped to the side. "I didn't say they were."

"That isn't what I meant." Her French accent curled around the words. "What I mean is, they do bad things but only to bad people."

"How did you meet Luke?"

Maddy pressed her lips into a closed smile and shook her head. "That is a very long story, and one that is hard to understand. It would prove that he is a good man, but perhaps you would need to know me longer before you thought I was a good person."

Victoria thought about how she'd tried to rationalize shooting Ivan, knowing that Locke would take a bullet, and how long that argument went on inside her head. "You might think the same thing about me."

Maddy stood up and smoothed her fingers over the comforter. Outside, the sound of little kids tearing into the backyard filled the air. "That's my cue to go put on my suit. I hope you join us. It'll take your mind off things if you need it. And if not?" She shrugged. "You've already met the Winters's kids. Rocco and Caterina have a hell-raiser running around and a little one if you like to squeeze babies. Plus when Mia walks outside in her bathing suit, it's going to be a hoot."

"Why's that?" Victoria asked.

"Because she's pregnant again, and it's going to be hysterical watching the guys try to figure out if she has a baby on board or not."

CHAPTER ELEVEN

RYDER THREW THE rawhide, and Winters's dogs took off, throwing themselves into the lake and splashing, one over the other over the other until one dog triumphed and raced out onto the beach. It wasn't so much a beach as it was the sandy area that Winters had cordoned off for them to relax, kick back, for kids to play, and barbecues to be had by the water. Ryder let his toes dig past the top layer of warm sand into the cool wetness underneath. The dogs raced up and dropped the rawhide at their feet. Ryder tipped back the beer in his hand as Rocco reached down and snagged the toy from the sopping wet dogs.

Winters, Luke, and Rocco had all spent enough time with women who had been hurt that he could ask their opinion of how best to talk to Victoria. But he wasn't quite there yet. He didn't even know what he wanted to ask. And he didn't want to tip off that hanging out with her was pushing his buttons but not in a bad way. She got under his skin. Again, not in a bad way. He wanted to help her—more than he should.

Ryder tipped back his beer again as the cool bottle sweated in his hand, and the hot sun blazed on his bare shoulders.

"Thirsty, much?" Luke rolled his beer bottle between his hands, noting that Ryder's was nearly halfway empty.

"Relaxing, mate." He raised his eyebrows, giving his bud a pointed look. "Suffering through this brew you Americans call beer."

"Hey, don't knock my beer." Winters laughed. "Or you can ask Clara for a juice box."

Clara, Ace, and the dogs ran in the grass a couple dozen yards away. Ryder wondered where Maddy and Caterina were and he hoped that Mia had talked Victoria into coming outside. Victoria said she went upstairs to change out of her pajamas when Rocco and Cat arrived. When he checked on her after twenty minutes, she wasn't interested in coming back downstairs.

When Luke and Maddy arrived, everybody took the party outside. He decided to leave Victoria alone and give her space. They'd shared a lot last night. He had shared more than he had with anybody since Zoe, but more importantly, he'd learned a lot about her. *Everything but a last name.*

The back door opened, and Mia walked out by herself. Disappointment hit. The chances of Victoria joining them with Maddy or Caterina were nil, and if she wasn't with Mia, she probably wasn't going to get in the lake. A heavy weight settled in his stomach, and Ryder ran his tongue along his bottom lip. Caterina and Maddy walked out the door and let it shut behind them. No Victoria. *Damn.*

His disappointment was now flat out annoyance. Frustration piled on top of the discomfort that had already lodged in his chest.

"Mommy," Clara squealed out and took off running toward Mia, creating a train of activity behind the little girl as Ace, Jacián, and the dogs trailed.

"Mommy," Ace repeated as loud as he could. Both kids jumped on to Mia. Right before Ryder was sure Mia was going down, Winters stepped in and scooped Clara up, letting Ace catch Mia on her hip.

Despite the bathing suit cover that hung over her like a drape, Mia was a little thing, and one of these days, both those kids were gonna take her out. It'd be funny, and Mia would probably fall down laughing anyway. She seemed made to roll around with her children.

Rocco scooped up Jacián and took off into the water. The dogs changed directions and took off after them. The splashes went high and wild.

Ryder threw up an arm, turning away from the raucous fun, and ran away from the dogs as Maddy and Caterina with a baby over her shoulder walked down the hill. Cat waved to them in the water and called for Mia to join them. As Winters and the kids ran circles around her, she shrugged off the cover and made her way to the ladies.

Ryder narrowed his focus, gaze bouncing from Mia to Maddy and then Cat. Each woman wore variations of a black bikini, and he'd never been one to check them out, never compared and contrasted his buddies' wives, but he knew what they looked like, and Mia looked different.

Her stomach was… not normal, and then, awkwardly he looked around. Nobody said anything. The other girls hadn't noticed. Winters rolled on the ground now with Ace, so he couldn't have said anything. But it would have come up since he'd been staying here lately. Wouldn't it? Ryder glanced back at Mia. Her stomach definitely looked funny. *Right? Or no?*

Funny wasn't the right word. Bigger? No, that wasn't probably right either. Distended? *Fucking hell.* He looked at Luke, who was now searching the grass for… *nothing*. Ryder stepped closer to him, and cleared his throat. "Hey, what are the girls doing?"

"Dude." Luke didn't make eye contact. "Is Mia pregnant?"

At least Luke was the one to say it because Ryder never wanted to be responsible for asking that question if it wasn't true.

Why would Winters have forgotten to mention if Mia was pregnant? Surely that he wouldn't have held them out to dry like this, right?

"I don't know," Ryder mumbled. "Fucking hell. She's so tiny; maybe she just ate a damn hoagie."

Finally, Luke glanced up. "Or two."

They exchanged glances that said one thing loud and clear. They were both sworn to secrecy and would never mention the conversation they'd just had.

Winters left Ace and splashed his way into the water then back on to the beach with Clara. "I give."

"I'm catching butterflies." She ran back into the water to meet up with Jacián as Rocco stepped out.

All of the men with exception of Winters stood, paralyzed, having no idea what to say. There had to be some sort of bro code where this type of information was shared so that none of them put their foot in their mouths, particularly if that person's wife knew how to mindfuck them in ways they could never recover from.

Winters joined their gaggle, wiping water off his face.

"So Winters." Luke crossed his arms, tucking his beer bottle against his elbow. "Anything new going on in your life, buddy?"

"The only thing new I can think of is the bottle of beer I'm about to find. Anyone need anything?"

With two nos and one yeah, Winters sauntered away, stopping to kiss Mia on the cheek, and hit the cooler that was sitting by a table.

"That was an obvious ask," Ryder said. "And if Mia is and he didn't say, not cool, man. Not cool."

Rocco looked from Luke to Ryder and back. "What?"

"You don't know why the hell we're standing here like dumbasses?" Luke barely tilted his head, clearing his throat as though that slight noise might be a finger-pointing toward Mia who now had her back toward them.

Rocco's gaze ran back and forth, going wide and then narrowing back toward the women. "What?"

His voice was louder, maybe too loud, and Ryder's eyes bugged as he shook his head enough to tell Rocco to shut up.

"Dude." Luke took a step back, giving Rocco the same headshake.

Rocco glanced over again, but this time, something dawned on his face, and he smiled, his eyebrows lifting slightly. "How about that?"

That wasn't the tone of voice that Ryder would've expected, but each to their own when it came to kids. "So you think?"

Rocco nodded. "Yeah, I think."

"Do we say something?" Luke mumbled.

Rocco shrugged, not nearly as confused about Mia's stomach as he and Luke had been, but maybe that was because they had two kids. "She looks like she's doing okay."

Both Ryder and Luke took a drink of their beers, having no idea what okay might look like. Mia looked fine except for her stomach not looking the way it used to.

"I always thought pregnant people had these rounder stomachs," Luke finally said.

Ryder's face twisted slightly as he thought about this, and maybe that was it. Maybe he and Luke had just never been around a pregnant woman who didn't have her shirt on. "Yeah, I've never been around anybody in the sprouting stage."

"Same." Luke nodded. "If that wasn't obvious."

"Sprouting?" Rocco choked on his beer. "What the shit are you talking about? Cat. Nicola. Beth. Sugar."

"I don't think we went swimming with them when they sprouted."

"Christ, you guys need to get out more." Rocco laughed louder.

The back door opened and slapped shut and brought a smile to Ryder's face. He and Luke turned to see Victoria walking off the deck steps.

"Hey!" Winters laughed from near the coolers. "Come on down."

Victoria joined Caterina and Maddy, circling around Mia, none of the women seemingly noticing Mia's stomach, and walked down to join them along with Winters.

"Let's find out," Rocco said.

"Dude." Luke elbowed him. "Don't do anything—"

"Who's ready for the water? Winters, want to toss the ladies off the boardwalk?" Rocco asked. "Or we could go do margaritas? Anyone up for tequila shooters? Mia?"

Ryder froze in the sand and would bet money Luke was equally as stuck.

Suddenly, Winters laughed. Then Mia. Ryder cautiously glanced at her, as Victoria stepped next to him.

"Hey, you." She leaned against his arm. "I came to watch the excitement."

Excitement?

Winters grabbed Mia into a bear hug as Ace and Clara ran over, yelling. Mia's laughter became even louder. Maddy moved next to Luke, and Caterina handed Rocco the baby as their son curled into his mother's side.

A few inches separated him from Victoria, and even she laughed quietly.

"You knew?" He pointed at her with his bottle.

She nodded yes, and Luke threw his hands in the air. "Oh, come on! That's not fair."

"Life's not fair, good-looking." Mia blew him a kiss.

"*Touché*, Mia. Congratulations!"

"Another Winters baby." Rocco clapped. "Job well done, Mia. I don't know how you put up with that guy, but job well done."

Ryder closed the distance next to Victoria. Half a day ago, they were under the moon on the boardwalk, arms touching and whispering secrets about the past. Now, with friends and laughter under the warm sun, their bare arms brushed as he stole a glance at her wearing little shorts and a bathing suit top. They congratulated the whole Winters crew, the kids taking most of the attention now, and talked about the future. He couldn't help thinking that everything with her felt right.

"I'm glad you decided to come out." Ryder brushed his knuckles against the back of her soft shoulder.

Victoria shivered despite the sizzling summer air. "There was good news to be heard."

"There was." He couldn't help himself; his fingers ran along her arm, and her goose bumps followed his touch. A million things were happening around them, but that was all that he noticed. Her skin reacted to his touch. He sucked in a deep breath and held it. The last thing he needed to do was to *react* to her too. His way might be far more noticeable than hers.

"And maybe some laughs." Victoria fidgeted, taking a hair band off of her hand and pulling pieces of her hair into a bun. She slid sunglasses on top of her head. "It was so worth rushing outside."

He wanted to calm her thoughts, wipe away her nerves. But every little side glance she gave him pushed him toward touching her, teasing her, seeing why she fidgeted around him. He wanted to know what this girl was really made of, wanted to hold her again.

Ryder moved to her side so that he also faced Mia and Winters. His hand smoothed over her bare back, and she leaned against his side. His heart hammered. There was a difference between stealing private moments by themselves and whatever this was.

Fuck it, he didn't care. His arm went around her shoulders, and he ducked close to her ear. "Was it now?"

Teasing her, his lips against her hair, her back under his arm on this perfect lake day surrounded by his friends and good news, Ryder tightened his hold around her, touching her more than he should and not giving a damn. It was just for a second, totally on the fly. Everyone was distracted with the pregnancy announcement, and for those seconds, he wondered how much further he could push the line, how much more he could play pretend. Every now and then, they came home from jobs and each man on the Delta team turned to something to relax. They had to. They saw despicable crimes and witnessed horrors. Sometimes, Javier fought. Luke too. Rocco would go on reality show binges and would just watch TV for days on end as if he had no mind. Ryder would swim lap after lap after lap until his muscles ached and burned, until his mind was clear of wherever they had gone and whatever he had seen.

He stepped away from Victoria, letting his fingertips skip along her bare back. “Get in the water with me.” He took her fingers and began walking backward. She balked.

Laughing her refusal, she held out the other hand. “No way. We’re celebrating.”

He made a face, squinting and tossing his hand. “We celebrated. They know I love them and that baby-to-be. Come on.” He stepped back and linked their fingers.

Victoria gripped him, taking hesitant steps but still following, and he couldn’t tell if her smile and blush were shy and nervous or if that was the sun making her skin a little pink. “The water is cold, Ryder.”

Their feet splashed in knee-deep water now. “Not going to lie, love. It won’t be hot.”

Her sunglasses slipped down onto her nose, and her nose wrinkled. “Nobody else is swimming.”

They were thigh deep in the lake, and he pulled her close, stomach to stomach. “Do you care what anybody else does?”

She went still, and he pulled her sunglasses up.

“No,” she said quietly.

He let her go and rested both palms on her hips, letting his thumbs tease back and forth over the edge of her shorts, skipping close to the skin of her stomach. What the hell was he doing? Nothing that he should but everything that felt right.

"Come on, Iowa girl. You are used to the cold."

Her eyes danced, and she licked her bottom lip. "Doesn't mean I like it."

Hell. Ryder scooped her into his arm the way he had held her and walked out of the Mikhailov basement when her legs refused to carry her as her tears fell. But this time, she was all smiles and laughter. He spun around and ran into the water. Victoria wrapped her arms around his neck, her face buried into his neck until all he could hear and feel was her.

CHAPTER TWELVE

THE GOOSE BUMPS on Victoria's skin jumped, but it had nothing to do with the water and everything with the rush of adrenaline. The scruff from Ryder's cheek scratched her neck, and his muscles captured her against his warm chest in the best oxymoron she'd experienced in her life. His body was hot to touch, hard to hold, cut like steel, and soft to burrow against. His mouth was against her ear. Her nipples reacted to the tease of his lips before her mind could rationalize that even as she laughed and cried no, all of her moaned *yes*.

"Close your eyes." He held her tight, laughing even harder as she kicked her legs.

"Don't you dare."

"We're going under." They spun the other direction.

Victoria freed an arm and scooped as much water as she could, throwing it at him over and over. "You're a dead man."

"Three… two…" He tipped backward in slo-mo, taking her with him.

"Ryd—"

The water couldn't have been more than three or four feet deep, but Ryder was submerged, and she easily could have stood. As her feet fluttered for the sandy bottom, he sank like deadweight, and his palms slid from her side, over her butt, then to her thighs. Victoria stopped fluttering, if just for the moment, to let the delicious shock roll over her. His hands smoothed back up, wrapping around her back, and Ryder pushed off the ground, rocketing them out of the water. They shot into the sun, and her hair was everywhere, sunglasses gone.

Victoria flipped her hair back and wiped the water from her face, blushing and smiling because she couldn't help it. He even had a playful grin, a boyish I-felt-up-my-girl tease hanging on his face, and she didn't care that they probably an audience.

"You're a dead man," she whispered, catching her breath, having no reason to have lost it except that the man in front of her kept stealing it.

"I'd love to see you try, love."

It wasn't as if she was inept at a takedown, even if he had her in terms of weight and training. Victoria grabbed his arm and swung—the water buoyancy wasn't helping—and he pulled his forearm round. She pushed up.

"Ha!" She couldn't stop laughing because that move should have used her weight to counteract his defense, but she simply lofted herself up in the water. Instead, she pushed, he pulled, and they were face-to-face. Almost lip to lip. Breath to breath, her heart pounding, pulse thumping in her ear. The tickle of their breaths colliding made her roll her lips together. All she wanted to do was kiss him. Every nerve hummed, every thought drifted to their magnetic pull.

A football landed a foot away, shooting water in its wake. They jumped apart as someone from the beach yelled to Ryder, "Chill with the swim lessons."

Her face lit on fire. "Oh my God."

Still smiling but shaking his head and laughing, he cursed before snagging the ball and drilling it back toward one of his teammates.

"I just died."

Ryder winked as he turned back. "Ah, they're just fucking with us."

"I'm dead." She might never get out of the water. Did she almost kiss Ryder in front of a shore full of his coworkers and their kids?

He took her hand, dragging her to walk deeper. "Forget them—"

"Who wants in on volleyball?" Mia yelled loud enough that Victoria questioned how such a tiny person could exert that many decibels.

"Unless you want in on that?"

"I *am* pretty good," she admitted.

He changed directions, walking them back toward the beach. "Well, let's go because I don't lose."

As the depth became lower, she realized that no one was staring at her like she should be mortified for nearly making out with Ryder in the water. Heck, Luke and Maddy were making out, and right after Mia finished laying out the volleyball and net, Colby ran over and kicked the ball. Their kids and dogs chased it, and as everyone laughed, Mia picked up a squirt gun that looked like a bazooka and exacted her revenge. Not a hot second later, Colby had her disarmed and carefully in his arms, running after the ball with the kids and the dogs as Mia laughed.

Clearly, Victoria almost kissing Ryder wasn't going to make anyone uncomfortable, and this was the happiest place she'd ever been.

Knock. Knock.

"Come in," Victoria called from the edge of her bed.

"*Bonjour, mon amie.*" Maddy walked in. "Do you have a moment?"

"Sure. I was about to come back downstairs, but I thought everyone left."

"We came back. I wanted to check on you."

Part of Victoria's heart squeezed. She wasn't upset that Maddy brought up an ugly pain, but an indescribable sensation lodged in her chest that seemed to help her heal, even if it was microscopic. "Thanks."

"What happened to you, it can fester inside you or you can destroy it."

The two options were black and white, weren't they? "Destroying it would be nice."

"Don't let anyone tell you how it will fester, and don't think there's one way of destruction. It might take annihilation by a thousand tiny blows or one life-changing collision."

"Okay." Victoria breathed.

"Maybe a minute, or years… decades of time." Maddy gestured in such a delicate way that it was unnerving to see the polished woman discuss obliterating internal demons. "It means doing things you'd never do. Everyone—psychiatrists, therapists, family—they will all have their opinions, but the only person to listen to is you. Follow the voice inside."

Her voice inside said stick with Ryder, that he understood her. He let her talk when she needed to, let her feel safe again. Maybe Maddy had seen how she'd spent her time with him, seen that she wasn't shrinking away from his touch, that what happened to her hadn't made her repulsed by men, which Victoria had expected.

"How do you know so much about this?" she finally ventured.

Maddy gave a tight, sad smile. "I told you, you would have your reasons to hate me."

"And I could give you one of my own..." If she did now, Maddy might trust her more, or Victoria would lose this close advocate. "I had the opportunity to shoot my attacker, and I hate myself for not."

"Why didn't you?"

"Lots of reasons." She pulled in a fortifying breath. "There's a good chance, at that range, it would've been a through-and-through and hit Locke."

Maddy kept a blank face as she processed the information. "You didn't take the shot," she finally said.

"Ryder disarmed me."

"*Non.*" Maddy gave her a curt shake of her head, lips firmly pressed into a line. "If you were going to do it, you would have done it."

"I don't know."

"What you feel is regret for not having different circumstances." She stepped forward, taking Victoria's hand in hers. "But that pain in your eyes? That torture that you keep going back to? You have no sin to be rebuked for. You made no error for which you must find redemption. No evil of yours led you down a path that the righteous can point to and judge."

A painful knot formed in Victoria's throat. "You don't know my past."

"I don't need to. I can see the truth in people."

She scoffed as she recalled the ridiculous mistakes she'd made following the mayor's tips, working alone when she was too inexperienced to ignore warnings to partner up, and not fighting hard enough when under attack. "Don't be ridiculous."

"You're young, but so is Ryder."

"You're not that old either," Victoria cut in.

"No one on their Delta team is *that* old. It's a new team that needs to stay at Titan for a long time to come. Eventually, the old guard will retire, and this will be Titan, and they will hire up a new ghost team. But that's not the point. Age is a number. Maturity, intellect, ability: those are the things that matter."

Those were the things that she and Seven had always said about themselves, and Victoria had noticed that Delta was noticeably younger than those Ryder identified as Titan, even though he'd explained that everyone was Titan Group. She hadn't asked more.

"Victoria." Maddy made her name sound beautiful as her accent wrapped around it. "I was the daughter of one of the most influential human traffickers in the world."

Her thoughts ceased. Everything Victoria understood about the woman before her evaporated into a breath of smoke.

"I saw horrible things, I did horrible things, but I am *not* a horrible person. It, however, has made me a particular person, and because of life's experiences, I've found needs and desires that only my husband can give me. That was my healing process." She batted her hand. "Not important. What is important is that you believe me when I tell you to believe you."

Mind still spinning, Victoria agreed in silence.

"If you would like a woman to talk to who won't throw cutesy BS your way and will talk about how she got through her own hell, call Caterina."

Victoria's eyes widened.

"I'm not betraying her trust. She knows I was going to tell you about me, and she said to mention she was available."

"She didn't…" Victoria didn't know how to ask why the other woman wouldn't come up and volunteer her story because that was a silly question. Why would any want to volunteer or assume that someone was ready to listen?

"Maybe the better question is why did I talk to you," Maddy said instead. "And that's because there's a difference between being victimized and working on the offending side, though I won't say I wasn't a complete victim—"

"Ivan's daughter, she didn't want to. She tried to stop so much. And did."

"You did too, from what I understand."

Victoria shrugged a shoulder, immediately uncomfortable, and turned away.

"Ah, see, that's how I know you are holding on to a grievance. Your healing won't be as much about a man as it's a guilt about whatever you are blaming yourself for."

Wasn't that the truth? She glanced over her shoulder. "Got all that because I turned away?"

"And because you would've made out with Ryder in the lake if Grayson hadn't pegged him with a football."

Victoria's cheek flamed. "Oh, God. I'm so sorry about that. Kids watching and everything." She covered her face with her hands.

Maddy laughed. "*Mon amie*, these children are all raised that love is a good thing. Kisses are healthy. You are fine. No one noticed a thing."

"Except Grayson."

"Well… Delta team noticed that Ryder noticed you, and they haven't had many chances to give him hell." She lifted her shoulders. "They tease like brothers."

"He doesn't bring girls home?"

"No one brings girls home." Maddy lifted an eyebrow. "Special circumstances aside. But I haven't heard of him in a relationship—nothing more than enticing someone with that accent when he feels the need."

"That accent though…" Victoria quietly laughed, and Maddy smiled.

"I'm off then. I need to find Luke and head out again."

"Thanks for talking to me, trusting me, and… not hating me about Locke."

"Same." Maddy blew her a kiss and headed out the door as Ryder stuck his head in.

"Night, Madeleine," he said, and turned back. "You up for a minute?"

Victoria repositioned on the edge of her bed. "Sure."

He held up a blue bottle. "Need any aloe?"

"Actually, yeah." Despite using lotion all day long, her shoulders were a little pink. It wasn't much, and they didn't hurt, but she didn't want them to. Victoria hadn't changed into her pajamas yet, so she could easily apply the aloe with her tank top and still talk to Ryder.

"Turn around. I'll do your shoulders."

Or let him do it even if her heart began to race. "Okay."

The cap clicked open, and carefully, he dropped one side of her shirt. "Mia threw the bottle at me after she put the kids down and said to make sure you weren't in pain."

"I'm not in pain. Oh—" His hand made contact, and the cool aloe sent a frosty sensation skipping up her neck and sliding down her spine.

His warm hand stilled. "Did that hurt?"

"No. Just cool."

"All right." He gently rubbed the aloe in and replaced the shirt strap, repeating the process. "You have fun today?"

She scrunched her face, looking over her shoulder. "Was there a question?"

"No. Just checking."

Victoria dropped her head, sighing deeply as his thumb kneaded up onto her neck. Finally, his hand stilled. "Me too."

He let go of her and closed the cap.

"Thanks," she said.

Was she supposed to ask if he needed any? How did this work? When did she become so awkward around a guy? Probably the moment she began to have a crush on him and didn't know what any of it meant.

"What'd Maddy want?"

Saved by the change in topics. *Thank you, Ryder.* Victoria tried in vain to stabilize her rioting insides. "Girl talk."

He nodded, maybe wondering how they were supposed to act out of water and off the beach. They'd played a hell of a game of volleyball and crushed Grayson and Emma. Though Colby and Mia kicked their butts. Home team advantage, maybe. "I'm beat. You headed to bed?"

"Just about to change, and then yes."

"Could just sleep naked," he suggested with a wink.

She rolled her eyes. "All right. Good night, Ryder."

"Night, love. Try not to dream about what I sleep in."

"Out." She gave his sinewy back a little push, but now that he'd said that, did Ryder sleep naked when alone?

CHAPTER THIRTEEN

THE DARK HALLWAY surrounded Ryder. The cold weighed down his arms, made his boots heavy as his mind searched for where he was. Traces of Zoe's face seemed to flash in the dark, a transparent ghost of a whisper in his peripheral vision. But with his head on the pivot in the narrow passageway, he couldn't catch her, couldn't reach her, couldn't save her…

"Zoe!"

Zoe. Zoe. Zoe. The echoes of voices tortured his mind, and Ryder clung to his weapon, perspiring as he tried to breathe through the mission.

He blinked. He breathed.

He was alone?

Ryder spun.

No team? No one, and no more apparitions of Zoe. *Was she even there?*

Night goggle green illuminated his vision. Ryder stopped abruptly, confused—but there was Trace, mirror and flashlight in hand at the corner. Ryder focused on the job as confusion made his temples pound. He was at work with Delta, at the Mikhailov compound, and there was Luke.

"The women are down here." Luke beckoned Ryder to hurry even as every step seemed slowed by quicksand.

He couldn't move fast enough to help. Ryder growled through the strangling efforts to keep him away from their targets.

Luke waved him closer. "One of them has a gun."

A gun… Civilians. Victims. They were armed. Ryder blinked, and he was in front of Locke—and a woman with a gun trained on Ivan Mikhailov. "We're here to help. Here to help. Don't shoot. Here to help."

The words were thick on his tongue, but a woman's voice responded.

Goddamn it, Zoe. He couldn't make out her words. His heart tore. She was out of reach. He couldn't help her when she only wanted to help others.

"Stay still." The woman's anger was so raw he could feel her wrath. "You ruined my life," she yelled at Mikhailov.

Ryder watched the events like a television show as Locke talked to her. *Victoria.* Her tears echoed in his ears. The missing pieces of who she was and what Ivan had done to her were clear.

She was going to kill Ivan.

She *should* kill Ivan.

But Locke… Locke was in the way, and Ryder… the hallway spun.

Ryder couldn't see. He couldn't make the words come out of his mouth. He needed to stop her from shooting his teammate, but hell, the only thing that made sense in Ryder's mind was that he wanted Ivan to die.

He couldn't get the words out. Locke's eyes were on him. Victoria's sobs were next to him. Ryder's disgust for Ivan grew and grew, more than he could imagine for a man he didn't know—

He bolted upright in bed, sweat tickling his brow and his heart slamming in his throat. His gaze darted around—not Russia. *Not in Ivan Mikhailov's compound.* "Fucking nightmare."

As Ryder glanced around Winters's guest bedroom, he took a breath, relieved that he wasn't reliving the hell of Victoria's decision all over again, and he scrubbed his palms over his face as the hatred he harbored for Ivan grew. He hated that the excuse for a human was still alive.

Slowly, Ryder's heart rate came back to a normal pace, and his eyelids sank shut, remembering Zoe's appearance in his nightmare. "Christ."

He dropped back to the pillows. A soft knock sounded on his door.

Ryder propped up on an elbow. "Yeah, hello?"

The door cracked open. "Hi."

He heard her voice before she stepped into the room. "Victoria. Hey, did you need something?" He swallowed, his pulse still not where it should be, and his voice didn't sound right either.

"I thought I heard you," she whispered.

"Oh, right. Bit of a nightmare, I guess."

She clung to the door. "You're okay?"

"You checking on me?" He smiled, chuckling, and folded himself upright.

The covers piled around his waist, and her chin dropped down. "Guess so. If you're okay then."

"I didn't mean to wake you."

"I wasn't sleeping."

"Are you okay?"

She shrugged without lifting her head.

"Something's up? You're staring at the carpet like it's amazing."

"You're not wearing a shirt, Ryder."

"Oh," he laughed. "I don't sleep with a shirt on." His hand searched the top of the bed for a shirt to pull on but came up empty. "And I don't know where a handy one is. Sorry."

"I'll go."

"You're going to leave because I'm not wearing a shirt?"

"I… I don't know." She shrugged again. "Feels intrusive. I didn't mean to bother you."

"You're not bothering me." He patted the side of the bed. "We went swimming earlier. You've seen me without my shirt on."

"True, I guess. I'm sorry."

"I told you before, don't apologize. Want to come in?"

Though now she'd mentioned he wasn't wearing a shirt and he'd beckoned her to his bed, he was tempting himself. Not that he wanted her in his bed. She'd been victimized. Hell, he wasn't a monster. But the idea of her curled against his bare chest?

He sucked in a breath and held it, puffing out his cheeks before he let it out.

"Do you get nightmares?" she asked, still not moving.

"I'm not having a conversation with you one foot out the door."

Victoria picked her head up and held his eye. "I should get back to my room."

"Why?"

"I don't know."

"Yes, you do."

She pulled her lip into her mouth. "Because I want to sit on that bed with you more than I think I should."

Ryder kicked his legs from out of the covers and hit his feet before he could think of reasons to stop. In three steps, he found himself in front of her and took her hand, his thumb gently running over her knuckles, and clasped her fingers. He hadn't moved abruptly, but he had been fast. That was the sniper in him. *Smooth.*

She didn't balk, only dropped her hold on the door she'd clung to like it'd been her life raft. The thump of his heartbeat reached his eardrums, but no other sound surrounded them as Ryder reached behind her and tapped the door shut. They stood there in the dark, Victoria in the cute pajamas she'd been sleeping in and him in his boxer briefs. Thank God for the cover of darkness because he was half-hard just standing there, and damn it, he didn't get it. Nothing about Victoria screamed, fuck me. Nothing inside him said he wanted to. But they had a connection that urged them together.

"Sit with me," his voice rasped. He gave an easy tug, and she followed. Ryder let go of her hand and crawled back to where he'd been burrowed before and propped himself against the backboard.

Victoria gingerly sat on the edge of the bed. He didn't want to push her, didn't know how much of this was nerves—figuring out what this was. He had no clue. How much stemmed from what happened to her at the hands of Ivan Mikhailov? *Maybe none of it.* Perhaps Victoria was a woman who wouldn't be caught dead in a half-dressed man's room in the middle of the night, and this was too much to handle. Not that he was making a move. What was this? Hell, Ryder was lost as he sensed she was. But her saying that she wanted to be there? He'd make it happen.

"Do I scare you?" he asked.

"No."

Did she tense saying that? Maybe he made the wrong move asking her to sit down. "I made you uncomfortable. I didn't mean to."

"You didn't."

"Then why do you look like you're going to run?"

Victoria pivoted. "You don't have to take care of me."

His eyes went wide. "I know."

"If you feel some sort of responsibility, you can stop."

"I don't. Or I do, but it's not a bad thing."

"You shouldn't."

"I—is that what this is about? You don't think I want to be here?" He leaned forward and took her hand. "Because you're right. I don't have to. I could've popped in, checked on you, and left. I'm here because I want to be, because I like spending the time here."

"Mia and Colby are your friends."

"I have friends all over the world, Victoria. You're not there." He squeezed her hand. "You're here."

Her rigid posture eased, but she didn't relax.

"You want me to walk you back to your room?" he asked.

"No."

"Want to head back on your own?"

She shook her head.

"I could call Mia..." He was out of ideas, and she seemed miserable.

"I don't want to leave." She inched back on the mattress, turning to face him. "I like being near you."

"You look as though you're going to fall off the edge."

A sad laugh fell from her lips. "I don't trust myself. My thoughts. My... me. I'm so lost."

She didn't want to sit on the bed, didn't trust herself—just like when she confided about her job, thinking that she was a sham and couldn't go back home.

"Give yourself a break. It's alright to feel however you do."

"Maybe."

"What is it that you want? That you don't trust."

She looked away. "It's so stupid."

"Try me, love."

"It sounds terrifying, and it's not. I know it's not because I sort of almost had it."

"When did you almost have this mysterious thing?" he asked lightly, urging her on but not playing down whatever terrified her.

"Last night."

His stomach dropped, not expecting that answer. "What was it?"

"A hug. Being held." She lifted a nonchalant shoulder that was anything but. "You put your arm around me, and it was fine. Asking for a hug sounds as silly as it does scary…" Her voice trailed. "But it was nice."

He squeezed his eyes shut, and not for the millionth time, he said a prayer that would let him seek vengeance against Ivan Mikhailov. "Not stupid or silly or anything you might worry about."

"Logically, I know."

"You dealt with a lot over there. It's bound to creep up in ways that don't make sense."

"Mia mentioned that."

Thank God Mia had a conversation with her about that. He didn't want to press, but having a therapist in the house was exactly what Victoria needed. Yet another reason why Titan and the Winterses were likely letting Victoria stay as long as she needed: Mia could offer counseling whenever. "Good. Mia's helped a lot of people work through a lot of things."

She fidgeted on the edge of the bed.

"Victoria?"

"Yes?"

"Do you want to come up here?" He held an arm up, needing her to make it her move.

"Yeah," she whispered.

The hoarse neediness of the plea nearly killed him when she scurried close to his chest. He repositioned and angled down as if she were to lie next to him. Ryder scooted down also, wrapping his arm around her back, and Victoria laid her cheek below his shoulder. She wrapped an arm over his torso, and her fingers flexed into his side as she clung to him.

"Easy." His lips brushed the top of her head. "You're okay. There you go." He wrapped his other arm around her, hugging her close. "You good?"

Nodding against him, her hair tickled his chin. "Mm-hmm."

Hugging her until her iron grip on his side began to relax, he hummed a lullaby he knew by heart. He wasn't sure where it came from, only that it came easily, and it repeated over and over after the last note drifted off his lips.

"You give the best hugs," she murmured, and he didn't know if she was awake.

That wasn't the first time he'd heard that, and finally, he remembered where he'd heard the song he'd hummed for the last ten minutes. Growing up without parents, he'd bounced from home to home, one orphanage to the next, and there were always the kids who were smaller than him, more scared, and he'd tell them it'd be okay—even if it wouldn't—because they needed to know that, in that fearful moment, it'd be okay. Eventually. And hugging some kid he didn't know would make it so.

CHAPTER FOURTEEN

VICTORIA WOKE SURROUNDED by warm strength. She couldn't place the safe, secure feeling as she blinked her eyes open until she realized that Ryder held her close to his chest, and she had spooned her way over his body.

She should be embarrassed, but this was the second time she'd been this rested in so long, and the last time was because of similar circumstances.

Ryder's warm skin stuck to hers, and she closed her eyes again, breathing him in. He smelled sleepy and masculine, familiar and… sexy. There was no doubt that hard, steel-cut muscles wrapped around her, and a man who'd rescued her was a turn-on, but she couldn't wrap her mind around that. Days ago, she didn't think that part of her existed anymore, and now it was consuming more of her thoughts than it should.

She couldn't sleep without him? *Not healthy.*

And she could wake and feel this way? Whether that was healthy or not, Victoria didn't know. People who'd been assaulted, weren't they… ruined? She thought so. Her inner arousal had false bravado. Whatever it was, it was a farce. Her mind wanted to act normal even if it didn't know better. Who on earth wouldn't find Ryder attractive? That accent and those arms holding her tight…

But it was the memory of him humming her to sleep that made her stomach flip. Her pulse picked up, and the replay of his low rumbling voice tossed through her memory, rolling across her senses and awakening her nerves.

"Morning, love."

She jumped in his arms. "Oh, hi. Did I wake you?" But if she hadn't woken him before, startling like that now would have made sure he was wide awake.

Ryder loosened his hold on her, possessively repositioning but not letting go. "No."

Oh, no. What if she kept him up all night? "Did you go to sleep?"

"Sure." His silent chuckle barely shook her.

Lying next to him was too comfortable, too familiar when there was nothing to base that on. She couldn't shake the feeling they'd known each other forever when even their breathing seemed to follow the same pattern, as though their lungs held hands and skipped along the same path. What was she doing here? What was she thinking? Yet, here she was, noticing the slight tickle of his breath, the delicate touches that sent her careening toward a dead man's drop.

Victoria peeled herself from his sinfully warm, sculpted body, and he released her from a bear hold.

"Thanks. Again. I slept great." She nervously stumbled over her words, not sure where to focus her attention. *His bare chest. His beautiful face.* The stubble that she wanted to touch, his mussed hair… She couldn't give any more attention to how the man simply inhaled and exhaled.

"You needed it." His hands drifted over her back, her side.

God. Goose bumps prickled under his touch like a shadow trailing after his palm, and another batch of them simultaneously leapt to life at the nape of her neck and slid down her spine. "Perhaps."

Even her insides were… awake. The free-falling spin her stomach had just started was a wicked combination, knowing that Ryder was wrapped around her. And he was. She wasn't making that up. She was as awake as she could be, and he wasn't moving. Just like on the deck, dangling their feet over the water, she had the urge to move closer, touch him, feel him, even if right now, she was tight in his arms.

Maybe he didn't mind that she spent the night against him. Victoria flicked a quick glance his way. Eyes closed. *So, so very beautiful. And hard. Fierce.* Odd that the two could be equal parts while the man simply lay there.

Did he want her there? *Maybe… Or maybe not.* She'd practically knocked down his door. What was he going to do? Shoo her away? The free-falling stomach froze at the realization, and disappointment weighed down her feelings, her thoughts, every part of her from eyelids to burdened shoulders. "Go back to sleep, Ryder. I'm up. I'll go find breakfast or—"

"Do you want to leave?" His voice bottomed out against her earlobe, setting out a frighteningly powerful reaction coursing down her nerves.

Damn, would she have a reaction to his every question? If they were posed against her neck, maybe. Victoria steeled her thoughts and wondered if all American girls shivered and quivered at the Aussie accent whispered against their bodies. "Mia probably has coffee and breakfast ready."

"Mmm, true." He squeezed her closer as if she were a blanket to be tucked closer. "She loves to cook. It's a hobby of hers."

"Lucky us."

"Are you ready to get up?" He reworded what he'd originally asked, but the intention was still there. Did she want to get out of his bed? Was that what he wanted to know? Would she have this insane inner monologue if Ivan hadn't assaulted her in Russia?

Damn it!

Nerves ate at her insides. She couldn't get a handle on what was up and down, right and left—flirting or not. They were twined together in a bed! He wasn't wearing a shirt, but he hadn't made a move, not so much a step past an innocent hug, when all she wanted was for Ryder to hug her, hold her, kiss her, and make her moan into whatever came next.

If anything came next. Could she even go there?

No.

Victoria was jacked in the head. *Damn Ivan all over again.*

That was why Ryder wouldn't make a move. He was there to help her, protect her. He didn't see her like that. The man was simply on duty to keep her safe and sound. All she had to do was tell him if she wanted to get up or not. *Such a simple question.* "I—"

But she couldn't answer one way or another, didn't trust herself not to ruin everything. She wanted to be here, and it didn't make any sense. If she'd been violated, she shouldn't want anything to do with a man, right? What was wrong with her?

Victoria twisted from him, focusing on the framed row of pictures on the wall next to the bed and decided not to answer his question. "Did you have any more nightmares?"

"No."

"Good." She drew in a shallow breath as tears pricked her eyes. *Such a wimp.* She couldn't look at him. All she had to do was say she wanted to stay where she was. "Are you ready to get up?"

"I'll answer if you stop staring at the wall."

Was she that transparent? "I'm not."

"Should we start lying to each other?"

Stinging pricks of tears burned her eyes, and she blinked back the stupid reaction. "No."

Silently, he nodded, letting his hands drift over her side, a hushed request for her to break away from the hard stare at the wall. She faced him, shifting against the soft pillows and the thick weight of his muscled bicep. "You?"

"Me neither, love." His eyes narrowed. "I don't want to get up."

"You don't?" she whispered.

"Not if you want to stay with me for a little while longer."

Her heart climbed into her throat. What did he mean? What was he asking of her? Or the better question, what did she want?

She wanted *him*. She liked him. He made her feel safe. There was no denying how attractive he was. And sweet. Caring. Nice. But not that nice. He'd already explained he was a contract killer. As jobs went, that maybe disqualified him from nice at all. But he was nice to her—and she liked that a whole lot. Respected it too.

Ryder inched away. "No worries if you want to get up and run down to Mia's cooking. I don't blame you. Once you have a Mia muffin, you'll appreciate what I'm saying."

"No."

"Then what is it that you want, Victoria?"

Come on. She wanted them to stay exactly like this. Couldn't he read her mind? With his arms around her…

"Tell me," he urged.

A hug. A kiss? Yes. A kiss. Her cheeks flushed. No—her entire body did. Even her pussy clenched at the thought. But she couldn't tell him, and instead, leaned close, absolutely terrified to admit that she wanted his lips on hers. Wordlessly, she burrowed against his side.

"I want that too." His sun-kissed arms that she'd had no problems clinging to in the dead of night wrapped around her back, folding her close to his bare chest.

She took what felt like the first sigh in a decade, relaxing as if he had lifted that burden of decision-making from her shoulders. *That wasn't so hard.* He wanted her here, and not to fuck and be used, like Ivan, not to be a burden like she feared she was. She needed to trust her thoughts. How she felt… how they felt because, tame as this was, it was about as good and sexy as she could handle.

Even relaxed and lying back, his muscles were taut and distinct. Her fingers toyed with the light smattering of chest hair that covered his pecs, and she studied the rise and fall of his breathing. "Staying here was a good idea."

"Agree." One hand carefully stroked her side, his finger scratching over the pajama shirt.

Staying here was just one inner thought. But she voiced it, and a shocking amount of confidence bloomed after he agreed. Victoria inhaled. She was finding her way back to herself simply by spooning.

"Doing okay?"

"Better than I expected." She tilted her head back, and her forehead scratched against the morning whiskers on his chin. "Mm."

"Mm, what?"

His stubble was a gentle reminder that Ivan Mikhailov hadn't broken her. She could feel. Sense. Be. Honestly, the idea, that pinprick of awareness, was enough to celebrate because not too long ago, she thought she was empty inside.

Victoria drew back and let her fingers touch Ryder's chin, following the prickly line of his jaw.

"I need to shave," he murmured.

"It works on you." She inspected her fingers' path. His sharp chin and full lips were inches from her own as she planted her chin on his shoulder.

Ryder repositioned, pulling one hand back and tucking it between his pillow and head as he casually continued to rest with her against him like it was no big deal she was inspecting him, touching his face. His eyes were closed, and he had the longest eyelashes. They didn't flutter. And those lips… perfect. Pink. Full. *So perfect.*

"You're staring," he mumbled with a slight smile.

"Your eyes are closed," she whispered. "How did you know mine weren't too?"

"You can tell when someone's looking at you. Can't you?" Still he didn't open his eyes.

"I don't know. I think so."

"My senses are on point."

She inched closer. "What are you sensing?"

Was he as relaxed as he seemed? She wasn't. With every passing breath, her chest tightened with lust-pounding arousal that was to blame for this boldness. She was a victim, but in Ryder's arms, she didn't feel that way.

Her hot breaths accelerated. Even her boiling blood ignored warning signs her brain dropped as she was transfixed by his lips, making her mouth water, wondering how it would feel to brush hers to his. *Soft. Plump.* He probably kissed as amazing as he sounded. Smooth and seductive… Holy hell, her panties were wet. The realization hit her across the face.

"I'm in the moment, love." He drew in a deep breath, making his chest expand. "Enjoying my time with you. Whatever happens, happens…"

What did that mean?

The innermost intimate muscles of her body reacted as a thousand thoughts raced through her mind. He wanted more? But the move was hers—because of what happened to her. The tender tissue under the silk of her panties throbbed. Her clitoris wanted attention. Her slit wanted his fingers stroking her slick skin the way he'd teased her back and side all morning.

Victoria didn't care anymore, not about Ivan or what happened—fuck, she did. But not now, and pushing that hell away, she wanted to kiss him and dipped her head close, hovering her lips above his. But didn't, couldn't, and still, he didn't move.

The control that man had—more than her because she wanted to scream and explode over a kiss that hadn't happened yet. Ryder's warm breath tickled the pout of her bottom lip.

A millimeter of charged space was between them, and he wouldn't. She knew that now. It had to be her. Had she ever kissed a man first? Probably. It wouldn't have mattered before. What did she think about that? She was… *maybe frightened, definitely excited.* Victoria chased away the final worry of nerves and let her lips dance across his.

Ryder groaned a satisfaction that rushed through her like white water rapids, and his mouth parted. The weight of his heavy arms wrapped around her.

"So sweet, love." The hot touch of his tongue pressed into her mouth. He wasn't just awake. He was alive. Hungry. Needy. A throaty groan rumbled in his chest, and she felt it flow through her. Ryder rolled on his side, taking her with him. "Easy. C'mere."

"Mm-kay." Her legs threaded with his powerful ones, and his huge weight of muscles and confidence surrounded her.

"You okay?"

She nodded into the words-tangled kiss. Everything that she'd imagined about his lips paled in comparison as he slowly teased her tongue with his. Velvet slices tangled and danced together, and her hips moved in motion with the rhythm of their mouths.

She opened her eyes to find Ryder peering down at her. He wasn't on top of her, but leaning over, and there was a depth to him watching her, like he was worried she might break.

"This is a good way to wake up." His lips seemed pinker than before, and his eyes glowed greener than she remembered.

"Yes." The heat of a blush rose off her neck, and Victoria cast a glance through her eyelashes. "I kissed you."

He chuckled, low and deep, pulling her to him, his kiss brushing across her lips before his dangerous mouth moved to her ear. "You kissed the hell out of me, love."

"Ryder! Oh my…" She teased against his chest, groaning and gasping as his tongue licked the underside of her ear.

"Oh my?" He pulled her tighter, his body straining against hers through the covers—his erection pressing against his leg. His quiet chuckle grew into a throatier laugh. His lips quickened down her throat.

"Ryder," she laughed even as her eyes rolled back from the dangerous work his lips did on her neck.

"Oh my? I thought you were a Midwest beauty. That sounded like the American south."

"Oh. My." She kept teasing, but that was so damn good. His tongue stroked. Her amusement transformed to an overwhelming hunger. Her pussy clenched as his attention focused a deadly hit on her collarbone.

"Oh my." Teeth scraping, lips kissing, the jokes disappeared.

"Oh…" Her lips parted, breaths rushing. "That's amazing."

His strong hands massaged her pajama-covered back and ran up her neck, threading into her hair as hers caressed his chest, kneading the warm flesh stretched across him, dipping across the carved muscles of his body. Nothing but carnal pleasure flooded her senses, and arousal continued to dampen her panties.

"You're okay?" His strained voice killed her.

"Yes. Fine." Failing to control her erratic heartbeat, she rolled her hips and embraced the high. "Please don't ask me again."

He stilled for a minute and nodded. "Roger that."

She pulled the covers that separated them away, tangling their legs. She wasn't going to sleep with him. She just needed to be next to him. Touch him. Feel him. Something. Nothing more. Hell, she was dressed like a girl scout compared to him in his boxer briefs!

But sweet mercy, his warm body under the covers…

"Victoria," he growled. "Easy."

Her nipples pricked tight under her T-shirt, and she had on too many layers. "I just need…"

Something.

Anything.

She needed to come was what she probably needed. Or she needed to slow down. Not because of what happened, but because sleeping with him seemed like it *wasn't* the right thing to do? She didn't know. Maybe it was? Though if she didn't know, it wasn't. God, she was dying inside though.

"I don't want to have sex," she blurted out.

He pulled back. Quickly. *Fuck.*

"That wasn't my intention, Victoria."

"No." She cringed. "I know. God, my head is all screwed up. It won't make sense if I say it, but God, I shouldn't have said that."

"Try me."

She shook her head. "It barely makes sense in my head, and I doubt I could explain it."

"Try me."

Victoria laughed. "So stupid. I'm overjoyed, I think, that I'm turned on. I was worried that, after…" She gestured. "I would be—I don't know—unable to be aroused." God, that sounded so frank and almost medical. She dropped her head in her hands. "We kind of have good chemistry, I think. I'm worried that I just said too much." She glanced up, feeling nuts for confessing. "Sorry to drop the feelings bomb on you."

"Eh." He shrugged. "Feelings don't scare me."

"No, huh?" She smiled hesitantly.

"No. Feelings scare away pussies. That's it."

"Oh." Cheeks on fire, she dropped back onto the pillow.

"Nothing wrong with those things. Taking it slow. Whatever." He leaned over her. "But, fuck, I like kissing you. You okay with that?"

Her cheeks were still hot. Neck too. *Everything, actually.* "More than okay."

"C'mere."

Deep lust she hadn't expected to spring back into her blood so fast warmed her neck in an entirely different way than her embarrassed flush, heating her in all the places she hadn't expected to feel so hungry, so alive, under his steady touch. She liked how the hint of desperation fed her need her to remove every last slip of air between them.

His weight leaned on her, pressing her hip into the mattress as Ryder leaned over.

Every kiss lasted forever and never seemed long enough. Tension built so tight she wanted to scream, and Ryder knotted his hand in her hair. She startled, shifting.

"Sorry." He released the strands too quickly, and the feeling was gone.

It wasn't that it hurt or that it reminded her of before, just that it was closer to what she needed. Her body ached with the need to come. His too, probably. This was torture.

"Don't say that." Victoria rested her hand on the one he was sliding away. "It's the one thing I really need from you."

"I'm not going to lose control, love. Promise."

Please. Lose control. She gripped his hand, all of her clinging to him, needing so much from him that she didn't know where to start. Victoria opened her eyes, and Ryder was still on his side, she was still on her back. "I trust you."

He let his fingers drag down her chin and walk along her jaw line.

"Why are you watching me?" she whispered.

"It's becoming one of my favorite things to do."

She melted on the inside then wanted to curse him for letting her feel that good without touching her body. But instead, Victoria wove her fingers with his and pulled his hand to her chest. Her heart beat a quick cadence. "Touch me."

"I'm dying to."

She held her lungful of air as he separated their hands and ran over the mounds of her breasts. Her eyes fluttered shut as her breath exhaled. Ryder massaged and teased, pulling moans from her as she relaxed and fell deeper into the throes of arousal until his palm rested on her tummy, his fingers feathered out, rubbing over her pajama shirt.

"Ryder..." She inhaled and touched his forearm, praying he knew she wanted his hand further down. "Please don't stop."

He held her eyes before slipping his fingers under the waistband of the pajamas and underwear. The pads of his fingertips carefully drifted south, gently teasing over the bud of her clit and stroking back across her folds. "Soaked, love."

"Yes." Ecstasy nearly over took her, and he'd barely touched her. "I am."

Ryder let the back of his knuckles rub over her nub as he drew his hand back, and her clit enjoyed the slight touch. She cupped her hands to his cheeks and pressed her lips to his as Ryder began to stroke her in time with how she kissed him until she couldn't any more.

"Oh…" Her mouth gaped when he spread and teased her entrance. Mind spinning, her body thundered from the inside out. She widened her thighs.

"Such a sweet one." Gently, Ryder eased a finger inside her body.

She needed his invasion. Wanted. God, she hadn't been able to breathe for so long. Finally, she could just because he'd breached what Ivan had been taking without permission.

"Ryder."

"Slow, yeah." His husky voice massaged her senses as his deft finger that moved in painstakingly circular motions, still easing up and down. He was doing such wonderful things, playing with her until he eased another finger into her. "Yeah, you like this?"

"Yes," she promised him. Her hips rocked in time with the rhythm of his wrist.

With every careful thrust, Ryder erased part of the past. Not that she'd be able to escape the memory of Ivan, but she'd never thought this would bring her pleasure again. Ryder deepened and let his fingers curve.

"Oh, that's so, so…"

"Good?" His graveled voice rumbled close to her ear.

"Good?" She nodded, mouth agape. "Mm, yeah."

"Mm, yeah," he growled. "Looks good. Tucked safe under your clothes. Safe against me."

Safe… Yes. Dizzy with sensation overload, her eyes fell back in her head as he picked up the pace. Her ass cheeks clenched, her pussy too. Legs trembling and heels pressed against the mattress, Victoria grew too hot, too wanton. Her clothes choked her, as desperation fueled and teased the climax that was too far away.

"Do you want to come for me, love?"

"Yes." She tossed her head side to side. "But. I can't." Sweat tickled under her pajamas. She was on the cusp, but her head was half in the game and shocked that she was even there. Maybe she wasn't as bad off as she'd thought? Maybe she was totally screwed up. Maybe, maybe, maybe—

"Relax," he crooned. "Open those beautiful eyes."

She squeezed them tighter, turning away, and *oh, damn*. Ryder shifted closer, fingering her deeper and faster, until she vibrated with a need to orgasm. Her mouth hinged open, hanging as she gasped for breath, her hips rocking side to side, her pussy grinding against the butt of his hand.

"Eyes."

She gave him what he asked, and a barely-there smile pushed her to the teetering edge of orgasm. "Ryder." Not coming was nearly painful, and she wanted to give up. "I can't anymore."

"You're getting in your own way."

"I—" Was she?

"Slide your fingers with mine." His intense stare said he knew she was right there, ready to come.

His barely-there smile went full bloom.

"Scandalous," he whispered against the shell of her ear, and again, she almost fell apart.

She dropped her hand on top of his sinewy arm, feeling it flex and strain with every finger fuck until her fingers slid under her clothes, and the pads of her fingertips massaged her clit.

"Victoria." Ryder sucked in a breath then ducked down, moving close to her ear. His fingers pumped into her as she played too. "Sweet, tight pussy."

Her eyelashes fluttered. Had she ever been with a man so vocal, so in tune with her? *No. No.* "Ohhh."

His hand pumped faster, the fingers not inside her brushing against the tight bud of her ass, sending illicit electric shocks shooting from the inside out. All of her was on fire. Her hips rose to meet him, her fingers spun her clit into a frenzy. "I'm going to come. Ryder. *Ryder.*"

Her canal clenched him, the spasming orgasm taking hold as her legs shook and white lightning blinded her. He moved on top of her, a searing kiss planted against her lips, not stopping as her muscles clung tight to his fingers, rolling and milking, gripping and pulsing. Victoria bucked against him, needing this release more than any climax in her life.

It was real. True. Pleasure. It was beautiful. And he washed away part of the pain. It was perfect, and she was high. Adrenaline surged. The drugged elation of hormones in her blood reached every inch of her body.

Finally, his kiss stilled as his hand did. Victoria held him, hugging. And small cry caught in her throat that she refused to let escape. She wanted this time, this euphoria without any complication as Ryder wrapped her in an embrace.

"You're okay? You're okay," he quickly promised.

"Yes," she admitted when she had control over her thoughts and knew she wouldn't risk a teary revelation. "I needed that."

"Still doing okay?"

"You must think I'm a huge package of drama," she whispered.

"No."

"What do you think?" Victoria squeezed her eyes shut then stared at the ceiling.

"That you needed to come, love."

She looked at him out of the corner of her eye. "I did. Hard. Thank you."

He laughed. "You're welcome." Ryder leaned over and kissed her forehead. "Getting you off was hot." He rolled away. "Why don't you get some breakfast, and I'll meet you down there."

"Oh." She bit her lip. "Don't you, um, want…"

Again, a hearty laugh fell from his lips. "Yeah. I want." He readjusted boxer briefs that didn't leave much to the imagination about what he was talking about. His hand covered an impressive bulge, resting there after he moved the jutting cock. "But, I don't know. You're right on that edge. I didn't know which way you were going to go, smile or tears. This was a moment to erase the past more than me nuttin' off." He winked. "I'm going to shower off and meet you, all right?"

"Sure." She didn't know what to say, now more confused than ever.

CHAPTER FIFTEEN

RYDER PACED THE bedroom after Victoria shut the door. *Right move, wrong move?* Who knew? What they didn't need was for her to fall apart, to end up more fragile than she was when she showed up in his room.

Hell. He was harder than when she left. He could probably do push-ups with his dick. His phone rang, and he walked to the nightstand, his hard-on leading the way, and grabbed the cell. Number unknown. Great. Not that many people had this number to begin with. Ryder swiped the screen to answer. "Yeah, hello?"

"How is she?" Maddy's no-nonsense voice came through the phone still holding an air of sophistication. He liked how she was like street-smart royalty. The woman knew far more than he'd ever want to know about human trafficking, rape, and sex crimes, and she had the capacity to know how to vindicate the crimes. But Maddy also had the ability to love and care for people. He guessed she almost had to in order to handle the horrors she likely had seen.

"How's she supposed to be?" Ryder flopped backward in the bed, his chub slowly dying.

"She's however she's supposed to be. Recovery has no set rules or agenda." Maddy paused to let that sink in. "But you knew her on day one. That's your baseline and tells you how far she's come. We don't know who she was, so she'll have to direct how much healing there is to do."

He grumbled. "Why didn't you call me from your cell phone?"

"Because you wouldn't answer," she replied, knowing the truth. "Now, I'm going to ask you again. How's she doing?"

"Ask Mia. She's the shrink."

"Don't play me for stupid, Ryder."

He rubbed his forehead. "Mia and Winters see her as much as I do."

Maddy laughed in his ear. "And I spent all day with you both yesterday."

"Same," Ryder raised his voice slightly. "Along with Mia and Winters, Rocco and Cat."

"They're not going to sleep with her," Maddy snapped back.

He squeezed his eyes shut. "Who said I am?"

"What are we? Children?" She let out a string of French words that he could only assume were curses. "There's nothing wrong with forming a connection with her."

"I didn't say there was."

"And there's nothing wrong with having feelings for her."

The pressure in his head moved to his chest. He rubbed his bare sternum. "Feeling deniers are pussies. I've already had this conversation with someone recently. Good to know you and I are on the same page."

"Ryder—"

"Maddy." He sat up. "She was raped. What am I supposed to do about that?"

"That doesn't make her *anciennes nouvelles*."

"English, Madeline," he snapped, pressure getting the best of him.

"She's not old news. Not used up. One attack—"

"Multiple attacks—"

"Might not define her. It might. But it might not, and I saw the way you two were together."

"So?"

"I know sex. I know people. Sex and people. People and sex. Connections. That's what I know."

"Well, I didn't."

"Sleep with her?"

"Yeah, mate. I made sure she got off. Loved every second of it." He sucked a breath and pinched the bridge of his nose, remembering how she clung to him like the very next seconds of her survival were dependent on him delivering a true blue, screaming orgasm. "She did too."

"Good," Maddy said approvingly.

"You should talk to her, all right? I'm not the one who needs the pep talks."

She clucked. "You need to know what you're doing."

"And what is it that you think I'm supposed to do to make this better? She's got to get through this herself. I figured that out myself, Maddy. I got her off. Showed her she could still go there."

"That's not enough," Madeline *tsked* him, letting her French accent thicken.

He shook his head, finally releasing the pinch on his nose. "Then what?"

"Next time?"

There wouldn't be a next time. Right? He did what she needed: got her off. Then he didn't know what to say. Hell. He'd panicked, nearly choking over how badly he wanted Victoria. But what did that even matter? She was leaving, and he was part of a ghost team. "Sure. Tell me about next time and how I might be anything good enough to deserve that." Madeline hung onto that silence longer than he expected. "Maddy?"

"*Oui*... I'm here." She let out a soft breath in the phone. "You are good enough, my friend, and when you have her? Don't mistake making love for actual love."

His eyebrows reached his hairline. "Thanks for the pro tip."

"Bury yourself deep, and never let go of her eyes."

A quick sweat broke over Ryder at the thought. "Roger that, Maddy." The thought of burying his cock deep inside Victoria's sweet body was going to send him over the edge. "Is that why you called?"

"To check on her."

"She's doing all right."

"She is if she had a sexy Aussie make her moan before her first cup of coffee."

"Either way, she's fine."

Maddy laughed. "Sometimes, you forget who I am and what I know."

He stared at the ceiling. "No, Madeline. You know sex and people. I got it."

"*Au revoir.*"

Ryder tossed the phone on the bed and couldn't face Victoria now, even if he hadn't wanted to hide in the shower before. "Ahhhh." He stretched high overhead, then dropped his hands, pulled off his drawers, kicking them toward the wall where his bag was, and padded naked into the bathroom.

He slapped the water on, and waited for the steamy air to wrap around him. *Bury in her…* Shit, if Victoria wrapped her legs around him, if he could sink into her tightness… "I'd never survive."

CHAPTER SIXTEEN

Australia
Four Years Ago

ZOE WALKED ON the railroad rail, one foot in front of the other, holding Ryder's hand. They had three hours until they needed to be back at their house, and they'd walked for the last hour one way down the rails. Now they had to head back to where he'd stashed his motorbike.

If it were his call, they'd do nothing but ride the back roads with her wrapped around his waist, but that cost money, and petrol wasn't cheap.

She jumped off the rail. "Let's walk into town."

He eyed the streets and would rather she didn't. But telling Zoe to not do something would only make her want it more. He knew what they would find: homeless and hungry blokes who sometimes weren't much older than they were but weren't as tuned into where to scrap for food—or skilled enough to lift it.

Zoe like to help as much as she enjoyed the rush, and given the choice, she'd choose the safer option, but she never refused a tough choice because the odds weren't stacked in their favor.

They rounded the corner, and as Ryder expected, two boys their age but living behind the buildings were hunkered down. He recognized them, and Zoe trotted up to say hello. Ryder scooped down, nabbing a rock, and skipped it into the street, taking his time. He didn't want to talk.

Zoe spun back. Her bright eyes said she was now a girl on a mission.

He caught up to the three of them. "What's going on?"

"They haven't had anything great to eat in days."

He could've called it.

"We'll be back." Zoe yanked. "Don't move."

"Zoe," Ryder cautioned, but he knew there was no point. They moved farther up the block and onto the main street. The end of the day would help out their prospects. Shops would toss leftovers, and they'd grab what they needed.

"The bakery closed half hour ago." She pulled him toward the back alley off the main street.

Time wasn't on their side. If this wasn't a sure thing, Ryder was going to have to sell her on leaving those guys to fend for themselves. If they didn't want to go to a shelter or figure it out on their own, they couldn't wait for his girl to feed them. But still, he felt for them.

"Look, there!"

Piled on the back entryway of the bakery was the days' worth of food to be discarded. "Not tossed yet."

"But it will be."

This was when word on the street was gold. The rule was to shoplift it, grab it from a dumpster but not from a loading dock or back breezeway. He didn't know the specifics, but something about that was a big deal, where a look-the-other-way crime became about taking a business's merchandise. Ryder didn't pretend to understand or even know if it was true, but he knew he didn't want to test the unwritten code.

"Let's find a shop that's dumped already." He grabbed her hand.

"It's right there." Zoe checked around them, and the backdoor light was dark. "No one's around."

It was almost as if he could feel another set of eyes but couldn't see them. "I don't know. Let's go."

"Come on." She dropped her hold on him and ran toward the stairs, summiting the bakery's platform, and grabbed an armful of their stash.

Out of the dark, an arm reached, grabbing her shoulder, and Zoe yelled. She spun and pushed, but the arm didn't let go.

"Shit!" Ryder sprinted, hopped the rail, and bounded up the stairs, ripping the hand off her. "Run."

They took off, him keeping his head on the swivel, back and forth, as the man emerged, hollering for the girl to stop. They didn't. They ran as fast as they could until they rounded the corner, and heart bursting in his chest from fear of another's hand on her, he erupted. "Zoe! I told you!"

She clung to the food, eyes wide, her breath racing for what had to be many reasons.

"I didn't see him," she finally admitted.

"I know." He urged them forward. "I never should have let you."

She stopped abruptly. "You never could have stopped me."

Wasn't that the truth… "Fine. Let's go. Come on." Time was ticking away. They jogged back to where the other guys were, and their faces lit up at the sight of Zoe's offerings, so much so that he felt like a fuckwit for complaining.

"We have to go," Ryder grumbled.

After she said everything she needed to, she joined him walking down the sidewalk. "Are you mad at me?"

"Not thrilled."

"That was a rush." She wrapped her arms around his neck as he pulled her behind the building. "Ryder. Ryder?"

"Never—" He stopped and pulled her close, kissing her as his name fell from her lips again. "Do that again. Never."

"It worked out though."

"Not my concern. You can't go around saving the world if it's you who's put in danger."

She leaned back, her fingers knotted behind his neck, and let her weight hang. "Why not? You love it when I do."

She was right. *Fuck it.* She was always right. The looks on their faces when she handed them food… His chest compressed at that exact moment, even as he wanted to yell that they needed to go. Ryder tugged her close. "Then do it safer."

Their stomachs touched, and he hugged her until the silliness wiped from her face.

"Who would have thought two orphan kids like us would have found each other?"

"I would." Ryder gave her sides a squeeze, hanging on to the special girl in his life, the one he could show he wasn't all tough guy and foster-kid fights. "I was supposed to find you that first night—"

Zoe laughed at the memory. "That was almost so bad."

"Almost." That night could have gone a much different way, but all he did was help her out, and it changed his life. He could see how she wanted to help people out all the time, and maybe she hoped it changed their world.

She stared up as if she'd read his mind. "Got my best mate and my boyfriend. That's a two-for-one deal when I didn't have anyone in the world. All because you helped me out when you didn't have to."

"I love you." The sound of the city faded away as he waited to see what she would say even if he knew what she would say.

Still, he'd said those words a thousand times, positive it would come out rushed, and she'd miss it. But he'd been wrong because he'd been slow, articulate. Like every time, "I love you," raced through his head had been a practice round.

"I love you, too." There was her smile, plus a happiness Ryder had never seen. She glowed. *Like an angel.*

Calm washed over him. She was his place in the world. He might've been a no one to everyone, an orphan kid bounced from home to home, but when no one had ever loved him before, having one person want to remember him was like an anchor dropped, and his future came into focus.

He pulled her close and kissed her because he loved her, because she loved him, because she did good things for people when neither of them had the ability to do a lot of good. She was the best, and the best was worth kissing as long as he could.

"We have to get back." He took her hand in his. "What do you want to do?"

She swung his arm back and forth. "Make a list of everything we'll do when we grow up."

"After I do my time. That's a guaranteed job. Money. Things we need to get set up."

"What if you love it? Being in the military?"

"Then I guess that'd make you an Army man's wife one day." He squeezed her hand. It wasn't as though they hadn't talked about the future. Together forever. Today just seemed more real.

She beamed. "Guess so."

CHAPTER SEVENTEEN

Present Day

THE MAN IN the mirror stared back at Ryder and mocked him. Victoria was downstairs having breakfast, and Maddy had just hung up on him after telling him he should be having sex with her. There was no question that he agreed with Maddy. But yet, he was alone, staring at a very keyed-up man who was within an inch of his life in need of an orgasm.

Getting Victoria off wasn't just about getting her off, though, God, if that hadn't been insane. He could hear every gasping breath and feel every tightening muscle. He needed her to know that she could, that it wasn't about him. Everything about that was for her because so much had been forced from her for someone else.

Ryder stepped into the shower and dropped his head back, letting the spray hit his face. The waterfall of heat cascaded over him, rushing over his knotted muscles. He'd seen Victoria with less clothes on yesterday when they were swimming, but in those pajamas, covered ankles to neckline, she'd never been sexier.

He gripped his cock, stroking as the blood rushed to the engorging member, stiffening under his hold. Nice and easy, his fist slid back and forth, until he paused long enough to glance at the options of fancy fucking soaps, grabbing the closest one and lubing his hand. He took hold of his throbbing erection again and closed his eyes. Victoria was front and center in his mind. The idea of thrusting into her and holding her eyes, all while he stayed buried deep as he could for as long as he could stand it—before, goddamn… He stroked, nearly gasping at the thought of sliding out of her wetness.

Ryder flexed his fingers around his dick, pumping, his hips jerking—

Knock. Knock.

"Fuck," he breathed out, molars grinding. "Yeah?"

"Hey, it's me," Victoria called through the door.

Who else would it be? "I'll be out in a minute."

"Can I come in?"

Fucking hell. She was going to come in, and he was at a full mast. The door cracked, and he saw her lips pressed to the edge of the doorjamb.

"I had something to say."

Ryder reached for the bottle of shampoo. "Almost done, love. Give me two minutes, yeah?"

He rubbed the soap into a frothy lather and dug his hands into his hair, quickly sudsing it when he heard the quiet click of the shower door opening and the burst of cool air rush along his back. Bubbles dripped down his forehead as he looked over his shoulder at the woman clearly in his personal space yet averting her eyes to the ceiling like she couldn't look at his ass.

"Everything okay?"

"No." Her eyes faltered along the side of the wall, and she leaned away from him. "Not really."

Damn it. He should have controlled himself. At least now his erection was less raging and more in the state of semi-erect. Still, the big guy wasn't down for the count, and she wasn't stupid. If she caught a glimpse, she would know exactly what he'd been doing.

Ryder maneuvered, maintaining an iota of cock coverage. "Let me wash this out, and I'm done."

He dunked his head back under the shower, running his hair clean then reached for the faucet, wiping the water out of his eyes—her hand found his, and his insides jumped. Shocked, his face shot her way.

Water sprayed over her shirt. Victoria's fingers bent over his as she still clung to the glass shower door.

"I was just getting out."

Her gaze swept slow and lazy down his neck, his chest, idling on the muscular V that led to his dick. "Don't."

Hot water trailed over his back, running rivers down his arm and their hands. The shower steam was escaping, but not before its humidity kissed her cheeks and painted a pink flush on them. A dewy damp sheen of water glistened across her skin, and he longed to see that same fresh sheen of moisture wet her breasts, her stomach, leading him the way to what he wanted to think about: her, wanting him, soft and wet.

"C'mere." He tugged her into the shower, clothes and all, and shut the glass door. Steam swirled around them, and he put his palms on her cheeks, feeling her jaw open as she peered up, lips parted. His heart hammered, and he thumbed away water droplets from her eyelashes. "Tell me what's wrong."

She didn't say a word, only slipping her eyes shut and dropping her head back with a sigh that bordered on a quiet, hungry groan.

Victoria was right. There was nothing to say. He took her mouth, letting his lips find hers, and his greedy tongue sank into a hungry, hot kiss. She moaned. Her hands moved to his chest, her fingernails scraping down his pecs as she kissed him back, more alive than she had been in his bed. A gasp caught in her throat and vibrated through both their bodies, and still he didn't let go of her cheeks, holding her face to his.

Her arms went up, languid and loose, and only then did he break away, tugging the soaked T-shirt over her head. His thick erection pressed between them, and Ryder took Victoria's mouth again, his hands skimming down her shower-soaked back, teasing up to her shoulders, and down her arms so that he could run his hands over to the perfect little breasts that had tortured him since the moment he saw her erect nipples behind a swimsuit top.

She inhaled deeply, head falling to the side while he teased the light rose tips of her tits. Victoria tugged at the sopping wet pajama pants as he plucked, watching her breasts become fuller and tighter as though they reached for his touch.

But her pesky bottoms clung to her thighs. "Want help?"

"Yes." She grinned, straightening to face him.

"I'm a useful bloke." He yanked the water-soaked fabric until the pants piled at her ankles, and she stepped out, kicking them to the side of the tiled shower floor.

His hands ran over her smooth hips, the curve of her ass. He couldn't stop touching her, feeling how soft, how perfectly she fit in his hand. His hard-on bobbed between them, and if he could will her hands to stroke his dick, he would. But her fingertips grazed back and forth, outlining the ridges of his stomach muscles.

Ryder ran his hands under her hair, and Victoria let her palms travel to his shoulders, the space between them gone and the soft skin of her stomach smoothing against his shaft. He ground his teeth, focusing on what she might need, praying that it might get him near what he most craved, but scared as fuck to come anywhere near hurting her. His hand wrapped into her hair, damp and dripping. "You had something to say?"

With a bite to her lip, she nodded. "Yes."

Ryder tilted toward her ear and whispered, "What?"

"I was wrong earlier."

Trepidation warred with anticipation. "About?"

"I do..." She squeezed his shoulders, leaning closer. "Want to have sex." She paused, her beauty and truth overwhelming him. "With you."

"Victoria." He almost choked on her name, not sure how fucked in the head she was or if this was a good idea. His earlier anticipation celebrated and exploded into lust. Carnal yearning nearly blinded him. A throbbing in his cock screamed to shut up, that he'd regret any word that shut down her invitation. Ryder swallowed away the uncertainty, nearly in pain with wanting to feel the slide of her sweet pussy.

"I was sitting there, drinking coffee, thinking that we'd erased something ugly, and one day, I'd be able to erase the rest."

He dragged a steamy breath in, trying to remain lucid as she swayed against his dick. "You have reservations."

She froze. "I did—but I don't know what I'm waiting on."

"Don't rush it." Doing the right thing sucked. Doing the right thing hurt. God, it sucked and hurt, and he didn't want to hurt her. He wanted to erase her pain, make her come again and again. Ryder wanted to be inside her body more than he could ever remember wanting to be with a woman.

"Why?" Beautiful, inquisitive eyes pushed him to answer a question he wasn't sure he could voice. "I'm not supposed to want it? I'm not supposed to want you? Because of an unwritten rule about how I should feel?"

His breathing was too heavy to go unnoticed. Water dripped down his face, but he didn't want to move. "I don't know."

"Where's the rule book?" she asked, dead serious.

He hated she'd had this happen to her. *Damn it. So much hate for Ivan Mikhailov.* "There isn't one."

"Am I supposed to wait a year? Two years? Then assume someone I trust to stop the second I breathe the word—the way I trust you—would just be there?" She shook her hair, letting more of it get wet. "I didn't do anything wrong, and my assaults haven't screwed me up in that way. Other ways, I'm sure."

Even when Ryder thought he couldn't hate Ivan Mikhailov with any deeper of a vengeful disgust, he learned it was possible.

"I want you." Her voice dropped low as if laying that truth on the line was harder than everything else she'd said. "I think you're attracted to me?"

This girl was killing him. "Yes, love. You got me there."

She dropped her hands, wrapping her fingers around the erection that couldn't get any harder if his life depended on it. Ryder tried not to come like a uni boy with his first girlfriend.

"There's a condom in the back pocket of my pj pants."

"Premeditated." He raised an eyebrow, working his jaw to the side as her grip stroked carefully.

"I'm a planner."

Hell, so was he, and everything he was going to jerk off to would happen in the shower.

He ducked his head and rested his lips on her perked tit. The tip of his tongue ran circles around the tight bud, and Victoria's back arched. Her hands sifted into his wet hair as she propped against the wall.

He kissed his way to the other breast, this time pulling her nipple between his teeth gently while his fingers began to stroke her slippery slit. She was wet, naturally lubricated, and his fingers parted her folds. Ryder teased her entrance, sucked her tit, and listened to her gasp as hot water rained over them. He slid his two fingers inside her, making her hips writhe.

Her inner muscles gripped him, and he kissed up her neck, nibbling her ear. "You good?"

"Yes," she gasped, rocking her hips as if she wanted more.

"Good girl."

He wanted more too. Gently, his fingers plunged, a pattern developing of taking her to the edge, circling her clit, entering her again, and bringing her to a high point. Making her come was fun. He smiled and decided to deliver on the torture he was creating. This time, he didn't stop and move to her clitoris. Ryder kept the pace, watching Victoria lose control and let her head thrash to the side.

She rode his hand, her breasts swaying until her mouth opened, a silent shout falling from her lips as if she couldn't make a sound. Her pussy clenched his fingers, climaxing powerfully for him.

She shivered despite the heat and hot water. "That was heaven."

Her fiery lips met his neck, her tongue licking over his thumping pulse as he strained to control the lust in his veins. Ryder palmed her breasts as she whispered, "I need this so much."

Him too. He swooped down in the water, grabbing the pajama pants, and extracted the condom. He held it between them, asking if she was sure without a word. She nodded.

"You change your mind…" Ryder tore the foil packet open and sheathed himself, tossing the crumbled wrapper over the shower door.

"I won't." She worked against him, fingernails scraping his back. Her leg crawled up his thigh, and Ryder kissed her, tongue stroking, lung searing, until he had her backed against the wall. Her leg hitched high, and he caught it in his hand.

His forehead touched hers, their eyes met, and he tried to read her, making sure her words had been the truth and not that she was forcing away a hated memory. All he saw was crystal-clear desire that mirrored his own. He guided his sheathed cock against her pussy.

"I…" *Never wanted this more. Never needed something so bad.* He didn't know how to finish as he nudged his blunt head into her soul-stilling heat. Even through the latex, he was close to coming undone. Restraint was his gift, but his limits were tested as Victoria arched, beckoning him to fuck her.

Tension burned in his muscles.

"Oh, that's…" she gasped.

"Good." He flexed against her, and water sprayed their faces. "And tight."

Water sprayed against the back of his neck as, inch by inch, his dick slid into heaven.

Victoria's gaze never wavered as though the strength of his stare was enough to hold her up.

"Sweetheart." He carefully pumped into her, at a loss for words. "You're beautiful."

Her eyes closed, and her head dropped back, tipping against the tiled wall. "Ryder, God, this…"

Finally, dizzy with sensation and seated fully inside her, he leaned forward and whispered the rest of what she hadn't said, "Was what we needed."

Because it wasn't just her. He'd been on the edge, clawing at the need that roared beneath the surface. Biting her earlobe as gently as he could stand, he stretched and slid his shaft from her and committed to memory her knee-quaking gasp in his ear.

"You like me inside you, love?"

"I need you inside me." She kissed him, biting on his lip, then let her tongue dance with his even as her body strained to accustom to his size, his girth. Every gasp proved that she loved how it felt.

She moaned and begged, faster and harsher, the teaser of orgasm far away enough to torture her with what she'd had recently, and Ryder wanted desperately to feel her pulse, planted deep in her body.

He drove back. Stronger. Deeper. She clung to him from the inside out, and his molars clamped. "Victoria, love. Grip me like that."

"Yes." She panted uninhibited as she clung, holding him tight, rubbing him, kneading him, goddamn, driving him wild.

He thrust, capturing her to the wall, keeping her leg high in the air. She began to tremble. Her nails dug into his skin, and he wanted her to leave marks.

"God, Ryder. *God.*"

Her convulsing pussy muscle milked and spasmed, rolling over his cock like thunder. He couldn't take it—too much, too powerful—and her addictive climax tore through him, dragging him toward the storm. His muscles tightened. His mind spun as lightning strikes ran down his spine, and white-hot electricity pulsed in his veins. He came hard, the most excellent, most intoxicating release straining into her shuddering body.

He collapsed forward, his elbow catching him against the wall over her shoulder while he gently released her other leg and held the limp woman to his chest.

She was a mind eraser. That had been so ridiculously good. He tipped her head back, landing a chaste kiss on her lips then stepped them apart. "Never met the likes of you before, love."

"I could say the same thing." She let lips move to his neck then left a trail of kisses with long, lazy strokes against his skin.

He could be in this shower all day—

She stopped abruptly. "Ryder?"

"Hm?"

"I need something from you."

"Anything."

The easy roll of her relaxed posture straightened, and Victoria's sated gaze had dampened. "Tell me everything will be okay."

"Victoria." His heart jumped into his throat. "I promise. It will be okay."

His chest constricted, and the pounding lust made way for something just as strong: the responsibility for having saved her. It landed deep in his heart and made him ache in a nostalgic way that didn't make any sense.

CHAPTER EIGHTEEN

RYDER WALKED ACROSS the kitchen and stopped short, taking a few steps back to look in the living room. Jared Westin was not who he expected to see, especially when his wife, Sugar, and the kids weren't there.

If Sugar had been there and in mom-mode, Ryder would've felt slightly more at ease. Or, even if she'd had been on the couch with her former-ATF, now-weapons-specialist hat firmly in place, he might have assumed she was there to consult on a Titan/ Delta op. But Sugar, in all of her sassy, va-va-voom glory, was notably missing.

Jared and Brock sat, elbows on their knees, heads facing down, fists holding up their heads. That wasn't a good look. Ryder had a sinking suspicion that they wanted to talk to either Victoria or him, especially if he didn't see Winters or Mia in the room.

"Hey, Ryder. Get in here, would you."

Jared wasn't asking, and Ryder hustled the few steps backward into the living room. Both men made faces that Ryder knew meant shit was about to suck.

"Bad news, huh, mate?" Ryder tried for a casual grin, but it failed. "This is gonna suck."

Brock ran a hand over his face, groaning, and leaned back on the couch. "Yeah, it's going to suck."

Jared rolled his bottom lip into his mouth and gnawed on it as he cracked a few knuckles, nodding with Brock's assessment. "Look, here's the deal. Ivan Mikhailov is back in business."

Fucking hell. Ryder didn't expect that. He had no idea what he was about to hear—maybe that it was time for Victoria to get her butt in gear, figure her shit out, and go home. Maybe they were about to tell him that

Victoria No Last Name was a real piece of shit, though he didn't think that would be the case. But Ivan… That hadn't crossed his mind.

"We knew it was only a matter of time. But—"

"But that's really fast," Ryder said. "I mean, I know the fucker's a billionaire. But maybe more than a few weeks? And what does back in business mean? He's running women again?"

Jared slowly nodded his head. "Delta dismantled his network. We crushed their suppliers and netted arrests in four different countries—"

Brock blew out a frustrated gasp. "And fucking hell, man. Those were big dogs too. Some of those guys, you couldn't get any bigger, any more important than the pieces of shit we took down."

"Apparently, there's always going to be more pieces of shit that important and that powerful who want to buy women," Jared grumbled. "I just didn't expect him to open up shop at all, much less this fast, again."

Ryder stood there, stunned. They had saved so many women from Ivan, but that goddamn country and that goddamn culture and the belief among some people with more money than they knew what to do with and an incredible lack of respect for life—he couldn't stomach it. "I should've let her kill him. Fucking hell. That asshole should be dead, rotting in hell."

"She would have hit Locke," Brock said.

"Would she? That's what I keep telling myself. But is it an excuse? Or is it the truth?"

"You were never gonna risk Locke's life," Jared snapped. "You know that. He knows that. Brock and I do too."

"Then we should have let her take care of business after Locke moved out of the way." Ryder paced back and forth. "It would've made her no different than me. I would've done it. I would've taken the shot. I should have taken the shot. It doesn't matter if I'm up close or far away."

Sitting there in silence, neither of his bosses disagreed.

"We made the wrong choice, didn't we?"

Brock stood up. "It's done. It wasn't the wrong choice. You don't let civilians kill other people. There's a fucking difference between you taking a shot on a target and letting somebody you don't know go willy-nilly with a fucking Russian-made pistol."

Ryder paced back and forth, the arguments on both sides of the situation storming his thoughts. He wished Sugar was here for an over-the-top, in-his-face snark. Something harsh and shocking that would kick start his mind into gear and make him focus on his job, which was to eradicate sick, devious fuckers from the face of this earth. But damn it, he'd let that one go. The person who'd violated Victoria was walking around free.

Ivan was back to business as normal. It was bold. It was a fuck you to Delta team, practically serving up two middle fingers, begging them to come back and take him down again. "What are we gonna do about it?"

Jared shook his head. "Nothing. At least, not right now."

"You mean to tell me that we know there's a trafficker out there, and we're not gonna go—"

"Do you know how many human traffickers and sex trafficking cartels there are out there? On how many continents? How many countries, how many billionaires to street thugs are doing this? We have to pick our battles."

"Right." But it didn't feel like the truth was supposed to be that way.

"We went after Ivan before, and we were able to take out so many spokes in that wheel, but we're not going to hop on a plane and go—"

Ryder stepped forward. "It doesn't have to be a 'we' thing. It can be a 'me' thing."

"No," Boss Man said.

"I'll go." Ryder kept pleading his case. "I'll snipe his ass from a thousand yards out. The only thing I need with me is a rifle. You'll have complete deniability. I won't even say another word."

Brock sat down and leaned against the couch cushion. "Do you want to know who she is?"

"I know who she is," Ryder snapped back. "I know what she's told me. And when she's ready tell me more, I'll know more."

Jared nodded. "Do you want to know how she got there?"

Tension sprang in the back of Ryder's neck as his molars ground down. Of course, he wanted to know how she'd ended up there, but the rage that pulsed inside of him at the thought of her ending up as a

Mikhailov sex slave made him ready to kill. “Yeah, sure. I’m interested.”

“If interested means homicidal, you look interested,” Brock added.

“You know, brother.” Jared cracked a knuckle, making Ryder wait for whatever advice Boss Man was conjuring. “When it gets emotional—”

“It’s not emotional.” *Fucking hell.* Ryder wasn’t waiting on advice about being emotional.

“And if it was?” Jared asked.

He fought away a grimace and forced a solemn face. “Then you know I could tamp that shit down. Nothing but the job is my only focus when I’m on the clock.” He eyed them. “And you both know it.”

They exchanged looks, and Brock nodded. “Our Aussie sniper is stone cold. I’ll give him that.”

“Next question is,” Jared said, “do you tell Victoria?”

After what Ryder just promised her in the shower? That everything would be okay? “No. Absolutely not. She doesn’t need to know.”

“You sure?” Brock asked. “Maybe I need to tell you a little bit about who she is.”

“No.” Ryder shook his head. “I know who she is, where she’s from, and what she did. None of that matters because I made a promise to her that everything would be okay. And *that* is not okay. Nothing about Ivan going back into business and selling women is okay,” Ryder’s voice was so low it rumbled and growled. “She’ll never know, at least not right now. And I’ll let her know when the time is right. But it’s not right now. It’s for her own good.”

CHAPTER NINETEEN

Australia

"LOOK," ZOE POINTED as they walked up the drive. An unfamiliar car sat by the house, and a suitcase waited by the front door. A lamp lit the parlor window, and the room was never used unless there were potential parents looking at the kids. "Looks like someone's here for their little bundle of joy."

"Yeah."

"Sorry." She squeezed his hand. "You know there's never enough homes."

"I know." Ryder hated that he still felt the sting of pain. Sixteen years stuck in these horror shithouses, some nicer than others, but none ever met the standard of having a family. Babies and the little ones were who potential families came to see, and no one ever took an interest in him. Eventually, he stopped caring. *Maybe.* Still, it hurt. Zoe was right, though. There wouldn't be as many kids as old as him in the homes if there were enough people to adopt them. But not everyone started in government care the day they were born…

"Come on," she said as they ran up the stairs, cutting it close to curfew.

He'd dropped her hand when they rounded the corner. The rules didn't allow them to be boyfriend and girlfriend. Maybe some other kid had guessed, but mostly, the grownups assumed they were just close. Or they didn't care.

Bright lights in the entryway got under his skin too. He shouldn't be jealous of anyone getting a home, and he wouldn't be. They ignored the adults standing to the side, heading toward the stairs—

"Here she is," Ms. Briddle, the head of services, said, and Ryder's blood ran cold.

Zoe stood on the first stair and glanced into the parlor room, maybe searching for whomever they'd missed, but Ryder's eyes were glued to her.

"Come over, Zoe. There's someone we'd like you to meet."

His eyes dropped to her white knuckles gripping the stair rail. She didn't move, frozen in place.

Ms. Briddle, that matronly old hag, turned toward an older couple who looked more like grandparents than parents, and said, "She's not shy. Zoe?"

"Yes?" Her voice shook.

"Come down and meet Mr. and Mrs. Wards."

"Why?"

The adults chuckled as if they thought her terror was cute. Ryder put his hand on the railing, bracing himself, fencing her from them.

"Why?" he growled.

"Because it's time for her to meet her adoptive parents." Ms. Briddle's forehead pinched.

A tidal wave of nausea hit him, and Zoe swayed. "But I've never met you before."

"That's fine," the old lady who wanted to adopt her said. "We just need someone around the house."

"What, like a worker?" Anger boiled in Ryder. "You don't get *workers* here. You get a *family*." Something he always wanted and never had. Something he *was going to have* with Zoe, as soon as they escaped this place.

"Zoe, come over here," Ms. Briddle demanded firmly, fake smile in place and an ass-kicking bent to her words.

"I don't want to."

Displeasure marred Ms. Briddle's oval face. "It's for your own good. Come here."

Ryder stepped closer to her, putting his other hand around her waist. "She doesn't go anywhere I don't go."

"I don't want *both* of them," the old lady said.

"That wasn't part of the agreement at all," the man agreed.

"Zoe."

They had to run away. Could they make it out the door? That old guy was older than dirt, but he was big and looked meaner than hell, the type to chase Zoe if he wanted to bring her home. They couldn't get out the upstairs windows, so they had to turn around and go back out the front.

"Son, why don't you run along?" The man came closer.

"Why don't you bugger off?" Ryder snapped back.

"Manners!" Ms. Briddle snatched her hands to her chest as if it was the first time she'd heard that from him.

Ryder squeezed Zoe aside, one step below her, and his mouth was near her ear. He whispered, "Run."

He dropped his hand from her waist, and she spun to his side. Ryder was a protective barrier between hell and his future. The old man lunged at Zoe, and he jumped on him, wrapping an arm around his meaty throat and knocking his face with a fist, over and over and over.

They spun, and Ryder's back smacked against the wall with the old man's full force. The air left his lungs. He couldn't breathe. Couldn't gasp. Couldn't punch. And found himself on the floor, pushing up as his breath came back.

Ryder gasped, smirking. She was gone. The door was open. *Thank God.* She was safe. He pushed back against the wall, catching his breath. Whatever punishment was to come would be okay because Zoe knew where to go and who to talk to until he could get to her. She'd made more than enough friends.

Ryder glared at the adults who directed the same look back at him until their faces changed, and the old man laughed, his eyes on the door. Ryder pivoted, head snapping that direction—and his heart stalled.

"No," he whispered.

A cop stood with Zoe in hand, pale and shaking. Tears streamed down her face. "Sorry to barge in your evening, but it turns out as I was coming in to look for this young lady, she was coming out."

"What did you do now?" Ms. Briddle muttered.

"Lifted bread."

"To feed starving kids," Ryder nearly shouted. "Old, stale bread they were throwing out."

"Wasn't yours to lift, son." The copper gave him a look that made rage hollow him out on the inside.

"She was helping," he pleaded, silently adding, *just let her go.*

"Well." The old man stepped forward. "We just adopted this 'un, sir, and it won't happen again. If you hand her over."

"You did?" He looked at the house director. "That right?"

"No," Ryder answered. "It's wrong. They're up to no good."

"The paperwork is complete," the director said.

Zoe sobbed, shaking hard as she cried in the cop's arm and pulled down, struggling as he tried to hold her.

"Don't do it," Ryder begged. "Lock her up. Give her a few nights. But don't give her to them."

The old lady walked past Ryder, not acknowledging Zoe nor speaking directly to the cop. "I'll put her suitcase in the car."

"No," Zoe wailed.

The old man's heavy boots echoed in Ryder's head as he walked by, and the two men handed Zoe off as though she were an oversized raggedy doll. Burning tears blinded him. Pain seared his throat.

He lunged for her, and the cop clotheslined him, wrestling him to the ground, pinning his face to the floorboard as a hand wrapped against his throat, cutting off his air.

"Ryder, help."

Ryder, help.

Ryder, help.

Ryder, help.

Ryder's hell replayed over and over until the room went black.

Present Day

DELTA TEAM WRAPPED their training drills, and they filed out of the training center at Titan HQ, heading into the locker room. Ryder pulled his bag over his shoulder, fishing out his cell phone and dropping the towel he'd used to wipe the sweat off his face. Grabbing his phone was now his favorite thing to do when done with work, as it had been for the past two weeks since Mia insisted Victoria take one of Winters's temporary cell phones from his tech room stash. Each time the text message notification pinged, he had an automatic Victoria-induced high.

The text message notification showed a partial message from Victoria, but this one stopped Ryder in his tracks, and Colin slammed into his back.

"Jeezus, dude. What are you? Three? Learn to text and walk." Colin slapped him on the back, maneuvering around him.

"Got it, fuckwit," he mumbled. The first few words Ryder had seen were *It's about that time…* Dread told him the words he hadn't wanted to read for the past couple of weeks were on the other side.

VICTORIA: *It's about that time. Heading back home today.*

The text should've been a great one, something he should go high five her over, but he wanted to mope.

Trace walked up next to him and punched him in the shoulder. What was it with people hitting him right now?

"Why ya standing there, asshole? You look like your dog died."

"Bugger off." He walked off, ignoring Trace's what-the-fuck grin.

RYDER: *Not without me swinging over there.*

VICTORIA: *I wouldn't leave without saying bye.*

RYDER: *Good.*

VICTORIA: *I'm going to miss you. You know that?*

The words hit him in the chest. Yeah, she was someone he'd miss too. Hanging with her since Russia hadn't been easy, knowing what she'd been through, but it'd been quite the experience.

RYDER: *That's what good sex does. Don't worry, love. You'll be fine.*

VICTORIA: *I know.*

VICTORIA: *BTW, thanks.*

RYDER: *For the good sex? No prob.*

VICTORIA: *For everything. <3 You really are one in a million.*

RYDER: *Not too many badass warrior women out there. See you soon.*

He read up, and it seemed casual. *It was* casual, but as he dropped his phone into the bag and pushed into the locker room, it also seemed like it sucked.

Trace came in behind him as Javier and Colin headed back out.

"Brock said get your Aussie ass upstairs in ten." Javier knocked the door open.

"I gotta bail."

Javier stopped at the door, keeping it halfway open, and Colin nearly ran into him. "What's up with people stopping today?"

"I've got a thing." He wasn't getting into details with anyone. Hell, he didn't know how to explain the details about Victoria with anyone anyway.

Trace grumble-laughed. "Yeah, that'll work."

Brock walked around the corner, probably coming out from the back office, and it wasn't as if Ryder wanted an audience when he told his boss he was going to bail.

"Ryder." Brock lifted his chin. "You're done for the day. Get out of here."

Uh... "Yeah?"

"Yeah. I don't want to see your face for the rest of the day. Go." Brock kept moving, pushing past Javier without a backward glance. "The rest of you assholes, the clock is ticking. T-minus seven minutes. War room."

As soon as Brock had cleared, all eyes jumped to him.

"I have no fucking idea," he lied then hustled to the shower for a quick rinse off. He didn't want to miss one minute of seeing her for the last time and wouldn't show up sweat-drenched. His chest ached, and if there was one thing he hated, it was goodbye.

Actually, three things: being helpless, acting helpless, and goodbyes.

CHAPTER TWENTY

RYDER PUSHED BACK in the ultra-deluxe leather seats of the Audi R8 V10 as he eased off the gas pedal and let the horsepower mellow out on the drive to the airport. Earlier, he made the premium sports car earn its reputation by eating the miles from Titan HQ to Winters's. But now, Ryder was taking his sweet time, enjoying having Victoria in the passenger seat and wishing to hell she wasn't going back to Iowa. "Maybe just one more romp, for old time's sake."

She laughed as he pulled into the parking lot and found a space. "What are you thinking? Maybe I just jump on over into your seat?"

"Yeah, love. Hop on over." He parked then patted his thighs. "Or the hood. Always wanted to root on the hood of a sports racer."

"Really? Good to know you have a healthy imagination."

Still laughing, he raised an eyebrow. "Did I leave a question in your mind about that?"

She shook her head, eyes shining with unshed tears, smiling because they were still joking around. Then her lips pursed, and her face fell.

"I know," he said, feeling down too. He reached over and unbuckled her seatbelt for her, unfastened his, then held up his arm, and she leaned in for a hug. Ryder wrapped his arms around her, holding her to his chest. "Going home is a good thing."

She nodded against his shirt, sniffling. "I have things to do, people to catch up with."

"You have your life, love."

"Yes." Her tear-soaked voice scratched.

Victoria took a deep breath and unburied her face, leaning awkwardly over the center console, and he moved his arm, keeping one draped over her shoulders.

"I have to tell you something, and it won't make sense." She shifted in her seat. "But I still want to say it."

Wasn't that the name of their game? "You go, then I'll try too. How about that?"

"Okay." She studied her fingernails for the longest time before she gave him her trusting eyes. "When I waded into hell and you pulled me out, the first thing you saved was my soul." She looked out the window. "Dramatic, I get that. Too dramatic. But you became more than a friend, you were my foundation, and you're forever woven into my heart for that."

If he never forgot what she'd just said, he would grow old happy with everything he'd done in life. Ryder had met hundreds of people over the course of his time with Delta, maybe even thousands. No one had ever had such a profound effect on him. "I don't have anything that's nearly as perfect as that, love."

His cell phone chirped with an alarm reminder of what time she had to be inside the airport—just in case he found himself distracted—and he cursed the bloody thing. He turned it off. "A few more minutes, then we head in."

She settled back against the crook of his arm, still draped over the console, and they stayed with their thoughts until he forced away himself from her.

Victoria shut her door, and without any luggage, only a small bag Mia made her take, she walked around the hood of the sports car and pressed a paper into his hand.

"What's this?"

"Basically, what I said. A note, in case I chickened out and didn't tell you what I thought."

Nostalgia rushed over him, but he pushed it aside and stared at the woman in front of him. "You are a very special girl to me. I hope you know that, and I'm going to visit you."

A doubtful grin teased her lips. "You'd better."

"You can count on it."

Ryder walked Victoria as far as checkpoints would let him go, and he kissed her goodbye—not some stupid, sweet, take-care kiss, but one meant for a helpless goodbye, the kind that lit his soul on fire and made the woman next to him blush.

As soon as he couldn't see Victoria any more, he found the closest row of benches and tore open her note.

Ryder,

Because of you, I've relearned what I already knew.

I believe I met you for a purpose, and you are my reminder, my educator, my reason for my being me.

I learned, again, that things break, but they can be repaired. That things go wrong, but they can always be made right. Almost nothing is permanent, and if I can't remember that, and believe it for the future, then maybe I can for just a minute, then the next minute, then maybe longer and longer until the future doesn't seem shattered.

You found me in hell and held onto my soul when I wasn't strong enough to know how tired it was. You gave me the strength I needed when I was building myself again, and that has to be the basic foundation of the most honest friendship I have ever had. Thank you.

All My Heart,
Victoria

P.S. Thanks for all the OOOOs. That was a lot of fun too.

Powerless to fight their circumstances, he ran his hand over his face, half-smiling from the postscript, half-numb from the rest. There was nothing left to do now but work.

CHAPTER TWENTY-ONE

RYDER REVVED THE engine one last time before he powered down the sports car in the underground parking garage at Titan's headquarters. The emptiness in his chest still held its paralyzing grip, making his limbs ache with heaviness. This was what Delta did. They saved people, rescued them, returned them to their real lives. And then Delta disappeared like a wisp of smoke, never to be seen again.

Already, Brock and Jared made a special exception for him, and maybe that had been the wrong move. He dropped his head back against the soft leather headrest, closing his eyes, and he breathed in the extravagance of the vehicle. Nothing about this car, this life was what he ever expected.

The passenger door opened, and Ryder startled to attention as Brock eased himself into the Audi. Maybe Ryder should've taken something a little less flashy, but he needed speed, and this baby had a serious set of wheels and get-up-and-go packed under the hood.

"She make it on her flight okay?" Brock asked, likely already knowing the answer.

Ryder's last text from Victoria had been from her seat. A selfie. She also gave him a quick update on who she thought was traveling as a federal marshal in plain clothes. Then she had to power off her phone. He donned a placating grin and forced it to stay long enough to be believable. "Flying back to the heartland."

"Do you know why we recruited you?"

Ryder snorted, not expecting that turn in the conversation. "Because I'm a hell of a shot and had no one."

"Because you were a hell of a shot and were going to spend the rest of your life in prison."

Ryder's eyes narrowed, and he sucked in his cheeks, not daring to say a word.

Brock cleared his throat but didn't carry the conversation either. No one knew what he had done. *No one.* He wasn't going to prison, and there wasn't proof—no evidence, no witnesses. Nothing.

"Was that part of your decision?" Brock finally broke the silence. "To take the job with Delta?"

Ryder's molars ground down. Of course not! No one knew! Delta team was a once-in-a-lifetime opportunity to do amazing work, something that mattered more than his piddly shit at home. "Not sure what you're talking about, mate."

"It was a deciding factor in hiring you." His boss frowned in thought, lines deepening against his forehead.

Irritation scraped under Ryder's skin, testing his limits as memories percolated. "Whatever you're talking 'bout, I'm sure blackmail *wasn't* one of the things I thought you hired me for."

Brock shook his head. "On the contrary."

Ryder glared, teeth steeled together, his nostrils flaring as he tried in vain to control his response.

"You were a top contender for recruitment." He shifted in the passenger seat, crossing his arms. "As you know, we learn everything. Nothing happens that we couldn't find out."

Ryder's heartbeat slammed in his chest. Bile churned viciously in his stomach. "What are you getting at?"

"A sniper is as good as his kill shot. His accuracy. But we didn't want just the best. We wanted someone worthy of being on the team that carries out Delta operations." Brock tilted his head, his severe dark eyes grabbing on to Ryder's and not letting go. "You were thoughtful, thorough. Calculating and premeditated. It was justified."

Ryder couldn't breathe. His lungs seemed at capacity as his nostrils flared with each drowning inhale. Even if he wanted to respond, his jaw had sealed. Nothing was moving except the jumping, thumping pulse at the veins in his temple. Brock knew. Titan Group knew.

"You're just a kid, Ryder. But life didn't give you a childhood."

Sweat trickled down his back, and he willed his heart to slow the hell down. "I wouldn't change a thing."

"Because then you wouldn't have had *her.*"

He looked away, his throat burning at the memories of the past, wondering why they were even having this conversation. "What're ya getting at?"

"You have a good moral compass."

Ryder twisted toward his boss, confused as hell. "You just called me out for premeditated murder."

"And anything that could ever prove that—if there was anything—doesn't exist. You ran an op that needed running. We had your back."

His brows arched, stunned.

"Stay in touch with Victoria." Brock opened the car door. "I've never seen you so focused at work since you met her."

"We're a ghost team." They weren't supposed to exist outside the smallest network of people and never to their rescued targets.

"Every ghost needs a reason to disappear."

The car door shut, boxing Ryder in with his memories of Zoe and feelings for Victoria, trying not to compare and contrast the two, but he couldn't help noticing the one similarity that roared above all the noise in his head. They both gave him a sense of comfort and a closeness that felt like a bedrock of stability. *What a gift for an orphan kid to receive.*

CHAPTER TWENTY-TWO

THE AIRPLANE TOUCHED down, and suddenly, Victoria was desperate for a ball cap, a disguise, anything to hide who she was. As soon as she made her way into the airport, there was the chance someone was going to be from Sweet Hills, and she was sure that her face had been plastered all over the news after her disappearance.

Then again, maybe she looked like any other young twenty-something. Who knew anymore? Her internal barometer for reality was skewed. But talking to people she didn't know was also high on her not-interested list.

Not ready to talk was an understatement. Mia was right. She had to go home. Yet home seemed like a foreign concept. The only place familiar was hundreds of miles away—or more. No telling where Ryder was. She could text him, but obviously, their time together was done. Whether or not he'd actually visit, she had no idea, but he'd always hold a piece of her heart since he'd helped anchor it back in place.

A long breath slipped from her lips as she followed the line of people deplaning. She found a hat at the first gift shop, tucking her long hair in and pulling it low—not the greatest disguise, but her face was hidden.

Without any luggage and only a small duffel bag, Victoria skipped the crowds and headed for the taxi stand, holding her new phone and a couple twenty-dollar bills that Mia had given her. Everything she had with her was courtesy of Ryder or Mia, and she wished they knew how grateful she was. Words didn't seem to make a dent in the spectacular amount of good things she hoped they received in life.

A thirty-minute taxi ride later, she was at home and using the spare key from the fake rock in her front yard to let herself in. It was obvious investigators had been inside. Seven had been there too. Victoria's things were searched and reorganized. Then there was the telltale sign of Seven. The blanket on her couch was refolded in the way her best friend liked. A sudden, heart-tearing pain shredded her insides over how selfish she had been, and tears fell uncontrollably. People she loved were worried about her. "Oh, God."

She'd screwed up. Big.

The enormity of her selfishness collapsed on top of Victoria as her weak knees crumbled, and stumbling, she made it to the couch, wrapping her arms around the blanket Seven had folded. She pulled it to her face and hid from her decision to stay at Colby and Mia's without calling her friend to update her on her safety, all because she couldn't stomach what people thought of her capture!

"Ahhh!" She threw the blanket across the room. "I hate him! I hate him! I… hate… him…"

Other than during the actual attacks, she couldn't have hated Ivan Mikhailov more than she did while all alone, in the safety of her home. Tears flowed, and she couldn't make them stop. His name poisoned her mind.

Victoria rolled her shoulders back and wiped the tears with the back of her hand then grabbed her cell phone, needing to call Seven. But she didn't know her best friend's number by heart. It'd been programmed in her phone for years, and come to think of it, she knew no one's number. Instead, she pulled up the web browser and searched for Perky Cup, Sweet Hills, Iowa.

Up popped Seven's coffee shop and the icon to call now. Victoria pressed the screen and listened to it ring.

"Yello, Perky Cup," Seven said playfully, laughing.

"Seven, it's me."

"Victoria?" The sober whisper sounded as if Seven had covered her mouth. "Where are you? Are you okay?"

"At home."

"Oh my God. Are you okay?"

"Yes." *No, not in so many ways.*

"I'm coming over—can I come over now?"

"Yes—"

The phone rustled in Victoria's ear. "Last call. Finish your mocha, frappas, whateva ya gots. You gotta go, my friends."

"Seven! You didn't have to do that." Her mom probably needed her to keep the place open every chance they got. "No one else is working today?"

"That doesn't matter. You've been missing for weeks," Seven hissed at her. "I'll see you soon."

Something struck her as odd about the conversation, and Victoria couldn't put her finger on it—then it hit her. "Seven?"

"Ycah, sweetie?"

"You're coming alone?"

"Sure, unless you need someone?"

Victoria glanced about her living room and wondered who had been in her house for the missing person investigation other than the expected detectives. The sheriff? She wanted a word with him, maybe even the mayor. He butted his nose into everything. "Why aren't you calling the police? Or demanding that I do?"

Seven paused. "You haven't?"

"No."

"You should." She faltered.

"I will when I'm ready." But for as bright and colorful as her friend was, she was also reliably predictable. "What aren't you telling me?"

"Nothing. I'm on my way."

"*Seven.*"

"You didn't want to come home," her best friend whispered quietly.

Victoria's heartbeat lurched. "I what…?"

"And they were worried you weren't thinking clearly."

"They, who?"

"Two men flew out here and talked to the sheriff, and he roped in the mayor. You know how Mister Chatty Pants is. He talked to me quietly, so I'd stop worrying so much but also so he could have someone to talk to about you. I'm sensing major guiltage from City Hall."

Victoria didn't know whether or not to scream or rejoice. She was as furious as she was elated.

"Are you mad? Don't be. I promise it was coming from a good place." Seven paused. "They said you needed time to yourself, that you were exhausted. They didn't want any resources being used that could be used elsewhere, and they wanted to let your loved ones know you were safe."

Victoria couldn't comprehend the thoughtfulness behind protecting her reputation from what had happened to her.

"I would've called bullshit on the whole thing, but apparently, this Titan Group is the real deal. You should have seen the sheriff. He looked like a teenage boy about to shoot his load when they talked about it. The guy even reenacted the handshakes, talking about how they're head honchos in the world of getting shit done."

Victoria choked on a laugh. "Yeah, apparently."

"Are you mad?" Seven asked.

"No." She was floored.

"My last customer just walked out. I'll worry about dishes and shutting this place down later. I'm headed your way."

BY THE TIME Seven arrived, Victoria had tried to check her email but lost herself on Google. The search history was a simple list.

Ivan Mikhailov

Ivan Mikhailov corruption

Ivan Mikhailov rapist

Ivan Mikhailov billionaire

The news made her sick, and sheltered away from the real world, she'd never once attempted to catch a TV show, surf the web, or see what might be found on Ivan. But what she found now said one thing: he was untouchable.

And despite the Delta team raid on his estate and compound, the Russian propaganda news arm made their high-ranking government official sound as if it were a friendly visit. Nothing came of it other than hopefully, he wouldn't try to start that type of *business venture* up again.

Her career as an investigator led her to believe it would be a tough sell.

Would his clients come back? Discretion was surely something they paid dearly for, and he'd not been able to provide that.

Seven's shoulder hit the door as she tried to push through the usually unlocked front door.

"Whoops, sorry." Victoria jumped up from her office desk, pushing through the French doors. "Coming."

A quick unlock of the deadbolt and Seven rushed through the threshold and wrapped her arms around Victoria's shoulders. "I am *never* letting you go."

She didn't want her to.

"I have sandwiches next to my purse. On the porch."

Victoria pushed back. "You have to let go for that."

As if on cue, her stomach growled. Seven's pierced eyebrow mocked Victoria before she turned for the front door, calling over her shoulder, "You know I'm going to ask..." Her best friend disappeared, grabbing what she'd left on the white-painted floorboards then joined Victoria back in the kitchen as she pulled plates from the cabinet. "What really happened?"

Victoria let the bright blue plate clatter on the table, even though she knew the question was coming. "You don't want to know."

"I do." Seven tore open the bag and pulled out two sandwiches, tossing them onto the plates in a way that would make anyone hard-pressed to believe she'd successfully taken over the Perky Cup. "Not even in a sicko, voyeuristic way."

"That's not true. I know you."

Hurt registered in her eyes, and damn it, Victoria didn't mean to say that when she knew Seven had the best intentions.

"No," Seven spoke softly. "Not when it comes to you. I'll keep my train-wreck-watching interests to others. You, babe, I want to make sure you're really okay."

"I'm not going to tell you, so we'll have to leave it at that."

Seven twisted her lips. "Just tell me if you are okay. For real."

It wasn't mental pain that caused her heart anguish, though there were bouts of vivid memories that made her pulse panic. What really scared her was her quickly forming obsession, the need to find the son of a bitch who sold her out, the bail-jumper that caused this hell to begin with. Victoria almost itched to push Seven out the door so she could throw herself back into her work. If the jumper had been taken into custody, she'd exact her revenge one day. But the two men in the bar… She wanted to find them, hurt them. She wanted to go back to the Ice House, look the bartender in the eye and—

"Victoria?" Seven broke the spiraling trance of adrenaline-fueled anger. "Are you okay? Then, now?"

"No." An acidic taste coated her tongue, and Victoria inhaled, letting her nostrils flare, calming her heartbeat. "Not at all."

Seven assessed the physical reaction, and clearly, it was visible, but she had her own demons. Victoria never pressed her on those and let her self-medicate in her own way, whether it be bright hair and piercings, or wild nights with Mayhem that neither of them would talk about. "What do you want more? A hug or a hoagie?"

Victoria pondered the options and decided that food won. "Hoagie."

"Atta girl." Seven went about unwrapping the sandwiches then grabbed paper towels off the counter. "Now, the question no one has been able to answer…"

Damn it. Seven wasn't going to let it go, might even point blank ask if she'd been raped. Everyone would assume, but she didn't want to say it. "Get it over with."

"Do you know who abducted you?"

"You bet your ass I do."

"And what are we going to do about it?"

"*We* are going to do nothing."

Seven went to a kitchen drawer and extracted a knife, handing it to her. "You, what are you going to do?"

Methodically, she sliced the sandwich down the middle, taking too much time to appreciate how the lettuce and tomatoes crunched under the blade. "Time will tell."

Seven took the knife, cutting hers, and together, they ate in silence before Seven pushed back in her chair. "Flavored waters. Hang tight." She fished out two bottles, placing one in front of Victoria's plate. "What is that look?"

Lost in a thought of hoagies and knives, she glanced up. "What look?"

"That one, right there."

Victoria shook her head, unable to admit where her head had been: Ivan, rebuilding her business, what people thought happened to her, how they might judge her… The list went on and on. "I didn't have a look."

Instead of digging in deep, pouring out her soul to the girl who knew her every waking dream, she cracked the top on the bottle.

"Not revenge…" Seven studied her like a puzzle. "More like—I don't know—you're hellbent to fix something." She tossed her cap in the air, catching it, then chugged her water as Victoria gaped. "What? That's a look. You can't tell me you're not bugging out on the inside."

"I met someone recently who said eerily similar words." Maddy's thoughts on needing redemption rang clear. Victoria had thought that encouragement was focused on Ryder and sex, but perhaps Maddy meant at home and righting what went wrong with the bail-jumper.

"I don't think that's a good idea," Seven said. "Don't do it. Don't even go there."

Victoria felt surer in her next step than ever. Obsession surged in her blood. "You don't even know what I'm thinking."

"Don't do it, Victoria. I never tell you no, and everyone told us no when we started."

She remembered. The town had clucked on and on. They were too young. Seven needed to deny her Mayhem roots if she'd wanted a chance as a business owner. Victoria'd had too little guidance growing up—how could anyone trust her cavorting with criminals when one had raised her? But age was just a number. Seven managed her family's undeniable connection to outlaws with wisdom beyond her years, and Victoria's lack of parental involvement had made her a serious child, enamored with the law. "Don't start now."

Brightly colored hair fell over Seven's worried face. "But that look on your face coupled with the very little I know about what happened to you… We've always been smart."

"Calculating."

"We did things for the greater good, for our success. To live a life we wanted to have."

"Agree."

"Revenge was never us." The plastic bottle in Seven's hand crackled under her grip, and they both jumped. "No revenge."

"None. I won't, I promise." Revenge wasn't what she wanted. Only justice.

CHAPTER TWENTY-THREE

"EASY DOES IT." Javier's quiet voice had been in Ryder's ear off and on for the last six hours. Now, their target was in sight, and Ryder had one shot to take out a terrorist who had found safe harbor with a lieutenant in the Leyva cartel.

Sweat trickled down his back, his neck, teasing and tickling along his face where the humid night was breaking to dawn. Two hundred yards away was a solid location. He ignored the mosquitos the size of hummingbirds and jungle temperatures that were already climbing to hellacious as the morning sun turned the black sky deep purple.

It was a windless day as he stared at a soulless man surrounded by a booby-trapped thicket of leaves and bushes. Ryder kept his heartbeat still, even as his trained pulse wanted to jump for joy that the uncatchable terrorist was now in his crosshairs.

"Target identified," Ryder reported. "Are we still a go?"

"Affirmative," Jared replied from Titan HQ.

From that point on, no one else would utter a word unless the mission was aborted or critical. A woman remained close to his target, and Ryder wanted a clean shot without risk. There were enough windows, and their behavior was unguarded, so he wanted to wait.

The man disappeared from sight, and Ryder's trigger finger caressed the familiar pull. Patience was his, and the dead man walking had no idea he should be making right with the Lord.

The target came into view, alone, second window on the north side, a cup of coffee in hand. Ryder focused, aimed, waiting to find the right cadence of his heart rhythm. All sounds around him were gone. There was nothing but Ryder and a point of entry. A kill shot. His job.

He pulled the trigger. Then he breathed.

"Confirmation of hit," Javier reported.

Ryder could've told them that, but then, what would his mate have to do? He wiped the sweat from his face, pushing his numb body into action, and policed the brass round his rifle expelled.

"Let's move," Brock ordered in his ear.

"Roger that." Ryder had his gear in place, and he covered any signs he'd been there for hours.

"Do *not* forget the perimeter is wired, triggered, and trapped," Brock repeated for the umpteenth time.

But the reminder was always a good one. "Yeah."

"Air support is incoming. ETA two minutes." The logistics report came from Parker Black at Titan HQ. "Hustle to rendezvous. Should take you a minute-thirty."

"Be there in less than that," Javier jabbed.

Parker laughed. "Got you both on thermals, and I say you'll be on time."

"Prove you wrong."

"Be smart, dick," Brock snapped.

"Smart, smart, all over the smart, brother."

"Jesus fucking…" Brock's muttered reply cut off.

"Ryder, eyes up." Parker's voice turned serious. "Something's tracking you. Doesn't fit human form or pace."

"Great." He kept his gaze on the pivot as he pushed forward, still keeping eyes up for trip wires.

Dogs howled in the background.

"Canines out and heading your way, hot on your trail."

Great, though expected. "Yours, who?"

"Both. Closer to Javier though. If you hear traps tripped, it might be them. Keep moving," Parker's even voice stayed steady. "But seriously, Ryder, your left, ten, fifteen feet, something's ran ahead, and closing back in on you. You see anything?"

Fucking hell. He pulled his sidearm as he pushed toward the rendezvous. "Not a thing, mate. I'm about to start shooting—"

A blast detonated to Ryder's front left. The roar of fire hit his ears before the bright light and blast made sense. The reverb threw him back, his head ringing as his feet lost their grip.

Ryder blinked. Breathed—couldn't. His ears screamed. His eyes teared. They burned. Smoke and charge filled his nostrils, and he coughed, finally, rolling to his side, gripping his ribs, head spinning for stability. He needed a baseline to get up and keep moving.

Then he was. The jarring harshness of the move didn't help him stabilize, but the realization that his screeching earpiece wasn't helping did. Javier had grabbed him, and Ryder yanked the busted comm speaker out of his ear as the jumbling fast pace came to an abrupt end. Ryder blinked and was on his back again.

His head fell to the side, and Ryder rubbed a heavy hand over his face, wiping open his eyes. *The clearing.* He pushed up onto his elbows, focusing on his surroundings as Javier popped a squat beside him.

"Ready?"

The near silent helo seemed suddenly there, and hell, if Ryder's head took a hit. "Yeah."

He tried pushing up and needed Javier more than he wanted to. Wrapped into his teammate's arm, getting to safety under his direction, Ryder somehow found himself in the belly of the stealth chopper.

"What the fuck..." His mind tried in vain.

"Some big-ass jungle animal tripped a wire too close, bro."

Two men Ryder didn't know pushed Javier out of the way on the pretext of checking Ryder out, and Javier let him, joking that it was nothing but a scratch.

"I'm fine," Ryder mumbled, elbowing them away. Nothing seemed broken. *Disoriented. A concussion.* A few days off were coming.

"Our chopper. Our SOP," One said.

Great. He pinched his eyes shut, hearing Javier chuckle as he strapped in. The wind rushed through the open hatch as they gained altitude and headed home.

The crew stripped off Ryder's shirt and body armor—Zoe's note, which Ryder kept against his chest on every mission, whipped into the air current. His lethargic arms reached for it, and as the crew assessed that other than a few scratches, nothing was bruising or seemed broken, Ryder watched in slo-mo as it tossed in the wind.

"Wait." He reached half-heartedly for it as it flew into the sky. No one noticed, and Ryder stared at the open hatch, waiting to feel upset that her note, one of his most treasured and only possessions from his teens, was gone.

But it didn't come.

His heart smiled. That was the way Zoe would want to go, flying high in the clouds on the day he beat death. Somewhere, up there, she was soaring with the angels, no matter how much he wished she'd beat death too.

"Are you in pain?"

Ryder blinked, focusing on the man inches from his face.

"No." He pushed the bloke away. "I'm—" Ryder eased up, sore but confident nothing was broken. "Fine." Ryder muttered that their standard operating procedure check boxes had all been met. He grabbed his shirt and pulled it back on, then strapped in next to Javier and donned a headset.

"I'm back," he said to whoever was listening.

"Javier mentioned you were having a private moment," Brock said from HQ.

"Shove it, fuckwits."

The laughter died down, and then Brock added, "Plan on a visit to Doc Tuska when you get back today."

"Roger that." Tuska wouldn't tell him anything Ryder didn't already know, but what everyone knew was if he blacked out or there was a question about a head injury, especially for a sniper, Delta would mandate downtime. He almost couldn't hide his smile, not the reaction he expected, mostly because he planned to be on the first plane to America's heartland. Time to find out about the flyover states—or state—he'd recently heard so much about.

CHAPTER TWENTY-FOUR

THE SMALL OFFICE in the business park had been easy to find, and there was only one light on in the building at seven in the morning, only one car in the parking lot. There wasn't much in way of security for the building, but the office park, just off of a strip mall in safe-and-secure, middle-America, where most everyone likely left their doors open at night, didn't seem to have top-level security. Whoever came in the building first unlocked the front door. Their three-story professional office didn't have an elevator but was clean and economical—exactly the type of place a private investigator might set up shop. *Somewhere with no fuss.*

Ryder already had a folder of details on Victoria, where she lived, where she worked, what she drove. When she hadn't been home, this was his next stop. *An early bird.* Somehow, he hadn't expected that. But learning about her was half the fun—just like learning about this town. Sweet Hills, Iowa: a place he couldn't say he thought he'd ever visit.

He bounded up the stairs to her third-floor office. Maybe surprise wasn't the best idea. *But, yeah. It probably was.* After all, she'd said to give her time before he dropped by. Who dropped by Iowa? And she'd said it with a tinge in her voice that he couldn't place.

Either way, Ryder didn't listen. He didn't want to be that far away from her. He liked how she smiled, how she kissed, how she tasted. And even if she didn't want someone to check up on her, he wanted to do that too.

The office doors had names etched into clouded glass, and he passed by an accountant and a legal aid office. Their dim shadowed doors bespoke the time of day, but the end of the hall, one door was lit.

Victoria Massey: Investigative Services

His lips curled. It was cool. There was a streak of badass in her that he admired, and it didn't matter that she'd hit a mental road bump. The girl had been sideswiped with a hellacious hit. But still she stood, ready to get back at it. *Badass and admirable.* Parker had mentioned she taught self-defense at the community center. Again, he grinned. She knew what she was doing and wasn't greedy with the know-how.

He knocked twice before twisting the doorknob, but it didn't turn. He pulled out his wallet and a credit card, sliding it between the doorjamb and lock, letting himself in. "Hey, surprise. Guess who."

The sitting area had a small couch and end table with a lamp and an office off that. Her head popped out the door opening, wide-eyed and mouth gaping. "Ryder!"

"Hi ya."

"What are you doing here?" Wild, round eyes and outstretched arms were the first thing he took notice of as she surged from her office, not questioning that he'd let himself through the door and jumped into his outstretched arms.

"Thought I'd say hey."

Her eyes assessed the scratches and a cut on his face. "I'm glad. Really glad to see you."

Her nose buried against his neck, sugar-sweet lips trailing against the collar of his T-shirt in a way that ran straight to his groin. "Me too, love. Me too."

He lifted her in a hug, breathing her in. It'd been too long since he'd dropped her off at the airport. "I needed to see for myself."

"See what?" Her clinging arms held tight around his neck. Nothing about the distance or space of a few days had made the burning desire to get her naked any less strong.

"That you were settling back in okay."

She squeezed him once more, and he set her down, prying himself loose.

Her eyebrows bounced playfully, her tease tormenting him. "You didn't have to do that. I could have told you." She tilted her head. "Everything is fine. But what about you? Run into a rosebush?"

"Yup, that's it." He snorted, walking farther into her office, putting his hands on her sides because he liked the feel of her hips.

"Mighty mean thorns." She twisted to inspect the deeper cut along his temple. Her finger traced the edge of the cut. "This one especially."

Not five minutes in her office and she had his blood picking up the pace with nothing but one little finger running down his cheek, its pad sliding to his jawline before teasing away. Ryder inhaled deeply. "That one was a nasty little fucker."

"Hmm."

He grinned, quietly snickering. "Is *hmm* like *fine*?"

"How so?"

"Fine—isn't that the definitive buzzword for 'don't believe that bullshit'?" His fingers drifted away and hung, empty and missing her. "I wanted to see you, see what Iowa was all about."

"Riveting place." She stepped farther away and held out her arm. "Well, this is my office."

"Nice digs." He curled his right hand, working his trigger finger, needing the tension that ran up his forearm to dissipate.

"This is the sitting area." She pivoted on her heel back to where she'd come and the source of most of the light. "My office. It's not very big, but I don't need a lot of room. I'm out more often than I'm in. Paperwork is the bane of my existence."

"Makes sense." He hitched a grin, letting his smile pull up on one side. "I can't see you chained to a desk."

"And that's the tour." She stepped back as he followed her in. "Much like Sweet Hills will be. Not a whole lot to see."

"It's not anywhere near as small as you made it sound."

"But it feels like it sometimes, though."

He'd been all over the world. The largest metropolitan cities could feel like they had the power to strangle a person under the right circumstances. He wouldn't push as to when that feeling emerged, pre- or post-Russia.

Victoria took a seat behind her desk, and Ryder stood in front, glancing down at the strewn paperwork covering where she'd been working. Her laptop had gone to sleep, and the cell phone was facedown. None of that was interesting, though. His gaze was drawn to the printouts of maps, with coordinates and locations that had been highlighted and red and black lines connecting pinpointed locations.

His gaze casually slept across all of the investigative material. "You picked up a job already?"

She'd been back in town a week. No matter what she had said, her reputation hadn't been sullied because of the asswipes who'd hurt her. Maybe she'd start to believe that now.

"Not really." The fun, flirty girl who'd jumped into his arms moments ago stiffened. She reached across the desk and grabbed an unmarked purple folder. "Just some stuff."

With giant sweeps, she gathered what looked to be tracking information. *Odd for how expertly she'd had it arranged. Forget the specific order.* She slapped the papers shut in the purple folder.

"I can look at this later." She toed open a drawer and deposited the folder in a side drawer.

"You okay?"

"Yeah, why?" With a quick kick the drawer slid closed, and she slid back into her chair, pulling her hair off her shoulders into a ponytail.

"If you were busy…" He traced a finger along the now nearly empty desk. "I can come back."

Victoria reached back to her hair, pulling at the hair band. "It wasn't a new job. I was looking over the notes from someone I used to know."

Ryder ran his tongue along the inside of his bottom lip. Why was she lying? He wasn't born yesterday, and obviously, he could tell the difference between new and old materials. Even the papers had a sharp crispness to them—until she'd scrounged them into a pile and slammed them in a drawer, and not that Ryder had intentionally searched the printouts, he was fairly sure one of the maps showed reference to yesterday's date in the corner. *Or maybe not.* Either way, the paperwork seemed new, and that was a silly thing to skirt the truth about if he was correct—which he might not be. His gut said he was.

Maybe Victoria still had doubts about a career as a PI. Maybe uncertainty gnawed at her subconscious as to whether she could carry on as a legitimate bounty hunter. Those had been her concerns before.

Still, she had told him the truth about where her head was, even at the most uncomfortable of times.

"We're similar in many respects." He walked around the edge of her desk and eyed the drawer she'd kicked shut. "You know that, love?"

Her eyes flitted up to his. "How's that?"

He'd already explained he was a sniper. There wasn't much to say other than the obvious. But the maps, the coordinates—she was a bounty hunter earning a takedown for cash, and he was looking for a kill shot.

"You're tracking somebody down." Ryder lifted his shoulders, a nonchalant push that he knew what she was working on, no matter when she'd started on it. "That's what I do. I'm a hunter, a tracker. Sometimes, it's best to take a position and wait, but more often than not, an offensive move is more efficient."

Morbid, really, what he was saying if it was taken out of context. He didn't know who she was after, but he had only gone after the worst of the worst. And there would always be judgment on him as to whether or not he should be given such power, to take someone out, to pull the trigger, to decide if somebody lived or died, just because they were within the crosshairs of his rifle. It wasn't something he took lightly. But it was something that the world needed because evil existed in the form of men and women walking around, blending in with others, wanting to destroy humanity in the most depraved of ways. What Ryder did was for the greater good. But Victoria wasn't a sniper. And he had no idea who she was tracking or why. The more she fidgeted with her ponytail, the more he knew she didn't want to talk about it.

"Who are you hunting, Victoria?"

She glanced down and lied with a smile that didn't reach the beautiful eyes he wished would look back up. "No one. Like I said. Old files, reliving the glory."

He let her feed him the lie… for now. Ryder walked back a few steps, giving her the room to breathe around whatever mistruth she needed. "Are you glad to be home?"

A harsh laugh fell from her lips, but she tilted her head up, letting him see her eyes. "I haven't decided yet."

At least he knew that was a truthful answer.

When he'd showed up in her town, he wasn't sure if he was going to make himself known to her. But who the hell was he kidding? There wasn't a chance to be this close to her and not say hello. Part of him wanted to make sure she was adjusting back to life and not screwing up, but the other part of him couldn't keep his hands to himself.

Parker had provided him lists of her acquaintances, friends, and business partners. To date, Victoria had only reached out to one person. Ryder had wondered about that the entire flight to Iowa, and the more he replayed her desk full of paperwork, the more he noticed the twinge of concern tightening in his chest.

Victoria had confessed the truth about her family, her terror about Sweet Hills accepting her back, and yet she'd lied about the papers scattered across her desk. *Why?*

"When will you decide?"

Her eyes dropped to the drawer. "Probably when I find some type of closure."

Damn. The dots connected. That wasn't any old job or paperwork. It was her outstanding bounty: Yuri Maysak. The Russian gunrunning bastard sold her out to the Mikhailovs.

The unease in Ryder's chest expanded into his stomach. Worry bled into his muscles. "Victoria, who was in that folder?"

Her pupils dilated as she straightened then toyed with her cell phone with nonchalance that didn't fool him. "I told you. I was just looking over old files."

"Fine." He ignored how he cared for her, the level of attraction that he had which could hide every flaw and conceal every question, and Ryder stared at the raw realness behind the desk. Dark circles under her eyes. Stress lines that hadn't been there after the hell of Russia. Was she paler? Had she lost weight? In a week? Victoria wasn't sleeping.

"Want to take a break and get some coffee?" He stepped closer, still assessing what was now becoming obvious and apparent.

"Sure."

He couldn't decide if there was a hint of hesitation in her agreement. "I'm not asking to play tourist in your hometown. Let's just go grab a cuppa and breakfast." He rapped his knuckles against her desk. "You can't ignore basic human necessities like food."

Her stomach growled as if on cue, and he raised his eyebrows.

"My stomach is a traitor," she laughed.

"Whatever that means." He smiled. "As long as I get breakfast in the heartland."

"Would you settle for the best coffee ever?"

"How about this? I'll make a bet with you."

"What's that?" Victoria leaned forward on her desk, and for the first time since they got comfy in her office, she looked interested in something other than whatever she buried in that bottom desk drawer.

"You take me to the best coffee ever, and then you let me prove you wrong."

Victoria stuck out her hand. "Over breakfast tomorrow morning."

Ryder grasped hers, not giving a damn even if he knew he'd win coffee wars. "Bet."

CHAPTER TWENTY-FIVE

THE COFFEE CHALLENGE was on, and Victoria basically asked Ryder to spend the night. He'd just surprised her in Iowa, so it wasn't like she was being too forward.

"What's so funny?" He put his arm around her shoulder.

"Nothing much." What was Seven going to say when she walked in and introduced Ryder? "We're headed to my best friend's coffee shop."

"Yeah?" He leaned against her. "Maybe you want to hide me away."

She laughed. "Seven's eccentric."

"Her name is Seven?"

"I'm so used to it, that's not even what I was thinking about." Victoria leaned back against him, and his casual hold squeezed tighter as they made their way across the parking lot.

They walked to the passenger side of his rental SUV, and Ryder tossed a set of keys in the air with his other hand, caught them, and pressed the button on the key fob. The lights flashed, and the doors unlocked before he opened her door. Victoria stepped forward, but he tugged her back. He was still behind her as she turned, and Ryder caught her mouth in a good-morning kiss that would make the asphalt melt. His tongue made the sun's sizzle feel like it drew its heat from him, and his hands were tight on her sides.

Her hammering heart jumped into her throat. Flushed, she was speechless as he drew back.

"In you go." Ryder's closeness was addictive, but she forced herself into the SUV as he shut the door. A moment later, his door was open, and he hoisted himself in.

"What's that look for, love?" He reached over and brushed her hair off of her cheek.

"Everyone says I have looks lately."

"Who's everyone?"

"Well, you and Seven."

"Did hers come after kissing you and grabbing your ass?" His brows inched up.

"No," she laughed. His fingers brushed against her cheek, and the humor faded as her eyelashes fluttered. This touch-and-tease that he had going on was enough to make her pop the seatbelt off and crawl across the center console… But she refrained. Inviting him to spend the night was enough forwardness. "And I don't have a look."

"You do." He pulled that sweet hand away and put the key in the ignition, turning the engine over. He shifted into reverse and checked all of his mirrors then turned back to her. "I like it, too."

Her insides went haywire. She did too…

Ryder pulled out of the parking space then headed out of the parking lot. "First stop, coffee."

"Make a left, two stop signs, and then you'll see the light," she gave the familiar directions. "That's Main Street. You can make a right then park anywhere along the road."

Ryder nodded and then followed her instructions. Nerves quickly replaced the lust that had colored her cheeks because even though she had been home, she had been hiding and working. She'd made no appearances in public, though if she was going to go public, it was nice to have Ryder by her side.

The familiar scenery of Sweet Hills passed by her window as she watched. Ryder quickly found a spot and parallel parked.

"Ready?"

Her mind screamed no. What if she saw people who expected her never to have lost a law enforcement battle, but she smiled yes.

He chuckled. "It's like ripping off a bandage. You just have to do it once, and we'll make it fast. Plus, there's caffeine. That's always a bonus."

"I'm focusing on the bonus." With that, she released her seatbelt and opened her door as Ryder did the same and stepped out onto the sidewalk.

His tall stride ate up steps, and he confidently grabbed her hand, leading them toward the coffee cup sign that dangled over the shop.

"The Perky Cup," Ryder read the sign aloud. "That's cute. Nice. Other than Seven, nice people inside, I assume. Or not?"

"Nice enough." It was only Seven, and her outspokenness could scare outsiders.

"You're tense because you don't want to see anybody? Not just the Perky Cup people." He gave her hand a squeeze.

"It's fine. I've just been hiding," she said as they stood in front of the coffee shop's door. She rested her hand on the old, worn brass handle. "Thanks for coming with me, though. It's nice to be with somebody I don't have to explain anything to."

His eyes seemed to understand, and he gave her a lift of his chin before she pulled the door open, oddly comforted by the familiar jingle of the doorbells. The cool air rushed over them, as did the strong smell of coffee and sugary pastries. The Perky Cup was decorated with eclectic, artsy placards and signs, mismatched tables that looked good together, and all of the mugs and plates also were intentionally unmatched. The entire shop was covered in bright, bold colors, and it had an energy Victoria had always appreciated.

When Seven's mom first had her stroke, the coffee shop had been on the verge of closing. Seven turned it around.

"Hey—*hey*." Seven bolted from the counter and nearly ripped Victoria from Ryder's hold. "I didn't know you were coming in." Seven broke the hold, eyeing Ryder. "Or that you were bringing guests."

"Just one guest," Ryder offered, moving close to Seven.

Seven's eyes went wide then wider. Yup, that was about the reaction Victoria expected of her friend.

"Well, hi, person from Australia."

She loved Seven like a sister. She'd known her for her entire life, and this was exactly what Victoria could have predicted. Maybe she should have warned Ryder. But making him pause, mouth agape for a hair of a second, was worth it.

"Hiya, Victoria's pink-and-blue-haired mate." He extended his hand.

"I'm Ryder Hall."

He was the kind of hot that made people look over their shoulder when they thought he wasn't looking, and when he opened his mouth and dropped in an Aussie accent, nobody could be held liable for what happened. Though Seven was barely liable for what normally happened on any given day.

"Oh, shit," Seven whispered.

Add in Seven's lack of the occasional verbal filter, and all Victoria could do was hang on and watch the show. "My best friend, Seven."

Seven gave a sideways glance as she shook Ryder's hand. "Do you think, perhaps, you left something out when we were making crucial life-altering decisions like hoagies or hugs?" Their hands dropped, and she smiled back at Ryder. "Welcome to the Perky Cup."

"Thanks."

"There will be further discussions about this one," Seven made obvious head-tilting and eyebrow-waggling gestures at Ryder. "Over something stronger than coffee." She turned back to him. "Until then, darlin', what'll it be?"

"Coffee, black, a muffin and butter on the side. What do you want, love?"

Seven's pierced brow arched on *Love.*

"My usual."

"Good." Seven plastered a dramatic smile in place. "I was beginning to think everything I knew about you was questionable."

"Nope."

"I was going to go outside, and the sky would be green. The roads orange."

"Dramatic, isn't she?" Ryder winked.

"Seven?" Victoria rolled her eyes. "Never."

"I don't know. Victoria hiding a hot Australian model in her backpack or something is worth a little dramatics, don't you think?"

"Well, hot model." Ryder laughed, dipping his face to Victoria's. "That sounds like it could work."

"Oh, no. This is how she charms you." Shaking her head, Victoria laughed as he pulled her in front of him.

"Hot model?" Ryder teased in her ear as Seven came apart behind the counter. "Seven can charm all she wants, yeah?"

Victoria playfully jutted her elbow back.

Seven pulled herself together long enough to give Victoria a look that said all kinds of things, but mostly, why had she not dished about him? And mostly, that was because she didn't think she'd see him again…

"Give me two minutes, and I'll bring it to you, okay?" Seven waved them toward an empty table.

"Could we get ours to go?" Ryder asked.

Victoria turned. "Where are we going?"

He shrugged. "Iowa is all new to me."

"Sure thing," Seven said over her shoulder.

"Where's the closest national forest?" The wheels were turning, and she had no idea what he was up to. "Or public-use open land?"

"You could ask me." Victoria nudged his shoulder.

His eyes danced. "What fun is it to plan your own day?"

"Holy shit." Seven looked one hot flash away from a puddle of pierced and dyed goo. The girl was going to melt in a puddle of Ryder-induced hot flashes—and she wasn't the only one.

"That means you know some place?" he followed up on her cursing.

She nodded like a girl in a trance. "Go down Main, turn left on to Old Clover, and then you will see the 352 Bypass. Take that for ten miles or so. You'll start seeing signs for a national forest over there." With that, she handed Ryder a bag that held far more than one muffin. "In case you get hungry on your adventure, I packed sustenance."

He gave her a wink and a grin.

"Sustenance?" Victoria almost shook her head. "What is it you think we're doing out there? Hiking the back forty?"

"I don't kiss and tell. Why would I ask you?" Seven cocked her head innocently despite what she'd just said.

Victoria's mouth fell open, but unless someone was going to shove a croissant in there, she had nothing to say, and gaping wasn't doing her a bit of good.

"Your latte," Seven offered.

She closed her mouth. "Thanks."

"For the sustenance," Ryder quipped, and Victoria elbowed him again.

He took his coffee from Seven and went to the side station to doctor it or grab napkins. Whatever, Victoria didn't pay much attention. She was too busy shooting eye daggers at her friend. "There will be payback."

"I hope so, and I'm putting a request in that my payback also involves an Aussie."

Pretending to mutter, Victoria did her best to hide her amusement behind her coffee as Ryder came back.

"We're off. Thanks, and nice meeting you, Seven." Ryder walked ahead of her as Seven made a whispering noise for Victoria to turn around. She did, leaning on the counter.

"That accent…" She bobbed her eyebrows. "Figure out a good way to need *sustenance*."

"I can still hear you." Ryder laughed.

Seven blew him a kiss. "If you stay in town long enough, you'll find out I don't care that much." Her eyes dropped back to Victoria. "I can't remember the last time I've seen you smile like this."

Victoria shifted so that she could see Ryder waiting for her by the front door.

"Why, in the name of bad boys who are good men and good men who know how to make you scream bad, bad things, are you not running toward that man?" Seven whispered, quiet enough this time that only Victoria could hear.

She had absolutely no reason not to follow him. "I have no idea."

"Sustenance…"

Victoria gave her a side-eye and a quick lift of her latte to say goodbye then walked straight to the man with the Perky Cup bag waiting by the door to do who knew what for the rest of the day under the sun. *With sustenance.*

CHAPTER TWENTY-SIX

THEY FOLLOWED THE scenic highway, and what had been flat roads and open skies shifted. Lush trees, the slope of hills, and peaks of mountains appeared in the distance. The sign for the national forest directed them to turn off the main road. Ryder slowed as they hit the asphalt driveway and followed another sign at a fork in the road that led them down a more secluded gravel drive. Large boulders lined the way, and they wound through the landscape, past some markers that explained the significance of the area, and came to a deserted parking lot. He parked and drained the last bit of his coffee.

"I didn't realize we were going for a walk today," Victoria said.

"We're not." He smiled, enjoying that she had no idea what they were about to do. "Finish your coffee, and then I will show you."

She took a long sip of her coffee and held it between her hands in her lap. "How are you going to show me something when you didn't know this place was here?"

"The location doesn't matter. Are you ready?" The truth was, he was really excited. He'd never actually done this as a date before and didn't know how it would go.

But he thought she would be into it, though the surprise was about to be up in about three seconds. It wasn't as if he could hide a rifle under his shirt.

Victoria took one more long sip of her coffee and held up the bag of muffins. "Should I bring these?"

"You bring that..." He unfastened his seatbelt and jumped out, walked to the back of the SUV, and opened the hatchback. "And I'll bring this."

She turned in her seat, taking off her seatbelt, but couldn't tell what he had.

"Come on, love. Get out."

Her car door slammed shut, and a moment later, she was by his side, eyes wide open and the bag of muffins dangling loosely in her hand. "Holy shit..."

"Is that a Sweet Hills thing? Or do I just make everybody in this town say holy shit?" He joked.

She tore her gaze from his rifle case and playfully jabbed him with the bag from the Perky Cup. "You're going to let me shoot your long gun?"

"I am." He ran his hands over the case and turned it sideways, popping the latches on either side and opening it for her. "My most prized possession. My livelihood." He ran his finger along the inside of the case. "No one's touched this before. I don't like to share my toys."

"Ryder," she breathed out his name quietly. "This is so far advanced for me. I can do handguns. Pistols. I mean, I've shot a rifle. But it was my dad's hunting rifle, and it's been a long time. I don't know what I'm doing with something as souped up as this."

"You don't need to. That's why I'm here." He winked. "You'll blow off some steam, get rid of some of your stress. Want to?"

"Do I want to? Hell to the yes. Yes, please. I want to."

He tossed his head back and laughed then straightened, taking his hand away from what was his most prized possession and wrapping his arms around her. He pulled Victoria into a hug, holding her against his chest and letting his lips rest against her forehead. Her tension relaxed and melted against him as they stood alone in the middle of nowhere.

A breeze picked up, and the quiet sound of the grass and leaves in the distances waved around them. They were in a private cocoon, locked away from the world, even if they were about to interrupt the quiet with a few loud blasts. All he wanted to think about was the light wind and how it smelled sweet, how she smelled summery and sweet. It reminded him of how she tasted. He closed his eye under the bright sun, and the midmorning glow was perfect. Ryder had never thought about what peacefulness might feel like, but now that it was in his head, it felt like this moment.

He'd brought her out there to relieve her stress and tension, but he hadn't realized that maybe he needed to find something too.

Chastely, he kissed her forehead then pulled back. "Ready?"

"Absolutely." He closed the rifle case and secured it, then grabbed his gear bag with what they might need: targets, ear and eye guards if they didn't want to use the silencer or if they wanted to use his other weapons. With all of that in tow, he slung it over his back and lifted the case, shut the trunk, and scanned the perimeter for where they might go.

After a few minutes of walking across an open field, he picked the flattest section, surrounded by brush on either side, then set up targets. All the while, Victoria sat in the grass and watched.

"So far," she said with a grin, "I'm enjoying the scenery."

He dropped down next to her, surveying the surrounding area. "Yeah, love. It's gorgeous out here."

She pressed her lips together, blushing and smiling simultaneously. "I'm positive that the scenery would be nice anywhere where you run around."

He laughed, and she joined in.

Ryder set up his rifle on a tripod, adding on the scope and silencer then dropped to his stomach to sight in on the targets he'd set up across the field. After everything was ready, he rolled over and stayed on his back, taking a moment to watch her appreciate his rifle. Then he folded up and sat next to her. "Ready?"

He walked through the steps, showing her what she already seemed to know, letting her find her comfort zone and appreciate what she was working with. Ryder watched as she concentrated on her target, eye against on the scope, finger caressing the trigger. "You see that; you feel that?"

"I do," she whispered.

"And you know that for some of these shots, we have to take in wind speed and other variables, but we won't get into that right now."

"Okay."

"And the smallest of movements can throw off your shot."

She looked away from the scope and nodded. "I've heard."

Ryder reached over into his bag and grabbed a set of binoculars, dropping down onto his stomach next to her. Victoria went back to looking at her scope, and he pressed the binoculars to his eyes, searching the various targets he'd set up. "You shoot between heartbeats. So still, you control your breaths." He slowed down his words and did what he was describing. "When it comes time, you take the shot between heartbeats."

He took a breath. Never did he want Victoria to experience the evils he knew existed, yet she also had a career in law enforcement. She was trained in her own area of expertise just like he was a trained protector.

"We don't have to worry about that, but it's still very cool to be able to focus that intently, to lie someplace for hours, sometimes for days, in nature, in the elements, and you only exist in one place."

Ryder dropped his binoculars to the grass and turned his head to stare at Victoria. She was someone he could spend hours thinking about. And that was an interesting revelation.

The corner of her eye crinkled as she focused in on the scope, and he watched her hold her breath. She pulled the trigger, and the rifle kicked back. Even with the silencer on, it sounded with the familiar noise, and Victoria drew back all smiles, taking a deep breath. "What a rush!"

Ryder picked up his binoculars and checked the target. "Bull's eye, love."

"I know." She beamed and grabbed his binoculars as she moved to her knees. With them held to her face, she saw the proof again. The target he'd placed out there shattered.

Ryder put his fist up and she bumped it. "You have a helluva teacher."

"I am awesome," she drawled.

"Won't get a disagreement from me." He took the binoculars from her and leaned over. "Grab your casing." He picked up the shell the bolt-action rifle had tossed and pressed it into her hand. "Pull this back and over. And… we're ready to go again."

She dropped down to her back in the grass and held up the empty shell overhead. "I'm going to keep this. Make it into a good luck charm or something."

How many times had he seen empty shells and never once thought that they could be a good luck charm? Then there was Victoria, taking everyday things and twisting them. He needed that in his life. She rolled over on her stomach and moved back to the scope.

"You ready for the next one?"

"No, not really." She shook her head. "I don't actually need two good luck charms. I got my rush, my good luck charm." She looked away from the scope and raised her eyebrows then tilted her head back toward the scope. "Got to see what it looked like when it explodes, which was pretty cool."

"What, so one and done?" He let his fingers drift along her back as she looked at the scope and over at him.

Victoria shifted and pulled away from the gun. "Oh, I'm sorry. If it totally ruined your plans, I'll shoot as much as you want me to."

He shook his head. "No, that's not why I said that."

"But if you had the expectation that I was going to do a bunch of shooting to feel better… I feel better right now with you because you were right. Pulling that trigger and watching the target explode? That was awesome, and I got a keepsake out of it. It only took once, if that makes sense." Her face scrunched. "Does that make sense?"

Ryder let his fingers walk up her spine. He scooted closer to her so that they were hip-to-hip, grass crunching between them, and his arm draped over her back. "Love, my job is successful only if I take *one* shot."

"Oh, right."

"I get it."

He watched how she registered his dark reality, wondering if it would ruin fun in the sun, but she was in a branch of law enforcement. He had to assume she understood his role in the grand scheme of things. Or he hoped. Still, she didn't say much past the "oh."

Victoria folded her arms in front of her and rested her chin on her forearm. He did the same, dropping his head into the corner of his elbow without pulling his other arm from her. A stray sprig of grass tickled his cheek, but he didn't move with the exception of the fingers he slowly danced along her shirt, playing with the ridge and dip of her spine.

"Why did you come see me?" Her eyes locked on him as a breeze picked up and lifted her hair, waving the tall grass behind them.

He drew in a deep breath, breathing in the warmth of summer, the scents of nature, and as he let it out, he turned over how they'd already been through the basics of that with the surprise hellos. He wasn't stupid, and that wasn't what she was getting at. "I missed you."

Sweet happiness moved across her face in a way that was hard to describe except her eyes closed as though that was all she needed to hear and could relax. Hell, saying that he missed her was unexpectedly as satisfying as firing a shot.

The anticipation.

The explosion.

The gratification.

"I missed you, too… more than I expected, and maybe more than I realized."

God, she was a sweet one, and he didn't even know he liked sweet. But there she was, eyes closed, lying in a field under the sun as the rays lit her cheeks and shone in her brown hair, talking about how she missed him. "It's been a long time since someone's missed me."

Her eyes drifted open. "How long?"

"A while."

"You didn't have family," she said, more reaffirming what he'd told her a few weeks back at Winters's lake, under the moon, so much like this under the sun.

He shook his head. "If anyone would have been family, she would have been."

"A girlfriend?"

Ryder nodded, wondering how he should feel about Zoe, why he was talking about her to Victoria, if he even should. He hadn't said a word about her since she'd been dragged from his life, and when he'd finally tracked her down, he had discovered that he was too late. He drew in a breath and dropped his head back. "A long time ago."

"I've never been in love," Victoria said quietly.

Lazily, despite what he felt inside, he rolled his head to take her in. Pity the men who'd missed out on her. And maybe, possessively, he liked that she'd never given her heart away, that she'd never been hurt the way he'd grieved.

"Have you?" she finally asked.

"When I was a teenager, I met a girl who was the only person I trusted. She was a real friend when those didn't exist for me." He shifted closer to Victoria. "Beautiful girl who made me laugh."

"Sounds like love."

"Yeah, I loved her."

"What happened?" Victoria asked the only logical question.

Ryder didn't want to answer—and he wouldn't, couldn't give her the entire answer because even if he said this much, some things he couldn't say at all. "She died."

A quiet gasp. "Sorry. I didn't know."

"How would you?" He brought his face close to hers, and his traveling hand stopped at the top of her back, running once down her shoulder. They didn't kiss, but they could have. They were so close their breaths tangled. His lungs felt full, and his lips tingled. Ryder licked his lip, watching her closely as her eyelashes fluttered. "I hope you never go through that kind of hurt."

Her empathetic agreement came without a word.

"But," he said, wanting to kiss Victoria more than he needed to change the subject, "I'm here because I missed you."

"Good."

He closed the distance, letting his lips touch her soft ones. Some kisses were like fire, others like coming home. This one, her lips melding to his, was like a calming breath that devoured his soul. The complex possession scorched and still comforted him as the sun warmed his shoulders. Ryder listened to her quiet mewl of anticipation as he slipped his fingers on the other side of her shirt, savoring the touch of her soft skin.

Sweet and innocent when she wasn't tough. Never in love—it wasn't always a two-way street. "Has anyone loved you?"

"No."

"The world has missed out."

Victoria touched the tip of her tongue to his lip, rubbing her mouth to his. "I didn't notice I was missing out."

Ryder took her mouth again, deepening the kiss as she opened for him.

Crazy, how familiar they were when they weren't that familiar. Weeks felt like years. A kiss felt as if his heart might explode.

"C'mere." Rolling to his back, he tugged her, surprised and giggling on top of his chest. "Better?"

"Think I was fine before." Staring down, her hair fell along both sides of his face, hiding them away from the world.

Ryder ran both his hands from her waist up her back and back down, stopping on her ass. His fingers curled, tightening over her shorts, and these curves… he'd missed them too. "Then I'm better." He gave her butt another squeeze. "So much better, love."

"Ryder." She laughed against his mouth. "You're only saying that because I'm on top of you."

"That's exactly why I'm saying it. Did I give you some other impression?"

She shook her head, brushing her lips against his, teasing him with her tongue each time. "I guess not."

"Temptress."

"Says the man who dragged me to the middle of nowhere, ran around flexing his muscles, and—"

He chuckled. "Not what I was doing."

"That's what I was watching."

"A temptress and a voyeur. I had no idea." His hands ran up her back under the shirt. "What else don't I know about you?"

"I've never been naked outside…"

Tall grass waved as though to remind him they had little shelter yet some cover. All alone in nature, but it was a public park. "Funny, neither have I."

"It's as though we have a bucket list to work on."

Pausing at her list reference, he let the idea roll over him then threaded his fingers into her hair. "I'll make all kinds of lists with you."

Victoria pressed her hips down, and the pressure rubbed against his hardening cock. He spun over, rolled over and caged her—and then thought twice, freezing in a panic.

Ryder was twice her size, nearly double in weight. He knew better. She been trafficked, traumatized, hurt, raped, and now he had her pinned.

"What's the matter?" Breathless, she blinked up, confused.

"Are we okay?"

Her brow furrowed. "Why wouldn't we be?"

"Because…" His guilt hammered hard as his self-irritation killed the mood. "I just pinned you."

"And I loved it." Exasperated, she wrapped her legs around his thighs. "Except, I still have clothes on."

Her strength and complaint affected him all the way down to his erection. Still, he didn't want to hurt her and ground his molars, forcing himself to double check. "Yeah?"

She lifted her hips, pressing against his cock. "You're bigger than me. Stronger. I liked it when you flipped me and held me down." Her chest heaved. "I want you to touch me. I trust you. I like how it feels to have a protective man take care of me."

Fuck, she had all the right things to say.

"Ryder, I don't care if you rip my clothes off because nothing you do will come from a bad place."

He would shred her shirt in a nanosecond if he wouldn't have to take her back to town naked. "Maybe I'll save the clothing ripping for tonight?"

"Good plan."

"For now." He rolled to his side and admired how beautiful she was. "I'll take my time. Touch you." His fingers danced over her stomach, sliding up the shirt to expose her bra. "Explore."

Ryder traced a line from her navel to her bra, skipping over the small bow between her breasts and dragging his fingers along the valley between her swollen, perked tits. The lacy bra showed off her erect nipples. "Slip your shirt off, love."

She leaned up enough to pull it over her head, dropping it to the side.

Ryder unfastened her shorts and slid them down to reveal unmatching, yet still lacy underwear. They caught on her shoes, and he took a moment to untie those as she giggled.

"Ticklish?" He brought her ankle to his mouth, letting his lips linger.

"Maybe."

His tongue worked to the side of her calf, and the laughter fell away. "I missed seeing you every day."

Victoria nodded. "Same."

He kissed up her thigh. She bent up and hooked her hands to his biceps, pulling him over her chest.

She wriggled under him, moving until they were almost in the same position where he had caged her before. "I haven't kissed you enough. Haven't felt you over me enough, and I need that."

Hell, she could have whatever she needed. Had he ever gotten off harder on giving a woman pleasure? No. With his forearms on either side of her head and planked over her, he let long, lazy kisses turn deep and hungry. He had her pinned, but she gave him directions until the directions were clear: take over.

Victoria's kisses consumed him. She gasped her breaths, and her hips rocked against him. He rolled them to their sides, unfastened her bra, sliding the straps free under the sun, and tore off his shirt.

His mouth found her nipples as his hand slipped into the lace panty, sliding along her slick folds. Flicking his tongue over the tip of her breast, he switched to the other breast and sunk fingers into her tight entrance.

"Make love to me," she whispered.

Ryder sucked her nipple harder in response, driving his fingers into her as she moaned in pleasure.

"Now." Victoria drew in a deep breath. "I want you inside of me."

He needed to be there too. Ryder withdrew from her sweetness, pulled the underwear down, and tossed it into their pile. With quick effort, he lost his clothes and grabbed a condom, sheathing himself, and positioned himself between her legs.

With her hair spread out, she lay in front of him, a hungry and loving smile innocently given to him in the middle of nature. Ryder leaned over her, encapsulating her in a protective cocoon of them, and kissed her sweetly, deeply.

He propped himself up on an elbow and guided his shaft toward her tight entrance as their foreheads touched.

Victoria inhaled deeply, arching as the head of his cock pushed into her gripping body. Inch by inch, he worked his thickness into her, staring into eyes that wouldn't look away. Her lips parted. Their breathing hitched. Ryder's short, careful thrusts toed the line of making love and needing this woman.

Until she grabbed his ass.

"Fuck," he groaned, grinding deep into her, catching her moan of a kiss on his lips.

Ryder drank that gasp and took another as he withdrew and plunged forward again. Making love didn't have to be soft—at least not with her. It had to be deep, and they had this connection, this soul-stealing, eye-locking, couldn't-stop-kissing desire to be together.

Her legs wrapped around his thighs, and her sounds made his heart hurt for not finding her sooner.

Victoria tensed, squeezing him with a brutal, fiery strength, and she bucked under him as she climaxed. Her pussy convulsed around his cock as a breeze blew over them.

"Ryder…" Her muscles went limp, and he slowed, kissing lips he couldn't stay away from.

He rolled them onto their sides, letting her rest on his chest, lazily still stroking her. Her eyes stayed closed until she eased forward, urging him onto his back. Of all the things he never saw coming—Victoria riding him in the middle of a semi-open field.

But she rocked her hips, using her knees to move up and down his shaft.

"Bucket list," he said. "And you're the most beautiful woman I've ever seen."

She opened her eyes, the pink flush on her cheeks darkening. Ryder pressed his fingers to her clit as she rode his cock. "Oh, God."

Again, her muscles tightened as her breasts swayed, and her mouth gaped. She milked his cock with the quivering build of her orgasm. He wanted to come with her. Victoria dropped down, pressing her lips to his, and he thrust into her, driving until incoherent moans fell in gasps.

Ryder strained into her, groaning his deep satisfaction. "Damn, love."

Relaxed against him, Victoria purred quietly, kissing his neck, and he wrapped his arms around her. They lulled into a post-high haze and drifted as he watched the clouds float by. *That was spectacular.*

"I'm not sure if I'll be able to handle it when you tear off my clothes." She slipped off of him and started to dress.

He laughed, taking care of the condom and pulling on his clothes. "You're the wild one."

Victoria finger-combed her hair. "What else should we put on our bucket list?"

He hooked her close, pulling her into a hug. "I don't know. Outdoors, round two?"

Tires crunching in the distance caught his attention, and Victoria's too as she pulled off of his lap.

"There's a car. Oh, my goodness," she giggled.

He pulled himself together, tucking his shirt into place as she tried to do the same. "You good?"

"Relatively speaking."

"Meaning?" he asked, eyebrows up.

"Interruptions stink."

He laughed, adjusting his belt. "Yeah, agree. Just in time to finish, though."

The new car parked near his SUV, and out popped a man and woman. Victoria stood, smoothing a hand over the backside of her shorts, and Ryder took an extra second to appreciate how her backside filled them out.

"Hi, mayor," she called. "And Marjorie."

Mayor. Well, fuck. Ryder stood up, not wanting to meet anyone, particularly the mayor and people she had to work with. They were out in the boonies for a reason.

She turned to him. "His wife."

Awesome…

"We heard you were out here," the man shouted back as they made their way over.

"I'm gonna kill Seven for all of her Holy Shitting gossiping," Victoria muttered loud enough for only him to hear. "We were just target practicing."

"A great day for it," the mayor called back.

A few strides later, the new additions had joined them. Introductions were made, and all Ryder could think of was less than five minutes ago, the mayor had almost seen a whole new side of Victoria. Literally.

"Do you want to join us for lunch?" the mayor asked. "Marjorie, my wife," he added for Ryder's benefit, "would love for you to join us."

That brought Ryder to the here and now, because he didn't want to go to lunch with the Sweet Hills' political who's who. He wanted to drop back to the ground with his girl.

"Sure." Victoria turned to him. "Sound good?"

"Peachy." At least she wasn't scowling over the desk, eyeballing intel that she wouldn't admit to. "I'm game."

CHAPTER TWENTY-SEVEN

YOU'RE BACK. IF Victoria had heard it once, she'd heard it a thousand times as their group made their way through town. The mayor had made a power move, and Victoria should have seen it coming. But she didn't. He parked nearly two blocks away from where he announced he wanted to eat, then walked her down Main Street like she was a circus animal.

But Ryder was brilliant and clued in by halfway through the first block. The first person who stopped them and gushed over her arrival home was virtually an unknown to her, and it was obviously uncomfortable. By the third time, Ryder had his arm over Victoria's shoulder and was dropping the thickest, sexiest accent she'd ever heard him work.

By the time the bells jangled on the diner's door, the talk of the town was the hot Aussie on her arm, not that she had been missing. *Point, Ryder.* He knew what was up in the mayor's gamesmanship.

The waitress sat them immediately at the mayor's favorite table as the windows rumbled from passing motorcycles. Mayhem was in town and rolling down with throttles set on level *Send a Message.*

She eyed the mayor and he stared at a menu which he likely had memorized.

"Afternoon," their waitress said. "Mayor, your usual, sir?"

"Sure," the mayor agreed. "Marjorie too."

His wife rolled her eyes and agreed then proceeded to change everything the mayor ordered for her.

Guess studying that menu didn't matter much when ordering the usual. Victoria glanced at Ryder who was in some kind of Delta team assessment mode. He wasn't his usual relaxed casualness. Cool eyes kept the mayor under watch. Ryder wasn't missing a beat.

They ordered, Ryder letting her order on her own, anything she wanted, thank you very much, and it took the mayor all of two minutes to jump to the Russian gunrunners and for Marjorie to offer prayers and clutch her pearls. *Great.* Gang activity leading to her sex slavery—not what paired well with a cheeseburger and a shake.

"Well…" Victoria searched for a generic answer that changed the topic.

"Lenora." The mayor's attention caught on the attorney in the power suit ignoring his call. He pushed out of the booth. "If you would excuse me, I have a Mayhem discussion to have."

"Mayhem?" Ryder tracked the man in hot pursuit of the motorcycle club's legal representation.

"All those motorcycles that just rolled through town? She's their attorney." Victoria shrugged. "Guess the mayor would like the window rattling drive-bys to stop."

The waitress arrived with their drinks. "I see the mayor is off politicking."

"Or something," Victoria muttered. "Always interesting, I suppose."

"Oh, honey. You're the most interesting thing in here." Their waitress winked. "The topic of every table."

Marjorie nodded in agreement.

"Nothing's a secret," Victoria said with a fake smile a country mile wide. "Tell them all I say hello."

"Me too." Ryder gave a quick wink back that wiped their waitress' just-in-fun, not-quite-crossing-the-line smirk away as Marjorie seemed unsure how to respond.

The mayor came back annoyed, huffing as their waitress did something similar, maybe unnerved by Ryder's unsaid order to shutdown the town gossip. Lunch was off to a great start. *Excellent…*

Victoria's phone buzzed with a text message, and she ignored it.

"Don't let us keep you from working, love," Ryder offered.

As it stood, the mayor and Marjorie were both face first in their phones, though the mayor's grumbles made it seem like his email reading might be similar to his menu reading.

RYDER: *How long do we have to stay?*

Victoria almost choked on a laugh. Wasn't that the question?

RYDER: *Also, holy shit, that was good earlier. As the locals would say.*

Marjorie put her phone down, and the mayor did as well. Still grumbling, he shot daggers back where the attorney sat down and leaned toward the table. "Mayhem and the Russians are making deals."

"The Russians have to sell to someone," Victoria pointed out then raised her eyebrow. "And if the law plays favors, ignoring what the MC does..."

"You're too young to know Mayhem's history."

"I don't know it at all," Ryder offered, a smidge more sarcastic than Victoria would've expected, yet it played perfectly with the mood at the table.

"Maybe I don't have firsthand knowledge of Mayhem's history, but I know what you know," she said as their food arrived—that and she had Seven, who was like an encyclopedia of all things Mayhem, though that was never to be admitted out loud.

The waitress pretended to ignore everything, but Victoria knew that woman was as good of a source as she'd ever had, and smiling, she made sure to thank her when the surly-puss mayor didn't. That might come in handy one day. In her business, she couldn't have too many acquaintances.

"No one knows what Lenora knows." As the mayor unrolled the paper napkin and smoothed it over his khaki pants, Victoria swore she saw their waitress stifle an eye roll.

Obviously. Attorney/client privilege. But Victoria would keep that to herself. Then their waitress caught her eye, and they almost laughed as they shared a knowing glance, and all was forgiven about the earlier, gossipy remarks about her being the lunchroom conversation. Bounty hunters and waitresses collected intel on the down low. There was a give-and-take to that kind of partnership. Victoria used what she knew to find people, and their waitress read a table to earn a tip.

"Sunshine, you having a bad day?" waitress asked. "Ice cream sundae on the house."

The mayor lit up like a kid. "Why, thanks." He turned to Ryder as she left. "That's why this is the best place in Sweet Hills for lunch."

Ryder wasn't a moron, but he played to the politician's ego as small talk flowed. Reelection, budgets, things she cared about, but in the end, not really. Victoria wanted to keep her home as Mayberry-like as possible, even if they were at the intersection of profit and smuggling, thanks to the simple logistics of America's heartland and the highway system.

Lenora caught her eye as she pushed from the table, leaving the motorcycle men still eating. Their eyes met, and as she walked by, heading toward the ladies' room, they didn't drop. Victoria was mid-bite into her cheeseburger, but it didn't matter. The attorney never slowed.

Table small talk continued when Victoria saw Lenora return to her table the short distance from the bathroom, where the polished attorney dug into chili cheese fries. Her two roughneck friends—*clients?*—wore motorcycle cuts and eased back in their booth, lunchtime beers in hand. Victoria was certain she'd taken down a relative of the man with the goatee.

Lenora's walk by and stare were interesting. If nothing else, there was a conversation to be had, but not when the mayor was so bent out of shape and Ryder side-eying the shit out of everyone.

"Anyone up for an afternoon tour?" the mayor asked.

Her phone buzzed, and with it, Victoria's pulse. She much rather go home and strip and was certain that's what Ryder's text would say also.

UNKNOWN: *We need to talk.*

Not Ryder. Victoria cut a glance to Lenora who stared her way and popped a chili cheese fry.

"I need to get back to the office." She declined the request and avoided Ryder's inquisitive stare. "Thanks though."

They took time to fight over the check until the waitress said that it'd been taken care of, leaving the mayor stumped and annoyed, complaining that someone would claim it was a campaign contribution. Victoria drowned out the remaining grumps and growls of small-town drama and politics until her phone buzzed again.

RYDER: *Sweet Hills is hopping with the drama.*

VICTORIA: **hop* *hop**

RYDER: *Be careful, whatever you're getting into with attorney evil eyes over there.*

VICTORIA: *You don't miss much, do you?*

RYDER: *Just trying to keep up. Let me guess. Your key is under a fake rock in the garden.*

VICTORIA: *A gnome.*

VICTORIA: *I'm questioning all life decisions now. Just so you know.*

RYDER: *So. Damn. Cute.*

Honestly, could she fall any harder for him? The answer was no.

CHAPTER TWENTY-EIGHT

THE OVERWHELMING SMELL of roast beef and more hit Victoria when she walked in the door. "Hello?"

Ryder sauntered out of the kitchen with a kitchen towel tossed over his shoulder and mesh shorts hanging low on his hips. His green eyes sparkled then he winked. "How was work, honey?"

God, he was delicious. The house smelled delicious. Everything about her life was freaking delicious right now. "Did you make dinner?" Shock hung on her every word, almost like an accusation.

He shook his head. "Nope. But I found a great place that made an order to go."

"Oh, you're a smart cookie." She walked into his arms, needing his bare skin against her hands. "A sexy one at that."

His mouth took hers, and she melted into his kiss. This was a future she didn't know existed. A man who kissed like a hurricane of need and held her like he hungered for it to last for hours.

When he set her free, Victoria was adrift in an explosion of arousal.

"I went exploring today." He walked his fingers along her arms. "Left to my own devices."

She tilted her head toward the kitchen. "Guess it worked out for us."

"Forget the food."

"Oh yeah?" Her eyebrows arched, unsure what he meant.

"I went snooping too."

A blush crept up her neck, still unsure what he meant, but the scandalous tone of his words had a heat that made her insides clench. "Where?"

"Come with me, love."

Ryder turned them from the kitchen and took her hand. At the base of the stairs, he moved her in front of him, hands on her hips, massaging her sides as he urged her to keep going.

Three stairs up, and she looked over her shoulder. "*Where* were you snooping?"

"You have *one* vibrator."

She laughed. "Yup."

"Don't you ever want to change things up?"

Her laugh deepened as she turned to face him. "It's more a functional thing."

"Trust me, love." He yanked her close. "Nothing about getting you off is functional. You enjoy the hell out of orgasms."

Her heart pounded in her chest, and the fire in her cheeks heated a thousand degrees. Not because she was embarrassed, but because he was right.

Ryder moved close enough to feel the warmth of his breath. His hands moved to her ass, squeezing. "And you biting that lip, looking at me like you're starved, says I'm right."

She released her lip, not even realizing that she was biting it. "Maybe you're right."

"When I'm not here, I want you to think of me." His fingers moved to the buttons on her pants. "You touch yourself, you better know I wish it was me doing it."

A stuttering breath fell from her lips. "I promise."

He unfastened her pants and tugged them down with her underwear, and she stepped clear of them. Ryder held her eye as his hand moved between her legs, slowing stroking her. "Because you better believe this is what I'll dream about. Your pussy. Wet for me."

The teasing was torture. The best kind where she never wanted the slow buildup to end. "I like that."

He focused his attention on her clitoris, rubbing circles, varying the speed, the pressure, then moved back to long strokes. "I like all of this, love."

Nodding, she was to the point that words were secondary to enjoyment.

"Sit down, love."

She didn't think as he eased her back onto a step, only mildly frustrated that his contact had broken away, but the anticipation of what was to come more than made up for that.

"Spread your legs."

She did and watched his eyes gleam and nostrils flare.

"I am going to worship the fuck out that pussy." He backed a couple steps. "I want your legs over my shoulders and you screaming."

Holy hell, she couldn't breathe. Her clit throbbed and her thighs quivered before he touched her.

Ryder leaned forward and spread her folds. "Sexy as fuck."

His tongue teased her clit, and she couldn't stay still for the simplest swipes of the hot, wet heat. His lips encircled the tight bud of nerves, sucking her into his mouth, and his tongue twisted like a crazed tornado.

"Oh, God!" She arched off the steps, and he held her up, bracing her to his face. "Ryder!"

Victoria was lost to the sensations. To the stubble on his cheeks against her thighs and how he changed tactics like the stealth sniper he was. Smooth and unseen, one second stroking her, sucking her, tongue fucking her. His fingers played. His tongue was magic.

"I'm going to come." When did her thighs go over his shoulders? Didn't matter any way.

And he wanted her to scream? God, she wasn't sure if she could breathe enough to make a sound.

He spun her into chaos, and she drew tighter.

"Mmmm," he rumbled against her clit. "Sweet."

His words vibrated slow and deep as his fingers and tongue pounded. Victoria climaxed on his tongue, arching as he grabbed her hips. Her eyes squeezed, and she clung to the steps, trembling as he slowed to slow kisses, murmuring words she could barely hear through the rush of blood in her ears.

He kissed her hips, up her stomach, pushing her shirt out of the way. "We can work on the screaming."

She laughed quietly, untangling herself from him, and took his hand. "Try, try, try again. Let's go. Dinner can wait."

And she led him to her bedroom. One goal: scream for him.

CHAPTER TWENTY-NINE

INSOMNIA WASN'T TO blame if Victoria never had any intention of going to sleep. She was exhausted, no questions there. But with a lot on her mind and wanting to get back to work, she was restless. She'd waited impatiently for Lenora all afternoon and didn't hear squat. But Victoria was able to obsessively try to investigate the moves of the Russians involved with her abduction and the original bounty. There was nothing positive that could come out of finding out more about the abductors, and she had to force herself away from it to come home to Ryder.

They went to bed hours ago, and Ryder snored slightly as he shifted and turned. Victoria peeled back the comforter. With her breath held and her blood thumping in her ear, she slid out of bed as though she was escaping—she was. She was absolutely sneaking out of bed to work on something she didn't want him to know. If she'd only gotten up to go to the bathroom, she would've thrown the covers off and plodded off in the dark, paying no mind to whether Ryder woke up or moved around under the sheets.

She put one foot on the floor and then the other. She pushed off the mattress and stood in the dark like a statue. If he were going to ask what she was doing, now would be the time. Nothing but easy, sleeping breaths met her straining ears.

Carefully, she searched for her clothes but gave up and went to her dresser in absolute silence, sliding the drawer open as though the quietest of noises would wake him up. He was a sniper after all, though an off-duty one who was likely well worn out. If her mind wasn't going a million miles an hour from all the work she didn't have a chance to bring home and trying to read into Lenora's intense stare, maybe she'd be in an orgasm-coma too, but for now, maybe working some would help.

Victoria pivoted, watching Ryder sleep in her bed. She couldn't see his chest rise and fall, couldn't hear him breathe, could barely see him on his stomach, his arm stretched toward her empty pillow as he slept with his own scrunched under a curled bicep. She liked this, not just him: the idea of falling asleep in his arms, dreaming big dreams next to a man who wanted to keep her safe.

He had big dreams too, even if he hadn't said what they were. But he had to… He was a specialist for an elite company. He came from little and became top tier. Ryder had to have an innate drive, some deep motivation. What motivated him?

What motivated her? Right now, Ivan Mikhailov and Yuri Maysak—or whoever was directly responsible for sending her to Russia.

But Ryder… They were both in their early twenties. If she'd been alone the way Ryder had been, would she have succeeded the way she had? Without her dad's reputation to prove herself against? Did she have the same inner fire Ryder did?

She closed her eyes.

Yes.

But right now, that fire said to go find Maysak and burn him alive. She tiptoed out of her bedroom, cognizant of every creaking floorboard, and waited in the hall for him to call her name, wondering where she'd disappeared to. Again, he didn't.

She quietly but quickly padded to the stairs, rushing down, skipping two stairs she knew would squeak. If Ryder was working, she knew he'd be a light sleeper, but he had his guard down, and she was taking advantage of that. "That makes you kind of awful…"

At the base of the stairs, Victoria grabbed the housecoat she'd had dropped when Ryder kissed her earlier. "Definitely going to relationship hell."

She should just tell him what she was up to, and that twinge of guilt that tickled across her arms would go away. Instead, she tried burying it in the silky fabric as she tugged it over her shoulders and tied the sash.

He'd want to help; he *could* help—except him helping would likely also be him saying, *whoa, stop*.

She slipped down the dark hall, looking over her shoulder like a teenager sneaking out at night, and made her way into her study. Only after she shut the French doors behind her and sat at the desk facing the door with her laptop open did she finally take a deep breath. Her finger ran along the side of the laptop and pressed the power button. The screen illuminated the small room. The laptop chimed, and she cringed in the dark and shook off her paranoia.

What was the deal? All Ryder would do was ask what she was up to.

Victoria turned on the desk lamp. "Lights mean I'm not sneaky. Talking to myself means I'm going nuts."

With a couple quick clicks, she logged into her email and made a mental to do list—

Lenora Appleton.

The email glared at her from near the top, and Victoria should have expected it after lunch today. It wasn't as though they hadn't worked together in the past. They shared a network of contacts and had done one another favors. What did Lenora want that warranted the subject line *Meet Only*?

Mayhem, in all likelihood, was one of the Russians' biggest clients. The better question Victoria had for Lenora was if she had expanded her clientele. Did she represent the Russians now? In particular, did she work for the assholes from the Ice House or the bounty she never captured? "Okay, Lenora, let's see what you have to say."

She pushed back from the desk and grabbed one of many burner phones neatly stacked against the wall. She unwrapped the box, opening the phone, and even though it came with a ready charge, she popped it on the charger before clicking open Lenora's email. As Victoria expected, it contained only a phone number.

Giving the burner a second to boot up Victoria cued up a message to the number and thumbed her response. *Sam's Deli. Mid-morning.*

She hit send and leaned back.

The burner rang, and Victoria scrambled to answer it before it woke Ryder. Her guilt raced as much as her surprise, even if it had to be Lenora.

"Hello?"

"Sam's works for me."

Her heartbeat pounded in her chest. "I figured as much, but I thought this was an in-person only conversation."

"I had one other thing. Unrelated."

"I'm sure." She rolled her eyes, heartbeat steady now that the normal wheeling and dealing of Sweet Hills was back on the table.

"There's an outstanding Mayhem bounty. Ignore it."

"I'm not working."

"The mayor didn't push you?"

"No. He pushed you?" *That son of a bitch.* Lunch hadn't been about welcoming her back to town. It was about sending a message, as much as was the message she heard when Mayhem rolled through town during lunch. It wasn't their style, the noon rolling thunder show.

"He put in his request." Lenora mentioned far too casually.

Victoria leaned back in her office chair, rubbing her thumb along the edge of the cell phone. "No one knew I'm back in town."

"I did," the attorney said, "before I saw you at the diner, and now everyone does. Don't pull that naïve fresh-to-our-world bullshit on me, honey. I know you and don't give two shits if you're twenty or two hundred."

"Not twenty," she mumbled, though she might've been acting like it, sneaking out of bed from her boyfriend—*boyfriend?*

Victoria set that shock of internal madness aside for a second and concentrated on Lenora. "I have a friend in town. I'm not working. Consider your man ignored."

"Many thanks."

Why did they have to have this conversation? It easily could have been done tomorrow. "So tomorrow, Sam's?"

"Yes."

"Lenora, what am I missing here?" Victoria finally asked. "Meet only and then a phone call. What's the deal?"

"I wanted to see what your state of mind was."

Damn it. The Ivan Mikhailov effect struck again. "I might've been kidnapped, but I'm still the same PI, bounty-hunting bitch you knew before."

"Never said you were a bitch."

"That's right. You implied that I was young," Victoria snapped. Maybe she should have stayed in bed. Lenora was a good resource, and there was no need to get on the attorney's bad side.

But really, what it came down to was screw the side effects from Ivan. No matter what, she would find a way to make everything right.

"Don't take that the wrong way. Age is a number. Attitude is everything, and you've always had the 'tude."

More like a will to prove herself.

"I'll see you in the morning." The call disconnected.

"I don't know about attitude." Gumption? Was that too old-school a word? Victoria pulled open a drawer and dropped the phone into it. She closed her eyes and rocked back in her chair, kneading her knuckles into her forehead. The door opened, and she startled, hand snatching the subcompact handgun secured in the ready-access holster under her desk. She drew and focused, pointing the barrel dead ahead.

Ryder.

He remained calm. Still. Bare chested and with pajama pants hanging low on his waist, he waited for her to realize that it was him and no one else.

Her finger slipped off the trigger and her hand fell, letting the weapon thud onto the top of the desk. Adrenaline flooded her bloodstream. "Shit. I'm sorry."

Ryder opened the French door all the way. "Easy there, love. Didn't mean to startle you."

"I couldn't sleep." She casually shut the laptop and took the gun off of her desk, sliding it back into the holster. "I'm used to being alone."

"I get it."

She could've killed him. "…lost in thought."

"Looked like," he said.

"Thank God for steady trigger control."

Everything that could've gone wrong raced through her mind, and the high of adrenaline was quickly crashing. Doomsday scenarios where she blasted a hole in his chest wrecked her vision. Guilt ate her alive. More than sneaking downstairs, now she'd nearly killed him.

"I shouldn't have snuck up on you."

"You didn't sneak up on me," she snapped. "I'm just jumpy. Reactionary. Maybe I shouldn't even be around people."

Ryder walked around the edge of her desk and put his hands on her shoulders, kneading and massaging the tense muscles. "Do you want to come back to bed, or do you want me to stay up?"

Every part of her wanted to tell him to run away from her, that she'd lied about why she was down here, right before she'd almost shot him. Her rigid muscles were as unforgiving as her mind, but Ryder seemed stubborn in her silence, letting his thumbs work up her neck, pushing circles under her hairline until finally, she couldn't take it anymore and she dropped her head forward, letting out a breath she'd held in as a protective barrier.

"That's my girl," he soothed.

God, what had she done to deserve him? Her eyes fell shut as his hands crawled back down her neck, and his fingers dug deep, almost to the point of pain, but it felt so good that she wanted to moan for more, wanted to feel that down her shoulders and along the length of her spine. The neediness was so selfish. "Your hands feel so good." She let out a languid sigh. "I love them on my body."

"I love them on your body too."

She hummed as he pushed along the length of her shoulders, pressing below her collarbone. "We should go back to bed."

"You finished working?"

Tension snapped her back into reality, and she stumbled for something that wouldn't be a lie. "Just saying I was back in town. It doesn't matter now."

"No?"

Not for a few more hours at least. "Let's go upstairs."

His thumbs pressed behind her ears and rubbed methodically before he agreed by taking her hand.

There might be a special place in hell for lying to Ryder. He'd given up his time, maybe the opportunity for work. She'd barely asked him about the scratches he had when he arrived, letting him fret over her more than she'd checked on him because she'd been so focused on what was becoming her obsession with vengeance.

RYDER HAD BOTH hands on Victoria's hips as she walked up the stairs, and he worried about where her mind was. Maybe she'd seen news about Ivan Mikhailov. Was she keeping tabs on him? Ryder had noticed that Ivan had kept a low profile in the press, and unless Victoria was searching hard and having the news translated, she wouldn't come up with much. Maybe keeping this information from her wasn't best.

At the top of the stairs, he wrapped his arms around her and rested his chin on her shoulder. "You want to share what you were really up to?"

Her stance went rigid, and her middle-of-the-night-tired muscles froze. "Not really."

"If you can't sleep, and it's on your mind, wake me up next time."

She turned her head, worry clouding her eyes and missing the connotation behind his point. "Why?"

"I can think of things to do instead of sitting in front of your computer." He let his hands run down her arms until one hand interlocked with hers.

"Oh," she whispered, melting against his back.

"Oh." He kissed her neck then led her back to bed.

Still, they both had untruths weighing them down heavier than the blankets they pulled over them. If she ever found out he had information about Ivan, she would never forgive him.

Victoria rolled over and curled under his arm. He tucked her close, breathing in the now familiar scent of her shampoo. It was distinctively different from how she'd smelled in his arms at Winters's place. Everything about her place in Iowa was hers, and learning the bits and pieces about her made Victoria all the more… Victoria. He even liked that she had a gun holster under her desk and her trigger control.

She twisted to rest her chin on his collarbone. "Are you laughing?"

"I'm not laughing," he said with his silent laugh coming stronger. "Maybe a little."

"Why?"

"Of all the places and all the jobs, my life flashes before my eyes in Iowa."

She laughed too then kissed him. "Sorry."

"Teasing," he said against her lips. "But I really am glad you're good on the trigger, love. I wasn't kidding about that."

Her laughter stopped. "If something happened to you…"

"Aw, come on. I was playing." He pressed his forehead to hers. "Tell me you know that."

"I know that."

"Say it like you mean it," he tried playfully.

"I know that," Victoria repeated.

"Tell me that you like this, love. You and me."

She straddled him. "I like this, you and me."

Ryder groaned as she slipped on top. "I do too."

He pulled her shirt over her head and bared her breasts. The erect tips had hardened, and his hands drifted over the small mounds. Her shivers made his cock harden, and Victoria leaned into his hands, lifting herself up and sliding her bottoms away.

"What if I *had* to go through the hell and the hurt to get to you?" she whispered.

"No." A pang of hurt sliced his heart, and Ryder wrapped her to his chest. "No, no, don't think like that." Would she cry or scream? He didn't know how to smother those nightmare thoughts.

Victoria kissed his neck, and not a little kiss—a hungry one.

She moved to his jaw, nuzzling her way to his mouth until she met his lips, and her back arched under his arms, her tongue slipped to his, and her hips danced side-to-side in a small-but-needy cry for him to join her without clothes.

He reached down and yanked off his boxer briefs, kicking them down his leg, and the arousal dampening between her legs met his skin. Victoria rubbed her slick folds against his shaft, teasing his head.

"I would've found you." He reached to the nightstand where'd he left his wallet with a condom. The need to be in her was overpowering. Somewhere, there had to be a cardinal rule of sex that said thou shall not screw without foreplay, but she was drenched, and he was going to die.

She murmured against his cheek as he tore open the condom. Victoria lifted her hips, and he slipped it on.

"Eyes on me," Ryder said.

Whisking a quick kiss across his lips, she listened, connecting their gazes, and it wasn't until she was entirely still, maybe even entirely focused on him, that he guided the head of his erection to her sweet pussy.

Ryder rubbed against her. "You're soaked, love."

"Mm-hmm," she agreed, not taking her eyes away.

"I barely touched you."

"You don't need to." The breathlessness of her words made his heart trip over itself as he tried to hold back. "I see you. I want you. I hear you. I need you. I feel you. I am ready."

This woman… He couldn't keep from fucking her if he tried.

CHAPTER THIRTY

RYDER WAS A beast in the kitchen. Victoria didn't have much in terms of groceries, and everything had come out of the pantry, but the man could cook. Somehow, normal pancake mix had turned into a fluffy, heaven-sent breakfast with the bacon she'd had in her freezer for a questionable amount of time fried up nicely. Even coffee was nicer when somebody made it for you. It wasn't that he was doting; it was just that Ryder seemed to take over everything he put his hands on. Like her. He'd rescued her, and here he was, in her life—in Iowa—though she wasn't complaining, especially when he made coffee like that.

"Why are you staring at your mug?" He crossed his arms over his chest.

Maybe the thing she liked most about Ryder here in Iowa was that he seemed as though he didn't like wearing his shirt much. When they were at Winters's place, he'd worn most of his clothes, except when they went swimming, which was to be expected. But today, he woke up without a shirt on and hadn't found a reason to put it back on yet, and Victoria hadn't found a reason to remind him.

"It's really good coffee."

"Secret ingredient." He winked.

"I don't know about that, but maybe I just like that you made it."

"No, for real. I have a secret ingredient." He laughed.

"Are you going to share?"

"Well, then it wouldn't be secret."

He could say all he wanted to. She knew exactly what she had in her house in terms of food and secret ingredients. There wasn't much, and she also knew what she took in her coffee—cream and sugar. Apparently, his secret ingredient was finding the perfect amount of each. Somehow, in umpteen amount of years of drinking coffee, Victoria had never found the right balance for cream and sugar and coffee, and it took Ryder one time. "Well, then you keep your secret ingredients. And I'll assume that I know what they are too."

"Ingredient. One ingredient."

She raised an eyebrow. "Okay, mister. But remember, I almost shot you last night. You almost died, taking that secret ingredient to the grave with you. Maybe you should share."

"That's a risk I'm willing to take."

She leaned back in her chair and finished the last of her secret-ingredient coffee, drinking down the remnants of the best brew she'd ever had. "I have to run a couple errands this morning. It shouldn't take that long, and when I get back, I can give you a tour of my town. Does that sound like a good plan?"

It had taken all through breakfast and a caffeine high to work up the courage to lie straight to his face about her plans to meet Lenora. Oh hell, she hated this, and she reached over and stole a piece of bacon from his plate and gnawed it even though she was too full to appreciate how good it was.

"I can ride with you." He dropped into the chair next to her, acting suspicious as all hell.

Which he should be. She took another bit of bacon. "It's just a thing. Won't take me very long." Now she was going straight to relationship hell. "You can hang here."

"No problem. I have to check in with my boss anyway." He leaned forward and took his mug, dragging it across the table, but coming short of picking it up. "Hey, look. I know I showed up to surprise you, and you seem surprised, like you want me to be here. But if you don't—"

"I want you to be here," she said as quickly as she could. And she did. The last day had been one of the happiest she'd had in a long time, and maybe the happiest she'd ever had in Sweet Hills. "It's just a quick errand."

"I didn't plan this out very well." He lifted a shoulder. "I came out here to check on you. And I could've done that and turned around and walked away, and that would have been fine. I'll take my lead from you."

"It's not you. I swear."

"Not worried," he said. "Just mentioning."

"You're not leaving here until I figure out what the secret ingredient is." She smiled, and he did too.

Ryder pushed his coffee out of the way and leaned across the table, planting a kiss on her forehead. With two of his fingers, he tilted her chin up and planted another kiss on her lips. "Be careful, love. Or you might never find out what the secret ingredient is."

He pushed his chair back as he stood then took his coffee, stealing the bacon back off of her plate and devoured the rest in one bite. "I'm headed upstairs to jump in the shower. When you come back, don't forget I'm here."

"Why would I forget?"

"Just don't want a gun pulled on me again." He picked up her napkin, balling it and swung back, aimed, and tossed. It bopped her on the forehead, and he smiled. "Bull's-eye."

She picked it back up and tossed it, also hitting a bull's-eye. "Go get in the shower."

Burning. In. Relationship. Hell.

CHAPTER THIRTY-ONE

VICTORIA DIDN'T EVEN have to think about where she was going on her way to meet Lenora. It was as if her car parked itself after driving to their normal meet-up location outside the incorporated city limits of Sweet Hill. They both knew the truck stop deli was open twenty-four hours a day, didn't have security cameras, and anyone who was there to recognize them would never admit to seeing them have a conversation.

She unbuckled her seatbelt and pulled the keys from her ignition. She leaned to the passenger seat to grab her purse and saw Lenora inside. Victoria went into the store, and with a quick nod hello, she grabbed a bottle of water and went to the register to pay.

It was Sam's deli, and Sam had a rule. They could have all the business meetings they wanted in his deli, but they had to buy something, even if it was only a bottle of water. Normally, she would have a little more, but right now, stuffed with pancakes, bacon, and the world's best coffee, Victoria was full.

After she paid in cash, Victoria joined Lenora, who seemed far grouchier, likely because she had not had the world's best cup of coffee or breakfast cooked by the world's sexiest man.

"Been here a while?" Victoria asked her.

Lenora wrapped the edge of the wax paper over the half-eaten breakfast sandwich and nodded to say as much. "I had another meeting this morning. Before we get into this, I just want to say—"

"Don't you dare say a word," Victoria beat her to the abduction-Russia pity conversation. "I don't want to talk about it. I don't want people to know about it. I don't want—"

"The people who are gonna know about it, they know about it."

"Then they know." Victoria rolled her eyes.

"And people like me?" Lenora's lips pressed into a thin line. "It could have been any of us. It could have been me. You don't deal with their type as often as I do. You don't traffic in the risks I do."

"Neither of us have a risk-free job. Maybe I have one that has more of a community-friendly face." Victoria refused to feel like a victim right now. "Though maybe not so much anymore."

"How so?" Lenora asked.

She snickered, hating how she doubted herself. "Who's going to trust me with their security when I can't even handle my own?"

"The same people as before. People who trust you, people who want someone to blend in, who need to share their deepest, darkest secrets and would rather ask you about a spouse running around on them than call up that asswipe Lee Morrow."

Victoria tried to hide her laugh. Lee was a dick.

"The douche hangs out with all of them down at the pool hall. We live in a small town with a big mouth."

"Not that small."

"The excuse of a Midwest, flyover state is our security blanket. Maybe we're not that small, and we profit off highway traffic and the commerce that comes through here—"

"Profit? Is that what we're calling it these days? Not legally profiting," Victoria said.

"How about a small-town feel with big-city problems?"

"I can agree to that."

"Sweet Hills has a Main Street and a little itty-bitty police department looped into our county sheriffs and judges and court systems, but the reason why we have bounty hunters and private investigators is because we have the MCs and drug trafficking and gunrunners. And you know that as much as I do."

Victoria cracked open the top of her water bottle and took a sip. "Lee is a dick." Right about now, that was all Victoria would say.

"Lee is also commercially successful at the same thing you are. Our little town with the brochure that shows perfect, charming little Main

Street and our perfect school system with the blue skies and the green grass, and everybody happy—if that little town is able to support the two of you?" She laughed. "And me because trust me, there is no shortage of work for me and the folks I deal with. Don't make Sweet Hills out to be some holier-than-thou place that's too perfect to sustain someone who's been through the hell you've been through."

Victoria rolled the bottle between her hands. "Did you want to talk about the MC? Or what? Tell me who I need to avoid so that you can tell me what I need to know."

"Yes, but not before I say one more thing."

"You certainly are chatty this morning, Lenora."

"Because it's important. And I don't think anybody's told you this."

"Nobody's told me anything," Victoria said.

"That's because you've been hiding. I had to hear it from somebody I had on payroll at the airport that you were back in town."

"Not true," she corrected the attorney. "I went to my office, the Perky Cup, the diner." Victoria smirked, annoyed that her baseball hat and quick getaway didn't help. "I have *not* been hiding."

"Fine. This is what I want to tell you. I hate that you were raped. I hate who took you. If you didn't have something to trade for this information, I'd still find a way to get it to you."

Victoria almost jumped back. No one outright said rape to her face.

"The second I knew something, even if it's not much, I had to tell you. You would do the same for me. And that's what I wanted to say." Lenora folded another edge of the wax paper over her sandwich and turned it over so that none of the edges would crinkle. She leaned over and pulled a small envelope from her purse. "These are the bounties you will ignore."

Her manicured fingers pushed the expensive linen envelope across the cheap, chipped table with smudged grease marks decorating the plastic.

Victoria took the envelope and unfolded the flap, extracting the piece of paper and reviewing the information. Both those boys were worth a lot of money. One of them, she might even recognize. Easy money fast.

"Now why do I want to do that?" She folded the envelope and put it in her purse next to the subcompact nine mil.

Lenora took a sip of her coffee and seemed to gauge whether or not she would finish the cup before replacing it unfinished on the table. "Vashchenko runs the Russian guns. He hasn't left town because he's protecting Yuri Maysak."

The mention of Maysak's name turned Victoria's stomach even if she'd been ready to go after the bastard again before Ryder arrived. "Okay."

"Lee Marrow didn't pick up Maysak's bounty, and he's gotten quite comfortable outside of Sweet Hills. The MC is using a trucker outfit to run a new drug supply up and down Highway 35, and they've struck a deal with Vashchenko."

Vashchenko was the head of the Russian gunrunners, the head of everything Russian and criminal for a hundred miles in any direction. "I heard guns. You're saying drugs." Why would the mayor want drugs ignored? Wasn't that the shipment he and the sheriff were playing games with? The one that landed her at the Ice House?

"It's both. But that's not important."

"You're telling me a whole lot about an asshole I don't care that much about, and now none of it's important." When really, all of it was important.

"The two brutes who knocked you out work for Vashchenko," Lenora said too casually. "Protecting Yuri is under his order."

"Glad you know the gory details." Victoria hated how the attorney kept acting as though they were friends, as though it might be more than a business deal, and kept jabbing her with sharp bits of knowledge meant to shock and stun. She tried to keep her face a blank slate. "Every Russian works for Vashchenko. Got it. You're not telling me anything I don't know or care about. So far, knowing this isn't worth ignoring them." She pointed to Lenora's list of Mayhem members she wanted ignored.

She pursed her lips. "It is."

What was Victoria missing? "You have to give me more, Lenora, because I don't care. The guy has no money on his head. I'm sure the sheriff could track him down if he wanted to; I'm not going to go narc on the guy for what? Any number of the laundry list of federal transgressions?"

Lenora let her lipstick-lined lips loosen with a calculated sigh.

"Come on and cut the doing-this-for-me bullshit." All the showmanship was fine for the courtroom, but Victoria wanted to get back home to Ryder. "I don't have all day for theatrics."

The expertly crafted smile curled. "Maybe a line has been crossed too close to my community. Even Mayhem has a line as to what they'll turn a blind eye to."

Victoria raised an eyebrow. "Spit it out."

"Vashchenko is running guns *in* country, and whispers have it that he's running girls *out.*"

Victoria's eyebrows dropped as Lenora's words tumbled through her mind. Why would the Russians be snatching girls? "Vashchenko has a partnership with who?"

Lenora shook her head.

"What have you heard?" Victoria's voice dropped to a whisper as she leaned forward, terrified to ask and needing to know. "You can't say that and not keep going."

"I heard one of their billionaire financiers took a hit. They're co-opting investments, specifically to bring in American women, and they're accepting partial down payments in some kind of partnership with a weapons dealer for large purchases."

"What kind of down payment?" But Victoria knew what was coming, knew who was hit and had the means to co-opt with weapons dealers for investment purposes. If Lenora said women, that was all the confirmation needed.

"In the form of viable, sellable pussy."

Ivan Mikhailov was going back into the human trafficking business? Nausea hit as the floor seemed to bottom out. She swallowed away the urge to vomit, flattening her feet to the ground as though that might right her world.

"Damn it," Victoria growled, angry, shocked, and sick all at once.

"With that kind of reaction, we're on the same page of thinking who," Lenora confirmed. "Take a sip of water."

She grabbed the bottle then gulped the cool water until her mind slowed. When she replaced the cap, Victoria mumbled, "That bastard."

"His time will come."

"For the two who took me too," Victoria promised.

"I think their time is coming, regardless." The attorney shook her head. "Major problems between the Russians and the MC lately. Might take care of itself."

"I'd like the chance first, if you could mention it to your clients."

Lenora rolled the cup of coffee between her hands. "That's a serious ask."

"I'm not asking for anything other than they don't kill anyone in the next few days." Victoria didn't know why or how it mattered. She didn't have a plan; she wasn't going to go kick someone's ass. "Seems that shouldn't be too big an ask, but what do I know."

"When it comes to Mayhem?" Lenora drew the question out oddly, almost dreamily. "Not much."

CHAPTER THIRTY-TWO

WITH THE MORNING sun now high overhead and at her back, Victoria walked into her house, still numb, and tried to fake any emotion that wasn't a mix of confusion, dread, and disgust. The floorboards still creaked where they should. Her walls were still painted the same light lemon yellow, and the house still smelled like bacon and coffee.

Everything, old and new, was the same, except the basic understanding that Ivan Mikhailov was back up and running, and Vashchenko was likely sending American girls to the same fate she'd endured. The hatred and heartache made her sick. Yet, somehow, walking back to Ryder, she had to keep it together and act as though everything was hunky-freaking-dory. If she told him, he'd say back off.

Hell, if she told him, he'd ask what she wanted to do about Ivan or Vashchenko, and the answer was, she didn't know—but something, anything that meant saving even one or two girls from the hell she'd endured.

Victoria numbly walked into her living room, and the picture-perfect version of what she'd always hoped for in life but didn't know she wanted until that moment was spread before her. Ryder was kicked back on her couch, reading a book. There was a blanket still folded the way Seven had the last time her best friend had been there, and her house smelled like breakfast and the world's best coffee. *This* was what she wanted. *He* was what she wanted. Needed.

"Hey, how was the errand?" he asked casually, laid a bookmark on a page, and placed the book on the coffee table.

God, she lied to him to protect herself, and *them*... It was selfish, and she wasn't sure if she could manage words. Even if she could, Victoria wasn't sure how they would come out. Nothing about how his visit to Sweet Hills had been the way he probably hoped. She'd pulled a gun on him and left him alone with her stash of mysteries and romance novels.

"You okay, love?"

No! If she'd killed Ivan, new girls wouldn't have been abducted. "Yeah."

That sin, letting Ivan Mikhailov live, would haunt her forever.

Ryder stood. "You're looking pale."

"My stomach's bothering me." At least that wasn't a lie. "I think I need to sit down."

"C'mere." Ryder tugged her onto the couch, and she pulled the blanket around her.

"Do you remember when you had that nightmare? And I walked into your room?" she asked.

"Yeah."

"What was it about?"

He sucked in a deep breath, holding her to his chest and groaning a little.

"Are you okay?"

He nodded. "I got a couple bruises at work the other day, and when I forget about them, they remind me they're still healing."

"What happened?"

"Wild animal tried to blow me up with a landmine." He laughed.

"Ha, ha, ha." She teased. "I'm sure."

"It's a crazy world out there. Someone's got to have the jobs like that."

Like her going after Vashchenko? She could help stop the gun running, and then she could save a woman or two… "True."

"That sounded deep," he said.

"Like your nightmare," Victoria pivoted away from that conversation and back to him. "Do you remember it?"

"It was about you, actually," he admitted. "In a way."

"Oh, great. I'm terrorizing you in your sleep." She dropped her head back, and Ryder stroked her hair, helping her relax.

"My arms and legs were heavy. I couldn't get to you—"

"We were in Russia?"

"Yes. You were going to shoot Mikhailov..."

"Which meant Locke too," she whispered.

"Yeah, that's what it meant." He paused. "But I couldn't stop you. I didn't want to stop you. I wanted Mikhailov to suffer."

"But Locke..."

"See why it was a nightmare? And..."

They sat there in their own thoughts for what felt like forever until she realized he'd never finished. "And what?"

"And I kept seeing Zoe too." Ryder shifted to see Victoria's face. "Is that weird to tell you?"

She searched his expression. "You didn't say her name before. Zoe was the one who died? What happened? If you want to tell me. You don't have to."

He pulled in a long, painful breath that tore at her heart. "She was adopted by abusers. Users. Scum of the earth."

"They killed her?"

Ryder repositioned, pulling her close to his chest. "They worked the system, adopting girls who were almost ready to age out, ones who had no legal recourse and who, when put through that kind of hell, would never turn around and report it once they were set free. If they made it."

"Oh... God." She didn't know the right words. "Ryder..."

Suddenly, he put both hands on her biceps and straightened her to face him. His hands cupped her cheeks harshly, until he seemed certain her eyes were on his, and her attention was nowhere else.

"I was older than she was. Soon as I could, I joined up. They gave me a gun. I was a good shot. I knew that already. But I was born to do what I do. I've told you that already."

Victoria nodded, but he held her head still.

"She didn't write me back. I never heard from her, and when I had leave, I went to find my girl." Hardness coated his face, despite the term, my girl. "I found out what she'd been through, and I hated myself for not learning sooner. *Hated.* But then I did what I know how to do, what needed to be done. I did it, and I will never regret that."

Victoria's eyes went wide. "What did you do?"

"I killed them."

CHAPTER THIRTY-THREE

Judge. Jury. Executioner. Victoria would either understand, or she would demand he leave her house. Ryder wouldn't blame her. That wasn't something some people could understand. They needed the law to handle criminal activity. The law did eventually come in and found body after body buried in the backyard. Zoe's adoptive parents had worked the system for years, maybe decades, pimping teenagers and peddling flesh.

Local news had sensationalized the shallow graves with multiples bodies, but there hadn't been a single loved one to claim a child. Not even a funeral. Ryder had held his own for them all, a ceremony of sorts. But it started and ended with prayers, and somewhere along the line, he also prayed for himself to find peace for not checking on Zoe sooner.

Peace had come over the years.

Delta team, he'd thought, was his final saving grace. His soul had been saved by the ghost team that focused more and more on human trafficking. Granted, they did the big money contracts, but they never missed out on the chances to help eradicate the dark web of people for purchase. Then came Victoria. He thought he had found peace, that he'd handled what needed handling about Zoe. But right now? All was right in his world. All had been *made right* in his world.

"Say something." After all, he'd just told her he killed two people in cold blood. The silence couldn't last forever.

Victoria surged forward, her lips landing on his. The kiss lasted forever as her arms wrapped around his neck. She finally broke her lips away, rolling her forehead against his slowly, side to side, then eased back. "Thank you."

Ryder pulled her back into his arms. He had no idea what he thought she'd say. He'd never spoken about what he'd done, except for the conversation with Brock that consisted of nothing more than I-know-what-you-did. That was different than laying it out there, the truth, the reasoning, his most vulnerable moment, his biggest secret. And she accepted him, understood him and his ugly, sad, lonely past because she had one of her own, different in so many ways, but yet, not.

Knock. Knock.

"Tell me someone isn't at my door," Victoria groaned into his chest. "I just want to exist in a world that feels like your arms wrapped around me."

Her phone buzzed from her purse on the floor, eliciting another groan. Ryder chuckled as he recognized Seven's voice carrying through the door. "Unless you're having crazy, wild monkey sex, I'm coming in."

"She has a key." Victoria pushed off her chest.

"What if we were having crazy wild monkey sex?" He laughed. "And Seven is loud."

"True." Walking toward the front door, she smoothed her hair. "She is that."

Seven's voice bounced through the front hallway as Ryder's phone buzzed on the coffee table. He glanced at the notification on the screen before it went dark.

BROCK: *Need you back here.*

Ryder dropped his head back and pinched the bridge of his nose. *Back to reality*. He was going to miss his girl, and no question, was headed back here soon as he could. What would Victoria think of that?

"JUST LIKE THAT, you're leaving?" Seven gave a nasty side-eye, to which Victoria gave her a glare to take it down a notch.

"Work calls." He leaned back on the counter. "Sorry to run."

"You just got here," Seven continued her protest.

But Ryder held on to Victoria's eyes. "You okay with this?"

"Sure." But after everything he'd just admitted, she decided she wanted to tell him about Lenora and Vashchenko, what she'd found out about

Mikhailov. That was a delicate subject, though, because it wasn't as if she could just throw out that she wanted to chase down sex traffickers and stop them. She needed a plan. He was a planner. But so was she.

There was a distinct difference between what she wanted to do and the act of private investigation or bounty hunting. What did she want to do? She hadn't decided yet. The only goal was to make sure she could stop others from being trafficked from around Sweet Hills or in Iowa. Not exactly a one-person job.

"You don't sound convinced," he followed up.

"I wanted to bat some ideas around with you, but I can do it later."

"Or with me," Seven volunteered.

"Or with you," Victoria said, which was true. Seven knew Mayhem better than maybe even better than Lenora. If Mayhem was her ticket to the Russian runners, Seven might be the answer.

Ryder's gaze narrowed. "What are you girls up to?"

"Oh, please don't ruin my fantasy of how awesome you are by being a patronizing, overbearing—"

"Seven," Victoria snipped.

Seven rolled her tongue out, revealing a new stud. "Okay, I'll just leave it at *holy-shit*-worthy, crazy, wild monkey sex."

"No monkeys," Ryder corrected her.

"Kangaroos?" Seven asked.

"You have a thing about Aussies, don't you?"

"You have a brother?"

He laughed. "'fraid not, no family."

"Oh, he's wounded and emotionally fragile." She feigned clutching her heart.

Ryder turned to Victoria. "Somehow, this is not who I would've picked out for your best friend."

"Yet, you are exactly what I would've designed to deliver the goods to my girl."

Victoria's face lit on fire. "Seven."

"It's true." She rolled her eyes. "Hey, what's the deal with the coffee?"

His grin went stratospheric. "You told her?"

"I kind of had to." Victoria cringed, hating to be in the middle of coffee wars. "It's kind of awesome."

He crooked his finger to Seven, and her eyes went wide.

"Please, dear Lord, tell me we're going to have a secret."

"Oh, come on. I want to know." Victoria crossed her arms.

"Shove it, bounty girl. You use a Keurig."

"And there's nothing wrong with that," she snapped back.

Ryder whispered in Seven's ear, and Victoria watched her jaw drop.

"Really?"

"Mm-hmm," he said, all kinds of proud of himself.

"It takes a lot to shock and awe Seven." Victoria scrunched her face.

"Are you pouting?" Seven teased.

"Definitely pouting," Ryder confirmed, then he locked his arm around her neck and pulled her in for a kiss. "Don't pout. I'll make you the world's greatest coffee whenever you ask."

That kiss sent fireworks exploding in enough ways that she almost grabbed hold of his shirt and kicked Seven out.

"Holy shit," Seven mumbled.

"Shove it, babe," Victoria mumbled back.

"I gotta go, love." Ryder ignored their antics, brushing her hair off her cheek, running his fingers over her skin as though he couldn't stop touching her. "Thanks for letting me drop by unannounced."

"Do it again?"

"Promise."

"Soon as you can?"

"I will."

He brought her in for one more kiss, and Victoria gave no shits that Seven was somewhere in the kitchen, or maybe the living room, making herself invisible now. She never wanted to let go of Ryder, and as he left, he took her heart with him.

CHAPTER THIRTY-FOUR

THE DOOR SHUT, and Victoria could feel Seven's eyes on her back as much as she could feel Ryder getting farther away.

"Are we going to talk about that man?" Seven asked quietly, all signs of silliness and snark gone.

Victoria leaned against the wall, not turning away from the front door. "What would you like to know?"

Her best friend walked next to her and laid her head on her shoulder. Pink hair mixed with her brown strands as she asked, "When did you know you fell in love?"

Easy. "When I held on to his arm like he was the only thing that could keep me breathing, and he held strong for days, until I knew I could on my own, even though he knew I could the whole time."

Seven hugged her. "I want that for you. Not what you went through, but what you just said."

"He's a good man."

"You weren't even looking."

"Isn't that how they say it happens?" Victoria asked as Seven dropped her arms. "I don't know. I don't think having a relationship has crossed my mind."

"We've been busy." Seven wandered into the living room and threw herself backward on to the couch.

"Speaking of which, how's your mom?"

"Eh... seen better days." Seven refolded the blanket. "You know what else we have to talk about?"

"Yes," Victoria admitted. "Do you know who I met with today?"

"Nope."

"Lenora Appleton." She took the blanket from Seven, unfolded it, and tucked it next to her side. "I'm not supposed to tell anyone."

"My lips are sealed." She grumbled, braiding her pink hair into the blue strands as the bangles on her wrist clinked. "I don't like that bitch."

"I know. Is the name-calling out of your system?"

"Maybe. What she want?"

"Gave me a bead on how I might…" Victoria gestured vaguely.

Seven perked up. "Really? Maybe not a bitch after all."

"Do you even know what I'm talking about?" Victoria asked.

"No—but, she's Mayhem's go-to legal girl. Mayhem and the Russians are wheeling and dealing every which way over every which thing lately."

"Sounds like you've been spending quality time with—"

"*No*, I am *not*."

"I think the lady doth protest too much."

"Yeah, yeah, that fire's so cold it's ice." Seven tugged the blanket partially over her knees, playing down the relationship that had nearly been prearranged. "Mayhem's come into more money, and they are also pissed at something going on with the Russians."

"I know you're not picking all this up at the Perky Cup."

"I won't reveal my sources."

"I bet not." Victoria wiggled her toes as she drew them onto the couch. "It's girls. The Russians are snatching girls. Ivan Mikhailov is a player in financing Russian weapons, and he's allowing purchases to be made with women as capital to make up for a loss he sustained recently."

Seven's eyes couldn't have been any wider. "What? How do you—" She blinked and stuttered to a stop. "How would you know that?"

Victoria sealed her eyes for a long moment before admitting the specifics she hadn't told Seven. "Because of what Lenora said and… I was Vashchenko's *gift* to Mikhailov. I saw the operation from the inside until it was shut down. I guess they're rebuilding."

"From here?"

"Probably from all over the world." Victoria twisted the edge of the blanket. "But the guns are here. Vashchenko is here. Their distribution partners for middle America are here—"

"Mayhem," Seven muttered. "East coast is too hot. That's why they're flourishing."

"That's why I have a job," Victoria confirmed. "Up from the gulf—then they can go anywhere in the US."

"Are they actively taking women?"

"Lenora thinks so."

"From here?"

She nodded. "Makes sense. Unloading to Mayhem. Empty cargo space. Highways. Easy to transport if they don't want to use airlines."

Seven let her tongue stud run along her teeth. She quietly grabbed Victoria's hand under the blanket. "I know when, maybe where, the next weapons meet is."

Victoria's head twisted so fast it might've popped off. "You do?"

"If they're grabbing girls, they've got them already."

"Does Mayhem know?" Victoria asked.

Seven arched her brows. "Maybe some members? I don't know. Business has been tense lately."

"What have you been up to?" She shook her head. "Never mind. One thing at a time."

Playing with the tongue stud, she nodded. "What do we do?"

"I don't know."

"Bullshit." Seven jumped that time, startling Victoria. "You know what we do."

"I don't know…" But she knew where Seven's mind would head. "You stay home."

"You wouldn't dare go without me."

"Of course I would. I work best alone."

"*I work best alone*," Seven said simultaneously, mimicking her. "Well, don't get yourself killed. There's a hot Aussie who'd be pissed."

"Fine. Now tell me what you know." Victoria grabbed her purse that she'd ditched by the coffee table after her meeting with Lenora earlier that day and extracted a pen and notepad. "Where and when?"

"Three weeks from tomorrow—"

"Really?" Victoria tossed the pen. "I got the impression there was something sooner."

"Oh, well tonight. But how much prep time do you need—"

Versus waiting three weeks? "If you help me, not as much." She tossed the blanket off. "Let's go."

CHAPTER THIRTY-FIVE

"IT'S JUST RECON." Victoria threw another protein bar into her bag. "Same as any other job."

Seven watched. A disbelieving frown had been plastered on her face for the last forty-five minutes. "Then why can't I come with you?"

"Because we've done this before. Twelve seconds into sitting there, you get bored, want your phone, and that won't work for me."

"You don't have night vision goggles for my nighttime phone viewing pleasure in your bag of tricks." Seven pointed at the bag as Victoria zipped it.

"Even if those existed, you'd distract me."

"We could put ninja warfare paint on our faces and barrel roll around—"

"And now you're slap happy when I need to concentrate."

"Okay, true."

Victoria walked over to the printed maps they'd pulled off Google and checked where Seven was sure the meet was going down. She'd heard Vashchenko had taken up a home base on what had been a working farm with, they decided, lots of places to stash a woman or two, if the Russians wanted to keep them there. They could store arms, bring in clients, make deals, move money, drugs, whatever they needed to, and organize cash-or-human payments to their suppliers from a central location.

If guns were coming out, they were going out. If Mayhem was going to place another order, like the one Seven thought there might be in three weeks, Vashchenko might keep some of the dough from Mayhem, send off women, turn a better profit, and make Mikhailov happy in the process.

Or not, and the whole night would be nothing but sitting in the dark, watching a gun deal go down and having nothing to do about it.

Seven popped up and paced. "All right then. I guess I'll let you get to work."

"Okay."

Seven nervously pulled on her eyebrow piercing. "I just want to remind you. This time, it's personal. You're thinking about this differently, so you need to take double care of yourself."

"What?" This wasn't the pep talk she needed right now.

"You're not spying for other people. You're trying to figure something out for yourself. You're not going to take what you learn and give it to someone else—you have said yourself, people can make bad decisions with good information—you'll just have it on your own."

"I get your point. I'm trained. I know what I'm doing—" She cut herself off, feeling suddenly stronger than she had in weeks. It was as if she needed this to remind her that she could do this job, that even if something went wrong, she was trained for it. "I expect my jobs to go bad, Seven."

"Obviously."

"Let's set Russia aside." Victoria regained her composure, working her arms back and forth. This was what she needed. "Things go wrong. I've been in pickles before. I've been surprised, jumped, bullied, maced—"

"None of which I like," Seven countered.

"Which is why you work at the Perky Cup, and I do what I do."

"You're an adrenaline junkie."

"A trained, savvy-as-fuck, adrenaline junky who needed this to get back on her feet."

"You sound like you want someone to come from behind and bop you on the head."

Victoria rolled her eyes. "Give me a break."

"Just sayin'." Seven moved about the room, putting her mild undiagnosed obsessive organizing skills into action with tidying and straightening things that had been just fine as they were.

Everything she was doing and saying was driving Victoria nuts. "Me too."

"Bop." Seven made the "P" pop as she flounced on a pillow, and Victoria stifled the urge to take the closest throw pillow and bop her. "Bop."

Barely stifling would be a better description. "If someone does *bop* me, I will deal with it."

"Bop."

Exasperated, Victoria turned to her best friend, who apparently forgot who the heck she was. "Are you done yet?"

Seven smiled like a Cheshire cat. "You bet your ass I am."

Then it clicked. Victoria had played right into her hand. "Well done."

"Go get 'em, tiger."

Her best friend believed in her, even if she got bopped on the head. "I love you, Seven."

"You love Holy-Shit-Aussie-Boy too. Now there's something to live for when you insist on running around and sticking your nose into trouble, all in the name of being a do-gooder."

That was so damn true.

CHAPTER THIRTY-SIX

THE LOCATION WAS rural, and cell service was spotty, but Victoria found the best spot. She drove a quarter mile past where she needed to be, grabbed her gear, and hiked through the fields to get closer, passing smaller farm buildings before coming upon a massive working barn that appeared to be the headquarters of the night's activities.

If she could get closer, all would be easier. Quickly, she moved through the field, staying low and out of sight. Despite Seven making fun of her, Victoria did have night vision goggles as she kept an eye out for Russians keeping an eye out for her. Seeing none, she advanced until she came to the first building. The door was unlocked, and a quick search yielded nothing but a heavy stench of unorganized tools, motor oil, and tractor parts.

Victoria skirted the edges of the splintered wood building and moved to the next. The larger was a two-level barn, and a bevy of expensive cars seemed to be parked in the front of it. To the side was a row of work vehicles. She moved by each one. They were in use, none rusted out, and all currently plated. A few had plastic bottles filled with dip-spit in the bed of trucks, while a Jeep Wrangler had a week's worth of candy bar and cigarette wrappers on the floorboards. *All in use vehicles.*

Whatever the Russians were doing at night, this was a working farm during the day, and a big one by the looks of it. How could anyone not notice if women were held captive inside a barn? Still, Victoria needed to take a look to rule out what was inside.

She crept to the corner and crawled up a wooden ladder to an abandoned hayloft hatch. The barn wasn't for livestock or horse use, at least not anymore. It didn't have the right scent, and she didn't pick up the sweet smell of hay recently moved inside during the summer months. Crawling along the side of a ledge, she worked her way to a window.

A set of headlights turned on, and she froze. Under the cover of the moonlight, she blended in mostly, but if someone drove by, she was done for. No way could she drop to the parking lot without injury. Instead, she prayed for them to turn the other way.

The car did, and her heart started up again. Almost to the window, she reached and pushed, dangling and pushing, reaching. She grasped the edge, swinging over. Maybe Seven was right; she was a ninja tonight.

Victoria pulled up. There were the Russians. She could've painted the pictures. It was almost too cliché. They sat around the table, cigars in their mouths, vodka on the table, playing cards. No girls though.

Except. What was that?

She pulled up and tried to see what was in the corner but couldn't. It was like chain link fencing. *Inside a barn?* Her stomach bottomed out. She was unable to see anything but suddenly knew everything. Lenora was right. The Russians had women. Who and how many, Victoria couldn't tell, but it was everything that she was so close to them right now, and they didn't know that help was on its way.

All she needed was a plan. There were a lot of them, and the easiest, safest way to go was to call Ryder. Maybe Delta could come in and clean house. Easy. She had a confirmation. She could tell them who, where, and almost how many, not that she had set eyes on the women. But it was a solid lead. Or she could tell the mayor or sheriff, though neither had her trust.

Either way. She had actionable intel, and now she was off to do something about it.

Victoria walked along the edge of the barn, easing her aching arms off the ledge. She took a breath on the side of the roof, letting her legs hang over the gutter.

Two mice scampered along the gutter, squeaking and squealing as they made their way. A large flapping came out of nowhere, startling Victoria. Something large and dark dove at her—at them—and the mice scampered. She covered her face as the animal—the bird—hit her, knocking into her with giant wings as it grabbed toward the roof. She curled into a ball, muffling her surprise, falling to the side. Claws scratched the gutter, and she rolled off the side, catching herself, dangling next to the downspout as an owl took off with its dinner.

Fuck.

The gutter bent under her weight.

No, no, no. Damn it. She repositioned her hand, trying to find wood. *Drop? Stay up?* Anything that wasn't semi-rusted out gutter to hang on? Better to drop. There was grass—

The gutter tore, screeching as she came crashing down.

Oomph. Landing on her back, air knocked out and dazed, she blinked hard, trying to roll hard to the side.

Victoria staggered to her knees. In a crouch, she surveyed the side, pivoting, and—*shit.*

"And who are you?" the man approached, weapon drawn.

Now this was going to make Ryder all kinds of upset if she didn't get herself out. "Vigilante chemical crusader, out to make sure farmers aren't using pesticides they shouldn't." Victoria smiled. "But you guys look all good. Guns aren't my concerns. Have a good night."

She turned confidently and started walking away. No way was that going to work.

Really?

She waited for him to yell or to hear the cock of the gun.

Just footsteps, and she broke into a run as he chased her. Pain exploded at the back of her head as the back of the gun struck in a swing. That... wasn't... a... *bop.*

CHAPTER THIRTY-SEVEN

RYDER PUSHED HIS earpiece in. "Say what?"

He wasn't cleared to do any gun work, but he could be the eyes for someone else, and right now, Cash Garrison needed his entire focus, not Parker breaking into Ryder's concentration.

"Can I get an update?" Parker repeated.

Cash was on another comm channel and wouldn't hear the back and forth. *Good.* Ryder focused through his binoculars, putting Parker's request on hold. Cash had the perfect shot. A madman had a knife against a child's throat, demanding a ransom that had made zero sense. Before he'd arrived and taken the hostage, he'd left a body count with that already bloody knife. Island police didn't have a hostage negotiator, much less one that spoke in tongues the madman would understand.

It didn't take long before Titan was called in for an off-the-books sharpshooter to end a spiraling ordeal.

The window shattered. The knife dropped. The child screamed as her mother ran forward, and the killer dropped to the ground. A two-day standoff was over, and the child lived. That was all that mattered.

"All right." Cash came online. "That's a wrap."

Ryder dialed in his binoculars, assessing the scene. "Good work. Clean shot."

They flipped to an open comm channel as the island sun beat down, and the sweet-scented wind drifted over the expensive row of beachfront mansions.

"Boss Man, you there?"

"Good shot. Wrap up, and get home," Jared said.

"Or you can send Nic and the kids down here."

Ryder didn't even notice whatever coconut-mai-tai-breeze kissed the air when they touched down after the warp-speed flight. His mind was still back in Iowa. Iowa, of all places on Earth. The thought brought a stupid-silly smile to his face.

"You can stay here." Pushing off the top of a rooftop of a nearby beach mansion, Ryder wiped his brow. "It's hotter than hell here. I'm headed back north to a suitable summer."

"Yes, you are," Brock confirmed.

He headed for the makeshift ladder, throwing his leg over the roof access.

"You had a phone call," Parker said.

Cash laughed. "Take a message."

"Not you," Parker followed up.

Ryder half-slid, half-jumped down the remaining rope rungs before he pulled down the proof that he'd been up there. "Me? Didn't know I'd reached rock star status like Cash."

"Cut the shit, you two," Jared snapped.

Pricks of sweats popped down his spine under the hot island sun. Between Parker almost interrupting a job before Cash took a shot and the uneasy edge of Jared's voice, coupled with who the hell would be calling him at Titan, or ever, trepidation sawed at his muscles. "Who called?"

"You know someone named Seven?" Parker asked.

Ryder stopped mid-step. "Where's Victoria?"

"She went out to recon a job and hasn't been home."

"What did Seven say?" Ryder's touristy, blend-in-with-the-neighborhood stroll turned into a run as he headed back to the meet-up. The sooner he got into that car, the quicker he and Cash could get into the waiting jet to take them home.

"Victoria thought a local gunrunner was making payments with women," Parker said.

"And?" Ryder cut down a sandy alley.

"She went to scout a location to see if there were girls."

"Damn it!" What was she going to do? Rescue them herself? No, Victoria wasn't crazy. She'd call in for backup. Ryder tried to focus on what he knew. She was trained, a beast at what she did. She knew the players, the politics. Still, she was missing.

"We have the location," Brock followed up. "Delta's already airborne, and we'll head you there first."

"I'm wherever I'm most useful," Cash added.

"Roger that," Jared said. "We've pulled everything from Seven. That girl has intel, and we're in a good place, working both back channels and official routes."

Roping in the government? Even in an off-the-books manner, that alone said how serious this was. "Meaning?"

"Meaning," Jared continued, "if this is something more than a neighborhood-level street thug she's stumbled into, we'll have intel on how to make our best move."

"I'm at rendezvous," Cash announced. "We'll be coming into the airstrip hot. Let 'em know we're less than twenty minutes out."

"Roger that," Parker said.

"Be there in less than a minute." Ryder pushed himself to run faster. Every second counted. He turned down a side street, the binoculars heavy in his board shorts, the two concealed guns, one on the other side of his shorts and one tucked in his back and concealed by the Bahama shirt, felt like a good weight to have, centering him with deadly force in an island of vacation and sunshine.

Ryder closed in on the waiting getaway ride, and when he grabbed the passenger door and threw himself in, Cash had the wheels spinning before Ryder shut the door. Cash looked over, dressed like he was a beach bumming tourist, but his scruffy face and blue eyes seemed more dangerous than Ryder could remember as he blew out a shaky breath.

"You good?" Cash pulled down his battered cowboy hat.

"Fuck no," Ryder mumbled. "Seven called Titan? I'm not good at all."

CHAPTER THIRTY-EIGHT

SUGAR THREW THE door open and walked in, taking in each surprised face after the table full of men craned their necks to see who interrupted. She put her hands on her hips and smiled. "Good morning, boys, I was told that I would be looped in on all conversations. This doesn't look like looped in to me."

Marco Nunez picked his jaw off the ground and stood. "Well, if it isn't Sugar Chase—"

"Sugar Westin," she corrected him. "But you knew that already. There's nothing about Jared Westin you don't know, isn't there, Marco?"

He dropped down and smirked. "Including how you had the reach to make this kind of intel request? Yeah, I know Titan has their hands all over this."

Sugar ignored him and kept her hands on her hips, swaying forward, one boot step at a time. Her high heels echoed in the cold, windowless conference room. "What I want to know is why I wasn't at the table *hours ago*." She crooked her finger at Marco. "Now that I see you're here, I have my answer."

"You were told that you would know everything you needed. You will."

"What do you have on Vashchenko and my girl?"

"Since when is Victoria Massey your girl?"

"Since I said so." Sugar blew a bubble of gum and let it pop, which she knew from years of working under him would drive him bonkers.

"The only thing I've got on Victoria is the Delta team Mikhailov rescue. Why didn't Titan slap security all over her?"

"Consider security slapped on her now."

"You?" Marco smirked and leaned back in his chair, pushing back so that the back two legs tilted, and the front two were suspended in air. "Maybe your old man is getting soft in his old age."

Sugar grinned. "You know what's funny?"

"What's that?" Marco sneered.

"Calling my old man soft?" She clucked at him. "It's not me who's gonna let him know that you did." Sugar danced eyes danced around the room, casually lingering on each man at the table. Marco's disrespect would get back to Jared; she had no doubt. "And even funnier? You worship the old bastard."

"Go to hell, Sugar."

An empty chair next to Marco shot back. She raised her chin, asking without a word about the solid invite to join them from the big black guy on the other side of the table. "Thanks."

He lifted his chin in answer. "Have a seat."

"Damn it, Deacon." Marco's lips snarled.

Deacon didn't bother to turn his head. "Nunez, if you think you're calling the shots, you're mistaken."

"Easy, boys." Sugar hooked her heel around the chair leg, snaking it over, and took the offered seat. "You know I get all hot and bothered when I see a turf war."

"I'm a fan of yours," Deacon continued. "And I'd be happy to talk about Vashchenko."

Marco slammed his fist on the table, making Deacon chuckle and extend his hand. "Deacon Lanes, I've heard more tales about Sugar and GUNS than I may've ever heard of one person."

Sugar took his hand and shook it. "Ninety-nine point nine percent are true."

He tilted his head with a sly wink as their hands fell apart, and she sat back into her chair. Another person at the table shuffled a stack of paperwork to her, and she said hello to the rest of the men.

"Of all the stories, what was that point one percent that wasn't true?" Deacon hummed.

"Everything is rooted in the truth somewhere. Just consider that missing percentage a gimme."

Deacon leaned back in his chair. "A gimme, huh?"

"You're a fed?" There were a lot of folks sitting around the table simply to be dealing with simple gang and gun activity. "Or do we have a DA who likes to jump into field ops?"

"Does it matter?" Deacon squared back to her.

Sugar narrowed her eyes and bit her lip. "I suppose not." She turned to the rest of the room. "All right… You're Marco's ATF newbie, and you are the agent in charge of training the newbie." She pointed to the other guys. "FBI. Lord knows the field office out there wouldn't let anything happen without knowing what was going on." She centered her gaze back on Deacon, apprehension suddenly tickling the back of her mind as to how this was about to get far more complicated. "Which makes you…"

Deacon's challenging smile said that she was correct about the FBI agents. "There are only two things you should care about when it comes to me."

"And they are?" *Damn mind games…* Sugar steeled herself for whatever was coming. Deacon had just dropped a level of cool in her opinion.

"First, when you have Nunez and myself in a room, I win," Deacon said, and Marco didn't disagree. "Always."

"Always, huh?" *Well then, he just bumped himself back up a level of cool.* "Always promising."

"And second, I go way back with your boy Jax."

Jax. Titan's newest recruit. What did she know about him? Not as much as she wanted to. "You were a military man, Deacon?"

"Do I look like I was in the military?"

"You look like you could do whatever you wanted to, my friend," she played along, assessing. But where did Jax come into play? He was a SEAL. Sugar scrambled to place the clues in the right order and figure this guy out—and that *was* her clue. He was a spook. *Everything was always a mind game.* "So you're with the CIA."

"We like to keep ourselves involved when we see peace-keeping opportunities."

"Is that what we're calling it these days when Langley plays God?" Sugar snorted. "Now that that's out of the bag, let's hear who Uncle Sam has decided to let live and die today."

CHAPTER THIRTY-NINE

"YOU'RE NOT GOING to ask about Jax?" Deacon dropped his chair onto all four legs.

Sugar leaned her elbows on the table, pushing her ass up. Did she look that simple?

"Jax…" She pursed brightly lined lips together and was aware that one of the ATF agents was intently watching those more than her face in general. "Is a dickhead."

With the exception of Deacon, the table's worth of men leaned forward, waiting on her answer. Collectively, they fell back, surprised she didn't fall for the CIA's gossipy bait, and they each tried to play it down.

"I want to know all about Vashchenko and Massey." She straightened. "If we could put all the bullshit CIA games to the side, that'd work for me."

"Fair enough," Deacon agreed.

The lip-starer failed to hide his smile, and Sugar got the impression that he hated Marco as well.

"I'm here to ensure the status quo," Deacon offered.

"Which you aren't ensuring," one of the FBI agents added. "Tommy Mondello," he added, giving her his name.

"Why is that, Tommy?"

"We are." Deacon's voice dropped. "Distribution and product levels haven't increased."

"But payment's changed." Sugar casually let her fingernails tap on the table, one after another, as every head in the room shot to her.

"What the hell do you know?" Deacon snapped.

"The reason *why* Victoria Massey is missing." She tapped her fingernails again, letting the pace pick up.

"It's getting out of control," Tommy snapped.

"You think pulling the strings and calling the shots means the Russians won't change the plays?" Marco laughed. "You boys gotta get out of Langley more often."

"If Titan Group didn't throw off the peaceful world order, we wouldn't have a payment issue right now." Deacon's friendliness was gone.

"Sorry that us saving pussy from plunder and pillage made your office gig a little harder." She rolled her eyes. "Why don't you stick to living in the drama and the politics of the drugs, guns, and trafficking, and tell me what I need to know to help rescue my girl."

"You can't stop the sales from going through," Deacon said.

Sugar gave him the finger. "Fuck you."

"There are bigger things at play."

She shook her head. "Don't care. I'm here about my girl. I didn't say I want to stop the distribution." Though she did. AKs or whatever hitting the street under the government's blind eye would kill her or at least require her molars to get capped as she ground them down. "I hope whatever deals you've cut recently are worth it."

Deacon didn't respond.

"About the rescue operation." Tommy broke the awkward silence. "If you'd like to coordinate—"

Sugar shook her head. "Not at this time. All I'd like is intel."

"We'd like to keep any actionable information admissible in court—"

"We're not going to take grenade throwers to an Iowa farmhouse," she snipped. Or she didn't think they would, technically. She hadn't seen any plans, so…

"They've only had her for what, less than twenty-four hours?" Marco asked.

The ATF trainee nodded. "If she was the cause of the cancelled gun sale last night, yes."

"They haven't moved her yet," Deacon said. "Vashchenko needs to make money from the sale last night, so it has to be rescheduled. We've given Mayhem approval to buy another weapons cache in three weeks."

She muttered.

"Sugar," Deacon snapped at her. "You have no idea who the end distribution is. Ease off the guns."

"No matter what Mayhem's doing, I think Vashchenko skimming off the weapons sales," Marco added.

"We haven't seen that," Tommy disagreed.

"I feel like we would've caught it," Deacon said.

Marco nodded. "Sure enough, someone will."

All of this seemed backward. Why weren't the Russians taking advantage of the East Coast, particularly the gang network and distribution channels along the 95 corridor? Or the West Coast, milking their South American cartel connections? "It hasn't been that many years since I left ATF. What am I missing? Why are the Russians doing it this way?"

Tommy twirled a pen between his fingers. "You've heard of old money and new money in the South?"

Sugar nodded.

"The Russians have had an influx of high-end investors since the fall of the Soviet Union, with many of them finding ways to work the free market. Every year since, their wealth and ability to amass it, albeit in questionable ways, has led them to search for the most favorable investments and offshore accounts. That pursuit of diversification and expanded portfolios has found their way to—"

"Moving guns up the middle of the US?" Sugar cut in, connecting the dots out loud.

"Using an established distribution network," the agent said.

"Mayhem motorcycle club."

The agent nodded. "That has charters all over the US, and in some places abroad. They took on something more akin to the opioid distribution line from the south. Cut out the cartels, the Irish, the other players who you'd expect to come from the coast lines, and you have a better rate of return."

"It's all about someone's retirement, huh?" Sugar let that sink in.

Tommy agreed. "When you have hundreds of millions or billions of dollars, and you can't yield the percentage you want, you look for new, lucrative revenue sources."

"These assholes don't care how it happens," Deacon said. "Then you have people like Ivan Mikhailov acting as a sort of hedge fund investor."

"He's the one involved with taking girls for partial payment." Sugar turned her attention to Deacon, and their waiting game started. He held the keys to making this rescue job safer for all involved.

"If you want your girl back," Deacon finally said, "I'll flag Mayhem to reschedule the buy for tonight. After every deal, Vashchenko and his men spend quality time with vodka and blowjobs. Any women they have locked down will be significantly less protected."

It was a double whammy. Sugar had accomplished her goal, getting Delta an easier opportunity to get Victoria out, but her stomach turned. They had to put guns on the streets. The weapons would be sold anyway. At least these were to save Victoria.

She turned to Marco, and he glared—not just at her or Deacon but the world. She knew he didn't buy into the greater good bullcrap. He didn't read the statistics or believe the handicapping numbers about how empowering one group over another would save more than it killed. Damn it to hell. This was one of the reasons why she was glad to get out of government. There was politics in everything—even saving people's lives.

CHAPTER FORTY

RYDER HAD MOVED to decaf coffee a couple hours ago, and he had long since turned off the TV and given up trying to read as he sat around the war room table. No matter which chair he sat in, he couldn't get comfortable. Sugar had left for her meeting with ATF twelve hours ago, and it was almost ten o'clock at night. He'd sleep on the table tonight and the next night, the night after that, and so on until she showed back up with details on Victoria or until somebody threw him out of the building with the bad news that there was nothing to be done.

The door bounced open, and Jared walked in, flanked by Brock and Sugar. Parker walked in behind them and shut the door as Ryder stood up with his eyebrows arching into his hair. "Good news I hope, yeah?" *That amount of time had to mean great news, plans, and logistics, deep and detailed intelligence.*

Jared took his seat in silence. Parker sat across from Ryder, and Sugar sat next to him.

"Hey, honey. Sorry it took me longer than I thought to shred them for everything I could."

Sugar being nice, and calling him honey made him nervous. "But you did, yeah?"

"Yeah, honey. I did."

Another honey. Ryder wished she'd spit out the information without the preamble.

Jared nodded at Parker who grabbed the remote to the flat screen, and schematics lit on the wall. "Thank you," Boss Man said. "The Russians and the Mayhem motorcycle club have a weapons purchase going down here. Bad news is, the place is covered with Russians armed to their teeth. The

MC isn't supposed to move the guns until after the sale, which was supposed to go down sometime next week."

Bile churned in Ryder's stomach. That many people covering a weapons depot would be all kinds of bad news. The girls would be collateral, and the weapons would likely have too many eyes on them. "If you tell me we have to wait until next week, she's gone or dead. You know that shit won't fly."

"I know," Sugar said.

"We're going in for her," Brock said.

"But Titan will also have to play."

"Two teams for an extraction?" Ryder rubbed a hand over his face. The more people involved in the job, the more opportunity for his teammates to get hurt. He didn't want to risk them, but he didn't care what resources were used to bring Victoria home. Damned if he did; damned if he didn't.

"This is the deal. Sugar has made arrangements for the weapons to be sold early—"

"What?" Ryder's head snapped to her. They were putting weapons on the streets in order to help Victoria? That seemed as though it fell within the two-wrongs-don't-make-a-right rule, and Titan would have a problem with that. Sugar sure as hell would. So did he. "We're going to help guns move? To whom?"

"That part isn't important right now," Jared said.

"Yeah, mate. It is kind of important. There has to be a way to help her and not do more harm." For as much as she meant to him, could he live with wondering if the nightly news reports about killing kids on street corners had anything to do with him?

"We're running short on options here, Ryder. You're going to have to trust me. Do you want your woman back?"

"What the hell kind of question is that? Of course I want her back." And that was the first time he'd publicly claimed her, to Titan, to himself, even to her. If she'd been here, it would've been a news flash. They hadn't worked out the semantics. But there wasn't really a question. All of Jared's relationship advice was null and void if Victoria ended up sold or in a body bag.

"Then you do as I say, and learn to trust me."

"Yes, sorry. I do trust you." Didn't he? Jared was the one who said that nothing could stand in the way between a man and his woman. But he wasn't without scruples.

"As I was saying, if some of the weapons move, all the manpower will also go. From there, it will be a simple extraction. I prefer to have you on the sniper rifle to take out anyone standing between her and freedom. If you're going to cause me a headache about that, I need to know now. And Brock can do some rearranging, but you're not the best man to pull her out of that building. You're the best man I have on a long gun's trigger."

Brock nodded in agreement. "There isn't anyone on Delta team I wouldn't trust to take a sniper shot. But Ryder, you're the best. It would be nothing but a selfish act to want to be the one who breaches that building. But brother, your woman, your call." Brock nodded again. "If you want to be the one who walks in there and brings her out, I won't stop you."

Ryder squeezed his eyes shut, and more than anything, he wanted to be the person who busted in the room that held Victoria, scooped her into his arms, and carried her out. But hell, this was why they had a team. This is why they were the best in the world and why he leaned on his brothers-in-arms. *Because of times like this.* "I'll stand sniper rifle. You send in who's best to do what's best. I trust Titan Group. I trust both of you with my life and hers."

"All right." Jared turned to Sugar. "Tell ATF, we are a go."

CHAPTER FORTY-ONE

VICTORIA CROSSED HER legs and recrossed them, trying to get rid of the pins and needles sensation she had long ago grown tired of. The section of the old barn she'd been locked in was hot. Sitting on concrete next to a few of the other girls, she knew they were all sweaty and hot. Her clothes stuck to her skin, but it was her limbs falling asleep that drove her the craziest.

"I am so hungry," Rosalie said from beside her. "And thirsty. It's so hot."

"Shhh," another woman hissed from farther down.

Victoria ignored the bitchy lady and patted Rosalie's knee. "The sun's going down, and everything will feel better soon."

"I'll still be hungry," she complained.

Her too, but saying that wouldn't help. "They'll throw us some food again. They did earlier."

The two men Victoria had watched from afar approached, unlocking a door in the chain-link fence cage, and tossed in a bag.

"Eat," one of them said, his accent thick and Russian.

The bitchy woman from earlier descended on the bag, and Victoria was going to make sure they each had an equal share of food. She had a bad feeling about the lady at the end.

The men rushed off. Before, they'd lingered, gawking. A prickle of excitement hung in the air. Rosalie handed her a bruised apple as she watched, waiting for any sign of what was to come—and then she saw it: more men arriving, their conversations quick and likely in Russian, and crates moved in past their cage.

She pushed against the metal wall, trying to see what they were doing.

But the deal was going down tonight. Finally, Victoria pushed away and saw the women watching her.

Rosalie's eyes trembled as she gnawed on a muffin. "What are they doing?"

"I don't know," she admitted. "Preparing for a sale of some type, I think."

"Great," the bitchy woman mumbled. "Two master's degrees and now this."

"I don't think we're for sale." *At least, not tonight*, but she didn't add that.

"Well, we're not stuck here for our own enjoyment."

"I came here looking for you," Victoria explained. "And someone will come looking for me."

The bitchy one tossed her hand. "My loved ones haven't found me, and I've been gone over a week."

"Same," Rosalie said. "Four days."

Others mumbled. Victoria would have stopped the downward spiral, but the distant rumble of motorcycles made her turn toward the wall. "Mayhem."

"Great. Bikers. Even better," the bitchy lady complained.

"Would you shut the hell up?" Victoria snapped at her then went back to staring at the wall facing where the bikers would pull in. She could almost see the pack of bikers, their leather cuts and hard faces ready to do business as they parked their bikes and strode off to meet the Russians. Last night's deal had been rescheduled for tonight.

Two of the men who had thrown food to them earlier quickly walked back with a wooden box. They strained under its weight, still rushing, and passed their cage without a word, running back to the front of the barn.

The entire deal took twenty minutes by Victoria's estimation, complete with name-calling, chest thumping, all around male-versus-male pissing contests. She wanted to roll her eyes at the uber-alpha showmanship unfolding behind the barn doors, but then money apparently exchanged hands, Mayhem backed in a vehicle, the stash was loaded, and the deal was done.

Motorcycles roared at they rolled away. Victoria wondered if Seven had noticed she was missing yet.

THE RUSSIANS WERE out of sight, but their celebratory cheers and congratulations were exuberant, more than Victoria would've thought for a simple deal, but what did she know? Big money was big money.

"They're drinking," the bitchy lady noted, though everyone could probably already figure that out. "Of course they are."

"Probably had a good day at work." Victoria walked over. "Are you going to be grumpy and snippy about everything? We're all in the same boat."

The lady rolled her eyes and moved to another area as the voices came toward their cage. Cold dread washed over Victoria. She was terrified that *they* were also part of the winnings.

The group walked past without looking over, and she gasped for a breath, backing up, her hands finding purchase on the wall before she could stop shaking.

"Are you okay?" Rosalie asked.

"I'm going to get us out of here." She had to. No question. No chances. Victoria came here to help them, and no way would she be hurt again.

The Russians cheered and what sounded like back-slapped from the back room. They came back, all smiles. Some puffed cigarettes. Some gulped vodka from the bottle.

What was back there? Victoria peered the opposite way from where the men went—just storage as far as she could tell. She turned to look the other direction, watching them praise the men who carried the box.

Had they shorted Mayhem?

No… That'd be a death sentence. Some gangs, maybe, yeah, that was the price of doing business. But not with Mayhem. She couldn't imagine they'd ever let a supplier rip them off with any kind of shipment, much less a weapons one.

The majority of the Russians acted as though they were leaving to the complaint of the younger ones—two, who likely had to keep watch over the cage of girls.

Victoria took a seat, wondering if she was reading it all wrong. Why would the Russians steal from the sale? To prove dominance? Make more money? Either way, they were celebrating now. Or nothing of the sort had happened, and the sale and the backroom cheers were two separate incidents.

Rosalie chitchatted for the next five minutes as Victoria answered, trying not to read into every little thing like it was the answer that could provide their escape. Both the remaining Russians' cell phones rang. Their semi-drunk, celebratory hellos changed to panicked questions, then rapid-fire, worried tones.

What were they saying? Even the other girls picked up on it.

"Something's going wrong, isn't it?" Rosalie asked.

Shit. "I think they shorted Mayhem in the sale."

"We're all going to die," the bitchy lady said.

"Would you shut up?" Rosalie screamed, shaking, and her face red.

"Easy." *Oh, easy, damn it.* That instantly reminded her of Ryder always telling her to calm down. "I'm going to get us out of this cage. We're going to walk out of here."

That time, the bitchy lady kept her bitchy comments inside, though even Victoria knew what she'd just said sounded nuts.

The chain-link fence was soldered to the bottom concrete floor and to the rebar above, but there was a window about the second- or third-floor level above. The gutter she'd fallen off was above the lone strip of grass, and everywhere else she remembered that might have a window was above a parking lot area or concrete strip. Jump or falling might sprain her leg, but that or even a break, she could handle.

Victoria tried to reach a notch in the wall to lift herself up to the barn's open framing but couldn't. "Rosalie, can you come here and help me up?"

"Are you insane?" she hissed.

"Probably." Victoria nodded. "But something's about to happen, and I have to get us out of here."

And now everyone was going to jump out a window. Her gazed tracked to the keys to the cage door's padlock. She'd seen the Russians use it to give their group food. But how would they walk out?

After they got outside, who knew what to do next? If Mayhem was coming back hot and the Russians were hauling backup in to defend what was theirs, this was about to be a gang war. All of this was a big guess, but she'd been in the game long enough and had grown up with a criminal as a father long enough to sense when things were stolen and about to get ugly.

She caught sight of the lighter, and her game plan formed. It would either work in a spectacular, maybe-gonna-die kind of way, or it wouldn't, which was fine because she didn't plan on dying. But if it didn't work, the Russians would send her to hell. "I'm going to unlock you then make it look like it's locked again."

Rosalie's face fell as her eyes rounded. "Why?"

"From in here, I'll go out the window—"

The bitchy lady scoffed. "You'll break your neck."

"Thank you for your optimism," Victoria said. "Once you hear them run out to check on things, you all *go*."

"No. No way," the bitchy woman in the corner snapped.

"Then you stay here." Rosalie put her hands on her hips. "If she thinks she can get us out of here, that's better than anybody else has done."

Victoria went over to the woman who'd been nothing but a bitch and knelt down. "I know you're terrified, and you don't know me from Jack."

"Don't try to psychoanalyze me."

"But this is the second time I've been locked up by these assholes." Victoria sucked in a breath, hating to admit that. "I don't know if that makes me the worst person to give advice or maybe the best, but I'm all you've got right now."

The bitchy lady seemed to listen.

Victoria continued, "I think some shit is about to go down. I have somewhat of a professional background in dealing with these guys."

"I know who you are," the lady said.

"Then you probably think getting caught by them once was one time too many."

She shook her head. "No. You can't outsmart evil."

Rosalie nodded her head. "That's the truth."

And that's something Victoria had never thought about before. "Okay."

"Do what you can," the woman said. "I support your efforts."

"Thank you," Victoria said, however much she didn't like how "your efforts" sounded. "Keys first."

The good thing about the chain-link fence was that it was very secure. She walked over and shook it. No rattle. After watching for the two men running around the front of the barn, she jumped up. "Here I go."

"WELL, THAT WAS a first." Ryder had successfully watched a Russian smuggler meet up with an American motorcycle gang, go into a barn, and apparently, come to an agreement. Then everyone went their merry ways.

The MC backed a black van into the barn, and minutes later, the men jumped on their bikes and escorted it out. The Russians had themselves a cheery toast, bottles up, after the MC blokes rolled away, and eventually, they climbed into their expensive Mercedes and sped away.

Everything went according to plan, as detailed by Sugar and the American government. What the hell they were thinking? Ryder didn't know. He didn't understand, and he was going to reserve his headache-inducing, screaming comments because Delta team had just let a motorcycle club run off with a cache of illegal, untraceable weapons without serial numbers that would probably be on the streets before dawn.

But at the same time, he had to ask the question, who the fuck cared? He was going to get his woman.

Stress pounded at his temples. The government had done it. Ryder didn't let them go. They did. They were approved. *Some kind of new world order. Or same world order. Fuck it.* He didn't get it.

What Ryder needed to do was concentrate. He had a go-to provide sniper cover for the team executing extraction, which was more than he thought he'd get, considering that he'd had recent head trauma and was personally involved with the high-risk target.

He pulled his night vision binoculars from their pouch and checked the landscape as the team moved into position. The circumstances were better than they'd hoped. Grayson was moving on one end as Colin secured a better vantage point for Ryder in case he needed a set of eyes from the south side. Luke and Trace were ready at the back, and Ryder had as near of a direct line of sight on the barn as possible.

One side of it was lined with work vehicles, and other than the occasional window, the scenery was drab. *Large but boring.* The property had many outbuildings and a silo, entrances and egresses, wild brush and maintained fields. In theory, it could be a logistical nightmare. But he was adequately pleased as he moved his rifle into place and resized the legs on the tripod.

"Still no thermals from inside?" Grayson asked.

"That's a negative," Parker reported from Titan HQ.

"What, do they have lead-lined walls?" Trace quipped.

"I suspect they're suffering from a case of the didn't-do-shit-itis," Parker said.

"Is that so?" Ryder mumbled.

"'Fraid so."

"I'll remember that," he said.

"Brother, so will I," Parker agreed.

Ryder dropped to his scope and dialed in then went back to his binoculars. "It looks like an old wood barn to me."

"That's what we're seeing on the ground," Luke agreed.

"Not very often does someone get on my shit list," Parker said. "But when they do..."

Minutes ticked by as they waited for Brock to make the call. Grayson would create a distraction. By their count, there were two Russians left on-site. He could subdue both, and Luke and Trace would find and release the women. Ryder was the eyes in the sky. Colin could be deployed to hit the barn at a moment's notice or feed Ryder actionable intel.

"Delta, all ears on," Brock broke in, requiring everyone to listen, and listen good.

"Sugar's contact just got a hold of her. They checked out their merch before they left but not all's in the shipment."

Ryder blinked, dumbfounded.

"Russians shorted Mayhem?" Parker regurgitated.

"Mayhem's of that opinion, yeah."

"Fuck," Trace growled.

"Parker, I need locations. Now," Brock ordered.

"They're gonna circle 'round, clocking in at a hundred miles an hour, if I had my guess," Trace continued, not helping Ryder's nerves.

"No one's there," Colin tossed out. "They're going to show up, find the two leftovers, kill 'em, take their stash—and fuck it, I don't know—leave the girls? They're not going to take the girls."

"They don't know who's in there," Javier said. "Mow the place down."

"Fuck," Ryder tried to keep his mind where it needed to be.

"Shut the fuck up," Brock snapped. "How far away?"

"Ten, fifteen minutes but there's no telling if they can knock a few minutes off of that. There is a lot of traffic on cell phones I've connected to the Russians. They've been tipped off."

"Are you pulling their locations?"

"Yeah," Parker grumbled. "Yeah, fuck. I have Mercedes coming from one direction, Harleys from another. Both are flying."

"Goddamn it," Brock growled.

Panic squeezed Ryder's heart.

"Sure as shit sounds like they're about to come to blows." Brock's voice steadied. "Get those girls out of there. Parker, get me a sat feed, and everyone else, gimme a position confirmation, or get your ass in place."

QUICKLY, VICTORIA SCALED the two stories worth of chain-link and crawled to the side toward the ductwork. There was an open section near the rebar where she needed to scoot through, and now that she got closer, it might have been a tiny bit smaller than she'd thought.

Shit.

She grabbed hold of one side and pressed her feet on the other, pushing and pulling with all of her might, hoping to God the rusted pieces of metal would have some bad pieces that gave. They didn't.

Shit, again.

Very high up, the angle gave a new perspective of their cage. She worked her way along the top edge, searching for a soft section of more pliable metal bars until she found the part not reinforced by rebar.

"We have a winner." She spread the steel wires apart from the edge of the chain-link fence edge. "Ow, shoot."

Victoria sucked her breath in pain as she tried to ignore the stab of the fence and began to descend the other side. The keys were freedom, and that pushed her to move faster, giving her a high. Finally, her feet touched the ground.

Everyone cheered in silence. Even the bitchy lady smiled.

Quickly, Victoria ducked down and ran to the key that hung on a chain from a nail. She paused long enough where the men kept their stash of cigarettes and lighters to take the cheap disposable and give it a flick to make sure the flame would jump. Then she made her way to the door of their prison cage and came back inside.

"Rcady to help me out?" she asked Rosalie.

"Your leg's bleeding."

"Is that going to keep you from boosting me to the window?"

Rosalie knotted her fingers together. "Let's go."

A minute later, Victoria used Rosalie's hand as a step stool, and Rosalie pushed her into the air. She caught the ledge, dangling to make sure it would hold her. After the last ordeal with the gutter, she felt less trusting. She swung her leg over to push off and reach up to the window. It was on an axle, and she was able to push halfway out and decided that jumping was going to hurt like hell but was the only escape. She ducked in for a quick second. "Give me a minute for the distraction."

"Which is what?" the bitchy lady asked.

Victoria had no idea, but it likely had something to do with the lighter she'd just snagged. "You'll know."

"I'll let you know," Rosalie told the bitchy lady in a tone that was a shade nicer than shut the hell up. She beamed, maybe on her own adrenaline high. "I always knew cheerleading would come in handy one day. I just didn't know it might save my life."

CHAPTER FORTY-TWO

"BOSS," COLIN INTERRUPTED as Brock almost finished ordering the operation a go. "Requesting additional assessment now."

"Hold up," Parker said on top of Colin.

"What in the bloody hell…" Ryder narrowed his eyes into his scope then grabbed his binoculars, tightening the focus. The night-vision-green image of a nightmare was taking place, and he threw them down, getting behind his trigger in case Victoria needed cover. Russians and Mayhem were going to be there within minutes. She wasn't just going to need cover. She needed an escape plan.

"Is your girl hanging out a goddamn window?" Locke questioned. "Parker, we might need info on the closest medical facility. Victoria's going to break her damn leg."

"Victoria's going to be filled with bullet holes if we can't get to her—"

"Javier, shut your face," Ryder snapped.

"Truth, dude."

"Three minutes for expected arrival," Parker added.

"Which one?" Ryder asked.

"Both."

"Awesome," Colin said.

"Luke, Trace, change of plans," Brock directed. "Northwest side of the building. HRT is on the move. Colin, get to Grayson. No one's alone."

"She's going to do it," Javier whispered.

Ryder switched back to his binoculars. Collectively, they stopped and watched for the seconds it took Victoria to drop the meters and crumple onto a parking lot.

Get up. Get up!

"She knocked out?" Trace asked.

Then she curled into a ball, pushing up. "No. She's good."

Damn it to hell. He loved that she wanted to save herself, but if she could just have given them a few more minutes, maybe she wouldn't have a shattered femur or something. Then again, she was smart. Maybe she had clued into signs that the Russian and MC deal had gone bad.

"We're on the move," Luke reported.

Where was she going to go? Victoria was going to either run into the fields, or she was going to run toward the road, down the parking lot, and out the driveway, which would be the safest bet. *Right or left, love. Right or left.*

She did neither. The woman sat upright, surveying the parking lot area and the line of vehicles, taking too long.

"Where are you, Grayson? Colin?" Brock barked.

"Not like this is a cute, little prairie barn." Colin's breath raced in his earpiece. "Big, long fucking work barn. And we're running through a muddy, fucking bog of shit."

"Literally, it's shit. I think," Grayson added.

Ryder ignored them and zoomed in his binoculars, trying to read the emotion and pain level on Victoria's face and didn't come up with anything that registered a medical report. What was going on with Victoria? Why wasn't she on the move? She ran forward.

"What's she doing?" Trace asked. "She just scooped a screwdriver."

"I have no goddamn idea," Ryder muttered with his heart in his throat. "Love, come on where you going? What are you doing?"

"Does she know how to hot-wire one of those old farm trucks?" Brock asked.

"Yeah, maybe." Ryder took the first breath in what felt like years.

She ran to the first pickup truck—and stopped.

"Get in the car," Ryder said out loud.

She pulled her arm back high overhead and slammed it into the side of the semi-rusted truck. Quick as she did that, she moved to the next Jeep Wrangler. Then she ran to the next work truck in the line.

"She's stabbing them?" Trace asked, bewildered.

At another work vehicle, she did the same thing—a stabbing motion—but it didn't work. Dread curled in his stomach. Victoria didn't do anything without a reason. Those were gas tanks. Each truck. Each SUV. She was immobilizing them? The second the Russians and Mayhem started shooting… this could be explosive.

"ETA, Colin," Brock asked quietly, clearly mesmerized by whatever Victoria was doing.

"Fifty yards to the corner," he reported, "then around the bend."

Parker, Javier, Trace, and Luke had a mixture of whispers ranging from "what's the point" to "smart girl." None of them had a clue why she was taking the time to drain those gas tanks. There were faster and more efficient ways to immobilize those vehicles. Spiking the tires could've done hella damage. Victoria was smart, and there was only one thing left to do with all that gas, but she didn't know that Delta surrounded the building.

"Pull back," Ryder warned. "We have to pull back."

"*What?*" Colin's surprise proved he couldn't see what Ryder could: Victoria and gasoline.

"A minute and a half for arrivals," Parker reported.

"We can hear the bikers hauling in the distance," Luke said.

"What do you want us to do?" Colin asked Brock.

Ryder stared as hard as he could through the binoculars at the row of cars and trucks and Victoria, transfixed in front of the creek of gasoline spurting from each vehicle.

"Abort," Brock ordered. "Back it up. Fast and now."

Victoria reached into her shirt, putting her hands between her breasts, and pulled out a lighter.

"No!" Ryder yelled, jumping up. "Don't do that!"

CHAPTER FORTY-THREE

THE OVERWHELMING STENCH of gasoline burned Victoria's nostrils. She saw the waves of fumes rising in the night. Truth be told, she had no idea if this would work. It was dangerous as all hell to start this fire, and she was putting her life in her hands over YouTube folklore.

But she'd heard that it was harder to light gasoline on fire but easy to light the fumes. It was either going to work, or she was going to explode alongside a dozen old trucks.

Nerves and anticipation tickled as apprehension made her worry. Perhaps she had gone overboard. Maybe one or two trucks would do the trick? But the goal was distraction, and all of the trucks were a huge distraction. It wasn't the time to be stingy. No do-overs.

Okay. Now, decision time. She turned, her ears certain they heard the rumble of motorcycles, lots of motorcycles. More certain than ever that the Russians had shorted Mayhem, she went back to the question at hand: did she try to ignite the fumes, the gas on the parking lot, or find a piece of trash or junk, light that on fire, and toss it into the fuel?

Why hadn't she spent more time on YouTube disaster videos?

Hell. Here goes nothing. She dropped down and put the lighter to the small river of gasoline. It took two flicks to get a flame. Maybe the first try, she'd been too nervous, but then she held it to the liquid and watched.

Fire.

It was almost beautiful as it skipped rapidly, almost benign looking. First, it was blue, and it spread, covering the top layer, yellow, red, orange, and white.

In her head, the whole thing should have become a raging flame that jumped high and, for some reason, loud. *But—whoa.*

The fire moved fast. Still skimming over the parking lot, it followed the fuel up to gas tanks. Black smoke started to plume. No longer was this beautiful. It was dangerous. It was a living, breathing disaster. She backed up and watched, terrified as the fire became flames. The licking lines of it started to shoot and jump. It'd taken seconds, but the heat was overwhelming.

The farm chemicals and items in the truck beds were on fire now, some smoking hot, others popping and sparking with mini-explosions. No telling what was in there to begin with. She took off, running away, feeling the soreness from the fall, worrying what might explode, unsure if a vehicle would explode. But the massive amount of accelerant was now unstoppable. The air was filled with the acrid smoke of burning metal and plastic. The wind around her was suddenly smoky and black. The heat of the fire traveled on the wind. She tripped, her head jarred and ears ringing.

Dizzy and discombobulated, she blinked, trying to get her bearings. She was on the ground. The sound of flames ravaging the vehicles tore through her senses. Victoria rolled on her side, ignoring the sting on her elbows and the sense of fresh blood from the cuts. She stumbled to a tractor on the side of the parking lot and ducked behind the giant ground-tilling blades as she watched the barn doors open and their two men run out with automatic weapons pointed toward the fire.

The flames raged, leaping taller than the barn as the two men paced the length of the building, shouting.

Rosalie ducked her head out the front of the barn door, not seeing Victoria or the men. She stood up, waving them on. Looking both ways, staring too long at the fire then deciding to move, Rosalie ran out the door, dragging the bitchy lady and the other women with her.

Goose bumps erupted all over Victoria's skin. *It worked.*

Motorcycles screeched down the farm's driveway. Headlights came from two opposite sides she knew were tractor paths but didn't expect the Russians to take in their Mercedes.

As long as the ladies saw what was happening, they would know to move from the front of the barn and stay low.

Russians came in from two sides and Mayhem from the top center.

Dear—please—God, let the girls have gone.

All the men rushed out, weapons drawn. Blood was about to be shed. Who knew if they'd be cordial enough to share a few words of explanation first? She leaned forward, oddly, maybe professionally, interested in how this would work.

"I usually watch from the sidelines, too."

The man's Russian-accented English startled her, and Victoria jumped, spinning around on her butt and fumbling backward.

"I… I, um." Vulnerable, on her bottom, weaponless, knew she could take him from this vantage. But damn, her leg was leaking a lot of blood, and she wished jumping out the window hadn't left her so sore—not to mention tripping and hitting her head. Okay, as long as she brought down her expectations, she could bring him down. "Please, don't," she begged, feeling around on the ground behind her for any kind of weapon. A stick. A rock. Another screwdriver someone had forgotten to put up would be nice.

No such luck.

"Do you know who I am?"

"Not uh," she intentionally stumbled over her words, though she didn't have a clue.

"My name is Yuri Vashchenko."

Her blood cooled, and all her rage and hatred focused on the man in front of her.

"And we've met before," he continued. "But you weren't awake."

She'd kill him—even as she bit her tongue. This was the bastard who gave her to Ivan Mikhailov as a gift.

Vashchenko gestured to the men in the heated discussion that she no longer cared about. "When I was your age, the thrill of it, that was interesting to me, yes. I liked to be involved. But sitting in my car, counting my money, that's of more interest to me now." He grinned like a sick dog. "And that you're going to make me money twice? I like that."

Victoria lunged up. He had more muscles than she expected, but that had never stopped her before. Her knee nailed him in the nuts, and the butt of her palm connected with his jaw as she pushed up, jabbing her elbow into a pressure point in his neck on the downward motion.

Unprepared, he fell back but didn't stagger away. He charged, roaring to life, swinging as she ducked, grabbing her hair and yanking her back. Victoria crushed her weight on to his insole and let him hold her hair, using his strength as a fulcrum as she pulled back and crashed onto his kneecap with both feet.

Stumbling, he went down, releasing her. She wanted his life, wanted to make sure he stopped selling women. Victoria dropped on top of him, wrenching his arm back. *Damn it!* He flipped her, but she twisted, crawling around his back, biting and clawing as he kicked.

She rounded his side and swung hard, punching his mouth and then clamped both hands on his throat. "You will *never* sell me or anyone else again."

His face turned red, his arms struggling. She had one pinned as his other flailed, and she couldn't shake her tunnel vision, couldn't get rid of Ivan's face in her memory, of him hurting her—then she blinked, pulled out of her trance and came face to face with the barrel of a gun.

"Let him go," the Russian ordered.

Maybe Vashchenko was already dead. She didn't care. "No."

The bastard cocked back and—fell over. *Dead.*

Stunned, she fell over, ducking from another unknown shooter, unsure what had happened, and saw that Vashchenko had a hole in his head too.

Gasping for breath, she stood upright, looking around and trying to figure out what in the hell was happening. Her guardian angel was somewhere nearby. That was the only thing that made sense. With as much of a deep breath as she could take, Victoria screamed, "Ryder."

CHAPTER FORTY-FOUR

By Victoria's count, there were more Russians dead than Mayhem. The whole place was a bloodbath, and she'd never seen anything like it. People joked about gang wars. They talked about it casually or in politics, but until someone saw the aftermath of what happened on this farm outside Sweet Hills, they didn't know. And she was pissed.

Was this something the mayor or the sheriff knew about?

Some kind of truce had been called. A meeting of the leadership was happening, and her very basic, civilian, non-gang, non-MC, non-trafficker world, it looked to Victoria as though Mayhem had won, and an agreement was on the table.

Now was apparently the time when each side gathered their bodies. What the hell kind of world did they live in? As the sun started to rise, her tears started to fall. Somewhere out there, Victoria was certain Ryder had been watching over her.

But yet, she was still here. They were still crawling all over the place, and there were two dead bodies within feet of her.

Someone whistled. "Up there."

She froze. Up there? Up *here?* What did that mean? "Oh, fuck." They were gathering bodies. She had two of them with her. Carefully, she moved from the turbine under the tractor, curling as small as she could and hiding behind the wheel.

The Russian came to the tractor, seeing one man, then the second, and cursed, confused. Both men looked as though they'd been killed by a sniper, unlike the bloody, pulpy masses that littered the parking lot.

He whistled, waving for another man to join him. They stood there for the longest minutes of her life, discussing the two men, crouching down to examine the gun she should've grabbed and the bullet holes in the face and back of head before calling up two more men.

Four Russians. Standing there. Feet away.

Victoria couldn't breathe as they examined the bodies, looked around, kicked the grass, even climbed onto the tractor before jumping down.

Her blood pounded in her ears. Despite the casual confusion, they seemed to handle the death of their friends. Or coworkers. They even had a few laughs as another man climbed into the tractor and, in his best American hillbilly accent, pretended to be a farmer.

Asshole.

Someone gestured for him to get down and for someone else to get the dead bodies. The asshole-wannabe farmer mumbled in Russian and—fell out of the tractor, landing on his hands and knees, opening his eyes to come face to face with Victoria. "Hello, pretty."

CHAPTER FORTY-FIVE

IF RYDER THOUGHT the last few hours had aged him, the last few seconds almost put him in an early grave.

Most of Delta team, minus Grayson and Colin who left with the women they'd rescued, had been glued in place for the last few hours watching everything unfold. There had been nothing to do short of walking into the melee, introducing themselves as there to collect their possession, and getting everything killed, except watch.

It. Had. Been. Hell.

And now, Ryder was dying slowly as the man yanked Victoria from under the tractor as Grayson and Colin radioed that they were back into position. His heart jumped as she was thrown like a rag doll, and Ryder caressed the trigger of his rifle, studying the man who had his hands on Victoria. He wanted to see his blood flow. This shot wasn't a calculated, emotionless job. Ryder wanted that to wear that death as a testament to what he would do for her. *Anything.*

"Let me take him out." He held his breath.

Russians and Mayhem both came to a standstill as the man led Victoria down the hill and threw her into the parking lot. The vehicle fires were burning themselves out, and the sun was coming out.

"That's a negative," Brock responded cautiously.

Ryder switched back and forth between normal and night vision, trying to see which one would give him the best picture of her state of mind. No matter which view he used, what he saw was tired and bloody.

One of the Mayhem members stepped forward, but not in a protective way. Ryder couldn't get a read on it. "What is going on?"

"Wait it out," Brock mumbled.

Ryder tried to come up with a good reason to hold back and failed. "Why the fuck would we do that?"

"We have orders."

He balked. "*Orders?*"

Brock gave Delta's orders. Hell, Jared did and took orders from no one. Ryder couldn't wrap his head around either man allowing Victoria to be yanked into a more vulnerable position without proper reinforcements.

"Can't get involved in their business."

"Boss," Ryder seethed. "She's *not* their business."

"She is right now."

"Fuck that."

"There's something bigger at play, Ryder. Shut your goddamn mouth and sit tight. I don't like this any better than you."

"What the hell does that mean?"

"If I could haul your ass in right now..." Brock muttered. "Listen up. The first and only time you get an explanation."

Ryder's head pounded. "Listening."

"We stay out of their beef because we have a partner that has requested we don't interfere with this play. Sorry your lady is in the middle of it. But even if I didn't give two fucks about a third-party request, if you start dropping bodies? She's dead. Victoria's in the crossfire."

Damn it, Brock was right. Ryder's headache intensified as he grew more helpless.

"We wait 'til we can get her—Make sense, bro? Anyone else have a brilliant fucking idea that won't get her killed?"

No one answered. His eyes sank shut.

"Soon as they break," Brock muttered. "We'll know who's taken possession of her."

To the victor go the spoils. Ryder dropped his head back as he realized that it was likely they were negotiating over who could keep her, what to do with her, knowing everything she'd seen.

Then the two groups started going their respective ways. Ryder held his breath as the last two leaders stood there with Victoria still on the ground. They shook hands, and the man in the leather reached down and yanked her up. *Not too nice. Not too mean. Not much of anything.*

"Our coverage in some spots is sketchy," Parker said, reminding them for the tenth time since setting up the temporary war room in Iowa.

They could go all over the world and not have a problem, but for some reason, communication was a serious headache on this job. Likely, it had nothing to do with Iowa and everything to do with the Russians and Mayhem's technology. Armed to the teeth and with their own surveillance and jammers, both gangs' tech scrambled theirs as well as each other's.

"Grayson, get ready to roll," Brock ordered.

"Already on it."

Ryder had done everything he could, protected her from afar, and now he came down to chasing after a van manned by Harley thugs. "I'm headed too."

He began to break down his station as he listened to the rest of the team to join the effort. *Delta team versus the MC.* They were going to have to physically free her without risking her life in a gunfight. After what he'd just witnessed, it was clear Mayhem didn't care if they spilled blood.

Ryder hustled and threw himself into the passenger seat of the idling SUV. Javier, Colin, and Luke took the back seats, bringing artillery with them. Mayhem's van and their escort of motorcycles were out of sight. Even with the windows down, they couldn't hear the throttle of Harley engines, and Grayson had been hauling ass to catch up as Parker directed them to the van he'd tagged.

"One hundred fifty feet ahead, hard right."

Ryder's eyes narrowed. There was no hard right. There was nothing.

"That's a negative," Grayson said. "No road."

The SUV slowed, and they pulled on to the shoulder as the occasional car passed in no man's land. There was nothing out here. Thick forest. A guardrail. That was it.

"Right ahead of you," Parker said.

Grayson and Ryder looked out both windows, shaking their heads, silently exchanging looks.

"That's impossible." Grayson parked. "There's no road. No nothing."

"I'm telling you..." Parker's annoyed voice bled through the overhead speaker. “I’ve got a tracker pinging. Now, not more than thirty-five feet.”

“Screw this.” Ryder pushed out the door. “If there’s a fucking road, I’ll find it.”

“What the fuck’s going on out there?” Brock snapped.

“Hard to explain,” Colin mumbled. “Might be better if you pull us up on the satellite imagery.”

That was the last thing Ryder heard from the SUV—nothing but lots of damn trees and a barrier rail. No access road. No place to turn. He hopped over the railing and stared into the thick forest. “Fuck!”

CHAPTER FORTY-SIX

EXHAUSTION HAD WIPED all sense of time from Victoria. Still, she had her survival instincts. After the initial shock, she'd gone into search-and-seize mode and mostly come up empty, except for the prize that she almost couldn't believe: a half-charged burner phone. Quickly, Victoria dialed Ryder's cell number from memory, and he picked up on the first ring.

"Ryder? Ryder? It's me," Victoria whispered into the phone that she had found, with her hand over her mouth, curled into the corner of the room at the Mayhem compound.

"Victoria."

The surprise and terror in his voice sliced through her heart. "I don't know where am. I found this phone."

"You found a phone?" He tried to hide his suspicion, but she shared it. *Too convenient. Too easy.*

"I don't care," she whispered. "I had to talk to you."

"That's fine. I'll have Titan start running a trace. Are you okay? Have they touched you?"

She shook her head, thinking about the disinterest that they had shown in her since the moment they dropped her in a corner. After a round of questioning and a discussion with a man she assumed was their club president, she had been unceremoniously dropped in this bedroom that smelled like sweat, sex, and dirty laundry. "It's not like that at all. They couldn't be any more disinterested in me. A bargaining chip for a rainy day maybe? But not right now." She squeezed her eyes tighter, wishing she done a thousand things differently. "I messed up. It took two life-altering screw-ups for me to learn a really hard lesson. I need to ask for help, and I don't know why I couldn't realize that beforehand." A sob caught in her voice. "I'm sorry."

"Easy," he hushed her. "You're talking to a lone wolf."

She hadn't thought of herself as a lone wolf, always surrounded by her community, always helping and trying to establish herself and her reputation, but he was right, just as Seven had been before. She liked that he understood. "I miss you."

"I miss you too, love."

She hung onto those words like they were his arms around her in bed back in Virginia when she'd needed him to feel safe and to forget about what happened in Russia. Now she knew them so well that she could imagine the contour of his chest and the slope of his chin as he tucked her safe into his embrace.

"Can I tell you a secret?" she whispered, gripping the phone like he might feel her handhold.

"We don't know much about this phone."

"Okay," she bit her lip nervously. "I wish you were here."

"I have a secret. It'll make you laugh. Want to hear it?"

She struggled with anxiousness over the unknown and tried to relax. "Yes."

"Butter."

"What?"

"Butter," he repeated.

"I don't understand."

"It's my secret ingredient." Ryder's low laugh came through the phone. "A little butter and coffee's like, whoa. Learned it back when I was a kid. Makes even the worst coffee the best."

It worked; she relaxed, smiled even as tears sprang. She couldn't wipe her grin away. "Ryder." Victoria clung to the phone. "I love you. I do. I can't explain that." The tears fell. "Butter. But God, I love you. Don't say anything. I know that's so much. In circumstances that are… so much."

She couldn't understand how she needed him when she'd never needed anyone before. She'd been able to take care of herself until Ryder showed up, yet Ryder showing up was what kept her sane. But that wasn't why she needed him right now—she loved him.

"I have every intention of setting you straight on how I feel when I see you, Victoria. But if you need to hear this now, love, *I love you.* And I will see you soon."

Everything was better. That she found so much comfort in a promise he had no ability to predict was insane, but her heart was overjoyed. Sniffling, she knew they were where they had to be for whatever awful reason. "I'll see you soon too."

"Do everything you can to stay safe," his voice dropped to a whisper, and with it, an almost desperate plea that she felt all the way to her soul. "Promise me, and I will see you soon, love."

"I promise."

An almost thankful breath of relief met her ear when he sighed—but it was cut short. "The phone's not giving much up on your location, but we're still working it."

She mumbled, "Expected as much."

Everything about this setup was suspicious. Finding a phone. A room that was dirty enough but free of weapons. Granted, they probably cleaned it out when she was coming in, but they wouldn't have left a phone, especially not a burner. Ryder was likely having these same thoughts. "No windows. No weapons. Motorcycle memorabilia, a bed, a burner phone in a drawer when I was going through everything, but no weapons, nothing."

"A phone and no weapons. Doesn't sound like any MC room that I can think of," Ryder grumbled. "Which means what…"

"That I have some help," she said, suddenly thinking of Lenora or even… "When's the last time you talked to Seven?"

"How'd you know I talked to Seven?"

"I assumed you would." Victoria focused back on the business at hand: getting the hell out of a Mayhem compound bedroom. "She knows Mayhem, and she knows who my local contacts are around here. This might be more of a local issue than anything else."

"What we saw last night wasn't something for a city council to take up, at least not your mayor."

True enough. She had no idea what was happening outside the incorporated limits of Sweet Hills. "Talk to Seven." She checked the battery. Half a charge, and no telling how old the phone was or how long it would hold the charge. "I probably need to hang up to save the battery."

"Okay, love. I'm coming for you. Don't do anything that could jeopardize your safety, but do what you need to."

"I will." Voices bled down the hall, and not wanting to worry him but needing to get off the phone, she said, "I'll be safe. Bye."

Victoria hung up, rushed to the dresser, replaced it, and slammed the drawer closed, throwing herself onto the mattress as the door swung open.

CHAPTER FORTY-SEVEN

RYDER THREW THE phone across the table and watched it slide until it stopped in front of Parker who never looked up from the wireless keyboard in front of him. He had arrived with Jared and Sugar sometime that morning after Ryder had some sleep. They were currently circled around a makeshift war room table in a local motel. There was a feeling something more was going on, especially with Boss Man and Sugar in Iowa, but no one from Delta was going to say a word as they nursed coffee and downed protein bars.

The small conference room door opened, and a few of Titan's main team walked in: Winters and Cash, which made sense if they were going to need backup. Winters knew Victoria, and Ryder and Cash did a lot of jobs together. But Roman walked in behind Cash, and if Roman was there, Ryder and Cash weren't partnered. Rocco, Bishop, Locke, and Jax.

He ran through everyone in the room, and with exception of the female operatives, Ryder was sure that all of Titan's main team had just walked in. What did that mean? Javier's eyes suspiciously watched the new activity while Luke and Trace kept their surprise more low-key. Grayson simply bumped fists with a couple of the guys. Colin drank coffee.

What the fuck was happening?

Parker stopped typing and grumbled. "Funny how the simplest, most basic technology is the biggest pain in the ass to crack." He stretched his arms overhead. "That burner phone's giving us nothing."

"What do we know?" Jared tossed down his phone and cracked an entire hand's worth of knuckles. Glaring at the silence, he shook his head. "Great. Nothing. No location. No weapons. No woman. No nothing."

"It sounds like petty, local bullshit," Colin mumbled.

"Except for the fact that it's not." Jared scowled. "You seen a bloodbath like that over petty and local?"

Colin shook his head.

"So what's the plan, Boss Man?" Sugar interrupted before he could go on a tear.

He looked his wife in the eye. "Find the girl and the guns, and take both back to where they need to be."

"That simple, huh?" She challenged him.

"You bet your ass, baby cakes."

Sugar raised an eyebrow. "CIA says don't touch those guns. Let them go."

"And you said that so that everyone in this room knows what the fuck we're getting into." He grabbed her chin, hauling her in for a kiss. "I owe you one."

"Like hell, baby," she said, eyes locked on Jared. "Get those weapons, and get them off the streets. No one in this room likes to play the CIA's farm boy games when they're warring with ATF. And Victoria?" Sugar leaned back. "You're telling me she helped a second set of women? Someone find that woman a halo because I'm already getting her a set of wings."

Ryder was able to contain the *hell yeah* brewing deep inside his chest.

Jared nodded. "Two teams. Two operations. Neither of which we have enough intelligence to make actionable. But we know our objectives."

Brock leaned back in his chair, shaking his head. "What do they want from her? She's local. Someone probably knows her. Nothing there but dirty laundry."

A quiet knock sounded before the door opened, and Seven's pink head popped in. "Hello? Oh, wow. There's a lot of you."

"Thanks for coming in." Brock stood as Jared did the same.

Both men could be intimidating. Ryder had to give them that, but Seven didn't seem to notice.

"Anything for my girl." She seemed more interested in the number of people in the room and hadn't yet walked away from the door. Her eyes landed on his. "Ryder. Hi."

Ryder decided to join Brock and Jared as they walked over to greet her, giving her a friendly face in the crowd. Introductions were made. Small talk wasn't so bad, and Seven stuck by his side, opting to take a seat next to him. Luke scooted over one to allow it.

Brock sat across from her, next to Parker, and all eyes were on Seven. Ryder had no idea if that was a good thing or not. Pink hair and piercings said attention seeking. Or did it say, strangers back the hell away? Either way, it said something.

"Seven," Brock said calmly. "We have two teams here. Both are personally vested in Victoria's safety."

"Personally because of Ryder?" She kept her eyes on Brock then turned her head to him and back to his boss.

"What Ryder does on his own time is his business." Brock pressed his lips together. "She's helped a lot of people out, some we were also trying to help, and we're in her debt."

"That's what she does," Seven said. "She's a giver. A fixer. One hundred percent other people before herself."

That part scared Ryder. "I think she has a solid self-preservation streak in her."

Seven nodded. "Only because it comes naturally. She's naturally a..."

"Warrior," he finished.

"Exactly," Seven said. "You know what you need about her. What do you need to know about Mayhem?"

After Seven answered every question they had, the response wasn't great, and she could likely tell. "I didn't bring new?"

"All news is helpful," Brock said.

"That's not what I meant." Seven let her tongue stud roll along her bottom lip. She leaned to face Jared. "What's the truth?"

Jared's face mirrored the same grim look as Parker's, and he was in agreement. "She's better off dead to them than she is alive."

CHAPTER FORTY-EIGHT

THE SCARRED, BLACK Mayhem bedroom door swung open, and Lenora strut through calm and casual as if it were any other day. Her demeanor could've been mistaken for lunchtime at the courthouse.

Victoria's eyes bulged. "What the fuck?"

Her shock wasn't just that the attorney stood there, seemingly of her own free will, but her clothes were far from the usual attorney wear. Lenora had ditched the power suits and conservative casual wear for torn jeans, a T-shirt with a torn V-neck, and bright red lipstick. Her hair was tossed into a makeshift bun and tendrils were pulled out in a windswept, back-of-a-Harley-hog way that screamed biker babe.

"This isn't a side of me I ever expected to introduce you to." Lenora's bright red lips turned up into an unimpressed grin. "You don't stay out of the way, do you?"

"*Who are you?*"

"Come on. Don't tell me you're the same girl at work as you are at home."

Well, yeah, she was. "You're their lawyer."

"Among other things." Lenora didn't hide her amusement. "Imagine my surprise when my man mentioned Victoria Massey had been won in a gunfight." She clucked. "Trouble finds you. Or maybe you go looking for it. Which is it?"

"The Russians had women. I decided that they shouldn't. End of story."

Lenora clapped slowly. "And *that's* the reason why I like you, kid."

God, she hated when people referenced her as young. But it wasn't as if she was in the best place to complain about that. "Since we're friends…"

Or something. “Does that mean I can get out of here?”

“I’m not sure that Hawk sees the value in letting go of a prize, but—” The door opened and two men walked in, one older who had serious disregard for Lenora’s personal space, and a younger man who lit a cigarette off of the butt of another cigarette. Could one of them be Hawk? What was going on?

The older man was wearing a Mayhem motorcycle cut. Victoria eyed his patch. Under the emblem read sergeant-at-arms. He greeted Victoria with a head nod. “Peaches.”

Exasperated, she crossed her arms, not caring if he had a leadership patch or not. “That isn’t my name.”

But he didn’t seem to notice that she spoke. Victoria couldn’t believe how Lenora was wrapped into this, and hell, did Seven know how Lenora was tied to Mayhem?

The older man whispered into her ear, and Lenora agreed with whatever he’d said. She turned to Victoria. “I gotta go.”

“Hey, wait. Get me the hell out of here.”

None of them acknowledged she’d spoken.

“Hey!”

They didn’t slow down, and the door locked behind Lenora.

“Bitch,” Victoria mumbled. “See if I ever help you again.”

CHAPTER FORTY-NINE

VICTORIA MAPPED OUT what she knew about her only potential ally. Lenora was a biker babe deep in the Mayhem world, involved in club business, and had a Mayhem man. She was an attorney who knowingly let them keep Victoria captive.

The situation was all kinds of screwed up, and the nerves in Victoria's stomach circled as she paced continual loops around the bedroom. How could she get out of the windowless room? There was nothing to pick the lock with, and waiting seemed to go on for hours on end.

The feminine click of heeled boots made its way down the hall. Fingers crossed it was Lenora, and they could finally wrap this up.

The door opened, and still, Victoria had a mental WTF reaction to Lenora's biker persona walking into the room. "Any news on when I get to go home?"

"My man came through with great news."

"I can leave?"

"Not quite." Lenora brushed by. "But I have an opportunity for you."

"No, thank you."

She bristled. "You don't even know what it is."

"I want to go home, Lenora. *That* would be great news."

Lenora tossed her hand. "The girls you helped free last night? They were taken by the same two men who grabbed you. The Russians' muscle has been busy lately."

How many others had there been? Hate wasn't a strong enough word for anyone who made a career out of abducting women to be trafficked. "What's the opportunity?"

The door opened again, and the two men from earlier walked in: Attorney, the sergeant-at-arms, and the smoker.

"Quite the Mayhem trio you three are."

The smoker let a puff curl with a choke of unexpected laughter while the older man's sun-aged, weathered brow tightened.

Unexpectedly, the bedroom door opened again. A woman about Victoria's age but with deep, brooding brown eyes that matched thick dark hair and a Latin complexion sauntered in, paying no attention to Victoria on the bed.

Funny how the interruption almost softened the old bastard in the leather vest with Mayhem insignia. Victoria eyed her. The woman was so casually beautiful in such an ugly place. Odd how eerily familiar she was since Victoria was sure she hadn't met her. She struggled to place the girl, coming up with nothing.

She didn't seem like she should be there. Yet with the jeans, tight shirt, and bandana pulling back her hair, she fit the part.

"Hawk says read this." The slightest hint of an American-washed Hispanic accent made the beauty that more exotic.

Lenora's man stepped forward and took the torn piece of paper. "Will do, Adelia. Move your ass."

"Bossy today, isn't he?" She gave a knowing glance to Lenora. It wasn't teasing or flirtatious, but caring… She was too young for him, much as Victoria would be, but the vibe wasn't that of an old hookup. Whatever the dynamic, she couldn't read that look to save her life.

"Don't talk to your Pops that way." Lenora eyed the ripped note more than the girl as she waved and left.

No one seemed interested in Adelia except Victoria, who made a conscious effort to pick her jaw off the filthy rug.

Pops.

There were a lot of questionable situations in the land of Mayhem, but she didn't expect their kids to be involved with abductions. Victoria couldn't wrap her mind around how Adelia appeared to look only ten years or so younger than the sergeant-at-arms.

Hell, maybe it was all a misunderstanding. After all, *old lady* was a term. Maybe pops was MC lingo.

Or maybe she was grasping at crazy ideas to make sense of what she didn't get—though that look she couldn't explain almost seemed like a teenager goading her father then a mother lecturing a daughter.

There was too much here that Victoria didn't understand. "Who was that?"

"My kid," he said nonchalantly.

The other man stubbed out a cigarette on the wall then put the butt in an ashtray, chuckling. At least he noticed that it seemed odd for a guy in his thirties to have a child in her twenties. But nothing further was said.

Instead, Victoria focused on the note. "Does Hawk think it's a good idea for me to leave?"

"You know Hawk?" the sergeant-at-arms asked.

Having said it out loud triggered the vague memory of Mayhem hierarchy, and Victoria knew that whatever was on that note, it had come from Mayhem's club president. "No. But I bet he wants me to leave."

"Sorry about your luck." He half-laughed, half-grumbled. "It says the Russians are having a pissing contest over their leadership."

Lenora's face pinched. "How does that affect my meeting?"

What was *her* meeting? Victoria bit her lip. Actually, who cared, as long as she could leave?

"It shouldn't change anything," the man growled. "Cool your tits."

Of all the things that she'd never expected to hear said to Lenora... *Wow.* Victoria couldn't tell by his voice if he was irritated, had smoked a few too many cartons of cigarettes this week, or if his concern level over the Russians' leadership scuffle was that aggravating. Lenora's face didn't give away the answer, and the other man was equally unreadable as he lit another smoke, sending a gray cloud toward the ceiling.

"It doesn't matter who they send. Nothing's going to change from our end. The statement has to be made."

Lenora jumped off the mattress. "Like hell. It matters who they send."

"A message is a message, whether the two you cherry-picked are there or not."

Venom danced in Lenora's eyes as they narrowed, and she took hard steps toward her man. "That wasn't the plan," she snapped. "I—"

"Nothing's changing right now. Club business ain't your business."

Lenora put her hands on her hips. "You are out of your goddamn mind if you think you're pulling 'club business ain't my business.' I had *one* request. Two men."

"I'm sure it will be two men," the sergeant-at-arms said.

"Specific men!" She slammed her index finger into his chest.

"Run your mouth to me." The man grasped her wrist, spinning Lenora into a chokehold as Victoria's eyes went wide. "And see what happens."

There were half a dozen evasive maneuvers to get out of that hold, but Lenora didn't try. She smiled and curled both her arms behind her head, wrapping around the man's neck. "Baby."

"Trying the cutesy crap," he groused.

What was happening? Victoria had no idea.

"You know I meant two specific men." She elbowed her man, and he snaked her to face him. "If you want to get rough with me, you wait till everyone's gone before you tear off my clothes."

His kissed down her neck, and Victoria looked away, unbelieving this was the attorney she knew. A minute later, Lenora flopped down on the bed as though she had been pushed, and Victoria snuck a peek to see a flushed-faced, lust-drunk woman who would probably rather no one else but her old man be in the room. This was the twilight zone.

"Two. Specific. Men." Lenora blew a kiss.

"I'll see what can be done." He crumbled the note into his pocket and sauntered out with the chain-smoker following behind.

When the door shut, Victoria gaped at Lenora as she dropped her head back with a lust – drunk grin hanging on her face she whispered, "And that's how it's done."

"Would you mind telling me what the fuck is going on?" Victoria said, exasperated. "If you won't, kindly lead me to somebody who will. I don't care who it is. Just bring me to somebody who can talk to me about what I need to know or let me leave. And Adelia? Tell me you two don't have a daughter ten years younger than you. I don't get that. I don't get anything!"

"That's the simplest thing here." Lenora rearranged a pillow that Victoria didn't want to touch and seemed ready to tell a story. "Club business does what club business does."

"Whatever that means," Victoria replied.

"Mayhem never touches women or children as a means to the end of earning a buck."

But guns, drugs, whatever else was okay. Yet, Victoria appreciated they had a code… of sorts. "Honorable, in their world." She left off, *I suppose.*

"It's in their rules, upheld by all charters, and, yes, whether you really do see how it's honorable or not, they have their own law."

"And Adelia was…" Victoria hated that the girl might've been trafficked or raped, and perhaps that was why she saw something familiar in her face that she couldn't place. Could she pick out other women who had been hurt like she had been?

Lenora scrunched the pillow and remained silent for several long minutes. Finally, she turned toward Victoria. "Do you think all people should operate under the same justice system?"

"That's an odd question coming from an attorney."

"Or maybe that's the best question coming from an attorney," Lenora mused. "I've seen it all. I know the system, the ins and the outs, who it best serves and most often fails. We both know how to make deals. We both know who never gets a second chance."

"Did Adelia get a second chance?" Victoria finally asked.

"She did and is one of the reasons Tex—that's my old man—takes awful personally."

"Because of Adelia."

"Not relevant to the meeting at hand today, but that girl, he found her on the market with a supplier south of the border right after he patched in." She gestured toward the ceiling. "First time he'd seen something like that. Mayhem does what Mayhem does, and that girl? She came home with him."

"As his daughter?"

"That's right. He's a good man—even when he was young, like you. Never had much family. Always held the burdens of others." Lenora's voice drifted as the respect for her man took her from the tiny room. "Bet he'll run the MC one day—but, again, not why I brought up a justice system outside the justice system."

"All right. Why?" Victoria pulled a strand of hair and wrapped it around her finger, dragging it across her face. It stunk like cigarettes, and she found it odd that she didn't notice until now. What else was she missing that was right in front of her face? "Why is Mayhem talking about Russian meetings in front of me?"

"You're a good investigator. I get why people trust you over Lee Marrow." Lenora chewed on her bottom lip. "Why weren't you an attorney?"

"Easy. Never went to college, and if I had, this would probably be my senior year. Or maybe last year. I don't know."

"You seem older than you are." Lenora flicked a piece of fuzz off the bed. "Very responsible and yet you're lying in a Mayhem bed with another woman."

She wrinkled her nose at the twist of a harmless situation. "That's the attorney in you, taking perfectly normal circumstances and making them sound awful."

"Speaking of normal circumstances that went awful..." Lenora flicked another piece of fuzz. "When we met at Sam's, I said it could've just as easily been me. We deal with the same folks professionally. You remember that conversation?"

"I do."

"Good. You need to know, it's time for justice."

Victoria propped up on an elbow. "Excuse me?"

"Today's the day," Lenora nonchalantly circled the air with a finger as though she were highlighting a date in her calendar. "For the club to enact their justice."

Lenora wanted specific people at a meeting... "You're talking about revenge against the Russians? For the trafficking? And for me?"

"It could easily have been me." She repeated that with a viciousness that Victoria felt deep in her chest. "Those two? Their job lately has been to grab girls. They got you, the women you saw at that farm."

"The meeting is a revenge hit." Did she even want revenge anymore? Ivan was impossible, and this... what did this do to help her?

"Mayhem is delivering a sentence. Simple."

Since Ivan had raped her and she'd been rescued, Victoria had focused on what she wanted to do in the future. She was done trying to prove her worthiness to her community as she had done because of her father since she was a little girl. But somewhere along this process of redemption, she realized that wasn't needed. No one was asking anything of her, and she didn't have a checklist or a burden to prove even to herself. As long as she could be happy and productive, she was fine. Maybe she wanted to do something more, like join the Rotary Club or volunteer on a city council committee because she enjoyed it, not to prove anything to anyone.

"Mayhem got a bad shipment from the Russians a few days ago. That's what triggered this shitstorm."

"Figured some of that out on my own," Victoria admitted.

"With new leadership, the Russians are concerned about shoring up their future business ventures with Mayhem."

"That's why they're meeting you? In good faith?"

"The criminal world is ugly and dangerous. You know this."

True. Why did she sound aghast that the MC was luring in the Russians? *Oh, because they were going to kill them. That whole two-wrongs-don't-make-a right mantra that was drilled into everyone since preschool…*

"Mayhem is sending a message about what we stand for and what we will not put up with. They were warned, and they didn't listen. There will be consequences."

"Lenora, you sound fucking insane," Victoria hissed.

She rolled her eyes. "Give me a break. Two criminal organizations with their own justice systems are doling out what needs to be done."

"You're a sworn officer of the law."

"Don't get all high and mighty on me. What happened to you in Russia will never see the inside of the courthouse, and you and I both know that. What happens between the Russians and Mayhem is governed by a set of rules and laws that you can't understand, but they can."

"What's going to happen?" Victoria asked even though she was almost certain she knew what the attorney was going to say.

"Vashchenko's already dead, so your two Russians with the grabby hands are going to die."

"Mine?" The hum of the air conditioning kicked on, and Victoria inched into the other woman's face. "The men who took me from the Ice House? You asked for them?"

"You bet your ass I did." Lenora's bright eyes held hers. "Justice is coming, whether you want it that way or not."

She couldn't say no, wouldn't say yes. "I'm not a judge and jury. You can't condemn people because of me."

Lenora sat up, pulling Victoria with her. "Honey, judge and jury are already done. Those two fucks are walking down death row as we speak."

"Someone's going to shoot them?"

Lenora shook her head. "The meeting is at the weapons cache. It's rigged to blow. Doors open, kaboom."

Victoria's heart jumped, and she hated the way her adrenaline mixed with anticipation. She didn't want to be happy over an execution. The confusion and guilt was almost too much to stand.

"Now, for why you're still here." Lenora's cheeks flushed with sadistic excitement. "I'm offering you the press of a button."

"Excuse me?"

"If you want to arm the system, it's yours. It's going to happen whether you do it or not. There's no question they're going to die." Lenora grasped both of Victoria's hands in hers and pulled her close. "If it was me, I'd do it. I'd get a cocktail. I'd find somebody to give me a cigarette, maybe even a joint, because I'd be celebrating."

"You're insane."

"Maybe. But I'd still have a little drink, press the little button, and know that I did it because of what they did to me." She squeezed Victoria's hands, almost hurting her. "But that's just me."

Lenora let go of her hands and stood up, brushing off her thighs as though she could swipe away all the germs in this room. Or maybe it was all of the sins and smoke clinging to her that she wanted to wipe away.

"I'm gonna find my man, figure out what's going on. When I come back, you give me your answer. Either way, no matter what you do, it will be done. After all of this is over, and we see each other again, you're the bounty hunter, and I'm the attorney. We will never talk about this. Do you understand?"

No fucking shit. "Obviously."

"What are you going to do?"

"I… don't know."

"Sure you do. Everyone knows. Whether they will admit it out loud, that's a different story, isn't it?"

That absolutely was. Did Victoria believe in justice outside of the justice system? She did.

CHAPTER FIFTY

THERE WERE SO many balls in the air. Ryder didn't know which one to focus on, so he chose the only one that mattered: his phone and the potential of Victoria calling back.

Delta team watched as Jared finished briefing Titan's main team. Boss Man was an attitude problem ready to explode. He was pissed about the weapons Mayhem had from the Russians and angrier that their intel said any number of local and federal agencies seemed to know about it and turned a blind eye. If there was one good thing about Titan Group, it was that they didn't often deal with bureaucratic bullshit, or at least that Ryder could see. Today, Boss Man decided that he wasn't dancing within the lines of those constraints. Titan was getting those guns.

As Ryder watched his phone, he also watched Seven. Actually, he watched Jax. The guy was a first-class dickhead, and there seemed to be a polar attraction pulling the unlikely coupling together. Jax leaned against the wall, foot propped up and arms crossed. Seven sat in a rolling chair, sliding back and forth. They didn't seem as though they were talking—more like a domino effect of conversational collisions had taken place. Jax had been a jackass, and Seven had volleyed his attitude firmly back. Ryder didn't think the guy saw a lot of rebuttals from women. He had a way about him that made asinine comments work in a way that seemed to make clothes mysteriously fall off.

Ryder rolled his eyes as Jared slapped the table and grabbed his phone. "All right. Location is confirmed. Let's secure those weapons."

Boss Man stood, and Titan's main team filed out, each slapping the doorway like they were heading into an arena for a football match. *One less ball in the air to focus on now.*

⊕

THE MAYHEM TRIO burst into Victoria's room, and she knew that this wasn't her get-out-of-jail moment. "What's wrong?"

Tex opened the dresser drawer and pulled out the phone, tossing it onto the bed. "Call your old man. Tell him to back down."

"What are you talking about?" Ryder was coming to get her?

"The guns stash. The company he works for is sending a team to get them."

Panic flooded her system. "Turn off the explosives!"

"There's no kill switch." He didn't seem the least concerned. "They're getting in the way of something they don't understand, thinking they're making a good play taking those weapons out of rotation—but they're wrong."

"No kill switch?" Her mind couldn't fathom the recklessness. Tex sounded reasonable, almost fair, and that was flat-out terrifying. "What kind of things is Mayhem moving? Shit!"

The two men exchanged glances. "The weapons the government won't acknowledge exist yet: magnetrons, sci-fi BS and IED-wannabe combustible crap." Tex ran his hand into his hair as if he were in awe of their capabilities. "I'd call your man and say, 'Back the fuckballs down,' peaches."

Her hands vibrated with rage and fear. Adrenaline. "Titan is going there? How do you know?"

"It's our job to know everything," the chain-smoker said.

"Call. Or not," Tex added. "I don't give a fuck. Deacon doesn't give a fuck. But Lenora does, and that's why you have your heads up."

Who was Deacon? The chain-smoker? He didn't react to the mention of the name. She shook with panic.

"Tick, tock, tick, tock," Lenora whispered. "Don't let them get there before kaboom."

Shit! Victoria lunged for the phone. Not much battery left as she hit redial for Ryder.

She prayed for him to pick up.

"Don't say anything that will tip them off. If they know what's going to happen, no telling who they'll tell, then this won't end well for you." Tex leaned close and growled then righted himself, showing the handgun tucked in his waistband. "Do I make myself clear, peaches?"

"Perfectly."

CHAPTER FIFTY-ONE

THE AIR CONDITIONING rattled, and some chairs squeaked. Titan Group's war room, this wasn't. But Ryder didn't care because it had everything Delta team needed: his teammates, Parker manning his keyboard, and all the technology Titan needed to set up a mobile operating center. Ryder had seen them pop up war rooms like this across the globe as often as he'd relied on an ear piece and a mic, yet his nerves were getting the better of him.

His cell phone rang, buzzing as the screen lit with an undisclosed number. With the approving eye from his boss and a go from Parker, Ryder swiped the screen and pressed the phone against his ear, praying it was Victoria with an update that Mayhem had simply released her. "Hello?"

"Hello, Ryder. It's me."

No such luck, he could tell by the sound of her voice that the situation was worse. Brow furrowing, Ryder ran his fingers into his hair as he shook his head, signaling to Brock no good news. "What's wrong, love?"

Parker pointed at Ryder. They had his phone tapped and could listen in via the phone system in the conference room. Parker counted down with his fingers. *Three, two, one* then he and Brock picked up handsets and listened into Ryder's call.

Ryder focused on Victoria and the out-of-place coolness in her greeting. Whatever her issue, her fear was serious and deadly. She didn't sound injured… but maybe trying to stifle panic.

"Listen to me. There's no time for discussion."

"Okay," he agreed.

"You have to back your team away from the Mayhem weapons."

"Wait, what?" Ryder's mind blanked.

Brock and Parker exchanged immediate glances. No one outside of this room and Titan's main team who was already on the move knew that they had decided to go after Mayhem's new stash of weapons. After what they'd witnessed between the Russians and Mayhem, Jared's decision was a simple one. No contract was needed. That was a greater good of society decision. Clean up the streets. Get the guns, the ammo, the goddamn bazookas—who knew what Mayhem purchased and planned to distribute?

Brock shook his head, cutting his hand over his neck like a knife.

Ryder understood. *Deny.* "I don't know what you're talking about."

"You have to stop it!" she demanded. "Now."

"Victoria, what're you talking about?"

"I said no discussion."

"*She knows,*" Brock mouthed.

How? But it didn't matter. Parker had a phone pressed to his ear and dropped his hands to his keyboard, fingers flying, likely trying to figure out the how. Or maybe better, why.

Brock rolled his hand, urging him to get more info. To do that, Ryder would have to admit to what was in place. The rest of the team leaned every which way to watch the three of them. Not even the air conditioning dared to rattle.

"Why would we try to stop that?" he asked.

"I can't say."

"One reason," he snapped. "One reason, love, why we'd walk away?"

The flat screen TV on the wall lit up with the main team's location on a live-image map of the middle of nowhere. They weren't more than a few clicks away from the target point. A tiny read-out in the corner of the screen announced that within ten minutes, the operational team would be on-site. They'd have their hands on those weapons, making the world a hell of a lot safer.

"I'm serious, Ryder!" she finally broke the silence. "Tell them to stand down."

Seven stood up, and Brock held his hand up as though he were stopping traffic. Brock pointed at her, at the chair that she came from, and gestured to sit her ass down—then he flagged Parker, who switched to Titan's comm system.

"Break, break, break, this is home base. Be advised, I repeat, be advised. Confirmation of hostile environment. Do you copy?" Parker kept his eyes on Brock who kept his gaze on Ryder.

"Got an affirmative from Winters," Parker relayed with a thumbs up.

Brock nodded, and Ryder took somewhat of a reassured breath. Still, not for nothing, Victoria was still on the line. "Love, you sound compromised as fuck."

"I'm not."

"Mayhem has a vested interest in not losing their merchandise. If you have a gun to your head, babe, spit it out—"

"God dammit, Ryder, back them off now. This is nothing more than revenge—"

The line went silent. Was she saying revenge? He couldn't be sure as Ryder stared at the blank cell phone screen of the ended call.

"What happened?" Brock demanded.

"Call cut," Parker volunteered. "Did it die? Or end?"

Ryder was at a loss. "I don't know."

"What the mother fuck is going on?" Brock growled.

"ETA, less than five minutes," Parker confirmed.

Ryder looked around the room as all of Delta team remained silent. Then there was Seven, her eyes imploring him to do something, and he didn't know what. "Seven, what is this? What's going on?"

Her pink-and-blue hair and eyebrow ring stood out in the row of men ready to go to war as she softly shook her head. "I have no idea."

His jaw ached from gnashing molars for hours on end. "You know everything about Mayhem—"

The softness abated, and she balked. "The hell I do."

The conference room door opened and slammed against the wall as Sugar stormed in, fury dripping in every leather-clad step. "ATF knows we're going after the guns? How the *fuck* does ATF know we're going after those guns?" She threw her arms out, dark pink fingernails acting like explosions in the air. "Can anyone answer me?"

No one said a peep, but everyone had to have thought, what the fuck? Mayhem knew. ATF knew.

"What the hell is going on?" Brock stood up, rubbing his temples. "What are we missing?"

"Three minutes out," Parker said.

"What don't I know?" Sugar's head snapped to him, her eyes narrowing as though she realized she'd walked into something.

"Mayhem knows we're coming. Now, ATF knows we're on a live op? We thought this was locked down airtight."

Sugar's jaw dropped before she snapped it shut. "Mayhem?"

"Victoria called Ryder. Direct request, abort mission now." Brock turned to Sugar. "Who was in the ATF meeting?"

"ATF, FBI, and friends." Sugar stood rigidly and appeared to be running her own mental what-the-fuck gymnastics, even as she kept her wording odd as if protecting a source.

"Sugar, cut the shit."

"Goddamn it, Brock." Sugar pointed at Seven. "Who is she?"

"A friend."

"Two and a half minutes," Parker said.

"Sugar," Brock snapped. "Is the CIA is involved with Mayhem? Now."

CIA? Ryder's mind spun.

Sugar glared at Seven, the lack of trust thick, and dropped her long, fake lashes to Brock. "Yes."

Seven didn't hide her audible gasp.

"CIA has moles in Mayhem." Sugar stepped closer to Brock, not taking an untrusting eye off Seven. "They're calling the shots."

"Bullshit," Seven said.

Shut up, Seven.

Sugar's glare was one of the best he'd ever seen. "Someone tell me exactly who sweet tits is?"

"Two minutes," Parker interrupted.

"Or." Sugar dropped her attention to Brock. "Let's focus on what I do know, which is what I don't. I *don't* know if CIA and ATF have talked. But let's assume obviously because ATF is pissed, and Mayhem was tipped off."

"In which case, we stay the course," Brock said.

"Or CIA doesn't want us to touch those guns. They found out we're on the move and are using Victoria to have us abort the mission."

Brock rubbed his temples. "ATF would've told us. If that was the deal, they'd have figured out what we were up to."

"Trust me. The points of contact on this at the CIA and ATF aren't on friendly terms. They have their panties in a wad over bureaucratic red tape."

"Minute-thirty," Parker announced.

"Ryder, thoughts?" Brock asked.

Neither of those explanations matched Victoria's voice. She was stressed and panicked. Ryder couldn't explain what wasn't tangible. Quickly, he caught Seven's gaze then looked at the faces of every one of his teammates.

Was he putting the woman he loved over the team? Over the mission objective? Was his judgment compromised? "The theories don't match her tone of voice."

Two deep lines formed over the bridge of Brock's nose. "You'd pull an op based on your girlfriend's tone of voice?"

"Forty-five seconds," Parker said.

Victoria was a warrior woman who wouldn't cave to a gang threatening her. "Yes. Kill the job."

Brock yanked his hand across his throat.

Parker radioed in, "Abort mission. Break, break, break. Titan, this is base. Abort mission. Pull back. Do you copy?"

All waited for a response. Parker remained intently listening.

"All operations have been aborted. Mission abort. Confirm. Titan, I need a WILCO."

Waiting on the 'will comply' response heaped pressure into the room. Nothing seemed to register as Parker typed on his keyboard.

"How do you copy?" Parker repeated in five-second bursts.

Ryder would've killed for a loud and clear at that moment.

"What's going on?" Sugar demanded.

Brock held up a hand for everyone to remain silent and calm.

"Radio silence," Parker said. "I've got nothing."

That wasn't unexpected. The team was set to go dark as they closed in.

"What the—" Parker switched the screen to a thermal satellite map, and the room's attention was pulled to the screen as a bright mark lit.

"What was that?" Seven asked.

She was the only one who asked because everyone else knew what an explosion looked like on a heat map.

The cooling color on the heat map did nobody any good. Still, Ryder couldn't focus anywhere else as tension continued its stranglehold. He had about as much control over his visceral reactions as anyone in the room. Blood pressure. Heart rate. Breath control. But still he struggled to maintain a clear head. Now it wasn't just Victoria that had his mind in tortured shambles. The radio silence from Titan's main team was deafening.

Once upon a time, Titan Group had lost an entire team to a helicopter crash. That was who Ryder had replaced. These things happened. *But not now. Not like this.* Not while they watched…

Sugar took a wary step toward the screen, the first time she'd moved in what seemed like years. He had never seen her scared, never seen Sugar without the tough-as-steel snark and sass that flowed as bright as the vivid pink on her slack lips.

"Titan, come in." Parker's requests never stopped. His voice echoed in Ryder's head on repeat for what felt like the millionth time. "Come in. Respond. Do you read?"

Silence except for the manic typing from the IT genius who was searching for information about an explosion in no man's land in the heart of America.

"Jax," Sugar spit out.

Ryder shifted his gaze to her. She was back to the hard-ass machine he was so familiar with.

Her jaw didn't move as she repeated, "Jax."

"Jax is with the team." Brock pulled his chair closer to the table, his eyes narrowing as he seemingly tried to guess her line of thought.

Ryder liked how Brock said *is* and not *was*. The simple verb tense gave a layer of reassurance that Ryder didn't want to let go of. Even with that, he tried to figure out what Sugar was talking about and came up with nothing. The way Sugar said his name—it was… accusatory.

"This is Jax's fault."

Parker didn't stop what he was doing, but his eyes tracked to Brock, and he let his confusion contort the already deep lines aging him. "What the hell are you talking about, Sugar?"

"Parker…" Sugar ignored Brock. "Where was Jax before he came to Titan? What wasn't in the file I saw?" Sugar walked behind Colin and but kept Brock's attention.

"Whatever you saw in the file, that's what was in the new recruitment file," he finally answered.

"What was in his goddamn file?" Sugar snapped.

Parker stopped typing, rolled his lips together, and shook his head. "I don't know what you're talking about."

Sugar spun on her heel. "Brock?"

"Chill. Parker's working on getting the team back online—"

"Assuming they're alive," Sugar said what no one had dared mentioned out loud.

"And," Brock continued, "a sat feed up. Let him work."

Her dark eyebrows arched. Telling Boss Man's wife no wasn't easy. Telling her no when it was Sugar was a thousand times harder, and double that when her husband was one of the men who wasn't coming back online.

None of Delta knew firsthand but all were well versed in the history between Jared, Brock, and Sugar. There had been problems of loyalty, safety, and friendship. For Brock to tell her to stand down could be dangerous, the repercussions of a civil war after Jared and Brock had made peace.

"Simple question: Tell me how is Jax connected to the CIA?" Sugar changed tactics, and Ryder didn't see that question coming.

Judging by a quick look around, neither did the rest of the room, except Parker and Brock. Both men kept poker faces. Jax and the CIA didn't sound as though they belonged in the same sentence. Seriously, the asshole was one of those irresponsible, couldn't-say-a-nice-thing Navy SEALs types, always looking for a fight.

"I can't," Brock said.

"Can't or won't?" Her smoky eyes narrowed into evil, lethal snake eyes.

Brock stood up, his chair shooting back from the table. "Stand down."

"Really?" She put her hands on her hips. "We have no comms, little visuals, and you're not even asking me why I want to know."

"Doesn't matter this second. So sit your ass down, or get the fuck out."

"I—"

"Those are your only options. I don't care about the who or how until I know if they're alive."

CHAPTER FIFTY-TWO

"IT'S DONE." TEX said.

Victoria watched the flashing box, the one that she didn't arm but hadn't protested when Lenora gleefully did, and felt peace. When Mayhem cut her call off with Ryder, tears had poured. She had never been more terrified that someone wouldn't listen to her in her entire life.

But it was Ryder. Despite the absurd ground rules Mayhem had set, not letting Delta know about the rigged explosions in case they wanted to be "save the day heroes" and help the bad guys in addition to clearing the weapons, Victoria knew that he'd make sure the right thing happened.

His team respected him. She'd conveyed what she could.

And now the Russians were dead.

Lenora lit her joint and took a long, slow pull from it, offering it to Victoria as she had a bottle of beer. Victoria graciously refused the joint as well.

"Feels good, doesn't it?" Lenora asked.

That two men had died? Would she admit to that out loud? "I'm glad they can't take anyone else and sell them."

Lenora rolled the edge of the burning tip along an ashtray, sculpting the red ember, then rolled the joint carefully in her fingers as she inspected her work. "I hope they burn first. Nice and slow."

Victoria did too. Maybe that didn't make her innocent or an angel. But she never claimed to be. "Maybe I'll take one hit."

Lenora passed her the joint. *When in Rome…*

SITTING IN THE motel conference room and staring at the same generic art pieces framed on the wall was almost more than Ryder could handle right now. But it was either that or stare at his phone, and Victoria hadn't called him back. He'd expected the phone would ring after they had proof of a blast detonation, but no, nothing.

Now that Sugar had been sitting next to him for the last five minutes, her tension and worry bleeding into the air around her, Ryder was hanging on by an imaginary thread that had wrapped itself around his neck and was pulling tighter and tighter with every breath.

Sugar's high heel tapped under the table on the carpeted floor. The beat began to line up with the questions in his mind.

Where was Victoria?

Why hadn't she called?

Was she safe?

"I'm getting sick of this shit." Ryder jumped out of his seat, surprising himself as the tension became too much to contain.

He rolled his shoulders back, pretending he'd planned to stretch when he'd surprised himself and made his way over to a pile of protein bars on a side table. He grabbed one, even though he had no intention of opening it.

Everyone's stares dug into his back, but the only one he couldn't feel was Seven. She was the person he needed to talk to the most. Making his way quickly across the conference room, Ryder shoved the protein bar in his pocket and asked, "Where is she?"

"You think I wouldn't have mentioned that by now?" Seven's chin pushed up defiantly.

"You know everything about Mayhem that the feds can't tell us."

"So?"

"You know what kind of cigarette butts are lying on the floor. Who's sleeping with who. Think, Seven, where do they have her?"

Seven's tongue stud pushed between her lips, running back and forth. "Still don't know anything new." But her gaze dropped to the side.

Seven did know something she hadn't shared. What the hell? "Spit it out. She's your best friend."

"You think I don't know that? I called you!"

"Why're you holding back?" Ryder shook his head, frustrated more than he could explain. "But is there a single good reason to keep your mouth wrapped around that damn tongue stud instead of telling me why you keep staring at the floor?"

"I don't—"

"Yes! You do!" he yelled.

"I only wanted to give you facts! It's an urban legend. I've never seen it." Her pierced brows arched. "I don't know anybody who's seen it, much less admitted to going there. Wherever there is. There is no there."

Ryder threw his hands in the air. "Just tell us."

"Tell you what? Mythical motorcycle drunken bullshit?" she yelled back.

"Yes! Anything and everything."

Her lips pressed together, half-cocked. "If I told you everything and anything I'd ever heard about these guys, you would be sifting through so much crap you'd never find her. Give me a break. Okay?"

"No."

"It's an imaginary place that goes along with all the rather boisterous bullshit."

He paced. "There's a difference between guys telling tales about getting laid and talk of a location."

That seemed to register.

"Where is it? What do you know?"

Her tongue stud ran along her lip again. "They call it Devil's Backbone, say it's in 'bullet country,' past the gorge, and you can't even take one of their vans back there. Accessible by bike only."

Ryder spun to Parker, his eyes wide and imploring, asking if that was enough to find a location somewhere in Iowa. If anybody could do it, Parker could, but Seven was right. That wasn't a lot to go on. *Folklore and local vernacular.*

"See, how do you even build a compound when you can't get a truck back there much less, I don't know, a bulldozer or something?"

"That doesn't matter." Parker typed. "They could easily close off a passageway after the fact."

"Well…" she mumbled.

"Not critiquing, just saying," he followed up.

"Like I said, I don't know anyone who'll admit to being there."

The speakers cracked and squawked. White noise garbled into the conference room. "Trying again—for fuck's sake." The speakers squealed, but the room held its breath as Winters's voice bled into the static.

One person accounted for. Everyone waited for more. Parker grabbed the speakerphone set, looping in the comm system for everyone to hear. "Winters, we read you. What's your status? Over."

"Everyone is safe and accounted for, minus one comm system." Winters laughed, and the room cheered.

"About damn time for good news," Brock said.

Sugar gripped the sides of her chair, muttered what looked to be a prayer. Then she stood and clapped, joining in with the rest of the raucous happiness.

"We read you," Parker said. "Glad to have you back online."

"For the most part, I've got this shit kinda working."

The room calmed, and a huge weight lifted off of Ryder's shoulders.

Static and white noise returned, squawking into the speaker again. "—Headed to—civilization—cell phones—"

Brock ran his hands flat back and forth over the table in front of him. "Suffice it to say, when they get somewhere where they can pick up a phone, they'll call in." He pressed his hands together and turned his head toward Ryder. "We'll get the details when we debrief, but it seems as though Victoria and Mayhem might've saved their asses by a hair."

"Was close enough, with enough reverb or interference to burn out their comms," Parker said in agreement.

"Now we're calling them good guys?" Javier stood up, pushing away from the table as though somehow angrier than before. "I'm gonna hit the head. Be back."

As Javier stormed out, Ryder tried to make heads and tails of that, the complicated situation with Mayhem, and Sugar's questions about Jax.

"I've got something," Parker said.

On the flat screen, a dated architecture drawing labeled "Schoolhouse" replaced the cooled heat map.

"You think Mayhem overtook some old classrooms," Colin snickered. "Someone would probably notice if they had Victoria trapped in kindergarten."

"Take a closer look, jackass," Parker said.

The screen zoomed in on what looked like the row of classrooms. They were adjacent to a larger section with other large rooms off the other side. "Use your brains, and tell me what's not right."

"The square footage," Trace muttered and then leaned back in his chair as the rest of the room leaned forward.

"Ding, ding, we have a winner," Parker said.

Each room that was set up in a style that looked like a classroom if you assumed the drawing labeled as a school was correct, except it was only about the size of a bedroom.

"Devil's Backbone," Seven whispered as if in awe of the mythical folklore that had been found. "Holy shit."

The speakers crackled and cleared, then Winters sounded, clearing his throat, "Let's try this: testing, testing, one, two."

"We hear you better, brother." Brock said. "Give me a confirmation. Is anybody hurt?"

"No, just a day of travel to witness some fireworks. And I've gotta tell you, impressive ones at that," Winters said.

If he was giving the rigging a thumbs-up, that said something since Colby Winters was Titan Group's go-to demolition and explosives guy.

"I hate to be impressed with something that almost cooked me," Winters chuckled. "But that was some solid shit. Would've appreciated the abort call, I don't know, a little earlier. But a little heat felt good under the summer sun."

In the background, sarcastic laughs and jabs were exchanged, and Ryder knew they were coming off the adrenaline high of the op. He watched Parker and Brock exchange glances, expertly communicating without saying a word. It was impressive, and Ryder hoped to God the next words out of his mouth had something to do with Victoria.

"Get Boss Man on the line," Brock ordered.

A jumbled, crackling minute later, Jared grumbled, "You'd better hope

Sugar doesn't find out how close that was."

"She did," Sugar snapped.

"Baby Cakes, bite no one's head off."

"I bite whatever the fuck I want to bite, Jared," Sugar snipped.

Boss Man chuckled. "Take it out on me later. I'll be ready for you."

That seemed to calm his wife down, and Ryder found the whole thing far too much info and still endearing. Damn, he needed Victoria in his arms.

"What's up, Brock?" Jared asked.

"The team's geared up. Nothing to do." The flat-screen TV switched to a new map with an approximate location for where Titan had been and where Devil's Backbone was located. "Feel like being rerouted?"

"My itchy trigger finger never even got a chance today, so that'd be a hell yeah."

Ryder stepped toward Brock. "If they're going, I want in." He wanted to be there. Hell, he *needed* to be there. "We're closer. Titan can be back up." Ryder spun back to the map and then pivoted to his boss. "We mobilize first and wait. You can't sideline me while someone else gets my girl. It's fucked up."

Javier came back into the room, glancing around. "What's up?"

"The team's back online. Everybody's fine, and they're going in to go get Victoria." Ryder crossed his arms, chewing the inside of his cheeks while he waited on Brock to make the right decision. "I want Delta to get in there first, and the other guys can be back up."

Javier stopped and leaned against the wall, shaking his head and rubbing his hand over his face.

"What's that look for?" Ryder flexed his fists against his folded arms, trying to hide his irritation at Javier's apparent hesitation.

His teammate dropped his hand. "Don't read that wrong, I'm not saying don't go after Victoria."

"Then you're saying what?" Ryder stared at Javier's revenge tattoo and knew there was no way the tatted-up street fighter would try to justify anything other than what Ryder had suggested.

Javier didn't just hate human trafficking—how women and girls were pimped and prostituted in a theoretical sense. He'd been personally affected like Ryder and others in the room. REVENGE stood out loud against the guy's skin as an inked reminder. What reluctance could he possibly have?

"Just like the Russians, these Mayhem fucks..." Javier scrubbed his hands over his face again. "I just walked out of here so I wouldn't tear this room apart."

Ryder knew there was a rage always boiling under Javier's skin. Brock let him take off to box or fight whenever he needed to take the edge off.

His dark, Brazilian complexion flushed as Javier paced. "I came back, and it's still there. These assholes want to sell women. They want to sell them the way they sell their drugs and their guns?" He stopped, shaking his dark hair. "I say we blow Mayhem sky-high like they tried knock off our boys."

He pushed past Ryder to Brock, with that same hatred Delta saw surface any time a reminder of his history came into play. A sister sold into the sex trade. A mother who was a junkie. A father who was nothing more than a pimp and gambler. Trafficking jobs made Javier rage like they made Luke worry over Maddy and haunted Ryder over Zoe. The world was an evil, evil place.

"Boss," Javier's low voice rumbled. "We scorch their world and get Victoria."

"Scorch their world?" Seven questioned quietly, trembling.

"Scorch it," Javier reaffirmed.

"What are we gonna do?" Ryder asked.

Brock looked at Seven, Ryder, and Javier. "Get your gear. Let's end this."

CHAPTER FIFTY-THREE

THE TIME FOR celebration and joint-smoking pleasantries was over. Even if Victoria would claim she never inhaled, Lenora definitely had. But that had come and gone, and the hope Victoria had Mayhem would let her go had faded now that she was back in the small compound bedroom. It seemed as though it was getting smaller, and she was positive that she hadn't so much as got a contact high from the weed that'd been passed around the room.

Victoria paced a U-shaped path around the unmade bed more times than she cared to count. After checking the cell phone's clock once, twice, and then a dozen times, she had given up tracking how long she waited for Lenora or anyone from Mayhem to come back.

The door handle jangled, and there was Lenora with her old man, Tex. Tex held his phone along with a pack of cigarettes in his hand, staying silent as Lenora greeted her.

"Why can't I leave?" Victoria asked, having no time for pleasantries, hellos, and whatever else she might have said.

The door opened again, remaining ajar, and the smoker from earlier joined them with a fast food bag stained with grease marks. Victoria's heart sank at the offer of food because it meant she might not be leaving anytime soon.

The smoker put the bag on the dresser with a grunt after she shooed away his offer.

"You can leave."

"Great," Victoria headed toward the door, but the quick hand of the chain-smoker stopped her.

"But." Lenora shrugged her shoulders nonchalantly as though Victoria wasn't locked in a room. "First, you have to help us with something else."

Always a catch. Whether the woman had her attorney hat on, or she was acting as an MC old lady, apparently, there was always a fucking catch. "What's that?"

"Everything happens for a reason, and you ended up here. That's better for everyone than my request for you to ignore those MC bounties."

Victoria's mind raced back to Sam's deli, where Lenora had asked her to ignore the two men that had never even raised her attention. "Why?"

"Go pick them up. They never meant to miss their hearings—"

"I'm bringing them in now?" Victoria asked, confused.

"Then I'll defend them," Lenora said. "You'll get paid. End of story."

"That's it?" Of course, that wasn't it, Mayhem was up to something, and Lenora was neck deep in corruption, lies, and motorcycle gang bullshit. But it wasn't as if Victoria was in a great position to point that out.

"As far as you're concerned, yes, that's it."

"But it makes no sense."

Lenora tilted her head, giving it a quick nod. "How much do you want to know, Buttercup? The choice is yours: ignorance versus club business."

Ugh, club business. That wasn't a good topic to be well versed in. But she was already mixed in deep. "I'm not doing anything unless I know everything."

Lenora looked over her shoulder at Tex, and he nodded to the smoker, who took a half step closer to the door and shouted, "Adelia, get your sweet ass in here."

"Club business it is then." Lenora inched back toward her man and squeezed under his arm.

Tex's daughter walked in. "You shouted." She smiled at her father and flicked the smoker off with both middle fingers. "Asshole."

"Here she is," Lenora said as though Victoria hadn't seen the woman before. "Club business."

Adelia was club business. "And I'm going to bring in those two because of her? Again, makes no sense."

"I need to send a message to someone on the inside, and the only way to do that is if they get put back into the system," Adelia explained.

Boom.

The bedroom walls that had been closing in on Victoria shook as an explosion echoed from somewhere far away.

"Goddamn retaliating Russians." Tex pushed Lenora toward Victoria. "Woman, stay here. You two, let's go end this shit. I want bodies dropped."

CHAPTER FIFTY-FOUR

THE DIVERSIONARY EXPLOSION echoed with enough reverb that Ryder was certain Winters was making up for a morning of blasts.

"You're a go," Brock said in Ryder's earpiece.

Grayson stood across from him and Javier behind him. Colin, Luke, and Trace were broadside and opposite Titan who was on the backside of the compound and responsible for the diversionary blast. Grayson slammed the battering ram, and the heavy door splintered off its hinges.

Ryder moved high left as Javier ducked low and right. Their assault rifles were drawn and set to rock 'n' roll, pointed to kill. They were ready for a gunfight, weapons strapped to hips and limbs, knives and extra rounds tucked wherever. They were ready for a full-force defense assault as they entered, even if Titan had lured Mayhem to the other side of the compound as Delta's team, split in two, entered on this side.

Grayson surged forward and moved for cover. "Delta two, in."

"Delta one, inside and moving," Colin reported.

Javier moved behind a pool table, and Grayson jumped behind a bar as Ryder moved broadside. There was a motorcycle standing on a raised platform. Framed mug shots decorated the wall behind it.

"Clear," Colin reported.

"Clear," Grayson did the same.

According to the plans that they had, Delta one should be moving down a hallway that likely led to or three meeting rooms. Both areas intersected and led to what he assumed were bedrooms. Titan's main team would stay behind the compound.

"We have tangos," Colin added.

His report met echoed Delta gunfire. Their silenced handguns echoed as *pew, pew, pew* from far away, mixing with the loud explosions of an inhibited shotgun and handgun shots.

"Hallway," Ryder directed as two men ran into the room, jerking back as they saw Grayson raise his weapon.

"Stand down. Drop your weapon. Drop your goddamn gun," Grayson shouted, taking an offensive position.

Javier moved in from one side, and Ryder moved in from the other. They had the two men from three points, nowhere to go, and—

A woman slammed into the older man's back. It wasn't Victoria. Ryder assessed her. *Threat? In danger? Armed? Trying to escape?*

The man yanked her to his chest and shoved the barrel of his gun to her temple. "Get the fuck out of my clubhouse."

"Stand down," Grayson ordered again. "We do not want to hurt your women."

"She's dead. Dead. Get out."

"Drop your gun," Ryder tried.

They moved closer, and the other man pulled his weapon on her too. *Fucking hell.* "You shoot him, I still kill the bitch."

She whimpered.

Damn it. They stopped their approach as if sensing escalation wasn't the right move.

"Get out of my clubhouse," the older man shouted.

Then the woman yelled, jabbing and rolling against the man's chest. A blur of activity spun between the two men, and Ryder focused on her, trying to keep her in his sights and his weapon aimed on the older man.

She pulled free, gun in hand.

The two men moved to defensive positions. *No! Offensive.* Grayson ducked and rolled, his weapon close to his chest but no longer on his targets. Ryder and Javier moved in.

"Drop your weapons—" Ryder gaped, stunned. What was going on?

The woman pointed the gun at him. She stood side-by-side with Mayhem, armed, as Delta to moved into defense.

Javier cursed, Ryder never saw it coming, and Grayson grunted as he dove for better cover. They had fallen for bullshit tricks.

Gunfire rained toward the bar where Grayson lay.

The old man fired shot after shot after shot, and Javier and Ryder fired back as the other two let loose their rounds. The woman fired at Javier, and Ryder aimed at the younger man, both picking their shots.

The scent of gunfire and sparks of bullets ricocheting and blasting through barriers added to the chaos.

"We don't want a fight," Ryder shouted. "I want my girl."

A momentary cease-fire dangled between the six of them, and the older man grumbled about not trusting Russians.

"Do I look like a goddamn Russian?" Javier said, letting loose a string of Brazilian Portuguese.

Goddammit. Where was Victoria?

The tense silence remained, and Ryder inched out for a better look—but it was Javier he glanced at and couldn't look away from. The out-of-place confusion marring his face settled Ryder.

Javier stepped from cover. "Keep your weapons down."

What the fuck was he doing? Javier kept going, moving too far from the safety of his protective position. His automatic weapon hung by his side, barrel pointed boots-down. His shooting hand didn't hover near his sidearm.

Ryder's pulse raced as Javier walked slowly toward the center of the shot-up room. Grayson's eyes met his. Neither knew what to do or what was happening. They both needed to pull Javier back. Mayhem thought they were Russians. He wasn't even moving to the old man in charge but toward the woman. This wasn't helping get Victoria back.

Ten feet separated them then five.

"Stay back," she ordered, pulling her gun up, cocking the hammer. "Back!"

"Adelia?" Javier whispered.

Ryder's blood ran cold. He was certain he had misheard, or maybe he was hallucinating because nothing made sense.

"Who the fuck are you?" Her voice trembled as much as the gun in her hand.

Everyone studied them. Dark hair. Dark eyes. Same chin. Javier was muscled and covered in tactical gear. She was clad in motorcycle jeans, cotton, and leather. But the resemblance was awesome, if there was ever a chance to use that word.

Javier reached forward, pushing her gun, and buried her into his Kevlar-covered chest for a hug. Her gun clattered to the concrete floor, and then the muffled, feminine sob shook Ryder's world.

No one spoke except Javier.

"You're alive." His native tongue flowed, and she sobbed as he held her, not letting go. "I should never have stopped believing that you were alive."

Eternity passed as they stood in near reverence at the reunion.

"Victoria's in the back room," the older man quietly said, pointing down the hallway. "I'd announce myself before I barged in. There's no telling with the woman she's with."

Ryder tore himself away from Javier and was on the move, leaving Grayson to figure out whatever was going on with Javier as Brock's conversations started fast in his ear. Ryder tuned everyone out as he carefully swept his gaze back and forth, not trusting Mayhem to be without other members ready to jump from the rafters, guns blazing.

He came to the row of bedrooms and banged on the first couple doors. "Victoria! Victoria, where are you?"

He was so far past the point of sly, surprise arrivals. If there was a problem coming from his backside, he was entrusting that Delta would keep him safe, and God help anyone between him and his woman.

The door at the end of the hall opened, and there she was. One of those life-flashing-before-his-eyes moments happened.

He always thought those happened right before he died. But apparently it happened right before he lived.

Ryder sprinted forward, the short distance gone in a few strides, and he wrapped her in his arms and close to his chest. He could finally breathe, and when he put her on her own two feet, letting their bodies stay together, their faces stayed cheek to cheek until their lips pressed together, and he kissed her. Nothing mattered as much as this woman.

Finally, he pulled away, stroking her hair, her face, unable to stop touching Victoria. “I love you. God, I love you.”

“I love you too.” She wrapped her arms back around his neck and held on tightly.

There were a thousand ways to fall in love, dozens of ways to have a family, more ways than he would ever know to be centered, to find an anchor, and to know his purpose. Victoria was all of it. There was only one of her. Every experience and person he’d ever been lucky enough to know had been preparing him to run down the hall to her.

CHAPTER FIFTY-FIVE

Two Months Later

THE NEW COMFORTER looked better on her bed than her old one, and Victoria liked the art on the wall too. The little touches here and there weren't a lot. But they were very Ryder. It was interesting that he didn't have a real home. He'd never had a real home: an orphanage, military housing, then rentals that Titan Group had arranged for—but nothing that was really his.

Victoria hadn't expected his excitement level when she'd asked if he wanted to pick out decorations for her house. Their house? Their house. She smiled, loving that they were in bed together, no matter the labels.

It wasn't that they were moving in together right now. He still had his place in Virginia for Delta to allow for meetings out of Titan Group's headquarters. How would a long-distance relationship work? She had no idea. Did he technically live with her? No… He was definitely based out of Virginia, but he could go anywhere in the world between jobs. So far, he had chosen Iowa.

Ryder readjusted the pillow behind his head, and she curled against his bare chest, scratching her fingers through his chest hair. "Nooners are fun."

"What do you call them when they last all afternoon and it's almost dinnertime?" He laughed.

"Fun." She leaned over and kissed him as his phone rang. "You call them lots and lots of fun."

Victoria had been worried that she would grow to resent his phone because it would mean that he had to leave. But she respected his work as he respected hers. Lone wolves. She was taking better care to be more cognizant of her surroundings on jobs, and she was good with needing backup, so Ryder respected her work.

Sweet Hills never questioned her either. They never asked her to earn their trust again; that respect she'd been so concerned about was just something she had to find internally after Ivan stole it—and she did.

Ryder answered the phone, and his lazy smile fell away, replaced by a hardness and anger she hadn't expected to see with a call to head in for work.

Victoria sat up, tugging the sheet around her chest, and watched him intently.

"Explain that," Ryder growled into the phone as his grip turned white.

Bad news. Bad, horrible news. What was going on?

"Whatever needs to be done, you tell me, and I'm there." Ryder listened for another painstakingly long minute before he hung up and tossed the phone down.

"What's wrong?" Victoria asked, terrified of what he would say.

"Cassidy was attacked after her hearing."

Victoria spun for her nightstand, grabbing the remote and turning it on to the first news station she could find. The scrolling news alerts talked about a woman attacked outside of a Congressional hearing. Her friend's face covered the television screen. But more than that, Cassidy was Locke's girlfriend and a woman who helped rescue her from Ivan's depraved hold.

Ivan? It had to be. Victoria turned to Ryder, tears falling down her cheeks before she realized that she was crying. "Ivan ordered a hit? How bad is it?"

"She's in surgery. It's bad."

"What do we do?" Anger bubbled more vicious than Victoria had experienced in weeks, since maybe the first time Ivan raped her. "Ryder?"

"Titan goes after him, and this time, we make sure he dies."

Yes! Lenora's words about justice and how some situations called for their own judges, juries, and executioners echoed in her head. With Ryder's promise, Victoria's tears stopped.

CHAPTER FIFTY-SIX

One Month Later

THE EARLY FALL breeze rolled off Baltimore's Inner Harbor, and Victoria was glad that she'd grabbed the light jacket despite Ryder's teasing. She had insisted on alone time, an errand, and needing to wrap a few small business emails, but the timing was perfect. He wanted to hit the gym then go for a run.

Unaccustomed to working with a team and technology like the ear bud in her right ear, Victoria rolled her neck side to side as she meandered through the touristy crowd. Again, she tugged on her earlobe. The earpiece was in place, and no one could see it, but it felt like a telephone book was hanging out of her head.

"Leave it alone," Locke's voice whispered.

How long would it take for her to get used to having a comm? Likely not long. It would just be like she had her iPhone's ear buds in, except for those were obvious and not as small and dropped into her ear canal. She lifted her wrist to her mouth as though scratching her nose. "Sorry. Last time, I promise."

There were only three people in the world who knew what she was doing right now: Locke, Jared, and Parker. Not telling Ryder didn't sit well with her, but this was need-to-know. He would eventually figure it out, and knowing her boyfriend, that realization would be almost instantaneous.

But the danger level and risk of tipping off anyone who might be listening was too high. The black-op job was sanctioned but would always be denied.

"The hotel is midway up the block on your left," Parker said.

Other than one meeting, there'd been no discussion. She hadn't been allowed to look up the location, map it out, or even check reviews of the hotel online. No evidence could exist that she'd ever seen the hotel.

Following Parker's instructions, Victoria moved further from the water as the crowd thinned, but not by much. It was a beautiful, sunny day, and tourist season never seemed to slow down in Baltimore. There were kids with their families, college students, and sports fans, all mixed on the streets. Victoria caught sight of the hotel and patiently waited to cross.

"How's Cassidy doing?" Jared asked.

It was a question Victoria wanted to know the answer to but was too terrified to ask Locke. The only updates that she'd had since Ryder had told her that Cassidy had been rushed into surgery were heartbreaking.

First, Cassidy had been in ICU, and no one knew if she would even make it. Then somewhere in there, Locke and Cassidy got married. It wasn't a huge celebration, though they probably didn't need one. How did it feel to have your hand forced? She couldn't imagine how Locke worried.

Yet, Victoria understood. If Ryder was on his deathbed, there would be nothing more that she'd want to do than marry him that moment. Ivan Mikhailov tried to assassinate Cassidy and tear Locke's future from him. Victoria understood why Locke was working this op as much as he'd married Cassidy the second she woke up.

Ivan Mikhailov was untouchable. Vast sums of money and corruption no one knew the total reach of made normal justice impossible. Ivan smiled when his government let him go for raping her, for trafficking women and children. *Children.* Victoria shook her head as she walked down the sidewalk. That sick son of a bitch was starting up all over again. How many people had died because of him? How many families had been destroyed because of his crimes?

Ivan knew there was no justice that could touch him.

But he didn't know her, and he didn't know Delta and Titan.

She walked into the hotel lobby and sat down at the first overstuffed lounge chair as though waiting for someone. Really, she scanned the crowd. Intel said he was here.

Twenty minutes later, she moved to the open bar where the early adults-only brunch crowd was taking advantage of mimosas and Bloody Marys. With a champagne flute of orange juice, hold the champagne, she casually moved about the lobby.

Someone tapped her shoulder. “Are you looking for someone?”

Victoria turned around to see a nicely dressed man smiling, almost smirking, and she realized it was an attempt at a wink. “I’m waiting for some friends.”

“Because I couldn’t help noticing…”

Whatever his pickup line was faded away as her skin prickled. She had been told so many times before there was no such thing as the physical touch of a man’s gaze. That was bullshit. Ryder could look at her, and she would melt, her clothes burning off her body with just his hot, Aussie glance. But this was different, and Victoria turned away from the man as he was still talking, waving him away wordlessly.

She heard him mumble bitch but didn’t care as she remained calm and casual and kept her eyes on the pivot. Ivan Mikhailov had her in his sight. He likely was fuming. After all, she was a possession that escaped, a special gift stolen from his personal collection.

Too bad… Victoria had tracked him, hunted him. Without the bastard knowing, Victoria had worked with all of Titan’s powerhouse resources. It was the PI-slash-bounty-hunting job of a lifetime.

Like a rabid dog eager to sink her teeth into a victim, Victoria found her target. Ivan was staying in this hotel. But Parker had found that he was traveling under heavy disguise because of everything that had happened. Still, he was too cocky to stay out of the United States.

“Where are you, you sick bastard?” She took a casual sip of her orange juice, keeping the champagne flute close to her lips. “He’s here.”

“I’m here too,” Locke confirmed.

Victoria moved casually through the crowded brunch crowd milling around the bar that spilled over to the coffee shop area. Her skin shivered with cold awareness of the man who’d intended to own her.

Ivan thought he was hunting her. Heart racing, pulse thumping, and adrenaline driving her keen senses, she tried not to look everywhere at once.

There he was.

A man looking not at all like the billionaire took a seat, positioning himself on a bar stool facing her. He looked nothing like Ivan. Wrong hair, wrong cheeks, wrong chin.

But the man's expensive casual clothes hung over the right size frame as he tracked her through glasses she knew he didn't need. The man sipped from a cup of coffee, sadistic hunger burning in his eyes.

Her stomach turned, and sweat dampened her armpits and underneath her breasts as bile churned viciously in her stomach.

The man stopped staring and went back to a conversation with the other person at his table as Victoria watched him drink coffee. They laughed, and she wanted to scream. His head tilted back as he listened, and she wanted to throw her champagne flute.

No question. That was Ivan. "He's at a bar table next to the column near the oversized plant. Khaki pants light blue polo shirt. Drinking a cup of coffee. Wearing glasses." Victoria had never been more certain of anything in her life as she stared at someone who looked nothing like Ivan.

"Victoria," Jared's voice was low and straightforward. "You understand that I'm not questioning you; I'm asking for a double check of your observation. Standard operating procedure."

Parker had likely hacked the hotel security system, and Jared and Parker were probably staring at the man she had pinpointed as Ivan Mikhailov, Russian government official, billionaire, trafficker of women and children, murderer, torturer, and her rapist many times over.

She closed her eyes and remembered every horrid, vivid detail. His hands, his wrists, the way they came down over her throat or how they drew back before he backhanded her. She recalled in intense detail the curl of his lips and the flare of his nostrils when she whimpered as he walked into the room. No amount of disguise and makeup could change that.

"Those are the fingers that wrapped around my throat. And that is the wrist I tore at with both hands, trying to break his chokehold. That head tilt, the way he gestures, the hungry, thirsty, enjoyable way he is taking his coffee and Danish is the same way he took me. That's him. I understand your standard operating procedures, and I'm not worried that you're second-guessing me."

Victoria drained her orange juice, and as, planned she stood up, taking a napkin and covertly wiping away her fingerprints. It didn't matter as a waiter immediately grabbed the glass from her and added it to a tray of many others.

Without a drink in hand, Victoria went and found a better seat and faced Ivan. Challenging her with a sadistic stare, he smiled, liked that she didn't know. Oh, she knew. It was him, that narcissistic son of a bitch, who would never dream of what was coming.

"Target has been confirmed." Jared said magical words in her head.

Like with Mayhem, she was the tracker and hunter, but not the judge, jury, or executioner. All had been decided and was out of her control, but participating with Delta and Titan, much like with Mayhem, worked for her.

"I have the target in sight," Locke reported.

"You are approved. Take the target at will."

Victoria wondered if Locke had promised Cassidy that he would seek vengeance. How long would Victoria have to wait? How long ago had Locke made this promise to Cassidy? What—

Ivan buckled, arching back and going limp in his chair.

She waited for shock to surprise her as people reacted. Victoria never heard the shot fired from wherever Locke was with his silencer. She knew that even a silencer gave off a noise, but the hotel was boisterous and had muffled the sound.

If Titan needed any further confirmation that the man was Ivan, they had it when his companion reacted like a Russian bodyguard and not a tourist, jumping to his feet and drawing a concealed weapon. That, more than anything, caused the pandemonium that ran through the crowd like a tidal wave.

People ducked, others ran as Locke reported, "Target's eliminated."

Victoria sat, savoring justice for a moment longer than she had planned then stood and swept herself into the chaos and fled into the street.

She made her way down to the bay again, letting her gaze drift to the barges that floated in the distance.

"Hey," Ryder called as she looked over her shoulder to see him jogging down the brick pathway.

"Perfect timing." She moved to her man.

His sweat-drenched hair spiked as he ran his hand through it, and his T-shirt clung to his chest. Everything about him physically was perfect, but it was the way he saved her that made her heart swell. It wasn't just a white-knight rescue, it was also how he let her fly then let her realize that she could save herself. That was why she fell so deeply, madly in love with him.

Victoria moved against his chest, wrapping her arms around his damp neck and hugging him close. "Hey."

Ryder gave her a quick, salty kiss and pulled back to hold her hand. "Something's going on back there. Lots of police and lights showing up."

She hummed noncommittally, as they walked along the Inner Harbor.

He slowed to a stop. "You're not even curious?"

Victoria smiled. It wasn't a happy one but rather more filled with contentment and certainty about the future. "No, not interested in what happened back there. Nothing there is my concern anymore."

His eyes narrowed, and she tilted her head to the side, pinching her fingers into her ear and pulling out the tiny earpiece. Victoria took his hand and pressed it into his palm, curling his fingers around it. With both of her hands around his, Ryder understood. Ivan was dead, and she was done with that chapter of hindsight, second guesses, and regrets.

"Special girl, you're my warrior woman." Ryder crushed the ear bud and tossed it into the water then pulled her into another hug. "The best and the worst day of my life is the day I met you."

EPILOGUE

Two Years Later

"YOU KNOW WHAT I've learned?" Ryder let his fingers run up her back.

Still sleepy, Victoria looked over her bare shoulder. "What's that? Brunch tastes better in bed?"

He smiled, burrowing next to her in the white down comforter. "Anything is better with you in bed, love."

She turned over, and his hand moved to her hip, smoothing over the silk pajamas as she relaxed. He'd been on assignment for a week, and it was so nice to wake up with him, look out their big picture windows and watch the last of spring's flower petals decorate the backyard.

"That's a good thing to have learned. It only took, what, two years for you to figure that out?"

"I think I had that figured out within two minutes of meeting you."

"Smart man," she whispered, sleepily. "What else have you learned?"

Ryder stretched over her, hugging her close. "There are no rules. No expectations. No… limitations."

"That's a good one. No limitations."

"Who would've thoughts an orphan kid from Straya would've found the greatest woman in the world?"

"Greatest woman in the world?" she teased playfully. "That's quite the compliment."

"I think you're the greatest, madam mayor."

"Deputy mayor," she corrected.

"Eh." He pulled her close. "Just a matter of time for the greatest woman in the world if that's what you want. Nothing you can't do."

She kissed his shoulder. "I've come to realize, there's nothing you can't do too."

"Like marry you?" He rolled her over so their legs tangled together, their faces inches apart. "I want to marry you. I can do anything I want?"

Her sleepy grin went ear to ear. "Are you asking?"

"I've been asking you to spend your life with me a thousand ways since the first morning you woke up in my arms." He squeezed her close. "But right now, I'm proposing."

Ryder took her hand—and only then did she realize her ring finger already had a diamond sparkling on it.

"Oh, you sneaky man." Victoria's eyes went wide as she faltered for a breath.

"Victoria Massey. I love you. Simple." He sat up, pulling an armful of her and the comforter into his lap. A sexy morning smile hung on his chiseled face. "You're my anchor and my purpose. Every day, there's a chance I could walk into a war zone, yet, you're the bravest person I know. I couldn't ask for someone stronger to be my family and future."

Tears caught in her eyes. Those weren't just words. They were a declaration of love.

Before he could say another word, she cupped his face, even as the ring glittered in the morning light. "Two lone wolves who find each other in their world of hate and hurt." She squeezed him. "I love you. Not because of everything *both* of us overcame, but because I was meant to find you. Love you. Kiss and hug you." Tears blurred her vision until she blinked them away. "Dreams I didn't know about have come true every day since I met you, and hell yes, baby, I'm marrying you."

ACKNOWLEDGMENTS

Thank you to the greatest readers! And, Team Titan, love ya! xo

Many helping hands made this book possible. Most importantly, thank you to my family, especially my children who put up with my writing at the oddest moments, and my parents. Dad had the killer catch regarding firing guns in national forests versus national parks, and Mom for everything from beta reading to typos. Book writing is a family business sometimes!

Thank you to the retailers who support indie authors! A huge shout out to the team that worked hard behind the scene: Hot Damn Designs (cover), Red Adept and All About the Edits (Editing and proofing), InkSlinger PR, AuthorEMS (iBooks uploading), BB eBooks (print formatting), Patricia Patti, Trish Kugle, and author Sharon Kay.

ABOUT THE AUTHOR

CRISTIN HARBER is a *New York Times* and *USA Today* bestselling romance author. She writes sexy romantic suspense, military romance, new adult, and contemporary romance. Readers voted her onto Amazon's Top Picks for Debut Romance Authors 2013, and her debut Titan series was both a #1 romantic suspense and #1 military romance bestseller.

Join the newsletter! Text TITAN to 66866 to sign up for exclusive emails.

The Titan Series:

Book 1: Winters Heat
Book 1.5: Sweet Girl
Book 2: Garrison's Creed
Book 3: Westin's Chase
Book 4: Gambled
Book 5: Chased
Book 6: Savage Secrets
Book 7: Hart Attack
Book 7.5: Sweet One
Book 8: Black Dawn
Book 8.5: Live Wire
Book 9: Bishop's Queen
Book 10: Locke and Key
Book 11: Jax

The Delta Series:

Book 1: Delta: Retribution
Book 2: Delta: Revenge
Book 3: Delta: Redemption

The Delta Novella in Liliana Hart's MacKenzie Family Collection:

Delta: Rescue

The Only Series:

Book 1: Only for Him
Book 2: Only for Her
Book 3: Only for Us
Book 4: Only Forever

Each Titan and Delta book can be read as a standalone (except for Sweet Girl), but readers will likely best enjoy the series in order. The Only series must be read in order.

Printed in Great Britain
by Amazon